Tearing Down The Statues

Brian Bennudriti

ISBN-13: 978-0-692-55348-0
Library of Congress Control Number: 2015917261

DEDICATION

This is for my dad, who probably still has stuffed away in a box somewhere the mystery story I wrote him in pencil, for when I got famous. Thanks for the long chats – it means everything.

CONTENTS

"When a story is old, it is powerful. If I write your myths simply and speak for your generation with things that seem new…if I tickle what you want to believe, and give you something to be, then when false details blossom and my myths live in the words of your politicians and artists, you will know I am flowering like a lily in spring. And I will seize your heart – not by your throne, but by your theater."

-The Salt Mystic, when asked if she could die

PROLOGUE

"Just bring me two so I don't have to wait. Right, big guy?" A flatrunner sailor slung his face mask onto the zinc bartop, smelling of chlorine. The regulars called him Munchy because he loved the dried fruit from the cinnabar bowls kept about in the resthouse. Two enlisted sailors and a young wide-eyed officer quickly slid next to him smiling and asking after his latest mission. Although all flatrunner sailors were considered a bit mad in those days, feverishly riding electrostatic charges ripped from the very salt of the cotton-white flats, scouts like Munchy would be the first to tell of furious smoking skirmishes in the shimmering borderlands of his patrol.

Munchy grinned and made up a stirring fancy about being separated from his squadron and coming across a war engine, only approaching the truth as the bartender pushed over his usual: buttered white ale, lightly sweetened as they take it in Mevin or Tobin, the twin cities of the salt flats. Afterwards, he was still smiling as he looked around at the faces in the resthouse.

"Ghost Dogs ooh rah!!." At this, those beside Munchy echoed his cry, smiling and holding up their cups in salute. It was only an ironic moment later when the chatter died off crisply as a stranger stepped into the doorframe shadows.

Tall and intense, in the old style military uniform only with the jacket open and the collar loose, he stood threateningly silent at the entrance scanning the room. It was commonly known there were wandering Rauchka generals left over from the last hot war, who never traveled alone and who were watched for controlling hand signals by still-loyal snipers and hidden troops. Several of those in the room fired up their weapons aiming directly at the stranger.

"Watch his hands. It's how he calls them", the young cinnamon-haired officer whispered to Munchy.

No one fired; and no one moved apart from the general as he walked slowly across the room towards the bar.

The young officer leaned more closely in, his face smelling of blueberry genever, "You never know how many there are. If he's really a Brigadier, then we've been infiltrated. He's got guys in this room."

Munchy scratched his nose as he looked at the familiar faces in the resthouse; and he wasn't the only one doing this.

"I know everyone here."

"You think you do." The young officer leaned back to an upright position as Munchy looked again at his face for a sign of how to take what he'd just said. It was only then, from the edge of his vision that he realized the Brigadier was walking directly to him.

The nation nestled in the mountains past the Yagrada river had been a smoking threat to the Salt Flat nation for a generation, since the days following the death of the last Warmaster, Old Man Talgo. As with the harassment and reconnaissance missions these sailors conducted every day, it was given that the Mountain and Salt peoples were in an irreconcilable and simmering cold war. The Rauchka were wild cards because their loyalty was, and always had been, unclear, particularly at this point as they no longer even constituted a coherent people. A wandering Rauchka general walking into a crowd of flatrunner sailors was unprecedented.

Ginger and timid, Munchy watched as the Brigadier strode to two paces in front of him, boots sliding and thudding on the barfloor's grit, and looked directly in his eyes. No one had left their seats; and it was softly quiet in the resthouse.

"Tell Cassian what I've done here today." It was a gravelly voice, breaking subtly but commanding even in its softness. His sun-leathered face was scarred and tired.

There was a moment where it seemed the Brigadier was waiting on acknowledgement from Munchy, an acknowledgement he only received as a confused furrow. Not everyone in the resthouse could hear what the general had said. He broke the trance and looked around once again at the array of flatrunner sailors, some staring in anxiety and some still pointlessly aiming carbines. Munchy surveyed the faces again with a slowly dawning understanding of what was about to happen…what the Brigadier had meant.

The general suddenly spun to walk towards the doorway, more deliberate and methodical than hurried, holding up his right hand with fingers bent like a stretched claw. At that, slaughter exploded the crowded barroom in a madhouse of thunder and confusion. Munchy dove under the zinc bartop and looked quickly at the young officer just in time to see his left eye and cheek opened up by a railgun slug. The carnage was quick and merciless, conducted by two men and a lady from within the room, familiar faces who'd drunk and laughed there for months. There were likely others firing from windows, it would have been difficult to say.

Some sailors tried to run for the back into the gaming parlor or to hide under tables. Some started firing their carbines madly, hardly aiming at all, their carbon breakers clicking and snapping as the room lit up with lightning. There was a man blubbering on the floor holding his jaw in place. Munchy had just closed his eyes and bent to the floor when the fury abated. It was silent again when he cautiously opened his eyes.

1 THERE IS NO SELF, ONLY THE RECORD

Although thinner than in previous years, crowds of onlookers still formed to watch the zeppelin shuttles glide softly to dock with the airpark tower, framed beautifully against the jutting mountains. Many of these were sightseers in to see the blooming algae gardens terraced on the gneiss cliffs and which speckled the majestic mountain city. A mildly hallucinogenic algae wine, sana drove the local economy on many levels, but particularly drew speculation investment in the hustling days before a holiday such as this.

A young Recorder stood waiting near the cargo bins, his forehead carrying the lava red and ash black tattoo of his calling. Stepping into place beside him was an awkward and gangly fellow who'd come perhaps not to obtain packages or to greet a traveler, but rather just to see the dirigible up close. His voice was squeaky; and his stomach pouched tightly in a sharp pear shape peeking out from beneath his shirt. A girl who was perhaps his sister, younger than him but attractive and clearly not sharing the young man's interests, was tagging along reluctantly.

"Daelin, do we really have to do this again? You're driving me crazy."

"Won't take long."

"You absolutely said that yesterday. I am not spending the rest of the morning staring at balloons again." She smiled at the Recorder when he glanced at her tan face. He liked that but wasn't supposed to.

"That's one of the Corsair class coming in. You can tell by the shape of the nose. This one has some really nice enginework." He hesitated and hadn't yet looked at the Recorder's face, though his tone and volume were certainly intended to solicit agreement or reciprocated enthusiasm. Instead, his eyes lingered on the mooring lines being thrown over black capstans ringing the heights of the docking tower like he was looking at ice cream.

"They used them for evacuations during the war…"

"Big toys, Daelin. Like you've got scattered all over your room. Let's gooooooo."

The Recorder glanced again at Daelin's sister, to which she responded by smiling again and rolling her eyes, shaking her head to signal how unfashionable she felt was this conversation.

"You wouldn't believe the lift capacity this thing has. Look at that on the tail there…" Daelin at that point glanced over as he pointed to ensure the Recorder's eyes were following him, but at last noticed the Recorder's forehead, recognizing him for his nature and charge.

"Oh…"

The Recorder still hadn't as yet said anything and remained as quiet while Daelin began to fumble a bit, "I didn't know you were…"

Daelin still pointed upwards toward the dirigible, but loosely and awkwardly, "It's got a uhh..it's got a hook to connect to others like it. They can make a train. Look, we need to go."

"That's it?" The young man's sister raised her eyebrows at her brother's discomfort. It wasn't uncommon, the fear of the Record.

"Yeah, we need to go do some things. Come on. Sorry, okay?" In a fit of escape, Daelin just turned and started lightly jogging away, glancing around himself trying to appear as if he'd intended to exercise all along and was hard at it now. He called again for his sister when she didn't leave straight away; and she lingered an apologetic grin and waved as she at last followed her brother. The Recorder watched her leave and then watched the place in the crowd where she had left. He squinted against the morning sun and scratched the back of his head before stepping around the tower to idly watch the stevedores slough packages.

A short line of awaiting passengers stood at the base of another tower, shuffling in position or scanning the top of the stairs for a signal they could board. Colorfully, there was a tiny twig of a boy in a uniform that was yet too big for him with a stuffed duffel bag at his feet and an anxious stare on his face. He was looking into the eyes of someone who might have been his father, leather faced and tattooed on his arms, skinny and traveled, who was giving him guidance on how to behave wherever the boy was going. The Recorder hesitated to absorb the moment.

Sometime later and of greater significance, as often happens in crowds an interesting face had caught his precise attention. With wide eyes and a mad open grin, a spiked shock of chestnut hair, a fellow bending down to leave the shuttle leaned against the black rails atop the airpark tower. It isn't important to describe all the details of sunlight and time, noises and colors, words said in the buzzing crowds and all, of which the Recorder made note because that is what they do and it goes without saying. What was new was that the strange grinning fellow was looking pointedly at the Recorder's face. He waved and started down the coal-black graphite stairway in a rush.

It is difficult to explain without describing the aggressive hypnotic and chemical training of a Recorder in their youth, their traditional role in the highest imperial and Warmaster courts, and the deepest integrity and dedication as was core to their collective identity why it was one didn't simply saunter up to a Recorder and say hi.

"Hi, Jo Jo. I can help you carry something if you like. Say, who is that sculpted up there on the mountain?" The stranger was still grinning as he pointed his thumb to a majestic carved figure of a man on a mountain face overlooking the wide Yagrada valley, sculpted from the rock with an outstretched hand through the rock fingers of which a natural waterfall flowed.

The Recorder tapped his forehead tattoo, "Perhaps you did not notice…"

"Jo Jo, Skipdance, Habilu…whatever. What do you want to be

called? My name is Ring. I certainly can't just call you, 'Recorder' –
what if another one walks by and I'm trying to talk to you? The
carving, man, who is it?"

Stunned and moving his eyes from the cascade then back to this
odd stranger, the Recorder started again.

"This Recorder is waiting on his package, then he is going to
leave. It is not appropriate for you to directly address a Recorder in
public nor is it seemly to suggest he bear a proper name."

"Right. Right. So I'll call you Misling, yes?" At this, the
Recorder's eyes locked for that was a word he knew well and it had
been nuanced correctly. It was a Mast word, a meta-language charged
with intricate layers of meaning and one which Recorders used to
transfer highly detailed information among themselves such as when
they preserved their pool of lives before dying. Ring looked casually
down the broad avenue leading toward the awakening marketplace as
if he wasn't aware what he'd just said.

"Listen, I'm not exactly sure where I am; and you probably know
lots of interesting things, so I'll just go with you." Ring nodded at the
Recorder like he was doling advice on how to remove a stain. The
Recorder examined this stranger again at full attention as he had been
indoctrinated to do when something potentially of some significance
occurred.

"You certainly will not."

Ring creased his forehead, "You know, you're a bit of a pain. I
mean, you won't tell me about the mountain face, you're stuffy; and
now you give me grief when I even offer to help you carry your
thingie – is this it?"

He leaned into the package chute and lifted a small wooden box
the color of barley, sealed with hemp twine, which the stevedores had
slid from topside out of the dirigible's cargo hold. With a final glance
to the cascading mountain face, Ring started down the few stairs to
the dusty market street leading to Alson's oldest marketplace,

mumbling along the way.

"…so you come across as really pretentious. I mean, I obviously don't know anybody, you could at least be neighborly and say a few insightful things – maybe comment on my trip or ask where I'm from. Something. It's obvious you're getting all feathered up-"

The Recorder, following within earshot, interrupted passionately, "This Recorder is NOT feathered up-"

"Sure you are – and you're stuffy too. Where are we going?"

The Recorder trotted quickly alongside Ring and seized the thin box for himself.

"This Recorder is not stuffy nor is he feathered up. You however are impudent and a troublesome busybody. Do you even understand what this means?" He tapped the tattoo on his forehead once again to make a point, the ancient wheels within wheels symbol of the Salt Mystic.

"I know it isn't an advanced apology for being rude and stuffy."

The Recorder huffed before pacing quickly toward the still silent market stalls. Resin automatons the color of thin milk twisted and bent fluidly, mutely arranging fresh vegetables, meats, breads and sana in terraces for display. There were vendors sweeping and talking to neighbors about the day's prices as the orange sunrise stretched long shadows across the cobblestone courtyard's masonry and ruined monuments.

The plaza traditionally exploded with noisy commerce once the market opened; but for the moment it was serene and pleasant with only the sounds of sweeping and murmuring and the bubbling of a ledgestone courtyard fountain. Two small boys and a girl sported around a morbidly obese sculpture commonly called, 'the market god', beside which were lanterns and an oak coin box. One of them was whispering into the statue's ear and giggling, ready to run clasping his own ears and await the first thing he heard said beyond the market's walls for a fortune or answer.

At the stalls, there was an official of some kind wearing a golden insignia on his linen collar, who was slowly making his way around to each vendor and taking notes as he went. As Ring watched standing alongside the Recorder, he caught that none of the vendors to whom the official had spoken seemed pleased with whatever they'd been told. Two or three actually shouted at the official as he passed.

"Misling, what's that guy saying?"

The Recorder cast an impatient look, then answered as was his obligation, "He is a market official and a representative of Judge Talgo charged with establishing Alson's commission rates and the pricing range for the day. Once he has gauged the market, he will update the glass board there and communicate today's rates and pricing, authorizing the vendors and customers to begin the traditional bidwars."

"What would happen if I updated his board once he's gone?" Ring stroked his chin.

"You are not authorized to update the board." The Recorder paused, no doubt pondering why Ring would even consider such a thing. No doubt, there were an obvious host of overly idealistic reasons that came to mind.

"It would be unhelpful to attempt to cheat the Judge of his commission…" Another pause.

"…or to artificially raise prices to benefit the vendors." After waiting a moment, watching the official, the Recorder glanced again to Ring to gauge his intentions.

"Or to artificially lower the prices to benefit the people. What is it you are intending?" Ring only nodded absently then changed the subject.

"Are you running an errand? Aren't you supposed to be

consulting for generals and judges and whatnot? What's that about?"

"This Recorder is property; and the gentleman to whom he has been entrusted requires…upkeep. Please continue along your way."

The market official perched on a stepladder, erased the frosted glass with a worn cloth, and wrote a series of prices and rates in the boxes using a charcoal pencil hanging from a leather string. He stepped down commandingly and briefly appraised the condition of the marketplace now that he had established the market's parameters. The sun-worn faces watching him looked bitter and angry at the figures he had set. Murmuring continued even as he raised both arms to signal the market's opening. This triggered an almost reluctant hurricane of bustle and motion as burly vendors and grocers, restaurateurs and tourists haggled heatedly over produce and meat, long sticks of fresh bread, and lime green bottles of shimmering algae wine.

The Recorder loosened the twine from his box and cracked it open for a cursory inspection of the contents before advancing into the noisy bidyard. There were tourists along the courtyard's perimeter, leaned against wrought iron fencing and crumbling stone arches to watch. Ring started laughing, and doing so almost losing his breath. The Recorder's face showed only indignation.

"There is no self, only the Record", Ring barely said as he tried to catch his breath from laughing, quoting a Recorder creed and looking at this one as if for the first time again. The Recorder's voracious attention locked again with surprise.

"That's bakas jerky, Misling…Salt Flat contraband. You can't sell that stuff in the mountains."

The Recorder shushed Ring and readied himself for a task he very clearly did not relish, targeting a set of opposing tables where two earthy rustics were haggling over crates shrouded in thick canvas fabrics. Ring caught his breath, likely with admiration for such disregard of propriety from someone charged with its maintenance. Although a young Recorder might have held as many as five lives in his Pool even at this age, the memories often had not yet unwound or become fully real. It was once an adage of such Recorders to 'trust them with diplomats, but not with your daughter'.

Ring touched his brow in a loose salute, wishing the Recorder luck, and started into the busy courtyard, disappearing in the market swarm seeming to ask for alms. The Recorder's eyes lingered for a moment on the place where Ring had been before inhaling sharply to enter the market.

In only a short while, as the Recorder was stuffing the price he'd garnered for the jerky inside a russet leather satchel, he was one of the first to notice a subtle change in the mood of the crowd, a mean spirit betrayed by angry stares and dying murmurs. Following the stares to the frosted glass board about which Ring had asked, he saw Ring himself wrapped in a linen overshirt with a golden coin attached to the collar and looking from the distance much like a market official with the proper insignia busily updating the prices and rates.

"That's ridiculous", someone shouted, for the commissions Ring had falsified for the Judge were exorbitant, more than quintuple what was set before. His price ranges were less than a fourth of the figures he was erasing as he made his way down the board. Not quite to the bottom row, he turned to hold his hands out to the sides and looks at the throng as if asking, 'what?'. He wasn't smiling, but rather was feigning formality as he turned to whistle and scribe more night-black figures. When a thrown yellow root smashed against his back, Ring turned to the crowd again and pointed in the direction from which the missile had likely come, looking fierce.

"Idiot", someone from the crowd screamed. "We can't make money at those prices. What's the Judge doing?"

Ring waved his hand dismissively, scratching the erasing cloth against the figures he'd just written and made a dramatic show that the new lower prices he was writing just then were as a result of the crowd's questioning him.

"You can't do that!"

Once he had raised the Judge's commission for aged sana sales twice over in retaliation for the market's rising furor, two miscreants banded together and rushed the frosted glass board to get him. Ring's eyes widened quickly; and he disappeared again such that the Recorder lost sight of him. As can happen in tense triggered crowds, those looking for a fight started one; and the marketplace bubbled over in chaos with tourists scattering from overturned stalls and madly rolling produce.

"Hi", Ring surprised the Recorder as he stepped alongside to survey the mess, out of breath and having discarded the linen overshirt and collar. The Recorder's eyes were somewhat wide; and his deliberate and methodical glances betrayed the highest level of awareness of which a Recorder made use, noting every scent and word, spatial relationships, and faces. As always in such a heightened state, he did so to the extent that even fifty years hence he could recount every detail of this single moment. He was still a young man though; and mischief can be exhilarating.

"Did anyone in there ever see anything like that?" Ring tapped the Recorder's left temple in reference to the lives in his Pool.

"You are an activist, likely a runaway from the Recorder academy."

"Not a runaway, no. I've never even seen the academy. Is it pretty?"

"Your show here was a hope to force a challenge to the prevailing system which you view as unjust or corrupt, yes?"

Ring creased his forehead in evaluation, "Wow, you're bad at this. That would have been iconic, though."

"Did you harm the real market official? Why did he not intervene?"

"I just asked some guys to keep him busy."

"And they did this just because you asked?"

Ring nodded as if that sort of thing happened to him often. The Recorder pressed further.

"Where did you learn the Mast word you used earlier, its proper nuance, and the Recorder's creed?"

"Misling, you ask an awful lot of questions for a Recorder. I think that's great; and we should chat it up; but shouldn't we kind of…poof?" Ring looked again to the mad courtyard.

"This Recorder is expected at the tent city by midday. He would not object to your joining the walk over while you explain yourself. He has cheese."

The two young men made their way beyond the market courtyard, passing the green copper domes of old observatories and theaters and the misty fountains of Vangeline park where white furred wanoa still pastured looking like cloud-white shaggy silverbacks. Ring scratched a female wanoa's head as he looked ponderingly into its violet eyes following the Recorder's comment that the serene beasts at one time long ago could speak.

"Misling, why do you suppose the people in the market so easily believed I was an official?" Ring stopped in place as he asked the question, planting his feet firmly on the broad avenue so as not to fall backward while running his eyes up the tall tower called Balcister. Although it officed those engaged in commerce and shadowed artists and street actors in the plaza at its base, the tower's skyblue masonry hummed softly with information and code. It was the best known building in a cityscape of minarets, slate roofs and walkways, with the exception of Judge Talgos cliffside palace, and was the only remaining computronium structure in Alson.

"The confidence with which you approached the task, perhaps…"

"Umm hmm. Guys in this town keep staring me down like I'm

supposed to be doing something they're stuck doing. What am I missing?"

Misling didn't answer as he watched and listened. Ring waited only a moment.

"You know, you're miserly with your local color knowledge. You should have been telling me about that waterfall thing this morning; and you could be chatting me up right now about Judge Talgos beef with Cassian in the Flats….but I get nothing that I don't drag from you."

Misling's brow creased, "This Recorder is not in your service nor in public service and is required to lecture on nothing. In fact, you did not ask about Marshal Cassian nor the Judge."

Ring nodded in agreement, "That's right. That's right. You could offer though, sort of in the general friendly spirit of our conversation. You knew where I was going with that. Is Alson at war?"

"Alson and the Salt Flat nation are in a cold war, marked by skirmishes and harassment. The mountain military forces are deployed for most of the year, either in forward tank battlegroups in the Salt Flats or in mog or submersible patrols locally and act to defend mountain interests against aggressors." Misling had answered in dictionary style in an automatic fashion, a prepared statement for Recorders. If asked again, he would repeat himself verbatim.

"Mm hmmm…." Ring had been idly watching four teenagers chatting in the sidestreet wearing military railgun thigh holsters. Misling stepped towards him impatiently.

"From where have you come?"

"How do you mean?" Ring stepped towards Balcister's deep blue masonry walls, touching his cheek against the computronium blocks and tapping to discharge the tingling static electricity.

"Do you know what Misling means? Do you know the Mast

language?"

"Sure, sure. Not hard. Mostly a lot of fables."

"How did you come to study the language? Where were you born?"

Ring looked back to Misling with a mischievous smile, still tapping against the tower. "You know, that's not strictly true."

Misling's left eyebrow lifted questioningly.

"Whether in public service or not, you're still expected to respond to questions. 'The day is kept whole for it is laden with treasures.' You've got to share; and all you do is ask me stuff. Who do you have in your Pool?"

Misling thinly hid his irritation at this question, one he was indeed required to answer, "This Recorder maintains the Record of four lives."

"Interesting; and who are they?" Ring scratched his cheek thoughtfully as if very intrigued by the pending answer. A chalk artist speaking with a businesswoman walked by, casting odd glances at Ring in wonderment at his ongoing conversation with a Recorder. Misling averted his eyes as they passed.

"Duke Exeter of Sarling in the days of the Brewing, Court Poet Phianna in the early days of Naraia, and Under Governors Faring of the Southern Red Witch Annex and Delton of the Fountain City."

"I have no idea who those people are. Faring sounds familiar. What color were Phianna's eyes?"

"Gray, and quite bloodshot later in life."

"Why?"

"Her only son was rebellious."

"What was the last thing she said?"

"I'd hoped they would stop by today." His tone was soft and tired, utterly different from how he normally spoke.

"Who was with her when she died?"

"Only a nurse named Tazia, a large woman apparently in a hurry to clean the room afterwards. It was winter; and frosty mud had been tracked about the tile floors."

"And what did the room smell like? What color were the sheets?"

"The room was cold and smelled of ammonia and iodine. The sheets were thin green linen; and the wool blanket was thin as well. An attendant had brought a bar of compressed lavender which was propped against Phianna's elbow because she enjoyed the smell. She coughed three times, looked out the window at the snow, then quietly shut her eyes."

Ring watched Misling's face for a moment, fascinated. "You didn't mention the Recorder standing right there in the corner who couldn't be bothered to put another blanket on the poor woman."

"There was no meaningful purpose to your questions apart from diversion from that which this Recorder asked you."

"That's not exactly true; but I'll let it go. Misling, I want you to do me a favor."

"That would only encourage you."

"I want you to introduce me to your employer. You freak me out a little, running illegal errands and getting all feathered up like you do."

"This Recorder was not 'feathered up'. You will not be continuing with him because you are irrational and nosey. It simply is not the way things are done; and you are neither invited nor welcome to attend."

Ring chuckled, sidestepping along the wall to the cross-street where he'd earlier seen the idle guards, sliding his fingers over Balcister's masonry as if he could feel the data of transactions, correspondence, and images.

"So you're getting picked up at the tent city, that's actually perfect. I'll meet you down there."

"You will not." Misling clarified in case there had been some unfortunate confusion.

Ring stood at last at brown, yellow and red graffiti scrawled roughly on Balcister's very wall, a stylized cartoon of an angry character in a jacket with flaming shoulderboards, a ball lightning carbine strapped to his extended right arm gripped with densely colored hands, and firing madly. It was evidently a boogeyman of some sort and had been the topic of the guards' chatter.

"Now we're getting to it…" Ring spoke to himself casually with a grin on his young face, leaning closely in and edging towards the youths whose curious notice he'd drawn.

Birds scattered from the cobbles as Misling stepped away. Years hence to desperate scholars and journalists, Misling would manufacture the backdrop of this moment to disguise the misfortune that he'd simply stopped paying attention as he glanced dismissively and walked past the fog-gray monuments surrounding Balcister.

2 LET THEM RAGE

Judge Wentic Talgos cliffside palace, with its slowly revolving stone turrets and sienna palisade, was repurposed from a very old imperial resort and had a commanding view of Alson's spires and rooftops. Impossibly, there were entire granite sections of the palace, pyramids and a massive statue of a winged figure, over which a thin film of water was trickled making odd dreamscape fountains.

In order to enter the palace in those days one had to walk through a broad plaza forested with shining colorful flags to a colossal arch over the keystone of which hung the ancient enigmatic image of a sad, translucent man seemingly imprisoned. Unearthly long in limbs and broad in its jaw, the image was traditionally explained as a fanciful illusion whose basis was preserved neither by folklore nor Recorder. It was always a controversial and at times superstitious event when the image would, in occasional years, move. As was typical, an immense crowd of protesters carpeted the plaza, shouting.

Following the morning reports and discussion of the unpleasant disturbance in one of the markets; and after Judge Wentic had dismissed the accountants and political analysts, he slid over the brass lever of a camera obscura pipework. The limewashed white bowl at the table's center flashed in miniature the image of the old library at the end of the grand hall. Only the pickthank, Revin, a guttersnipe and failed actor who merely listened well and found himself a counselor and head of armaments was left to hear the Judge as he frowned at the image.

"In the alleys, men warming themselves by barrel fires tell breathless stories about my brother Cassian's fearsome son...." Wentic was muttering at the bowl's image of Stendahl, his own bizarre son, laying on the top dusty stone shelf beside a stack of leather bound books with his shirt half-hanging out and unkempt. There were two Recorders sitting patiently on an oak bench, apparently answering questions when Stendahl thought to ask them.

"What's he reading there?"

"Those books are battle journals, torture manuals…first hand accounts of…you know….suffering. My father wrote most of them in his lunatic midnight rages. Stendahl wouldn't raise his fist to an insect! What is he thinking in there?"

"I've heard from some of the watchmen that Stendahl has the death touch of the Malthus."

"And that I buried his mother in a wall and sold his soul to the ghost of the old man, right. I feel like a fish bowl for ridiculous gossips to tap on! What do you hear about Cassian's son?"

"Outlandish stories about that one…hard to tell what's true. He's fast with a carbine. They say he fights close, almost like a fistfight with lightning. There's a bit of show to him…tattooed hands and burning shoulderboards."

"Burning shoulderboards…ridiculous. We need bloodier sports or something, to give the people something to talk about. I've not seen the boy since he was in cloths."

Stendahl's vivid image inside the bowl sat up. His hair was strangely white, his eyes a deep sea green. He was known to have meaningless visions that never came to anything, that never realized as an actual occurrence or bore any representation of true events. He monkeyed quickly across the gap to another shelf to find a book stored thereon.

There was once a time when Wentic's father, Old Man Talgo, thundered and shaped the times in which he lived. He was unpleasant in his personal habits and a cruel general; but he was imaginative in war and broke paradigms that froze strategic thinking. As the Naraia world government was burning down around him, the old man threw his two sons against each other in competition from their earliest competencies as his own way of nurturing boldness and character. It's important to know that only to understand the impatience and disappointment with which Wentic now was looking at Stendahl, buried in pointless volumes and chatting nonsense with Recorders.

"I'm a little early, Wentic." A woman in the doorway interrupted. Peri was standing with military bearing, her uniform the color of almonds all proper and pressed as was appropriate for head of the watchmen. As Wentic nodded and waved her in, there was only a curt nod between her and Revin. She joined them in watching as Wentic idly scooped Stendahl's image from the bowl with a folded piece of paper as if he were scooping soup in a ladle.

"I know how you feel about the tathlum testing, Peri; but I wanted you here for Revin's update. He's done some good work over there."

Peri rolled her eyes and began a protest, which Wentic quickly interrupted, "I don't need a power struggle between you two. Just sit."

"It isn't a power struggle, Wentic. It's an embarrassing drain of resources and an irresponsible provocation."

"None of your people agree with you, Peri." Wentic dropped the folded paper into the obscura bowl as if in emphasis.

"Because he's a con man who's with you every day. I don't blame them for feeding you junk."

"That's enough. Sit down, please. Revin, describe for Peri what we discussed this morning. Show her what you showed me."

Revin's polished descriptions began only when Peri had sat. In fact, it was common knowledge among Peri's staff that Revin's interest in experimental armaments faded following the selling of concepts. Testing was scattershot and biased; and his promised tathlum pods - transmitting projectiles fired into enemy vehicle armor which would embed themselves and inject artificial intelligence control signals - were unlikely at best.

"Peri, we think a lot of your frustration comes from not having a….you know…vision for what's going to happen when it comes to full scale conflict with Cassian's fleet…a fleet with more depth and firepower than we can face conventionally. Tathlum changes the game and…you know… turns their size against them." He raised a hand to forestall a protest from her that she was no longer offering. Much of this seemed to be a show for Wentic, likely repeating with emphasis any pieces that took the judge's fancy this morning, and targeted to hack at Peri's reputation.

Revin unfolded and laid out a spread of three paper drawings: one engineering design and two artist conceptions, all in electronic ink. He held his thumb against a circle in one corner to boot them up; and the images animated. The tathlum launch was a nightmare in black graphite, with tank tracks and a forest of antennas, lumbering over a hill towards an intercept of a roughly sketched flatrunner. He pinched a section of the image and widened his fingers, enlarging the line drawings. Penciled notes and figures appeared alongside the images.

"We're outgunned and outnumbered; and this is our chance to make nonsense of an invasion and turn Cassian's own fleet…you know… against itself."

"I know all this. What's the new bit?"

"…We've designed an expansion of the concept to include tathlum shot…a smart buckshot capable of embedding in human skin and overriding nerve signals with the object of sending affected foot soldiers and exposed battlesuit drivers back into their own troops like madmen. It may be possible to…you know…synchronize the AI signals and form attack wedges that coordinate troops and equipment." Revin's hands motioned wildly in his passion.

The tathlum launch drawing sprouted a swivel mount cannon and sprayed coal-black shot into a crowd of stylized footsoldiers. Peri rubbed her forehead and chin restlessly. As Revin spoke, she looked pointedly into Wentic's eyes with the expression of someone who was hearing a ridiculous fish story.

Peri looked at the Counselor as if he had defecated right there on the table, "What unnatural fear has you chasing such pipe dreams?" Both men nodded knowingly at each other, mumbling briefly about having foreseen her reaction at their earlier discussion.

"Wentic, do you respect my opinion?" Peri asked in a tone of old familiarity, recalling to mind years of commonality which Revin couldn't match.

"I've known you a very long time, Peri."

"This is absurd and unworkable. It's unholy and desperate. The people of the salt flats fundamentally disagree with our way of life; and they're landlocked without their own resources. It's certain that they're coming for us at their first chance. I can build a fourth squadron of ramships for the financing he's urinating on your goodwill."

"Give her the prototyping results on the pods." Wentic waved his hand at Revin.

"Keep it. I've seen his fluff; and I have people inside his group." Peri and Revin locked eyes for really the first time at this sitting. Wentic's forehead creased, the discussion not having gone his way.

"Marshal, perhaps you should review the data in private so you'll have more time to see the nuances."

Wentic casted an angry glance toward Revin and cut him off sharply, "Stop trying to make her look stupid. It's irritating. She's smarter than you are. Now I expect you two to come to some sort of agreement about a way forward. This is good stuff. Peri." The judge cast his greedy eyes back to the swirling ink; and Peri easily caught that his eyes and pointed finger were attracted to the image of the enemy arsenal ships in the background moreso than the intended prototype animation…his estranged brother's toys.

In an awkward moment following, Wentic suddenly became aware that Stendahl was no longer in the camera obscura image. Strangely, he looked to the door and found Stendahl there, picking idly at his lip and listening. He was unnaturally tall and haunting.

"Little Wennie."

Wentic lifted a puzzled eyebrow for this was a name he'd heard before albeit not from his young son, "Son, what are you doing? Are you asking to join us?"

There was only the muffled rush of an air vent from the corner, possibly some thin stray voices ghosting through a window from the protesters lining the courtyard. Revin lowered his head, rubbing a thumbnail idly against a pants leg, while Peri watched Stendahl closely. It wasn't clear at whom he was looking; and it went on until it was quite awkward. Stendahl at last slid quietly back from view and presumably down the hallway without further interaction. When he was clearly out of earshot, although one never knew that for certain with him in those days, Peri stood and spoke first.

"I'm going to go see what that was about." She pointed at the table, "You know how I feel about this. You're provoking your brother by pursuing it."

At last, she gestured toward Revin, "Ask this one who he's been talking to at the government building in Sullion.."

Wentic's eyes locked on Revin immediately at this, as Peri stepped through the doorway. She had some intelligence on amateur and unauthorized treaties Revin was negotiating with a cluster of small city-states beyond the Yagrada river, widely overstepping his authority. The judge would be displeased.

Around an old corner where a young prince used to hide behind the potted fountain blossom, Peri saw that Stendahl was still close by, his pale hand rested on the iron railing as he watched two housecleaners arguing. He broke off suddenly, his deep green eyes suddenly meeting Peri's.

"Joy and health, Marshal."

"And to you." She scanned him closely.

"What have you been asking the Recorders?"

Stendahl smiled, "About grandfather. He was intriguing and intelligent."

"There are differing opinions on that." Peri was careful what she said in reference to the old man, even in private.

"He mentioned you. As impressive. You reprimanded another cadet for crying during the gauntlet run; and your nose was bleeding. He liked your spirit." Stendhal articulated each word oddly as if it were the only one he had to say.

Ignoring his reminiscence, "Have you talked to the protesters outside as we discussed?"

"No."

She at once showed disgust, "Are you entirely devoid of leadership?"

His face was pale and emotionless, although possibly grinning very slightly.

"I don't need you to be a punk or a weirdo. Your father is confronted with morons daily, every one more dangerous than the moron in line before him. Revin is the worst of them. You're young; and people talk about you. Why can't you use that? Go talk to them. Give them some idea we're not setting their futures on fire. Say something inspiring. Am I really asking for that much?"

Stendahl was unearthly and odd. He moved his body and face slowly as if he were underwater. People of the time read about what he was wearing and bought merchandise in line with his passing interests. That odd fascination had swollen with his eccentricities in recent years. He was attractive in an entirely inexplicable way, and even here angry in this hallway and having known him from his birth, Peri still felt that distraction caused by his appearance.

"Let them rage. It creates."

Dully, like a dottering old street vendor at the end of a hot evening, Stendahl began picking at his lip again idly. He slid a worn leather-bound journal from the bullnosed rim of the fountain blossom pot and turned to walk down the rose quartz corridor, away from her and away from the steps to the courtyard, whispering.

"He goes by a name that shakes the earth when it rolls across a poor man's tongue…"

Shouting from outside was angry and in unison, although too thin to understand, almost as a melody only partially in remembrance. Peri shook her head while watching him leave, before descending the grand caparisoned staircase to head into the courtyard.

3 FIVE VISITATIONS

Rustic and boisterous like carnival people, those who lived in the tent city in those days were known for their cling to independence and freedom. In fact, the coarse fabric pavilions and collapsible apartments stretched thickly along the borderlands separating several principalities and city-states for the purpose of avoiding jurisdictions and tax districts. If disputes arose regarding such, the city simply moved in a marvelous night-time parade full of hearty mead songs and long, bright masks.

Misling at this point was shuffling quickly because he was hungry. His sponsor, Farmilion was laughing hard and staring at a soapstone statue the size of a thumb, seated across a freeform table from a fat fellow with the bohemian look of a tentman. Beyond them near a dropoff to the valley was a half-submerged rolling troop tower, rusted and stuck in the dirt as wreckage from a long forgotten siege.

"Farmilion, this Recorder has what was needed and is prepared to return home."

The old fellow looked up with a slightly faded smile, eyes blanking quickly and evidently fuzzy on the details of what was being referenced. For just a blink, a very short moment that most would not have noticed at all, the Recorder's face went very lifeless and sad.

"Joy and health, my little mystery talker…my bringer of enigmas. Surely someone in that cluttered curio of yours would turn a jug of sana with such disreputable alley cats as us!" The grinning fellow with whom Farmilion was drinking held forward a shining emerald bottle of the algae wine in offering, towards which Misling motioned his decline. As quickly as it had hardened, the Recorder's expression softened and relaxed, for whatever had come over him had passed.

"And in there…in that magnificently laden globe, would young master Recorder have any helpful principles or mind-expanding enlightenments on the ritual awakening of a…of a whatchamacallit?"

"A carab, my friend", the tentman said.

"Of course, I was just remembering that." Farmilion shut one eye and poked the soapstone figurine to his open eye as he would a gunsight. The mountain cities were from their earliest settlements peppered with trappings of oracles and superstition, largely lubricated through the hallucinogenic wine grown on their hillside terraces. Carabs were small stone men only brought to life in fantasy, through long hours of staring and of imbibing.

"Surely my precious little professor can shine his white light of wisdom on a dottering seeker and explain how to make this blasted thing say something funny…or wise….or perhaps just to burp."

The tentman joined Farmilion in a chuckle.

"Goodman Farmilion, perhaps there is an opportunity to discuss the carab in private during the return trip."

"My invaluable and priceless hermit, dashing at a gallop to sit and stare at his fat benefactor! Surely a bright day in the tent city turning a jug with Goodman Hastine here and unlocking the intriguing mysteries of the mountain common folk edifies more than listening to the odd voices in your crowded interior. In fact, my sly and mischievous elf, it haunts me and has surely not slipped your crisp view that you are obligated and pledged by your very honorable identity, now that I have asked, to explain why this confounding thing won't speak."

Misling watched Farmilion's smiling face, its puffed cheeks and wide nose shaded in pale pink from the drinking. It was a pause of almost awkward duration.

"Nothing in this Recorder's pool qualifies him to speculate on such a ritual, nor is it appropriate for him to do so, sir."

Farmilion's wide shoulders shook as he laughed again.

"A sly elf, no doubt, Goodman Hastine! Pour me another while we discuss your views on the matter."

Hastine's thick fingers upturned another flashing jade bottle of sana into a glazed ceramic mug as he glanced up past Misling's eyes to the Recorder's decorated forehead.

"No intentions of being offensive to your Recorder, my friend, but his calling unsettles me." Misling failed to sustain his neutral expression at the insight Hastine had provided Farmilion.

"I don't feel good about anything common I might say being recited in a hundred years."

"A fair though inelegant push, good sir. Certainly if my little elf could strike from the Record anything incautious you might let slip in an unguarded moment, I'm confident he would do so. Certainly the will is there, Hastine, though if not the liberty. I wonder if perhaps you could hold more closely to your bosom any further commentary which might upset young master Recorder. And on to this little beggar then…"

When it was clear Hastine and Farmilion would continue their winding discussion of the lifeless carab, Misling stepped back softly in his practiced fashion and sat cross-legged in the shade of a broad fountain blossom tree. Culturally in those days, a Recorder's sudden appearance or departure weren't events for which one spared concern or noticed. After a cautious scan for observers, he pulled from a pocket two umber sticks of bakas jerky and began chewing.

Misling watched the two fat men at their cups, absenting his gaze after a moment to linger on two beautiful children, a boy and a girl, riding their father's shoulders at once with out-stretched arms as he ran playfully. Misling took a deeper breath and intentionally turned back to burn the image of Hastine and Farmilion into the Record before closing his eyes in meditation. Exactly how long he was inside the Record wasn't something he could have answered thereafter.

At such times, when a young Recorder would unleash memories

in his Pool and allow them to unwind, he would recall the intricate and exhaustive sensory details embedded in the crystalline precision of Mast and flesh those incredible descriptions into moments as like any true moments lived personally. It was an awesome and terrible exercise, held in deep reverence for millenia, and even so, was still among the most misunderstood of rites maintained by the Recorders. Flashes in the timing and narrative of dreams bundled years of living: falling in love, fearing for an ill parent, killing in war, giving birth and a train of other moments which were destined for eternality because of the presence at one time of a Recorder. Collectively, the pools of memories maintained by all the Recorders of a generation was referred to as the Record; and even in the days of this story, that idea was among the highest and most perfect of human achievements.

Misling at last opened his eyes, distressed and sweating and evidently with the waxing sense of having been watched. He saw the little boy and girl he'd noted earlier now staring curiously up at him only a hand's width from his nose. He cocked his head, noting the girl's key interest was his forehead tattoo while the boy seemed taken with his nose. Over by the table, Farmilion was absent although Hastine was there in a lively dialogue with Ring and a coarse looking woman with her hand on Hastine's shoulder. Just as Ring noticed him and waved him over with a smile, the little girl tried to rub a smear on his tattoo with a tiny soft finger.

"Mine always rub off."

Misling watched her in order to acknowledge in his way, then eyed the boy to see what insight he could provide.

"Do you want to wrestle?" The boy's wide smile was pocked with two missing teeth.

Misling shook his head to decline, then wiped a stream of sweat with his thumb. Once the boy had run off, the girl's soft face hardened shockingly — wrinkled and angry, calling to mind the sudden onset of a black storm cloud shutting out the sun.

"You who have whored your freedom, taste the rape of the

chained!" Her tone was different and icy, like someone else was speaking through her. The Recorder stared on, suddenly lost.

"Stay away from the bell tower."

"Where is your father? Are you ill?"

"My daddy says you're a watcher and a listener; but you won't be when they're through with you. You won't be."

It was for him as if her words were garbled in rushing wind, "Who are these people? Why would you say such a thing?"

"They'll hear you breathing. It's hard to hold your breath when you're scared. Stay away from the bell tower, Recorder. Stay away."

She tapped his forehead once more before rising and sprinting in a zig-zag, darting in and out of the resin automata tending the fields, towards the direction from which she'd come. He watched, pale as a corpse, till Ring called for him. There was no warning, no evident or clear reason why this absolute stranger in such a form as a young girl who had so briefly before been lost in joy on her father's shoulders, had at once then turned dire prophet. The girl had by this point vanished into the barley fields; and Misling was startled and shaken as he stood and rejoined Hastine.

The woman took no notice of Misling and had pretty brown eyes although the skin of her face was rough and dry and unhealthy. Ring was sitting cross-legged tossing the thundercloud-colored carab about in his hands, only glancing occasionally at Misling. The three of them were seated around a stone firepit in chairs and at an intimate table with the unmistakable sheen of ProMat, a programmable matter which could readily be dissolved and tanked or repurposed into other geometries. They had evidently been there for some time and were deep into a discussion apparently driven by the passionate tentman. Misling only with some effort regained his stoicism – he straightened his shirt at times like this, when he needed balance.

"…your age have no idea the scale of violence that went on years ago. Pampered, and never having had to fight for your way of life. It's a different way of looking at your world to think someone out there doesn't want you to go on doing what you do every day." Hastine was continuing his discussion as if Misling hadn't rejoined.

"That's so, is it, Hastine?" Farmilion appeared coming back from behind a tent, straightening his fly after urinating. He was smiling mischievously; and now that they were all standing it was more clear how short and fat he really was.

"And that's what you were thinking in those days when Talgo was burning the shipyards, high and grand pontification on the unfortunate twists in the nature of man and how very courageous you were for facing it full-on, and not perhaps where there might be a quiet place to have a sip and talk to a pretty woman, ay Selisa?"

Selisa smiled at Farmilion as he gently tapped her chin; but Hastine kept to his agenda despite the chiding.

"Your grandfathers saw horrible times and times of the highest human expression…great wars, economic collapse, and disasters. Your fathers remember the deaths of great men or what they were doing when they heard news of events that shook the world. But your generation is left with nothing to believe in. We killed your religion and left you in those tall shadows. Whether it's blasphemy, I can't say. That's a matter of faith. But when we let slip the glue that founded and adhered our civilization for thousands of years, we truly failed you…because we replaced it with nothing.

"Really, Hastine." Farmilion chided him.

"So what do you stand for then?" He pointed to his right at nothing obvious, and in his urgency began to improperly include Misling in his eye contact.

"I stood at the Yagrada dock and watched a hundred thousand men submerge into the battle of Sarling. That's now just a date in a textbook – schoolkids don't even know why they went. When we're stuck with lunatics like old man Talgos sons and bloodthirsty fiefdoms clawing at our walls, your generation sits waiting on the next calamity to give them an identity."

Hastine and Selisa stood to follow Farmilion once he'd motioned towards the wrecked troop tower, indicating they would finish their conversation from its height looking out over the broad city. Misling waited till Ring followed suit.

"Well I'm not a local; but it seems to me everyone around here is drafted into the military, so I'm not sure where you're coming from. You seem to have a pretty clear vision of what you're looking for. What is it you'd have done?" Ring found a seat beside Hastine and rested his foot against a railing. Selisa rolled her eyes, no doubt having heard Hastine's answer to this before.

"Oh, you've done it now, little stranger. It saddens the tragedy that such well-intentioned and respectful curiosity is to be repaid with what is to follow." Farmilion patted Ring's shoulders playfully.

"Don't any of you start with me, he asked my opinion. War is not self-evidently evil, it's a function, like money or weddings or laws. Most are justified, I'd say. Sets limits for those who require them. Boundaries. It's naïve to think otherwise; and the need renews every generation when the limits age and start to be questioned – when it's not clear they still hold. My problem is the void of leadership in high places. When a soldier is laid as sacrifice for a hill or piece of ground, it wasn't Goodman Farmilion's twists in the nature of man that put him there, it was his general. We need better leaders; and I'm not sure democracy does that. I'm not sure dictatorship does that either."

"I'm sorry, did you answer my question?"

"We throw Judge Talgo out and his weird son. We keep that misfit, Revin as far away from the Judgeship as possible. Either put Marshal Peri in charge or better yet, establish a parliament and draft them from a pool of free citizens nominated by the city. Have them serve for four years, then return to being a private citizen with no chance to build an empire or get entrenched in ridiculous politics."

"Like a roaring burner to a balloon, you inflate my pessimism with your expectations of our countrymen, assuming such a deep bench of talent and motivation, such an ability to overcome steep learning curves in only four years that our nominees will be inexhaustible. I imagine only a handful of cycles in, we'll be posting wild wanoa from the field into offices and smacking their backsides in hopes of their relearning speech."

Farmilion continued, but broke into laughing, "Possibly, they're our only hope to simplify the taxes."

As they chuckled and shifted their positions for idle comfort, Misling looked again for the little girl in the barley field. Farmilion took the carab from Ring's hand and tossed it over the twisted railing.

"It's bugging me. Tell us your story; and let's give Goodman Hastine a chance to catch his breath. My little professor doesn't break from his introversion often; and you're a happy surprise. I hope we've not met, my memory is quite soft."

Misling engaged as he hadn't till this point, fully locking on Ring's face for an answer. Ring's knowing grin was different from before, as if he were deciding between a secret or a falsehood. He was looking out over the city, pocked with rises and towers, with ultramarine Balcister crowded among slate gabled apartments and alpine rises to the east and the bustling immigrant neighborhoods to the west. Much of the city was shrouded in its cluttered rooftops, drawing the fancy that one could walk from one end to the other simply on slate and copper domed roofs if not on its elevated covered walkways. Blocked only by the highest cliff with its sculpted waterfall, the view of the valley was beautiful. Ring's hesitation ended at last.

"I'm interested in making certain visitations…five of them. You'll appreciate this, Goodman Hastine. I want the world to be different because I was here…to be better…I want to be remembered; and I need to see certain things to understand the essence of the age."

"Five, is it? Will that quite do it? What's made your list?"

"Our tent city, no doubt, is one." Selisa joined in. "You worked the place like a politician before stepping in with us saying you were looking for the Recorder like he doesn't have a blazing sign on his head."

Farmilion continued when Ring offered nothing further except perhaps a slight sense that the guess wasn't right at all, "It sounds so mythological, I absolutely love it. And the central market, where the Salt Mystic first stepped from the flats to tell of her visions…you met the little professor there. That was on your list as well!"

"That's a fair bit of ground to cover in one morning."

"Blast it, Hastine! I'm trying to puzzle out his list. Keep quiet! The essence of the age…you'll need to hear from the military. A battlegroup then, perhaps one deployed in the flats."

"I spent the summer in the white fleet." Ring answered both Hastine and Farmilion at once.

"The Augur", Selisa added, drawing wide eyes from Farmilion, who stood and locked hands at his back hips to pace in thought as he mumbled an agreement.

"Have you spoken to it?" Ring asked Farmilion.

"I have no idea. Would think I would remember." He glanced to Misling, who shrugged in response.

"So the white fleet, the central market; and our own fabulous moveable village are in your bag. You've plans to pay a call to the Augur, a disturbing and mysterious experience I'm told. But I'm at an impasse to determine your fifth stop, my ambitious little novelty. Young master Recorder must join you in these final visitations, it's too intriguing to leave it alone."

Misling's back straightened at the news, his mouth inappropriately gaping. Hastine spoke before Misling could interject.

"What are you to do once you've sorted all this out, then? How are you to make a difference?" Hastine was impatient for details, but was ignored again.

"But where could your fifth visitation be? What would you pick apart to see the clockworks of our very times?" At Farmilion's question, they each looked at Ring's face. He eventually answered.

"The Rauchka sniper." He shrugged.

Each of them apart from Misling gave voice to their interest as they connected his dots. Hastine however, wasn't yet bought in.

"What could that thing possibly tell you of any importance? It's monstrous and irrelevant."

"What do you think, Misling?" Ring pulled in the Recorder, engendering curiosity in at least Selisa and Hastine. Farmilion took to the name straightaway before Misling could react.

"What did you call him? Misling…does it mean something? It's brilliant. I love it. Your name is Misling now. It's absolutely what you've needed, you magnificent and noble castaway."

The Recorder began to place his eyebrows against his thumb and index finger in order to process or perhaps unplug from what he was hearing; but Ring pressed for a reaction.

"Will you see the Rauchka sniper with me? I won't start any trouble."

Misling looked to Farmilion, who announced the plan's settlement. Hastine refined further, "Farmilion will be joining Selisa and I at Balcister the day after tomorrow for lunch. There is a café by the fountain where the event readers go. I'd like to hear about your visitation. If we're not there, we'll be in the tower at the bank. Just wait for us."

The four of them settled their arrangements, inviting Ring to sleep on board Farmilion's dirigible rover before getting started in the morning. Quite awkwardly, when he saw the group breaking up, Misling stepped in and gave Farmilion a clumsy hug, shutting his eyes just briefly before glancing nervously around himself. It was the kind of clumsy an ostrich or big crane might be, lumbering about on a cold morning.

Farmilion chuckled and patted his arm, "Dear boy."

It was a sweet moment, not lost on Ring, who only nodded and grinned. Ring and Misling stepped back down the curved ladderwell to have a look at it, leaving the others to a walk to the hilly paraball fields where an afternoon game was assembling. No one mentioned the hug; and the Recorder probably wouldn't have discussed it anyway.

Instead, Ring smiled widely as the two of them approached Farmilion's vessel, intrigued by the rover's eccentricity. He ran his hands over the colorful and grotesque figurehead on its bow: a sculpted very young girl's face and arms outstretching an icicle sword as if hopelessly warding off dragons. The rover had a sparse windshielded cabin, but a railed open area astern much like a pleasure boat, resting on a flat bateau-like keel rather than rails as more expensive rovers did in those days. There were visible patches on the hull and a bright green painted graffito along the starboard length which said, 'this too will pass'.

Four long and narrow gasbags the color of polished brass were arranged in a diamond when viewed from the front, providing better stability in high winds than a single larger bag. They were ornately illustrated with thin black celtic swirls and looked to be of greater worth than the rest of the ship as if they had been gifted or stolen. It was a vehicle intended for leisurely pace and lift sufficient only to raise it above rocks and terrain such that a drive fan moved it along. Ring sauntered directly to the helm, eyeing strange controls which looked to be an imitation brass.

"Please do not launch this vessel."

"Misling, when are you going to tell me what the little girl said to you? You were clearly out of sorts from the moment she left you; and you stared after her during what I thought was an incredibly pivotal discussion."

"Please do not launch this vessel. It is evident you have difficulty remaining still. Perhaps if you went for a run…"

"Why so nervous? It floats. What did she say?" Ring slid the lee helm throttle forward, drawing a deep hum from the drive fan, then smiled at his success.

"She seemed to be quoting something, or perhaps delivering a message. It was possibly a garbled threat."

"And her words were…"

"'You who have whored your freedom, taste the rape of the chained.'" At that, Ring's face showed he may have heard it before. He was put out a moment before slipping back into a grin.

"Odd. You're having a strange day, aren't you, little professor? Is that all she said?"

Misling hesitated, using the time to think while he looked out over the weed choked precipice leading down the mountain face into the valley, the direction the rover was beginning to slide.

"That is all she said."

Ring watched the Recorder's face a moment, judging something, then leaned forward over the chestnut helm wheel to look into the broad river valley.

"What in the world did she mean by that?"

"Rover vessels run low to the ground, and drift in high winds. One does not slide such a vessel down the side of a mountain.

Farmilion's intentions were for you to rest in advance of your visitation tomorrow, not to joy ride and place his property in jeopardy."

"Oh, we'll be fine. Air's thicker down there. We should sail over it like butter."

Misling bowed under the opening and headed for the railed platform behind the cabin to leave. Although the rover was only a moment from the mountainside, he stopped. Ring watched him, happily surprised he hadn't left already when the Recorder peered back through.

"It is irresponsible! Do you truly believe you can change the world?"

Ring draped his hand over the helm wheel to brace himself as the rover slid over the weeds and brush beginning to tilt.

"I have no idea. But it will be fun to try."

4 A CANNON OFF THE WHEELS

It isn't any longer common knowledge what Denai was really like in those days, a floating metropolis whose gleaming white towers and curves rose above the ocean encircled by a weathered stone wall. Like shaken hornets, merchant submarines and cargo ships swirled within its wide, crowded harbor. Invisible from the surface, long sleek buildings jutted down into the ocean eventually converging into a spoked wheel construction in the depths popularly known as, "The Reaches". It was from this seedy neighborhood of casinos, drug labs, and brothels that the real governors of Denai ruled, a cadre of untouchable dons managing extensive organized crime networks which outright bought the loyalty of the citizens.

A massive vortex cruiser had docked, its gleaming silver hull poised topheavy and impossibly high above the choppy water and hydrofoil rails balanced on invisible whirlwinds. Gulls scattered as dock workers tossed mooring lines and ran busily about tying off the vessel. A small crowd of onlookers had formed on the pier hoping to catch a glimpse of Cyprian, son of the Marshal of Tanith, who was said to have been on the ship.

His leather coat bristled in the sea winds as he stepped over the quarterdeck, the illusions of fire just larger than candle flames on broad black shoulderboards unaffected. His ball lightning carbine, the one with swirling celtic circles along the armature and which came to such fame later, was slung over a shoulder strap hanging from his back; and the ferocity of his expression was enough to turn celebrity watchers away awkwardly. With dusty boots, charred insulation on the armshield of his carbine, and a scar across his right temple, Cyprian clearly bore the look of a fierce fighter despite being a young man. A low ranking official was there to greet him.

"Welcome to Denai, Goodman Cyprian. My name is Ventrey. When the dons heard you would be visiting, they were understandably-" Cyprian interrupted his greeting by walking away.

"You will need to turn in your carbine and your knife. I'll see to it that-"

"Know your place, lapdog. You're an irrelevant functionary, act like it. Where are they?"

Chasing after Cyprian, Ventrey pulled a slim railgun and pointed it forward hesitantly, hoping the threat would shape events more to his expectations. Cyprian snatched it from his hand so suddenly, it nearly snapped the poor fellow's trigger finger. Certainly, it was too fast for a defensive reaction. He examined the railgun on two sides, evaluating its worth, then slipped it into one of the long pockets on his thighs while failing to even slow his stride.

"You're attracting too much attention; and you're armed. Your even being here is a problem. You can't meet them. It's like you don't even understand who you are!"

"If you say anything more to me other than, 'this meeting is arranged, follow me', I swear to you I will drown you in a toilet! Don't doubt me, lapdog. They've cost me a lot of money."

Continuing to hurry along toward the massive elevator complex, Ventrey held a finger to his throat to speak softly through a comm unit.

"The meeting is arranged. They knew you'd be like this. But you can't go armed, you'll have to turn over the guns. I'll hold your weapon within line of sight and return it when you're back topside. The knife too."

They had arrived in the giant atrium housing the central elevator complex, elevators which led to the undersea structures including the Reaches. The murmuring crowds flowed unevenly, breaking like a spent wave around Cyprian, whose height and appearance drew him out noticeably. He locked eyes with the man who was asking for his weapons, allowing only this pause as opportunity for a change of heart. When it was clear that was Ventrey's position, Cyprian moved quickly again.

Shoving the fellow into a column, Cyprian grasped Ventrey's hair and cocked his head to the side exposing his throat. He slammed a brightly tattooed finger into the place where Ventrey had accessed his communications just then and spoke into it himself.

"This will go so badly for you if I have to find you myself."

Following a tense standoff, Ventrey at last communicated his superiors' change of heart and the two made their way down into the serpentine corridors of the Reaches. The wide acrylic windows of the upper levels, opening to illuminated cobalt seas fluttering with moon-colored jelly-bells and predator fish, they disappeared in the lower levels. In fact, the Reaches were a dim nest of narrow hallways broadening into massive ballrooms housing loud casinos, bars, dance clubs and illegal theaters. It was a place of prostitution, slavery, abuse, and human horror fueled by grinning travelers and hard luck mineral miners. The handful of crime lords operating from these smoky backrooms led activities ranging throughout the mountains, salt flats, and beyond.

A dark old man stood to block Cyprian's way forward when they entered Moloch, Denai's largest casino. He was as tall as Cyprian with bulging eyes and the black skin of his face tight, almost looking cracked. He wore a gray hood and held forward as if it were a lantern a deep ebony carab-man the length of a forearm.

"All fortunes have momentum, young Talgo. Forces and players. Forces and players."

Cyprian frowned, lacking patience for this, "Step aside, old man."

"When that momentum sways against you, it is to be interrupted. Forces and players. Forces and players."

When Ventrey made an effort to gently coax the mystic to the side, the old man shook his head violently and held the carab higher.

"They turn their backs on a light that illuminated the world for seven hundred generations…true transforming knowledge…and gamble with its trappings! They bring us promises and distractions, pretty lights and beautiful empty people; but they bring us nothing for our souls!" The mystic shattered the carab against a wall angrily. While Ventrey stood shocked at the suddenness and anger of the old mystic, Cyprian was already continuing past him, entirely uninterested in whatever was the man's true purpose. The mystic called after him uselessly.

"Nothing for our souls, Talgo!"

On one side of the broad gaming floor, men playing the deadly card game, "Black Hallow" tried to catch knives thrown at one another. Beyond the dice and glass bead games in the central complex, there were lacquered oak doors leading to intense, sana-injected roleplaying games where people were said to lose their minds as losses. At some of the higher stakes games involving carabs and one actually involving an emanation, fevered men and women were betting their fortunes and body parts in mad frenzies. Cyprian only briefly surveyed the sweep of color and motion before advancing into the meeting hall to his right.

Inside, at least ten armed men actuated their carbines at once, clicking and sizzling in unison. The dons were assembled, three men and a woman lounging casually in expensive clothes. Apart from one of the men, who was young and had perhaps inherited his status, they were of advanced age and very relaxed considering the firepower in the room.

"Which of you should I be looking at?" Cyprian didn't acknowledge the ten weapons aimed at his chest, but rather scanned the four dons for a sign of authority, some indication of who would answer for the group or to whom deference was shown. The youngest of them answered in a defiant tone but with the voice of a very young man.

"We are all equals here." At that, Cyprian took a half step closer to the one who'd spoken.

"Then you can share in my irritation. Fifty cases of sana were to be delivered to Systelion Station. They weren't there; and my contact disappeared. You owe me for damages; and I'll take my payment now." Cyprian was immobile like granite, his voice commanding. The young don started a half-smile at Cyprian's boldness before glancing toward the others, then faded it quickly upon seeing their reactions. The woman crossed her legs before joining in with the grotesque and slow voice of a provincial grandmother. Although the dons relinquished their proper names upon rising to this level of power, she was known in common terms as The Sting and was perhaps the most dangerous of a group of supposed equals.

"Sweetheart, you're being a snit. Don't come in here and be a snit to us. That cargo comes from raiding parties; but things are all wonky with the mountain nation right now. You ought to know that since you're in the middle of it."

"If you lacked the courage, then why was an arrangement made?"

"You smart mouthed punk!" A pallid and thin don with white chest hair visible above his buttoned shirt interrupted. Cyprian pointed at the old don quickly as he answered in defiance.

"Watch your mouth, old man." There was a moment at this point when the old don glanced back to two of the armed men as if in anticipation of their coming at once to his defense at the insult. There was no movement, however; and Cyprian clearly noted the connection, which of the men belonged to this one. The woman, cool and professional in an expensive cable-knit wool brocade with her streaked hair piled high, watched Cyprian all along before stepping in again. Her face was only somewhat attractive, although powerfully confident and commanding; and her eyes were piercing blue like gas flames and cold.

"Let's be grown-ups. We're not going to gun down the son of a marshal, and certainly not a Talgo. You know, you could clear up much of our commerce through some pointed discussions with your daddy."

"You want to talk to Cassian, talk to him. It's nothing to do with me. I need to know you can be trusted to make deals. I tried to involve you, show you some respect; and you run away like children."

"Lieutenants made a good call based on the conditions. It happens."

"Are you lying to me? Don't walk away from your panic. If you're cowards, say so!"

"You embarrass your grandfather's legacy. You're a clown." The oldest don who'd insulted Cyprian before spoke, almost spitting his disgust.

"I told you once to shut your mouth. I can tell you're irrelevant to the others because of their reaction to you. I don't want to hear your voice again."

"Control yourself or this meeting is over." Ventrey leaned closer to Cyprian to whisper his warning, doubtless concerned with the rising tension in the chamber and Cyprian's own reputation for reckless violence. The woman clearly regretted the approach she'd taken with him.

"A snit. I swear, you just came in here looking to argue, didn't you? If we can get you off your agenda and pointed more constructively towards your daddy's bumbling, then maybe nothing nasty has to happen at all." The woman's voice sounded kind and disarming despite its dark undertones and context.

"He's built a bird's nest of pacts and treaties with silly parts of the world he's no business meddling with. He's promised Tanith's protection across the world and makes bullying noises at his brother. If world war doesn't break out in a backwater, it will happen in the shadows of those mountains. There's a whole generation out there waiting on their war; and your daddy is handing it to them. Big boots track mud, Talgo. You should know that."

"The point is that you need to do something with him or we'll do it for you." The youngest don spoke boldly, this time without gauging the reactions of his peers. Perhaps this was his first threat in this position; and he was relishing the words and the drama they entailed.

"I'm insulted." Cyprian spoke angrily through gritted teeth. "I'm insulted by your babbling and its implications that I can be manipulated. I'm insulted by this flunky you send to meet me and this room full of pointed guns. I'm insulted by this piece of filth here that speaks to me like he's bullying for lunch money!"

Several men in the back tensed again in anticipation. The older don shifted uncomfortably in his seat, glancing again to his guards as the young man took a step backwards slowly. The fourth don, in an expensive knotted wool cap slid low to his brows and sitting cross-legged in the corner, still had not spoken and watched placidly.

"You threaten my father to my face and ask me to run errands. If you were me, what would you do?" It may have been lost on some of those in the room; but subtly just then, Cyprian had actually asked that question of the men pointing their carbines at him and not of the assembled crime lords. His eyes lingered only a blink on their faces before looking back to the oldest of them.

"This isn't about your reputation, you self important punk. It's a world war we're talking about! If it starts anywhere, it runs out of control."

Cyprian touched his hand to the stock of his carbine, still hanging on his back but such that he could readily slide its molded assembly around to his forearm. That obviously wasn't lost on those watching; but the room was only hotter in its tension. He crowded the old man menacingly but spoke only a little more softly through clenched teeth.

"I told you to shut up, you fat donkey. I've had my fill of you; and I'll have an apology. Now. And I swear, you passed-over, swollen, hairy-eared, clotted old man, I will burn off your face if I hear anything apart from that. Understand me; and think carefully before opening your wrinkled mouth again."

It is difficult to imagine anything someone in that room could say to defuse what Cyprian had constructed as they all froze and waited for someone's first move, watching each other as if one of them were soon to shatter like a wine glass. Here was the scion of a powerful remnant of the shattered world government that once ruled the entire planet, goading into a frenzy an impetuous and short-tempered crime lord surrounded by his peers who in all likelihood would relish his death.

"I apologize for being late." At that moment, an out of breath fellow rushed in, armed with a railgun in a side holster strapped to his thigh. "I'm sure somebody's system broke down and I'm misreading what's happening in this room right now. Can't imagine such an assembly would be together like this without my being here. Look at all these important people, right?"

"Lanier." Cyprian nodded respectfully and in recognition of the old warrior, who it was commonly known was a dear friend of Grebel, the rough salt flatsman who'd largely raised Cyprian in the Marshal's absence or neglect. In these, the final days of Denai, Lanier was a peacekeeper and defender of the city, head of its limited fleet and militia. Many of the tactics he'd used in the last days of Naraia were still studied in war schools across the world; and his bold forays into front line combat inspired new leadership paradigms for mechanized warfare and supply line protection. It was generally held to be a sad end for such a great man to finish his career protecting a clearing house for wickedness; and he took his reasons for that decision to the grave.

"Cyprian." Lanier returned the greetings and scanned the guards, many of whom had lowered their firearms although none were at rest. He indicated the guards with a wave of his arm.

"Gentlemen and lady, make something sensible happen here." When the crime lords did not command a stand-down, Lanier addressed the guards directly. His reputation was already working on them.

"This young man is far more dangerous in a crowded room than one-on-one. You know that. You're not helping. Take their silence as agreement. Lower your weapons, right now!"

Muddled and at a loss for what else to do, the men did as they'd been asked. In fact, two of them slid their carbines to their shoulders and walked out of the room while a third stepped to a counter bathed in orange light and poured himself a drink. It was actually awkward for a few minutes while tensions settled at Lanier's unanticipated though timely arrival.

"My friend, Grebel is well?"

"He is." Cyprian granted a cautious deference to Lanier, taking his cue from the old soldier. Lanier's hair was peppered black and gray like steel wool; and his face, tanned and rough. "He is a woman. Tell him I said that. An annoying, farting old woman."

Cyprian loosely smiled as Lanier leaned confidentially, "I'd like this meeting to be over with. Is that something we can do?"

"No, it isn't." He fiercely watched the oldest don, who only waved his hand dismissively and went to pour himself a drink.

"If there has been any insult or offense, I apologize on their behalf. I'm sure a misunderstanding is at its heart."

Cyprian locked eyes with the woman known as The Sting, "I expect your people to reach out to me with compensation."

Critically, in a nuance only the most perceptive of observers would notice, rather than nodding in assent or addressing Cyprian's directed demands, the lady crime lord sought acknowledgement from the silent don in the corner before agreeing. Cyprian's eyes squinted at this move, indicating either the silent one held true authority, or The Sting sought to falsely communicate as such. Lanier failed to notice any of this, but rather seemed most urgent to get Cyprian from the room. He shepherded the young man towards the door and indicated three escorts in waiting.

"It was good to see you, boy. You've sprouted."

The escorts widened into an arc as Cyprian and Lanier stepped outside the lacquered doors into Moloch's main hall where frenzied joy cries were coming from the Black Hallow tables. Cyprian's demeanor was dark and brooding, restrained. Lanier edged him to a quiet corner where a milky white automaton squatted at rest awaiting something to clean.

"I know I'm a little crusty; but I'm not an idiot. Talgos don't come in person to argue about busted deals."

"Stay out of it."

"I fought for your grandfather; and I fought for your uncle. Listen to me, I earned that. I'm telling you, stop whatever you're doing. It's pretty clear you came to gauge their structure and capabilities, and maybe to do more. I don't know. The Old Man would have burned the room down and all of them with it to take over their houses, giggling all the while. I have an idea you may have considered something along those lines yourself. Please, next time you come for a visit, come to see me and not them."

As was common to many Talgos, Cyprian's appearance inspired a mild sort of awe. Where his cousin, Stendahl drew one in magnetically with deep green eyes, oddly white hair, and a gentle mysterious nature, Cyprian was frightening. His dark mystique was almost a third person there beside them, hovering in its intensity. He embodied the Talgo recklessness, ferocity, and command presence that in different times held together nations and drove screaming legions. And he was still a young man. As with his strange cousin, the common people were fascinated with his goings, although his lifestyle bred conspiracy theories and controversy. Lanier had cast his life before this young man's bloodline and had been there when he was born; but even now he clearly felt a pull, like the feeling of again seeing an old boss from years ago.

"I'll tell Grebel I saw you."

"A farting old woman…" Lanier reminded, pointing a finger in the air.

Cyprian grimly joined two of the escorts to return to the harbor topside. Lanier watched him leave, his mind no doubt conjuring pictures of other Talgos and the wreckage that was left in their wake. Those at Moloch's gaming tables and machines turned to watch him leave; and people throughout pointed and discussed him. Lanier at that moment showed in his face the helplessness of a man watching his house burn.

Out of his sight and along a broad corridor lined with tropical plants and painted softly with blue tinted lights shining through the acrylic sea windows, Ventrey trotted gently up to join Cyprian and the two escorts Lanier had provided.

"I've got this, guys. L wanted me to walk him personally. Head on back." His voice was chatty and routine; and the two escorts only nodded to do as they'd been instructed. Unseen by Ventrey, Cyprian grinned and lowered his head as he slowed his pace. When Lanier's men were out of earshot, four others stepped from the shadows and engaged their carbines. He was surrounded on all sides and stopped where he was, his hand resting tenderly on his own weapon.

Ventrey stepped close to make eye contact and puffed up his chest and shoulders, like he was setting up to say something threatening. He coughed.

"Did I upset you, lapdog?" Cyprian's voice was soft.

"You can't just threaten them like that. Jeopardizes the whole structure we've got here. You brought it on yourself, honestly. And I've got a lot of anticipation here; because I was just going to have someone put a slug in your forehead on the ship. A couple of the guys thought better of it to see what you could do."

"Risky."

"I don't know about that. Fascinating though. Nobody's going to start a war over you…the world isn't like that anymore, Talgo."

"Less chatter!" The guy behind Cyprian spat this out.

"You want to see something amazing?" Cyprian's grin was sinister, thrilled.

Another of those surrounding Cyprian, the one with a burn on his cheek, smiled wickedly, "Whatever. Rich boy."

The young Talgo watched the face of the one who'd last spoken, the one excitedly awaiting a show full of drama and color, swirling action and a thrilling recount for his friends. He did the same for some of the others and saw the same eagerness, a boyish delight in a playground brawl with the biggest kid in school. He had clearly seen this before and was maybe surprised at how alike these sorts of people are.

"I know your tricks, jay bird." A darker man to Cyprian's side spoke, one with an eye squinting more than the other. "Two breakers in your carbine – fires twice as fast. You prance around like a dancing idiot while we panic and try not to shoot each other because you're you. They write books about you, jay bird."

Ventrey had been watching the olive man who'd spoken, then at last turned back to Cyprian, "Give me back my gun."

Cyprian kept silent. He turned his eyes to each of the men about him, waiting on one of them to do something other than threaten. Impatiently, he raised his eyebrow and gently shook his head as if to signal, 'well, I'm waiting'. Perhaps they were only blustering. At any rate, when he moved, it was with ferocity.

Like a crocodile attacking, Cyprian leaned in and thrust his right heel behind him, crunching backwards the knee of the man approaching him there. The fellow quickly went down grunting like an animal and collapsing around that knee. Before he had even fallen, Cyprian had shifted his carbine to his forearm and slung a ball of lightning through the falling man's forehead exploding it in charred and smoking fragments.

Smoothly as if he'd seen their return fire in slow motion or on game film beforehand, Cyprian twisted the insulated shield of his carbine through the air blocking their shots in sequence. He spun a full circle throwing his carbine arm out to smash Ventrey's jaw with the barrel, drawing out a tooth and fired multiple precise shots off, throwing the others into defensive moves shielding themselves. Lightning popped and rushed around them and hissed as balls popped out of existence in searing flames.

In a blur and seizing their hesitation, Cyprian jutted his forearm toward the olive man, placing his barrel in line with and pointing into the other carbine's barrel. There was shock in the fellow's eyes as the two of them fired, Cyprian's firing twice, and exploded the weapon right there on the attacker's arm. He screamed like a hog as his arm up to the shoulder and the lower part of his neck burned away.

Cyprian fluidly blocked another series of return shots from the remaining two attackers, men who were by now firing wildly and wide-eyed. When he fired back, two of his shots bored holes through another of them, sending him to the ground smoking like a falling airplane. Cyprian shouted and rushed the remaining attacker, the one with the burn on his cheek who'd called him a rich boy. In his moment, his chance that he'd anticipated, he only froze and hesitated as a Talgo in full war cry came upon him and drove like a spear his fist and the flaming hot barrel of his carbine directly through the attacker's throat, bursting out the other side in a spray of blood and smoke.

Cyprian inhaled deeply and looked around himself. The railing along the corridor was lit up in St. Elmo's fire, whispering in puffs that sounded like a flickering cutting torch. Two of the attackers were still on fire. Ventrey groaned from the floor. The young Talgo stepped closer and placed his boot's heel on Ventrey's throat. He powered down his carbine and slid it back, then reached into his thigh pocket for the railgun he'd taken from the man upon his arrival.

"I'm important to them…" Ventrey's voice betrayed shattered

teeth and a swollen tongue.

Cyprian held the weapon up a moment, then turned it down to fire between Ventrey's eyes without hesitating or bragging. He widened his grip to let the railgun fall freely onto Ventrey's chest, then turned to leave, the sound of his footsteps echoing and the false fires of his shoulder boards casting long shadows along the broad corridors.

5 THE RAUCHKA SNIPER

"There you are, getting all feathered up again! That's what I'm talking about!" Ring was walking alongside the Recorder in a pine glade, both of them entirely drenched, their clothes stuck to them and dripping and their arms flared out. Misling's glare was his only response.

"Listen, I'm not a machine guy. I don't know why it got stuck up there. I would have thought the compressor doohickey would have fired up this morning after sitting idle all night; but it's cool. Why can't you just be excited that we got stuck over the lake so we could jump?"

"Do you have a map or some sense of orientation such that this journey is not subject to the whims of your attention deficit?"

"Are you kidding me? You have five people inside your head and not one of you knows how to get to the Cave City?"

"Please limit your responses to those which address that which was inquired."

"I have a general sense of wellbeing that emanates from this direction over here. We'll go that way. Should be close. How hard could it be to find…has a city in it, right?"

"You comfortably notify perfect strangers of your intent to mark the world with your presence yet you receive your direction from a general sense of wellbeing!"

"You know, Misling, what I find most endearing about you is how irritated you get. You love to tap on that tattoo of yours; but were you even listening in class?"

As they were walking, the clearing opened further through a gap in the fir and pine trees to a broad shining stream beyond the grassy bank of which was a weathered black statue one quarter sunk into the moss. It was of a commanding yet forgotten warlord from very long ago with his dark hands clasped prayer-like against the upside-down hilt of a cablesword, part of which was broken off near the monument's lowest visible portion. At its prime, it was perhaps three times life size; and its location said clearly this desolate woodland was at one time either a trade route or of some other importance and not at all as it appeared now.

"What's the deal with Farmilion…how did you wind up with him?"

Ring sat cross-legged beside the stream and skipped a flat stone across to the mossy bank. Misling admired the monument from its base, then began clambering up to get a closer look.

"Goodman Farmilion was at one time a respected dramatist. He gained a state protectorship when he lost his memory."

"Why, what happened to him?"

"That piece of the Record is sealed."

"Till he dies or forever?"

"That is sealed."

"Well who sealed it?"

"That is sealed."

"Come on!" Ring twisted to face Misling, who was curiously examining carved runes running alongside the cablesword's length.

"He wrote dramas…for the living theater, right?" Ring referred to the popular theater conducted in and throughout registered participant's lives with actors and magician's tricks, an art form that had once been very prominent and influential but had faded in its importance.

"He wrote satires as well. He was actually quite feared by many in prominence."

"Was it a Talgo who sealed his Record?" Ring watched the Recorder for a telling reaction, which was not at all forthcoming. Instead, the Recorder continued unaffected running his fingers along the night-black curves of the inscribed memorial. He scratched away a white spot of bird dropping with his fingernail.

"He was considered blasphemous and controversial, bringing new and scandalous conventions to the art. Much of popular drama today owes its boundaries to Farmilion's early works. For example, he was the first to include the Salt Mystic as a character in a work of fiction."

"Whatever. He seems nice."

Misling eyed Ring a moment, then returned to his scratching, "The bakas...it comes from many people who owe him great debts, and gold as well sometimes. He gives his proceeds to the poor children who inhabit the pier bridges and leads them in a dance to the markets so their parents do not take from them what he has given."

Ring smiled, "That's fantastic. What did he do for these people?"

Misling's voice went softer, "He does not know."

Ring watched him a moment, pondering, then idly resumed skipping stones as blurry curves rippled the silver stream, "How come you're not asking me what I really want from the Rauchka Sniper? Aren't I mysterious?"

It was silent but for the curling eddies against smooth stones and the croaking of insects; and Ring went to eye the haunting sculpture for himself, standing within its line of sight. The weathered face was threatening and powerful, evidently a chieftain or general of some sort from long ago. Armored and helmeted and taller than life, the impression was intimidating and inspiring. Although swept aside by the weight of history, here was a man who commanded his era.

When it was clear he would elicit nothing further from the Recorder, Ring thumbed his nose at the statue's face, wiggling his fingers disrespectfully and made a sort of flatulence noise with his lips.

"Cableswords were a mark of status during the time before the Brewing. Only the most promising student in each war college or monastery would be selected to train on the weapon. This fellow here led an uprising that evidently turned into a brutal dictatorship. He toppled a dynasty, but refers to himself as, 'The Iron Eye'" and demeans at length the insurrections he put down."

Misling traced his finger along the length of the coil and brushed aside clumps of soil and weeds into which the coil had been submerged following engraved lettering.

"'To you who will come…but for me, slavery awaited you'". Misling climbed out onto the monument's soiled and weathered right forearm to face it eye-to-eye. Balancing on the forearm by lodging one of his feet around a sculpted elbow, the Recorder looked for only a moment exclusively into the old warlord's blank eyes before shutting his own and engaging with his Pool once again. He was as motionless as an owl for some time, shuddering only occasionally as Mast memories crashed and roared, screaming inside his mind. At last, he accidentally slipped enough to shock him into awareness as he banged the crown of his head against the clasped hands and got his foot stuck.

"Oh." It took him a moment to free himself; and he almost came out of the monument's arms altogether in the attempt. Yet when he landed in the mossy creekside, it was clear something was wrong. Ring was missing.

"Oh. Oh no." He nervously paced in a widening circle, then climbed a fir tree for a possibly wider view with no sign of Ring. Misling was at once sweating and did what he could to uncover an instinct or follow a sign of Ring's passing; but nothing was clear.

Scholars and event readers, in their zeal to relish and interpret things in a Recorder's Pool often miss the obvious point that any embarrassing bits, and often any bits at all, which belong to the Recorder himself are passed by in the recollection and disappear from history altogether. Certainly this experience of Misling wandering in the glade for over an hour as lost as an orphaned kitten was something unlikely to be offered up for public consumption. He followed a broad plan of heading towards the rising elevation, certain that the cave city would be on higher ground; but his reaction to having been left alone was not one of courage and resourcefulness.

"Arrogant and pompous…self-absorbed…blabbering …concocting false mysteries…kidnapping and abandoning …troublemaking…deluded agitator!" The young Recorder continued along those lines, expressing vividly his perception of Ring thus far, all the while continuing through the evergreens in hopeless search for the cave wherein the Rauchka Sniper lived.

Although the cave city was referred to as such, it was in fact only the ruins of a village housed against the walls within a limestone mountainside which had been abandoned outside recorded history. The Rauchka Sniper was a relic of the wars that smoked and exploded in living memory; and he had watched over those ruins for two generations, playing hermit and event reader for visitors from the country. As Hastine had observed, it wasn't at all clear what someone so insulated and passed by could contribute to anyone's intentions of gauging the essence of their age.

"How come your clothes are wet?" A female voice came from behind Misling; and he turned quickly to see her. After an hour of hearing only insects and twigs cracking, it was jolting and unexpected. The young woman was a provincial, dressed unusually bohemian in a frilly skirt and high boots with buckles along their length. Her brown hair was streaked with pastel and glittered hairfalls; and she looked perhaps a few years older than the Recorder. She was carrying a cloth bag overstuffed with biscuits and fruits.

"Where have you been just now?" Misling took a single step

towards her.

"Following you."

"Why follow a Recorder?"

"Because you were going the wrong way." She answered in a curiously pitched voice, somewhat like what one would expect from a tiny person.

"Then why not just come from hiding and state that this Recorder was going the wrong way?"

"You wouldn't have believed me."

"What has changed now such that this Recorder will believe you?"

"Do you?" Her head cocked just noticeably to her left. Misling took a moment to assess both this new stranger and his situation, then at last changed his direction along the alternative path he'd earlier decided against. The young woman followed him casually as if they were shopping for new dinner plates.

"So why are your clothes wet?"

"This Recorder jumped from a stalled dirigible rover into a lake and was left alone to wander in this woodland. There are no clearly identifiable landmarks; and the cave city is well hidden."

"Most people coming down here don't have much trouble finding it." Her tone didn't change; and she wasn't laughing at him. Even so, Misling frowned at her implication.

"What is your name?"

"I'm Sylhauna. You're the first Recorder I've actually seen. Are you wise? You don't really come across as wise."

"Have you seen anyone else nearby, someone looking for the cave city very recently?"

"Oh yeah, your friend already went in." At that, Misling stopped short and raised his voice excitedly.

"It is close?!"

"Yes. But we're going the wrong way." Her expression was one of having been helpful despite the circumstances. She pointed in the correct direction and shrugged her shoulders at his consternation. Just as he turned away from her and began in the direction to which she'd urged, Sylhauna grinned.

Inside the massive cave opening, a faded painting of a burning man rose high along a flattened rock wall to the quartz crusted ceiling. Deeper in the sprawling caverns, bathed in electric light strung years ago for tourists, carved stone apartments and storehouses seemingly clung to the walls like thrown mudpies. Massive tunnels riddled the ground in checkerboard fashion under their feet. The nameless city had been abandoned for generations; and common knowledge did not record the significance once held by the burning man image although it recurred in numerous places throughout the ruins.

"I'll show you. It's a little creepy through here."

Sylhauna led the Recorder through to another cave mouth, opening up to a broader view of the sloping hillsides. At the perimeter of Misling's earshot, Ring was conversing, looking up at a gargantuan and grotesque fat man, easily an eighth as tall as the cavern itself and rolling with flesh. The towering stranger was wrapped in shimmering fabrics in places and bare in others; and perhaps a trick of the light caused his skin to appear a pale green. It was difficult to hear what they were discussing; but the man was evidently intrigued, bowing his massive head low to hear Ring when he spoke.

"Why is he so big?" Misling asked of the girl, who was looking in the same direction and possibly imitating the Recorder's posture and stance. She glanced at him questioningly.

"Because he eats a lot?" She shrugged.

"It is your charge to play caretaker to this man; and certainly you have been asked before the cause of his uninhibited girth and frame. What answer have you been instructed to provide?"

"I'm asked that a lot, so I try and say something different every time. Except I've said that before; and they laughed. I must not have said it right." Sylhauna pursed her lips idly. "But he does eat a lot. That can't help."

As the Recorder stood watching, his hands on his hips, he gradually noticed the odd girl was in fact mimicking his posture. She'd set her bag on the stone floor and was eyeing his thin legs to ensure her stance was similar to his own. Surrendering any notion of gaining context for the conversation, Misling went silently closer such that he could overhear and was followed by Sylhauna. Impossibly, he thought he saw movement from one corner of his eyes; but it vanished when he turned to look.

"Incredible question." The Rauchka Sniper's voice was deep and soothing. His face was puffed and round, kind with smiling eyes, but on a head closely as large as an entire man. In fact, his skin was a pale green. Strangely, he smelled lightly both sour and clean like pine or bleach.

"I have loads of them."

"This is the matter you've really brought, yes? I see now your line of conversation led a more direct route than I'd assumed."

"Yeah, maybe. I liked the chat though. What do you think?"

"The Augur came long before…even so, I can't quite put this notion of yours quickly away."

"All solutions develop eventually, yeah?" Ring scratched his eyebrow, leading the dialogue with his tone of voice.

"Inevitably…but to what purpose? Only torture and the tearing of nations resulted. If the Augur were a creature, dependent upon the minds of men for its sustainment, its advancement would require unity and continuity, not havoc. And how would you explain Talgos hatred and annihilation of the Rauchka?"

"I don't have to because I'm not sitting in a cave promoting myself as a guy with big answers."

"His unleashing of such horror in confrontations with the Clown Prince, Laoka…what would that advance? Still, if the Augur's nature reflects the nature of man…"

"There you go, that's what I'm thinking."

At that, without losing his interested smile, the hulking fellow rolled to his side and vomited something murky which pooled in a crevice and ran in tiny currents toward the cave opening. The Rauchka Sniper continued as if nothing had happened. In fact, he laughed at something that had apparently just occurred to him.

"I am old and strange and speak vaguely, and I am pretty good at sounding wise through hindsight. As a consequence, I'm brought silly questions about baldness and pregnancy, the acquisition of businesses and land and sometimes battleships. I'm asked about gambling and marriages, people whose genitals don't work. Even so, I've had cities founded at my suggestion. In all this, I've never been asked a question as profound and new as what you have asked me."

"Scratch some clay, then, you big green crazy." Ring gestured to the clay spread within an iron ring, the traditional work area of an event reader. The markings there were roughly smoothed over; and the iron was in places dented and rusty. It was quite a famous site, this circle; and perhaps it was surprising to see it in such disrepair.

In event reading, specialized figures were impressed into the clay with a stylus to reproduce complex dynamics of an event both in the personality types involved and the situational forces acting upon them. The purpose was to draw special insight into the flow of events like simulations in miniature. In the true heyday of event readers, their majestic declarations represented to seekers ecstatic glimpses into the workings of the human universe. In order to understand the Rauchka Sniper's next reaction, one must know that the revealed and, some would say, sacred method for running those simulations was to flush out similar patterns and transformations from the Pool of Recorders to leverage the repetition of history.

"Hello, Sylhauna." After this, the Rauchka Sniper glanced to Misling's forehead tattoo, then back to Ring. His eyes, like eight inch rolling sacks, widened.

"Your Recorder?" The voice was a bass rumble, beautiful. Misling watched Ring carefully, interested no doubt in how Ring would answer the Sniper's inquiry.

"He's my buddy. Four lives in his Pool. Knows all kinds of stuff."

The Rauchka Sniper lowered his incredible head to within the breath of Misling, almost touching foreheads.

"'I thought of the momentum of history as a fast ship on the sea, the wake of decisions rippling through the future as inset circles fluttering on an idle pond…the awesome, secret structure of coincidence tying designs from behind the hanging tapestry, and pulling back… like standing to appraise a chalk drawing, the whole of it falling into wheels within wheels…a clockwork of events the scale of mountains and yet also as the fuzz of an insect stumbling drunk from the flower…and suddenly I saw the shape of history in all its wonder.' Do you know those words, Recorder?"

"They are said to be the first spoken by the Salt Mystic when she stumbled into the great market, though it is considered unlikely she spoke with such poetry."

"And you are here, brought by a young man who asks me a question of profound depth which I've never before heard, relating to forces and players stressing our very times. A man of faith would say these are signs of turning points. But there aren't men of faith anymore, are there?"

Ring glanced to his side suddenly as Misling had done earlier when he thought he'd seen someone there. Misling noticed, perhaps Sylhauna as well; but the Sniper continued.

"Strange that we haven't seen any signs of turning points in the figures, Sylhauna. Maybe your old fat teacher is too unplugged from the real world. Obsolete and forgotten, yes? If the inputs to the figures are false, then so is the reading." He leaned over again and vomited as before, yet this time wiped the remnant from his mouth against a fleshy, rolling shoulder. Sylhauna motioned for them to sit on some oversized cushions closer to the iron ring, then handed them each a piece of cream-yellow fruit. She drew a net from an adjacent pool which held orange tea in glass bottles chilled in the mountain water and offered them. They declined to drink.

"Little Recorder, whose lives are in your Pool?"

"Duke Exeter of Sarling in the days of the Brewing, Court Poet Phianna in the early days of Naraia, and Under Governors Faring of the Southern Red Witch Annex and Delton of the Fountain City."

"Delton!" The Rauchka Sniper's huge face grimaced. "Delton was a spoiled and feckless irritant! How on earth did he rate a Recorder?"

Misling's face inappropriately showed his intrigued fascination and puzzlement at the implications, a fact which amused the Rauchka Sniper deeply and calmed his irritation. Sylhauna was impatient and short with the Recorder's slowness to dawn.

"One of the memories in your head is of meeting him when he looked different. Are you going to be able to keep up?"

"Fascinating, how the shape unfolds."

Ring chuckled as Sylhauna sat up quickly, a mischievous grin broadening, "Why don't you tell him your name?"

"I came to this cave to escape that name, dear heart. Whether it's a wheel or a force bringing it back to me, I'll not open the door for its return." At that, he playfully lowered his massive head towards her and smiled.

"I wasn't a sniper then."

The huge and mysterious man rolled his body over a couple of times till he dropped into the black pool, circled by a stone wall and steps engraved with images of a burning man and raised symbols. They could still see him from their vantage point at the iron ring, although only his head was above the water. The splashing and ripples of the water made lapping noises in the cave, joined by the gentle whistle of a breeze blowing through from the cave opening.

"I don't know the other three. You must be an inexpensive Recorder. Are you unbound, or attached to this mysterious smiling young man who brings me fascinating questions?"

"This Recorder is bound to Goodman Farmilion of the living theater, and was tasked to attend this visitation." Misling eyed the giant with his head cocked slightly, trying to place the face and voice unsuccessfully.

"He was lost outside." Sylhauna saw fit to add this.

"So are we right now, dear heart. You know, I dealt with him as most like me did, this Talgo you're asking about…long ago. He was a cruel general; but his times were very cruel as well. Is it unfair to judge him under our own values when so much has moved on?"

"Are you sure you're not rambling?" Ring flicked a pebble out into the valley idly.

"The core player was a strongman, no doubt, backed by two whisperers and a tinker embraced in mystique" Sylhauna smiled, kicked off her boots and squatted in the dun clay, madly sketching out the requisite figures with a curved soapstone stylus.

"Opposing was a reluctant strongman and libertine spearheaded by dreamers, rebels, and whisperers." Much of what the Rauchka Sniper described hereafter, though couched in the sacred runes and language of event readers, was common knowledge of events following the War of the Rupture and how Marshal Cassian and Judge Wentic came to rule the largest remaining pieces of what was once a cosmopolitan world government. His rushed descriptions formed a complex web of heroes, thieves, philosophers and clowns, the key personalities of those times leading to these, locked into a cuneiform design in clay that to a trained eye clearly formed forces driving these events by their arrangement and relative orientation.

Misling leaned delicately in as the Sniper solicited similarly oriented events from his own Pool, caught up in the beauty of a well-designed and informed reading very much in alignment with the hallmark principles and rules taught by the Salt Mystic herself so long ago. It was an intense and moving experience, solemn in its immensity of purpose; and in such readings one prone to fantasy and daydreaming could almost hear the roaring of machines and furious passions, the cries for mothers and lost loves, and the joy of the events indwelled in those strange clay impressions. As a result, none of the group recognized that Ring had in fact wandered off.

After some time when the creative and intellectual rush had faded, they paused to consider and process what the group had made. Sylhauna hopped out of the sod-brown circle gingerly and stretched her back, then looked around for Ring.

"What was his question?"

Misling scanned around himself, then mumbled something under his breath. The Rauchka Sniper had rolled his pale green flesh once again out of the well to gain a vantage of the figures. His expression, though smeared in its size and roundness, was clearly one of dawning surprise.

"Recorder, this fellow with whom you travel…is he familiar with your language and ways?"

"Moreso than is common, yes." Misling creased his forehead, folding the black and red design thereon. The Rauchka Sniper was lost in the figures, and possibly amazed at the intensity and clarity with which they had developed them. After a long and curious time where nothing was said for lack of direction on what could be said, the massive jiggling man broke into a fit of loud laughter that echoed across the abandoned cave city.

"What's that? Are we done?" Ring's sluggish voice came from outside, where he'd evidently been sleeping perched overlooking the wide valley. Awakened by the deep laughter, he clumsily flopped himself inside the opening. He'd slipped off his own boots and taken off his shirt to sun himself outside.

"Ooh." They watched curiously as he knelt beside the clay work area and examined the hieroglyphics thereon. The Sniper was chuckling, such that he was almost crying. Ring looked them over, then before crouching closely in as one would a fire on a winter's evening, he scratched his chin.

"Right, so this bit here…this is the meat right here, isn't it?" With his stiffened thumb, he pointed out one of the figures and circled a curved symbol adjacent to it, drawing flaky stubs of clay. Quickly, he twisted to have a look at the final figures they'd drawn, those representing the forces and players of their own times.

"What was your question?" Misling asked him, clearly intrigued but suspicious of gaining an answer. Ring looked at the Sniper, still chuckling from his own perch, and pointed. He grinned as well because laughing was clearly contagious for him.

"What's the big guy laughing at?"

The Rauchka Sniper cleared his throat, calmed himself somewhat, then got his companion's attention, "Sylhauna, I believe you should join this fellow and his Recorder. You should go wherever they go and listen. He's sure to turn the world upside down; and you might as well be there to see it."

Ring's eyes widened as he looked at Misling, casting an expression intended to say, 'I told you'.

"What was his question?" Sylhauna's face showed surprise, maybe frustration.

"Old man Talgo is long dead; and his sons are ruling, his grandsons possibly on the rise. The Augur has eroded into a dusty antique, visited only by the superstitious and the foolish not unlike myself. Both should be irrelevant and yet strangely are not. His question was whether the Talgo family's mystique is a tool of or product of the Augur, or perhaps its master."

"And your answer?" Her expression softened as if she didn't even understand the question; but his laughter broke out again.

"I don't know, my sweet girl. I just don't know."

She looked at Ring as if for the first time. Misling had stepped back from the group, eyeing events from his more typical distance, unobtrusively. Ring actually started to say something to her; but she at once mumbled something about having to pack and walked past him to climb down into one of the tunnels.

"That's a bit of a cop-out, you know?" Ring had stepped closer to the Sniper, leaning against a copper column made green in verdigris. "I mean, we came all this way."

The Sniper shrugged, "Isn't why you came."

Ring smiled briefly then changed his tone of voice, "Do you miss it…shooting people from buildings and stuff?"

The Sniper was examining Ring's face distractedly; and didn't at all answer the question, "It really is amazing."

"Yes, it is. Do you miss it, I said? Being a sniper."

"I do not. In fact, I have a higher and better purpose in doing this. I have been at it for some time now; and I can say now why the Augur works so well."

"And why's that?"

"They come to me and tell everything...both sides of every conflict, rattling off what they want and what they're afraid of. It's a comedy at which I must nod and sound supernatural as I repeat what I hear back to them. I would be useless if they'd just address this rot to each other rather than to me."

"Well you could stop throwing up. That's disgusting." Ring scratched his cheek idly.

"You're going to the Augur next?"

When Ring nodded, the Sniper touched his shoulder cautiously, his fingers like a man's calves, "There are no secrets there."

The two of them only watched one another, till at last Ring made a comment about checking on his new companion to see whether he could help Sylhauna pack. He urged Misling along; and both of them made their way down the tunnel into which the girl had gone before.

Faded painting and engraved friezes on the cavern walls showed wanoa armies in massive conflict, armored and riding machines. Possibly older and certainly more weathered were village scenes with human children swinging from rope ladders inside the cave city and other enchanting scenes of ancient life therein. There was no writing. Misling slowed to more closely examine each, running his finger along the cold stone borders and textured details, absorbing the images fully. Ring kept a hearty pace, all but ignoring them except for an occasional grunt to acknowledge Misling's fascination.

"Yeah, I know. Old pictures and stuff. It's great."

They each made their way to an inner clearing encircled with exotic potted plants and saturated in light from pipe holes leading all the way to sunlight. A bright cavern to their right housed a small bedroom which was spare with only a thick blanket for a bed and a canvas bag only a little packed. Cotton blouses and wool cloaks, boots and underclothes were thrown and scattered on the floor in piles untidily. From a window-like opening, they could hear the tinny gurgle of Sylhauna crying.

Ring poked his head outside to see her seated hugging her knees on an outcropping overlooking the valley and river, wiping her eyes. Misling followed suit till they were both sticking out like prairie dogs entirely unsure what to say or how to handle a crying girl. Misling made eye contact with Ring to spur him on to saying something. It wasn't a task for which he was best suited.

"You don't have to go with us."

He paused awaiting something, then started again when nothing happened, "It's completely your choice. I mean, you're welcome to come. But you don't have to. But you can."

She only looked up, her eyes red and her cheeks puffy.

"You can stay or you can go. I don't really know what to do with the crying. I mean, there's nothing to be upset about when you have this kind of latitude to do whatever you want, you know? It's up to you."

Sylhauna wiped the back of her wrist across her right eye again and sniffed. She was clearly trying hard to dry her eyes and stop it. Ring caught Misling's eyes for affirmation.

"Right? What did he say exactly?" Ring urged Misling on.

The Recorder's eyes were a bit panicked, "'I believe you should join this fellow and the Recorder. You should go wherever they go and listen.' That is what was said, indicating an intent and persuasive argument."

"So…so just let us know what you want."

Sylhauna inhaled and shifted position to a kneel facing the two of them. She paused and got control of her breathing and her voice before saying anything.

"I'm sorry. I've made you uncomfortable. I didn't mean to try and be funny earlier. I'm really sorry."

"'s okay. Don't worry about it. Everybody gives him a hard time." Ring jerked his thumb towards Misling, indicating him.

"This keeps happening to me; and I don't know why. I thought that here, maybe…" She looked out over the wide valley and shining river sadly, then back to them. She was evaluating their faces, their sincerity, perhaps whether they would laugh. They were solemn in response.

"It just keeps happening to me."

Ring and Misling awaited her, letting her decide the pace and the conversation. She stood suddenly as if recalling a place she needed to be.

"I'm making you wait. I'm sorry. I'll put my stuff in a bag." Quickly and in a disorganized fashion, she pushed past them and started stuffing what little was in the bedroom into a veined khaki sana-weave travel satchel. In little time, it was obvious she didn't have many possessions at all; and it seemed to cause her some embarrassment. A couple of times, her glances toward them seemed to ask that they not make mention of what they were seeing.

"My… nice stuff is somewhere else."

Ring only nodded, "You're looking at all I've got."

Sylhauna nodded back and looked a final time out over the valley, "Will you make me a promise?"

Ring nodded in agreement, "I'm in. What do you need?"

She awaited a similar nod from Misling before continuing, an unusual and inappropriate move considering his role. He nodded silently when he saw what she was doing.

"When you don't want me around anymore…when you want me to go…will you tell me what it is I'm doing wrong?"

Ring smiled, "Dear heart, that isn't a problem now, nor is it to become one. The big guy wasn't looking to dump you out like garbage – he's smelling something exciting. There are very big things about to happen – things that haven't ever happened before. It will be amazing. Well, parts of it will be very bloody; but parts…big parts…will be…amazing."

"Promise me."

"Okay, okay. I promise. Never going to happen though." He reached his hand outside the opening to assist her back inside from the landing.

"Like me and this guy have a reason to poke at someone else's crazy."

She stood before them in her frilly skirt and buckled boots, her blouse wrinkled and spotted from the limestone and shale, watching.

Ring dropped his voice confidentially, "Hey, can you keep a secret? Even from the big green fellow? I know something about your boss."

Sylhauna glanced at the Recorder, then nodded. Ring moved closely, right up into her ear and whispered so softly that only she could hear.

"His name is Isaniel."

6   INTERLUDE: HAMMERS

Although commonly spoken of as the Augur Temple, in reality the stone and foliage spire housing was a façade covering only a very old stairway leading beneath the earth and comprised only a small fraction of the massive temple complex. Molded openings in the blocks forming the spires held soil and greenery, giving the weathered beige a drape of emerald. Torches mounted inside spilled light through intentional cracks in the joints and caused the entire structure to glow in an unearthly manner. It was unsettling and solemn, as would suit an oracle. A large statue of the Salt Mystic rose from between three fountain jets surrounded by a stone basin.

Long lines formed once per lunar cycle leading to each person's appointed day of audience when the Augur would accept their inquiries. Lengthy participation in a dark room ritual with fasting and sana was required in advance of the audience; and those in attendance had most typically been on a waiting list for sometimes years. Crowded stores and marionette puppeteers, street actors and sculpture gardens competed for the attention of seekers in a huge campus that included a paraball arena. This ancient and hallowed swarm of activity and bustle was shrouded in a valley surrounded on all sides by desolate and awesome mountain ranges.

"Mommy, he hit me in the eye!" Two boys were pretending to play Black Hallow, using bright oversize cartoon cards and a soft silicone knife, squatted at the feet of a swaying woman holding a little girl. She looked coldly at the one who'd sought justice from her.

"That's what happens when you agree to throw toy knives at each other."

An obviously wealthy older woman standing in front of her turned to see the commotion, then smiled thinly awaiting eye contact. She wore numerous silver bands as was the fashion years before.

"You've got a handful, don't you?"

The mother nodded politely with an expression betraying ironically she was in some sort of hurry. She held the limp little girl just a little tighter and stroked her soft black hair.

"I've been on the list for an audience since last spring. It's exciting, isn't it? I'm not entirely sure what to expect." There was a pause for which the mother had no interruption, clearly driving some sort of awkward feeling for the older woman since she was determined to engage in conversation. The boys asked if they could join some kids their age they'd noticed; and the mother nodded her assent, assigning them the responsibility to remain within her line of sight.

"Oh, I would be so nervous to let my kids wander off in such a crowd!"

"They'll be fine. They're independent."

"Well I would be nervous."

"Don't let it get to you."

The wealthy woman idly shifted about, watching the eddying crowds headed into the paraball arena looking like stirred milk in coffee, then turned back again to re-engage eye contact with the mother. She motioned to the little girl, whose feet hung to the mother's hips, her head nodding to one side against a thrust forward shoulder.

"Such pretty hair."

"Thank you." Perhaps unnoticed by the stranger, the mother pulled the girl a bit closer to herself, ensuring the face remained hidden.

"So, how long were you on the list?"

"Since yesterday. I bought someone else's place."

This clearly wasn't what the old woman anticipated; and she couldn't help herself but to reassess the loose fitting cotton slacks and inexpensive fleece the mother wore.

"Goodness, that must have been costly!"

"I sold some stuff." The mother slid the little girl's weight over, either failing or pretending not to notice the old woman's consternation at the status shift that had just occurred. Some murmuring and shifting flowed through the crowd as the advance of another group into the Augur Temple allowed their own forward progress.

"I imagine your husband is a soldier." The mother nodded almost solemnly in response, drawing a sympathetic nod and smile.

"I thought as much, with you alone watching three kids on such an event as this. I do hope he's okay."

"I don't know."

"I see. Well bless your heart. How are the boys doing without their daddy?"

"They don't notice. He never paid them any attention."

The old woman's face went a bit cold, as if she was only now interested in backing away from this conversation as it had become decidedly unpleasant. Even so, she watched the limp little girl a bit closer, possibly noticing that the child hadn't moved even a little.

"Mommy, what's a Malthus?" One of the boys had returned and suddenly tugged the mother's fleece for her attention, inquiring about a street actor skit under way in the adjacent courtyard. She leaned over slightly to watch his face as she answered.

"An old timey go-to man for the Naraia heads of state, an agent…Recorders and the Augur helped decide on what to do, the

Malthus were the hammer to get it done. That's what they called shaping things…hammers."

"Did they kill people?"

"Sometimes, sweetheart; but if they did, it was okay because it was what was needed."

The boy stood on his tip-toes to get a vantage over the crowd at the red-robed street actor, a teenager masked in a cochineal bandana and skulking mysteriously around the milling crowds outside the arena.

"That guy says they could make things out of water and cause your body to create poison, even drive ghost-ships through the ground and pop up anywhere. Is that true?"

"I don't know, son. Go play. We'll be inside the Temple soon. It will be a long week once we go down those stairs."

"But could they do all that stuff?"

"I don't know, son. Please, just go play. Mommy has to get ready for the audience. Just go be with your friends. I can't do this right now." She shrugged again, shifting the little girl's weight again. The wealthy woman continued to watch curiously, even sliding to her side a bit to try and gain a closer view.

"Can I be a Malthus when I grow up?" Knowing he was trying her patience, the boy started a half step away from her to signal his imminent compliance. In an exhausted and beaten demeanor, she watched him again as she answered.

"The last one died before I was born. They're not around anymore. If we want to make things right, we just have to be our own hammer. You should remember that, son. Nobody's going to help you."

Their place in line had advanced once again; and the mother and wealthy stranger were at this point within direct sight of the dark and old earthen stairway leading underground just inside the stone spires. Some soft, vocal melody sounded from inside, sad and anxious like the feeling of summer ending. The boy ran off in the direction of his friends.

"Excuse me, darling; but I wonder if you'd mind if I see your beautiful daughter's face? I just love to see a pretty girl." The old woman's face betrayed her suspicion as she didn't hide it well. In fact, the girl still hadn't so much as twitched a foot.

"She's sleeping."

"I'm sure I won't wake her." The old woman reached in the direction of the girl's hair, drawing a sharp jerk from the mother.

"Don't touch her!"

"Let me see that girl." The old woman was more urgent, demanding. Several people adjacent to them were taking notice.

"I need you to mind your own business and just leave us alone."

"Where is your husband?" Her voice was accusing, her face almost angry.

"I don't know."

"Do you want me to call for a watchman? Let me see that girl."

"I told you, she's sleeping."

"She isn't moving. I can't hear her breathe. What have you done to her? Let me see."

"I haven't done anything. Please, just step back and give me some room. I can't handle this right now."

"Wake her up." Another stranger, a man who'd overheard thus

far, joined in. His wife stood beside him, judging and accusatory.

"I have to take her to a quieter place in line. Please, just give us some air." The mother started to step away; but the man grabbed her shoulder.

"What are you hiding? Wake her up."

"I'm not hiding anything. Please, you're going to upset her. Just let me go find another place to stand." Her voice was scared at this point, squeaking in panic..

"Honey, go get a watchman. She's done something to that girl." The wife implored her husband.

"I might do that."

"Please. I didn't hurt my little girl. I didn't do anything. Just let us go. We'll be inside the Temple soon; and I'll be their problem then."

"Let us see her, then."

Suddenly, the girl made a whimpered, seal-like noise. She twisted in her mother's arms. Those watching were surprised, at once silent.

"Sweetheart, just lay still. Mommy's got you. Don't look around. Mommy's got you. I'm not going anywhere."

The mother dropped to her knees to better hold the girl and shield her from strange stares. As she did so, a spot of blood pooling from the girl's thigh stained the mother's fleece. The tiny face was swollen and bruised; and her eyes were vacant.

"Sweetie, mommy's here. Daddy is far away. He's far away; and you don't have to worry about him anymore. Mommy's got you." She kept repeating that ever more softly, stroking the little girl's black hair.

When a watchman stepped up, asking about the disturbance of

which he'd been informed, the wealthy woman and man who'd questioned the mother told him they didn't know what he was talking about, that everything was fine. All the while, the mother sat there, concealed from the watchman's view by the couple and woman, swaying softly and whispering that Daddy was far away. After a moment, the watchman continued on his way.

"They're worthless in this." The old woman knelt and touched the mother's shoulder. "Especially when it involves soldiers. You've come to the right place, dear. I'm so sorry."

"We'll help you with the boys when we're inside." The man offered. "Are you going to ask where your husband is?"

"No, I can find him."

"What are you here for, then? What are you going to ask?" The old woman continued to touch the mother's shoulder, swaying her hand with her as the girl drifted back into silence and immobility. The mighty stadium roar of the paraball game lifted like an ocean talking, blending with the humming song from the Temple.

"I want to know how to hurt him." She looked up at them, squinting through tearing eyes.

There was nothing they could say; and they didn't make an effort to continue. Short afternoon shadows pooled beneath them as a dirigible drifted overhead bringing those seeking the final audience for this cycle. The couple embraced each other and looked into the uneasy blackness of the chamber ahead, sporting with flickering and ghostly torchlight.

"We're out of money again, lovey." An unattractive woman with a limp and a nose only a little twisted to one side accosted Revin beside the lobby statuary. 'Written on the Water' was a glamorous diplomat's hotel in better times, and one whose lobby side rooms and private dinner halls decided the course of nations over wine. In these days, it was only one of many obscure places to stay in Alson's glutted hotel district and so stood as a good place for meetings beyond public attention.

"When are you going to find out something?" Her teeth were stained and her manner familiar and common. Revin hugged her wide body, kissing her lightly. His personal Recorder stepped further to the side, a respectful distance.

"Don't you start again. I thought you were meeting with Rhelsea?"

"She changed her mind. I'm a little too posh for her now, I think."

"And Mendine?"

"Her too." He gauged her expression, clearly trying to read the depth of her disappointment in the failed plans. At last, he broke eye contact and glanced toward the glass doorway beyond a bed of smooth river rocks enshrouding dancing flames.

"I have a breakfast meeting right now. Where are you going to be?"

"You're boring. Maybe I'll go find me a man." She grinned awfully, purring, and twisted her hip to bump it against his.

"I'll come join you when I'm done." Revin looked at the woman expectantly, almost awkwardly so, attempting a communication which was lost on her. His bumpy forehead ridged like a sand dune.

"Is your idiot boss coming?" She asked this in a comfortable manner as she straightened some curls in her frilly blouse, betraying the commonality of such references toward Judge Wentic. Revin glanced urgently at his Recorder, then to the olive knotted carpet at his feet.

"I need you to go…you know…find something to do, right now." He raised his voice, driving her crooked smile to fade. She locked eyes with him and watched his face for a reaction.

"Maybe I'll have breakfast with you and your big visitor."

"I just need you to leave. Don't talk to me if he comes in. And he's coming any time now. Just go find something to do." The woman's smile was entirely gone, a hurt look filling its absence. She watched him, waiting on him to soften or apologize. He only glanced nervously at the door, suddenly inhaling sharply as someone entered.

The new arrival was in uniform, a sunset-red jacket studded with military ribbons and a gold braided aiguillette encircling one shoulder. He walked loosely, uncomfortably. Revin started to scurry toward him by instinct.

"You talk to me like that and walk away?" The woman called after him, louder than was comfortable for Revin; and he sped up. The uniformed man noticed; but only gestured a greeting.

"Joy and health. Rhodomontane?" Revin held his forearms forward, palms upward as if he were catching someone falling, in a salute that hadn't been used in a generation but which still appeared in fiction.

"Yeah. You too." Rhodomontane's rough voice and uncouth demeanor were oddly out of place coming from their well-groomed and sterile source. He paid too much attention to the awkward salute: a true gentleman wouldn't comment on it.

"We uhh…we don't do that anymore. You're Revin?"

"Armaments Chief and Judge's Counselor, Revin, yes."

"Yeah."

Revin eyed the aristocrat, jostling a bit for some sort of societal status. He took the lead with a wave of his hand toward the café. Rhodomontane seemed uneasy with the personal Recorder's attendance, but didn't request an abeyance.

"Into the sana shop for some conversation?"

Rhodomontane fluffed the back of his jacket before sitting, then ordered a hot sana. He asked that some of the algae be left in the glass and didn't remove his riding gloves. Revin had water. They chatted idly for a short time, mostly harmless observations on retail sales and welfare policies and that somewhat one way from Revin. It came quite suddenly when the tone of the conversation shifted.

"So, Judge's Counselor Revin, maybe you can tell me why you're so stupid." Rhodomontane's expression was dry and emotionless. Revin breathed in some of his water and coughed uncomfortably while awaiting his voice to dry out.

"I'm sorry?"

"Don't be a pansy. Own your actions. You've been play acting at alliance-building in Sullion and Rangel. Cassian's been watching that. You've got to be just awful at this to not know that."

"I routinely run…you know…diplomacy missions for Wentic, extending financial aid to some of the provinces. Your Marshal's information is bad. Please pass that along."

"You'll recall the fellow Dunsinore you met at Sullion? The one you extended financial aid to?" Revin nodded, pasty and watching too long the ripples in his water.

"I beat in his left cheek with a piece of steel. He remembers your visit differently." Rhodomontane's pallid face was solemn, menacing in his crisp and pressed uniform. His medals clinked softly as he shifted in his seat. Revin had no answer right away.

"It's an act of war, idiot. Does the Judge even know what you're up to…scooting about promising like a kid and playing mind games with heads of state?"

"You are entirely out of line, sir! You come from an enemy nation, presumably on a peace discussion, and make baseless accusations and blatant threats against me. In the presence of my Recorder. You will doubtless hear again from me and see the fallout from your recklessness!" Revin made to leave, but stopped short when he heard the Salt Flatsman's response.

"What is tathlum?" Rhodomontane was yet as calm as he'd been, although Revin was livid. Revin's fascination with the turn of topic was clear. Possibly, he saw leverage therein.

"What have you heard?"

"The woman you were speaking with when I entered is staring at us from behind that column. Can you please deal with that so we can get something done here?"

Revin turned bird-like and stood at once. He incautiously left the table without asking leave and stepped beyond the column to speak harshly to the woman. Their voices were uncomfortably loud; and the woman smacked Revin's face across the chin.

During the interchange, Rhodomontane turned to the Recorder, grinning thinly. He looked back to his glass to swirl the remnant sana against the curled algae coils, "I've got just a crazy surprise for him. You'll love it."

The shameless couple continued in their bleatings, Revin only occasionally glancing behind himself becoming increasingly impatient with the duration. At last, he pulled his right arm back and punched her in the stomach, causing her to double over and take a step back.

She was crying and out of breath, looking up at him horrified. He glanced back again and returned to the table. She wouldn't break her stare for a moment, then took a deeper breath and straightened her hair a bit. She rubbed her dark-ringed eyes and arched her plump back straight before at last leaving the hotel for the bustling sidewalk outside.

"Hard core, Revvie." Rhodomontane's hands were locked idly behind his head as he leaned back comfortably watching Revin.

"You asked about tathlum. What have you heard?" He was still catching his breath from the adrenalin, making his voice quiver like he was frightened.

"What is it?"

"Tell me the…you know…details of what's made it to you. It's very important. Be as specific as you can."

"Right. Mindgames." Rhodomontane leaned strategically forward for emphasis and impact. "I've heard, Armaments Chief and Judge's Counselor, that tathlum is a caricature and farcical piece of rubbish that you're using to retain your position. I've heard it's entirely fiction with no basis in reality. I've heard that it's a hammer."

"More details, less opinion. Recount the actual conversations please. Stick to the original words as much as you can. The details matter with this sort of thing."

"Start talking, fruitcake. Explain yourself."

Revin's slotted eyes squinted threateningly, "This isn't a…you know…palace intrigue. You're playing with someone of fierce authority and merciless reach. I asked you a question."

"I don't care what you asked. You're the one popping around with a bagful of stupid."

Revin let his voice take on an edge through gritted teeth yet still at a soft volume, "You've arranged your future with your disrespect." It came off as forced and false, however, like something from the theater which he was mimicking. Certainly, it didn't impact as had been hoped.

"Tathlum's a fairy tale, isn't it?" Rhodomontane watched Revin cautiously. "You're futzing with something on a bigger scale, something audacious…the kind of thing the Salt Mystic babbled about when she was withered and ridiculous…an event bomb, huh? Slow burning…dissolve a nation? You little creep, you wouldn't know what to do if it worked."

Revin grinned purposefully – whether betraying pride at a curtain drop before his masterpiece or a false lead seizing advantage, it was difficult to see.

Rhodomontane continued, "You're an idiot and a child. What does your little sissy heir apparent think about your dabbling? Does he even know?"

"I see our time together is…you know…without gain. You offer me no data; and your posturing is misguided."

"Posturing." At that, Rhodomontane slowly nodded, thought for a moment, then slid his right hand up to pinch his earlobe. Very suddenly, his face cracked clean through on his forehead, cheeks, and nose and peeled downwards into a spongy gray ProMat sphere, dropping off the grizzly mocha chin beneath like a raindrop. It plinked on the tabletop softly as he slipped off the riding gloves and tossed them into Revin's face.

"Grebel."

"Yeah, baby." For his part, Revin was clearly taken by surprise and fear, without a clear direction for where to take the conversation from here. Grebel had for a generation been right-hand to Cassian Talgo of the Salt Flats and had largely raised Cassian's impulsive son. His presence here, discussing acts of war with a Judge's Counselor was an era-shattering event that would shake two nations if it was publicly known.

"Why did you do that?"

"I don't get the glitzy Salt Mystic mumbo jumbo; but I can tell a loser in over his head; and he smells like you. Now, you're going to explain in high detail what you've been up to and why you're so anxious to know my mind about tathlum, in freaking writing with smiley faces on it if I say so…using words that make sense. And I swear, you sickening little polyp, if you give me any crap or start making up stories, I will smash in the side of your face."

"No." Revin watched clear ripples bounce against the glass in his hand. Grebel smiled widely, no doubt pleased at the prospect of pushback providing him an excuse for coercion.

"I'm not sure what restraint you feel is in place on me right now, little man."

"I didn't…anticipate. I don't understand why you would be in disguise. It doesn't fit your…I mean, isn't there really a Rhodomontane?" Revin had entirely lost his poise.

At that moment, the unmistakable rattlesnake sizzle of a ball lightning carbine charging up sounded and vibrated the cherry tabletop. Grebel's expression didn't change; and it was entirely unclear how he'd kept the weapon hidden.

"Not really planning to spend a lot more time jawing with you here, Revvie. What does Stendahl know about what you're doing?"

"He doesn't care." Revin's forehead had gone shiny; and he continued to watch his water. It was here that a dull and muffled boom sounded from outside. It was such a soft sound and so out of place that neither of them came off their discussion, though Grebel glanced for just a moment toward the glass doorway.

"Doesn't care or doesn't know?"

"You just wouldn't hide yourself, it isn't you. Why were you in disguise?"

"Momentum was against me. How much of tathlum buckshot is real?" Grebel immediately recognized his tactical mistake upon asking, reflected in Revin's eyes the old soldier's betrayal of how little knowledge he'd previously held. Some motion outside the glass caught his eye.

"You know less than you had let on", Revin said.

"What was Sullion about..." Grebel glanced again out the front doorway, which was misted over suddenly. His voice trailed a bit following his attention.

"What's happening out there?" Revin turned in his seat and followed Grebel's line of sight.

"Stand up." Grebel seized Revin's hair and jerked upwards, driving the counselor in the direction of the lobby's entrance. Ghost silhouettes of people were walking quickly and looking behind them, shrouded in the shadows of adjacent buildings. At some point, he charged down the carbine and slipped it around a shoulder holster, though continuing to grip Revin by the crown of his head. There were screams in the distance, audible even through the glass.

The Recorder slipped behind them as both men eased curiously outside, greeted by the char smell of smoke and dust and tiny shreds of singed paper. A cloud of smoke rose upward like a devil from the east.

"What's happened?" Someone in the hotel's colors had joined them. More city folk were herding by, some running in a stop-start fashion, all looking behind themselves as if the smoke were licking at their ankles and hungry. Grebel shoved Revin to let him go and stepped to a one-man wheeled vehicle.

"Balcister." Grebel said this, unlocking something on the cage at the base of his vehicle and pulling slender steel pins. With a dull metallic ping, the rounded cage tires parted and fell to the side, freeing the familiar curved paddles of a mog. These were light craft housing vortex generators for clinging to mountain faces designed for navigating crevices and outcroppings of the mountain ranges upon which Alson lay. He was preparing to leave.

"It's gone. It's just gone. Who would do this?" The hotel desk clerk was mumbling to no one, in absolute shock, as Revin looked with horror to Grebel for some sign of his involvement or of prior knowledge, some intimation that he'd at least prepared the way for such an abomination. It was oddly even more frightening a realization to find the same angry searching gaze looking back. Grebel had no idea who was responsible.

"My sister works in the bank…" The hotel man's voice was fading, his face drained of color.

The old soldier slid roughly into the swivelseat of his ride; and the vehicle jerked to life, snapping to the hotel's masonry wall like a spider. He shouted to Revin.

"Go find your Talgo, pansy! This wasn't an accident!" Once Grebel had turned his head, nearly vertical as the swivelseat had spun loose in its bearings, the mog ascended quickly out of sight over the cluttered gables and rooftops of the crowded hotel district. The counselor looked for just a moment at his Recorder.

"Stay away from the palace." Revin sprinted wildly in the direction of the Judge's cliffside palace, leaving the old Recorder in a massing crowd under the swelling blue dust and smoke of what was once mighty Balcister.

8 THERE'S NO HOPE FOR IT NOW, SON

Chalky and barren, the wide and blinding salt flats rippled in the heat. Nestled within, in a miracle of engineering and defiance, stood the twin cities of Mevin and Tobin which were collectively the nation of Tanith. This was the near empire of Cassian Talgo, Marshal of Tanith and brother to Judge Wentic Talgo. Native flats tribesmen even in those days still slung primitive hunting kites and housed themselves in the caustic wilds as they had for centuries. Yet the twin cities thrusted upwards like fists, shining in azure and aquamarine computronium which hummed and pulsed with data.

On this day, in the shadow of a mighty industrial craneyard and rising before a mass of seated and formally dressed spectators fanning themselves and whispering, stood a massive arsenal tank the size of a small town. It was at this moment dark and silent as a crew totaling a thousand souls stood at parade rest in gleaming and crisp uniforms behind the audience. The commissioning ceremonies were a proud and honored tradition common to what remained of navies which survived the War of the Rupture; and at this moment, Cassian was seated in a front row surrounded by his ministers and heads of state watching the rites.

"Alson has been attacked…brutally. Balcister is destroyed." A pink and fat, almost pig-faced fellow leaned closely into Cassian's ear and whispered. "We're not sure who is responsible."

The Marshal quickly gauged the expressions of his ministers while several of them rearranged their seats quietly to form a semi-circle. They clearly didn't wish to disrupt the ceremony, which right then consisted of an event reader spelling out the vessel's place in the order of the era…a formality that had outlasted its time.

"How was it done?"

"We don't know."

"Have you heard from Grebel?" Cassian clearly wanted some

clarity of purpose and advice from a trusted advisor; but no one was aware of Grebel's whereabouts. In fact, the pig-faced man looked at him with near anger at such an irrelevant question.

"Marshal, we need to raise our defense levels to the highest preparedness and institute draft proceedings immediately. We have to assume Tanith is also under imminent threat."

"Raise the defense levels, yes; but don't announce anything here. You think a draft is necessary at this point? Isn't that premature? We weren't attacked."

"Marshal, you have diplomats from all over the world here. Don't you think-"

"We don't want a gaggle of ambassadors making panicked calls home. We're walled up tight here. What about that draft – what are you thinking?"

"It will take time to staff up a response. We'll be calling up trained militia; but they have to be deployed." Another one of the ministers had answered here, scooting in his seat closer and already with beads of sweat stuck to his temples and cheeks.

"A response? We weren't attacked. To whom would you be responding?"

"Whoever! We can't dither on this. It takes time to get things moving."

"One of you tell me what we do know!"

"Balcister was blasted away this morning, taking a city block with it. Thousands are dead. The entire city is paralyzed – fires are breaking out in other areas which may be related. One rumor is that the Red Witch were responsible and have infiltrated Alson."

Cassian sharply turned to observe the night-black face of his own Red Witch body guard towering from the sideline observing the seated crowds, armored and cloaked in a duster. Those watching him didn't have what it would have taken to ask the nightmare to step out of earshot.

"One early report was that Wentic caused the blast himself."

Cassian was grimacing, soon to react to this last bit of chatter when a uniformed woman trotted up from the aisle and squatted near him.

"Marshal, the razor and claw squadrons are deployed."

"Eh? Deployed where?"

"Encircling patrols along Tanith's perimeter, Marshal. In accordance with defense protocols."

"What are their rules of engagement?"

"Marshal, are we going to issue the draft? There really isn't time to form an investigative committee or waffle on who our real enemies are."

"You'll answer my question or be relieved. What are the fleets' rules of engagement? I can't have any more misunderstandings with Alson when their own people are out for blood."

"Fire if fired on – what else would they be?" The pig-faced man answered too quickly, betraying what sounded like a guess, which Cassian apparently sensed.

"You know that to be a fact, or you're assuming those are the rules of engagement? Be straight with me!"

"Fire if fired on. You're looking for problems where there aren't any." The chubby fellow shifted in his seat and bore a disgusted expression for want of more decisive action from his leader. "We need to staff up a response quickly. Issue the order for a draft."

"Marshal, this could be another assault from the Rauchka brigadier."

"I can recite a list of possibilities too. It would be more helpful to have some sort of real intelligence. Don't we have people watching these sorts of things?"

"What does it matter who did it? Defend the nation and strike on Alson now while they're weak."

Cassian went quiet at that and looked at the short squat fellow who'd said it. This was a different strategy altogether from what he'd been thinking, or maybe at least he was glad someone else had said it first.

One minister agreed, "That's absolutely right. We have an advantage at this point. It turns things in our favor where they haven't been. We owe them; and it's time for a reckoning."

"They're filth; and they deserve it." The bland mumble of a group rose up in agreement.

Another of his counsel, the one who'd scooted in last, raised his voice beyond the theater whisper for which the setting called, "Look, your people need decisive action now. This mess with the Brigadier has cost us loyalty in the provinces. There are at least fifteen petty groups surrounding us smelling blood at any sluggishness we show. Alson was weak, so they were hit. We have to be strong."

The pig-faced man in his passion sat a little straighter, "You keep me around to tell you the truth; and this is it. I'd like to just get along too; but it's not the world we live in. It's not. We need to do something quickly and with overwhelming force before we are ourselves attacked with some monstrous tathlum abomination which we can't begin to counter. They're going to blame us – count on it."

The War Marshal looked to the orange sun, then towards the caparisoned platform. The lanky and wrinkled event reader had completed his flourish; and one of the commanders was recounting the history of his vessel's namesake. The junior commander stood in waiting for his turn, to be followed soon by a silent drill routine of carbines. It was a serene and out of touch with careening events beyond this echoing craneyard; and it is almost a certainty he was thinking of his trusted friend, Grebel.

Cassian addressed the woman who'd announced the fleet launches, "And what do you think?"

She was young and not expecting a direct address but rather likely a dismissal. Her red-streaked hair was a tight bun, her chin long and with slight wrinkles under her eyes. The other men were equally taken by this turn and looked at her uncertainly. Here was a woman, however, who wasn't at all uncomfortable with being asked for an opinion; and it was possible the fury of world conflict raged in waiting for her answer. She brushed a finger against one of her ochre eyebrows and looked him boldly in his eyes.

"We have every reason to believe Alson has been prepping an assault on us for some time." She leaned toward him, gaining in confidence.

"We know they are developing mass-casualty weapons the existence of which they deny. And they have aggressively forged alliances and treaties throughout the world in an accelerating and hostile fashion. Now that they have been wounded, Alson will be looking for all-out war with someone; and we will be blamed for what has happened to them. I don't see any other outcome. It is naïve to think we could somehow offer assistance or even just remain silent and not be drawn into whatever is to be their response. If there is any leverage at all in our hands, we must use it decisively. It's what your father would have done."

Cassian only nodded softly and scooted his chair to face directly forward, the legs scraping roughly against polymeric concrete. It was awkwardly still in the small group, their privacy somewhat cracking as many near them were being distracted. The woman eventually stood to pop her stiff knees, milled near for a moment, then drifted back to an empty seat several rows back for want of a better way forward.

The advisors tried to re-engage the War Marshal in the details of what came next; but he held up his finger to sign against it. In fact, the tight line of ceremonial soldiers was arrayed with carbines held high in salute when next he spoke.

"This next bit is my favorite. Very stirring."

A hunched old woman hobbled across the platform leaning on her walking stick. At the very moment her feet first tapped the stage, a thousand sailors formerly at parade rest came to attention in a snap of incredible precision. She was the haggard sister to old man Talgo, aunt to the ruling brothers and a woman who'd christened hundreds of war vessels. Her gait was ginger and unsteady, slow like a stalking cat. Those watching were in thrall or awe, some sensation driving silence and respect. When she reached the centerpiece flagstand, framed by the two officers, her cracked voice rang out clearly like a bronze bell.

"Soldiers and sailors of the flats…"Twenty soldiers lifted higher their forearms as one.

"…man our defender and bring her to life!" In response, twenty carbines fired blinding sun-yellow spheres into the sky, saluting her and the new arsenal ship before them. On cue, long clean lines of the crewmembers jogged down the aisles filling the massive warship at all the gangways. Shortly, the lifeless and still vessel began to buzz and whirl with activity as every device or instrument, every machine and engine was engaged to simulate the breathing of life into the ship. Hoses fired fountains into the air as weapons systems spun madly. Lights bathed the vessel in dazzling arrays. Eventually, several of the crew became visible through portholes and on higher decks, hurried in vigorous motion. Those in the audience stood in applause as the pennant representing Tanith rose along a cable in proud display.

Cassian stood along with everyone else, shaking hands and nodding to acknowledge congratulations. He watched carefully, methodically, as Nanny Talgo was helped off the platform by the commanders; and the crowd stirred like brushed bees once she stepped to the side of the platform hidden from general view. The commissioning was complete. The arsenal ship was a new concept in Tanith war planning, architected as the centerpiece in flatrunner and ramship battlegroups. Armed with overwhelming firepower, it climaxed a vision of short and decisive battles.

"Rosgrove, find my son and prep a runner to take me to him. As I understand it, he's returning from Denai."

"Out of the question!"

"War Marshal, you aren't going anywhere except to the government house. There is a prepared speech we'll customize; and the people will need to hear it from you. Certainly if there's to be an attack on us, you're the first target. We'll bring your son here." Many of them, including Cassian, looked suddenly as if the man who'd suggested bringing in Cyprian were instead suggesting they all build a campfire and sing.

"Where's Grebel?" Cassian's eyes squinted in his irritation.

"What does he matter, War Marshal? We can send somebody out for him; but he's likely passed out in a dumpster somewhere!"

It was actually a critical moment in retrospect, though none right then would have noticed, that Cassian's eyes fell on his old, limping aunt being helped down a small flagged stairway.

There was a time of which anyone interested in Cassian would have read wherein he as a very young boy had found a young shenna abandoned by its mother and crying for water outside his window. He'd squirreled it away from the sight of his teasing brother in a canvas satchel of sketchbooks and pastels. The tiny beast made squeaks of delight whenever it saw him; and it often would slip its silver head over the lip of the satchel to watch him arrange and rearrange his chalks till he was satisfied with crisp right angles in their layout. Incredibly, he would patiently straighten the chalks should the little creature bump against them to sustain regularity, though this wasn't a patience he would offer anyone else bringing such disorder.

Although Cassian nursed it with scraps from his own meals to better conceal the secret, old man Talgo discovered the shenna in his bath one evening but didn't force its release as Cassian had expected. He rather elaborately charged him with its protection. As a consequence, the boy was deathly frightened the one day he went back to his towering and cruel father cradling the little beast in his quivering hands asking what to do. The ill-looking shenna was quaking almost violently, even its red eyes, having done so all morning no matter what cure actions the boy had taken.

"There's no hope for it now, son. Take it out back and put it out of its suffering. Be a man, it's the only way."

Surely the boy wished the old man would deal this death rather than teach him lessons about manhood; but his father only handed him a knife and looked on. Cassian lingered and looked into its pie-round burgundy eyes, waiting until he was outside beyond his father's sight before the tears slid down his own nose. The shenna shook and wiggled as the boy hovered the serrated blade over one spot after another, over and again fitfully, setting the blade aside twice to cry and to rest from his failure to find the correct method and angle. He was entirely broken when the little beast looked blinkingly at him and tried to hold its position despite the shaking, dumbly sensing only that its master required it to stand still for something important.

At last, on the third attempt he drove the knife through to the rock below; and the silver creature went cold. He waited until the tears dried somewhat before returning to his father, anticipating at least the reward of the old man's pride at following through on a man-sized responsibility.

"Bad decision. You trusted advice without verifying; and that was a failure. Everyone giving advice has an agenda, Cassian. Shenna quake when they're pregnant."

The same wide brown eyes that stared in horror at the towering old man with his drooping gray moustache and thick eyebrows now lingered on the old man's aged sister, limping softly gripped to the forearm of a page. Her manner was stiff and unsteady; and the drugs and hormones that kept her coherent at all also assured the only thing she would say were she engaged would be a parroting of what she'd said on stage…over and over with no soul indwelling. Cassian took a very deep breath and faced the impatient advisors staring him down.

"Issue the draft. Don't attack anything. There will be a response discussion in the morning. Bring the shelf plans. I want a War Recorder and a statistics officer present. No journalists."

The assurance and surrender of his address sparked the ministers into a flurry of sidebar discussions, their collective chatter blending into a bland mumble as he was ushered into privacy for his protection. Cassian seemed to have been largely forgotten except as perhaps a figurine of a benevolent deity in which no one any longer believed but which was to be handled as precious even so.

Angry protesters shouting and leering viciously cowered and went limp as the massive Red Witch man motioned for them to back away, leading the War Marshal toward his flatrunner transport. Along the dockyard, shaded with a pale violet pergola over the covered walk, they overheard snatches of information about the frightful attack on Balcister Tower and the blackout of communication from much of the city. The rush of images and faces, the blend of voices and horror of what it all meant slowed the experience to a numbing dreamtime. It was only when he was inside the crowded runner racing over the desolate white flats that he realized he'd been clutching the forearm of his Red Witch guard.

As with all initiated Red Witch warriors, the guard's skin had been chemically turned black as a sunless cave; and his head was shaved cleanly. Growth hormones had swelled his size to massive proportions, not quite as tall as two men. The whites of his eyes were tattooed a blazing phosphorescent red, as were his teeth. He wore pistol railguns in both leather thigh holsters and a burned and dented carbine slung across his back. As their native language was so foreign and horrible in its worldview compared to the Naraian dialects, those from the Red Witch provinces rarely spoke outside their territories.

This one here sat and watched the Talgo silently as if Cassian was gripping the cold stone of monument inscriptions.

"Can you be trusted?"

The mercenary sat silently, watching. Cassian only then noticed he and the Red Witch man were the only people inside the cell of the runner, separated from the pilot by a privacy wall. He withdrew his hand and slid further from the silent man, pushed against the backwards-facing chair. They stared at each other for some time while streaked views of the arid wasteland flickered on the window, lit up spottily with electrostatic flashes.

"Are you going to assassinate me?"

Frustratingly, the enigmatic fellow only watched coldly, lightly stroking an edge of blackened insulation shielding on his carbine. At last, Cassian nodded, assuming an answer in his favor.

"I know what they want. And I don't think it's unnatural to want to settle accounts."

The Red Witch man was still as lake water but for the single finger.

"We've hated the hilljacks a long time; and now we're looking back on raids and night attacks, hostages. Of course we hate them now. Look what they've done to us. But if you were going to ask me what started all that...what it was in the beginning..."

His voice dimmed, washed in the rush of the flatrunner. Rubbing the grizzle of white fuzz on his sideburns, "When you're a kid and you're getting called names and pushed; and the other kids are yelling at you to go at the other guy...to hurt him...whether you do something or you don't...there's really no way to win that."

Cassian raised an eyebrow as he looked out the curved acrylic window, "I'll tell you what is truly unnatural, rooted in vileness."

He brushed stray strands of graying hair from his left eye and scratched the back of his neck, "In fact, it's only struck me just now. That's the most damning part: that it has only come to my mind now and not at the very first."

He let the curiosity of it hang for a little while, as their runner rushed closer to an approaching dock which led through some covered walkways to the government house nestled within proud Tobin. There were ghostly silhouettes of those awaiting him.

"Just now…when they told me about the attack…whispers in my ear…explosions, conspiracy, thousands dead…why would I not ask after the safety of my own brother?"

The two of them jerked forward, the flatrunner caught in the braking straps of the government house's dock. In only a moment, people from the government house would rush Cassian into hiding places and shrug him like a puppet for the rest of the evening, perhaps for days. He would be instructed on what to say and how best to show grieving and reluctant facial expressions, what his body language should convey, and in what time intervals he should eat or take rest to avoid perceptions of being callous to suffering. For now, in his final moment of peace in advance of those things, he locked eyes with the Red Witch man before him.

"I've tried to see it the way history will. I've tried to stay above it. You should know…" Cassian leaned in as he would at a campfire whispering of ghosts.

"It doesn't matter how good you try to be, you always wind up doing what the Old Man wanted anyway."

9 TO QUESTION IS A FEARFUL THING

Ring and Misling were sitting side by side, their hands locked around their knees, and watching Sylhauna on a grassy hill some distance off. In several directions beyond the lake, the foothills were green and beige ripples rolling to tall spiked pines in the distance and in large swaths frosted white with patches of meadowfoam. From their vantage, she was the size of a thumb, dancing alone and quite poorly. They were watching her twirling and gesturing with some abandon and not at all gracefully.

"She said she was saying goodbye." Misling leaned his chin into his palm.

"She's cuckoo. I like her."

At that, the Recorder stiffened his back and looked at Ring suddenly, evaluating him once again. Behind them, Farmilion's dirigible cruiser remained entangled within brush at the height of four men, overhanging a pink granite cliff rise which bordered the still black lake.

"The tent city was not one of your planned visitations."

Ring laughed at the suddenness and off-topic nature of the Recorder's address, "You're still thinking about that? Actually, I'd never heard of the tent city till you mentioned it."

They watched each other silently, then turned again to Sylhauna's birdlike prancing.

"Was anything that you have said true?"

"Every word of it. I don't lie."

Ring waited politely while the Recorder very clearly replayed the conversations from the troop tower over again in his mind in confirmation, to perhaps see if Ring had in fact agreed the tent city was one of his stops after all. His coffee brown eyes floated up and to his left when he did that. He nodded gently when he was done.

"Where is the fifth visitation to be?"

"Who sealed Farmilion's Record?"

"That is sealed."

Grinning, "So's my fifth stop, little professor."

Misling frowned, irritated. Ring let him simmer a while as they watched her flailing, then began again, "It isn't sealed at all, is it?"

Insulted, Misling gave a look of disgust. Ring noticed, and let it hang in the air a moment before continuing, "It isn't."

Misling's tone was acidic, "The day is kept whole! Unlike yourself, Recorders may not prance about the truth as if it were a spring frolic!"

"And yet, you're lying. He's losing his memory; and you're hiding it."

The Recorder went quiet, avoiding eye contact and suddenly uncomfortable.

"Every month, it gets worse; and he can recall less of what you're trying desperately to record. He contradicts himself and says things that sound made up; and you sometimes feel like the only thing between his having made a mark on the world and his irrelevance. And that breaks your heart because you never wanted the Record to be personal like that. And one day, you're afraid to your very soul he'll look at you and have absolutely no idea who you are. And then, you will be alone in a way that is worse than being by yourself."

Misling looked at Ring sharply, examing Ring's eyes for something to say how he knew this much and so intimately. He said nothing though. Ring waited, then nodded.

"I've never met the man, if that's what you're wondering. I just know exactly what it feels like."

Sylhauna had completed whatever it was she was about and was cartwheeling in their direction. It was enough of a break in the view to shift their subject once again, turning their attention to the crashed dirigible.

"She's on her way back. We've got to get this thing untangled. Why don't you climb up the cliff face and try to start that compressor again? I'll spot you."

Misling was lost in what he'd heard just then, "You did not select this Recorder from the airpark crowd at random."

"You're being paranoid. Rovers don't squirt on their own out of tangles like this – how about a hand?"

"Your dishonesty and evasion are tedious. This Recorder was tasked with observation of your pointless visit to the Rauchka Sniper. His obligations fulfilled, he will follow the Record while you address your unfortunate circumstances."

Misling sat cross-legged on a weathered stone by the muddy shoreline and shut his eyes, frowning. A little dip of flesh rose between his eyebrows. Ring smiled before making his way across some mossy boulders to the netting of vines and brush clinging web-like to the rock face.

"Pointless? You weren't paying attention. All sorts of things were happening. I worry about your share of the Record, sounds all muddled." The Recorder did not betray his curiosity, though he couldn't be seen clearly anyway by Ring who was gripping a small chalky outcropping and lifting his right leg to the rock face. It was quiet for a time but for the call of birds and lapping of shore water.

"Visiting your girlfriend, Phianna again?" Ring had already scurried quite far up and was to a point where he was grunting in exertion, reaching out over a bit of a precipice to grasp the mooring line they'd secured on their arrival.

"Please focus. Your irresponsible disregard for that which is predictable and mature has no doubt blinded you to the weak lift capacity of those gasbags relative to the mountain face above which they are to convey. Shuttles are available from Alson. This was a mistake."

"You're a rude little bunion, implying I don't have a plan for getting back! We're meeting Farmilion at Balcister yeah? I'll get you there. You really think the trip was pointless?"

"Entirely."

"Look at that reading again, you saw it. Look at it right now…all the stuff in transition, all the golems tramping along, the fatigue. The whole feel of it is structure and decay and old ideas that don't work anymore. They're waiting on something reckless. 'If it were a time of wild abandon, the people would crave order'-haven't you heard that?

The Recorder made a sound like, "Hmmph."

"And the knuckleheads at the heart of it all…it's like you could pry the whole bit up from one side and flip them all over, isn't it? You don't think things are all wobbly like that?" Ring was balancing himself horizontally, his boots pressed on a clump of bushes growing out of the rock and gripping the mooring line. Misling rolled his eyes while Ring busily went about his tasks high above as if his meaning were cast in the precision of a dictionary.

"Your statement is meaningless; and your implying otherwise is cruel. The visitation was pointless as no doubt was your time in the white fleet and the market, if in fact you have ever even been in the white fleet." Ring stayed in place a moment watching and possibly evaluating, then returned to his tasks.

"Wobbly bobbly!"

Sylhauna was suddenly beside Misling, drawing an embarrassing squeal from the Recorder at her suddenness. His squeal surprised her as well, eliciting from her a giggle.

"Does that freak you out?" She smiled in satisfaction. Ring waved at her from his vantage beneath the dirigible cruiser's smooth keel the color of buttermilk. Without slowing his advance, he threw a leg around the anchor line and reached to the extremity of his arm's length to find purchase on the keel.

"Hey, the little professor has checked out. Tell me what you saw in the-"

"Are you trying to start a religion?" Sylhauna smiled confidently, a purple and pink hairfall lilting over her left eye. Ring's grip slid such that he almost fell entirely.

"Uhh...no. Don't we have enough of those?"

"Where does suffering come from?"

"Wait…what?"

"All religions start with that, what's your take?" Sylhauna had a confident smirk about her soft face. Ring grunted, regaining a grip on the bullnosed gunwale of the cruiser's back deck. The cruiser tilted to one side and groaned like a whale as he did so.

"I don't know. Entangled consequences. Fishy odors."

"Not much of a religion."

"I'm not trying to start a religion!" Ring's voice rose as he leapt over the gunwale and entered the cruiser's deck. He leaned over the railing to see them below him.

"Then why are you cryptic? I think you're mean to him."

"I'm not cryptic." Ring glanced at the Recorder when he tilted his head, incensed, perhaps leaving Ring a heightened view of how he was being perceived since he at least acknowledged Misling's reaction.

"I'm sorry, guys. I have a lot on my mind."

Ring worked for some time silently, working the ballonet compressor's starter cord and leaning back and forth to free the graphite balustrade from its dry brush entwinement. He looked to them below cracking his mouth as if to make a pronouncement, then turned again to his task without speaking. Sylhauna stood between Misling and the cruiser such that Ring couldn't see her face and held a finger to her mouth to sign for the Recorder's silence. After a number of tries, the compressor fired and commenced inflating the ballonets embedded deep in the elongated gas bags. The cruiser tilted further, unsteadily so. He leaned over again and watched them.

"I told you the places I want to see. Mostly. I don't know about cruel...or pointless...that seemed a bit much. I told him something personal; and I never do that."

As he worked the last of the brush from the rails, he hopped three times in an attempt to right the dirigible. Their silence was working him; and the familiar excited grin was gone. Some stillness passed as the cruiser slowly crept lower.

At last, Ring leaned over the gunwale once again and looked directly into the Recorder's face. Misling watched him curiously while the strange young man seemed to decide something. When he had, he quickly slung his legs around the anchor line and spun upside down, dropping like a spider below the keel and facing the Recorder eye-level with his chin. When he at last spoke, his tone was different...older. If the Recorder had shut his eyes to listen, perhaps it would have sounded entirely unlike this new young man before him and instead like a weathered sea captain with a face cracked from sea salt or a leather-clad cowboy more at home in wild brushfires or blurry combat and wearing the years of experience.

"Our world is malleable, Recorder. The words we choose filter and sift what we see and what we hear, it's true. Just so, our words strike out and order that which is in flux." Ring watched quietly, without expression. Unprepared for this change of demeanor, the Recorder awkwardly forgot what his face was doing and left his chin and eyes to drift into embarrassing positions.

"Once poured, the water doesn't draw back to the basin; but we can loose from it a hurricane in a whisper. To question is a fearful thing, beyond the honor and calling of a bearer of the Record. Yet if you are braced to overstep your own boundaries, then so am I; and let loose the floodgates. One question, little professor. One straight and direct answer. Ask what you will."

Misling's amazement possessed him; and he stood at once, stepping directly to Ring. Sylhauna stepped closer as well till the both of them were close by. The solemn nature of a processional had at once settled upon them. Here was something new, something odd and out of shape...perhaps unwelcome. This was not the voice of Ring, not his vocabulary nor manner, and certainly not his way. The only sound was the white noise of the compressor and the gentle hum of the drive fan.

"You will answer with distractions and falsehoods. It is a careless and empty offer." These were the Recorder's words; but his expression didn't bear them out.

"I do not lie, Recorder." It was the same tone, mysterious and older.

They stared at one another, the Recorder's young face tight as if he'd been told a joke in church. Ring was without a doubt quite seriously steeling himself, his sparkle dulled. He looked almost frightened but certainly pained at what he was offering.

"I absolutely have one!" Sylhauna was standing on her toes, anxious. She was largely ignored, as the Recorder and Ring examined one another's eyes and eyebrows, the turn of their lips and the hue of their facial skin.

Deep in the third year of Recorder training in an exercise the young neophytes call, 'the liars' ball', faculty inflicted grueling sleepless challenges involving overly long recounts of events and anecdotes and lessons of the previous three years for students to repeat word for word. Spiced within the recounts were purposeful untruths which only unpromising novices would fail to repeat and would, in fact, correct unknowingly. The real lesson of the liars' ball was that Recorders weren't to alter the Record but only sustain it – a philosophy which left those who received their mark with the distinct inability to perceive untruths. Nothing in Misling's life staged him to see anything other than what was before him, which is why his Record was such an enigma to generations which were to come.

Ring's eyes were steady. Gripping a graphite cleat, Misling stared as he might at a famous painting, then suddenly slung his boots over and hauled himself clumsily over the railing.

"The offer will be exercised at a time of this Recorder's choosing, following due consideration." Misling's eyebrows and dimples betrayed his transparent pride at the reversal, his seizure of power.

Ring paused reluctantly, then nodded and righted himself. Sylhauna tossed him her satchel; and he helped her aboard. She fluffed her skirt and tossed back the colorful hairfalls before looking him in the eye.

"Weird religion."

Dirigible cruisers such as this one were often seen carrying tipsy city dwellers on holiday, drifting like soap bubbles close to the ground and carelessly following the breezes. Fishing and swimming tours hovered in linked masses over the Yagrada for most of each Summer, commonly encircled by catamarans and small boats with the inhabitants of which busily looking at one another. What was extraordinarily uncommon was for a dirigible cruiser to scale to an altitude of any consequence given the capacity of the gasbags. It exceeded the designs to go beyond the height of about two men depending on the temperature.

Nevertheless, Ring was supremely confident at the helm with a destination in mind as Sylhauna and Misling remained in the railed outside deck astern of the bridge. They drifted over country roads and speckled fields that went as far as the horizon, the tips of corn swishing lightly against the keel. Sylhauna lowered herself backwards and over the side to run her hands over the corn stalks. The Recorder stole a glance at her shiny stomach reflecting the sun before looking out over the swaying fields.

After some time, the Recorder watched some faded computronium ruins drift by, pale and depressing in their decades old resting place and swallowed by the crops, possibly the remains of a battle simulator for screaming warriors whose dreams had died in these rolling hills. Around lunchtime, Misling was twirling his thumb back and forth between his other thumb and forefinger, daydreaming or perhaps listening to ghosts as Recorders do, when at last he turned to see Sylhauna staring at him again. She smiled. Her legs and arms were oriented in precisely the same fashion as his own.

"This Recorder does not know with any certainty this vessel's destination."

"Okay." She said this as if that was obvious and wasn't what she was considering anyway.

"Do you not have a home or family you must let know you are traveling?" Misling asked.

"Nobody cares where I am." She watched him a moment, then changed the subject. "We're new friends now, right? Would you like a present?"

He watched her cautiously, unsure, which was his way of saying okay. When she at last understood that, Sylhauna sat upright and took a breath to continue.

"Shut your eyes tight and listen." She waited till he at last complied. It took a while for him.

"A quiet blue night sky full of stars…creamy piles of snow with only the occasional twig or bush popping up…puffy white snowflakes falling without a sound…on a half-finished covered bridge. Isn't that a pretty picture for you? Do you like it?"

"This Recorder does not understand what you have offered. Is it over?"

Frowning, "So how did your friend know Isaniel's name? That's crazy."

"What about the bridge? To which bridge were you referring? What is the significance of it?"

"Nevermind the bridge. Sorry. I just thought it was pretty. How did he know Isaniel's name?"

Misling nodded, still somewhat reluctant to let go of what she'd said, "If perhaps you could explain where the bridge leads…"

She glanced at him, as if to shush. When he saw that was the end of it, he allowed her change of subject, "This recent aberration aside, neither Ring's habits nor history, his knowledge, nor his true purposes are allowed to be known. It is an unwritten and senseless rule that in some manner bends to meandering discussions of no consequence with perfect strangers and the offering up of treasures and prized companions with neither question nor care for what Ring will do therewith. Strangers comply with his hidden purposes; and it is unclear why that is."

They both turned to watch Ring through the opening, at the helm and eyeing something off the starboard bow. It was quiet for some time but for the drive fans and the calling of birds, and at one point the laughter of a band of ragged children from the dockyards waving after them. Sylhauna was particularly pleased with that bit and fluffed her bright hairfalls for them, drawing cheers. Later, when it was awkwardly quiet again and she was staring at him, Misling offered what insights he could.

"Isaniel was the name of a ceremonial carbine manufacturer and painter in the Fountain City prior to the War of the Rupture. There were three embarrassing instances of conflict with Under Governor Delton, one very scandalized and quite destructive to the reputations of both men given the damage done to the dining area of the Mystick Public House."

"A woman?"

Misling shook his head, "A philosophy. It is difficult to accept what has become of his face and stature – there is only passing similarity."

"Well you didn't actually meet him, how would you know what he looked like really?"

"Mast." This was his only answer, as if he'd said he could see the Mystick Publick House even now as clearly as he was seeing her.

She frowned, "Depressing. How do you know we're talking now and you're not remembering me?"

Misling didn't respond but rather scratched his eyebrow to avoid that topic entirely.

Sylhauna paused in reflection, "I really don't know why he got so big."

"Treatments during the war" Ring shouted from the bridge without turning: the first he'd spoken in some time. "He could nourish a bit with sunlight so he could stay still for long periods to snipe; but he isn't supposed to stay in the dark and eat."

He turned then to smile at them, "How's that for cryptic? You guys are trading nuggets to establish a rapport. I can do that. And we're there, by the way. Have a look."

Spreading out in long filaments in numerous broadly parallel directions, cargo rail trams busily darted from a massive intermodal station linking seagoing vessels from the wide shining Yagrada and its crowded dockyards up magnetic tracks nestled inside gargantuan rips in the mountain face. Shipments from all over the world spoked into this facility, tracked in Balcister's shimmering masonry, and unloaded and stacked themselves by way of automatons of incredible size.

Ring grinned with satisfaction and amazement at the operation, before joining them on the deck and sitting between them, his elbows resting on his knees. "Tell me we'll never get away with hooking on and their security will arrest us."

Misling only looked on quietly in his unwillingness to participate; and so Ring glanced to Sylhauna in case she preferred to instead. With no takers, somehow, Ring was able to bound over the railing and down to a polymeric railed pad in one fast move without charging his leap.

Ring saluted them, catching Sylhauna's attention specifically, "It was truly a beautiful bridge."

His footsteps were echoing taps on metal containers as he made his way towards what was likely a dispatch station. She smiled after him, at last noticing Misling's eyes upon her.

"Your words were, 'I absolutely have one'. What were you considering as fit to place before Ring's newfound forthrightness?"

"Oh, I know exactly what you should ask him. Explains everything." Sylhauna stood and stretched her arms high toward the sun, her hair and its trappings hanging loosely against her back. She ran her hands through them, then leaned over the railing to spit. To her satisfaction, the white bubbled wad of saliva splattered within view.

"Ask him if he's the Salt Mystic."

In those days, superstition held that strong personalities of older times…emperors and generals and philosophers, were somehow locked in memories and stories carried around in the minds of the quick awaiting a time when they were most needed…perhaps intentionally embodied in Mast and transferred whole to Recorders. Neither supernatural nor religious, it was a deterioration of Salt Mystic principles envisioning a soul as a constellation of stories and something to be preserved like leaves pressed in a book. In the moment of their ecstatic return, the souls most suited to the unique needs of an era would indwell those who best knew their stories to champion the right, making a virtue of remembrance of the storied past. It came to general belief later that the day Balcister was lost was the day that belief lost its power to comfort.

The subsequent events were precious relics to the lost generation that followed, images and viscera that placed their own shattered history in context and which were to be savored. Yet a broad pattern of sweeping dreamtime lay across much of the Record from those days, no matter the Recorder. Such a sweep had of course occurred during previous times of upheaval: the Brewing revolts that toppled the old dynasties and laid the foundations of Naraia and the War of the Rupture which cast the mold for these very times being the two most notable.

"Yer boys. Yer boys did it, bunch of skinnies." The long man was bent over, hobbling with a lame left leg, mumbling to himself as he made slow progress down the length of the rail tram. It may have been difficult to believe he was speaking to himself given the direct address; but that is how it was with him.

"Funny business. Yer kind of funny business. Old Knotwhistle will get his piece." He squinted to his left as if he were appraising someone's understanding as he went. The way Knotwhistle widened his eyes stretched the skin of his face and lifted his dry lips off dark and yellowed teeth as if he were disgusted.

"We'll know how much they gave ye. Manifest change ain't right like that. Not like that. Old Knotwhistle will give ye a manifest change."

The old man aimed yellow and dimmed eyes at the now frozen loader automatons, idle and dark collosi shrouding out the sun. The rails were quiet; and no dirigibles flew in the sky. In fact, nothing was making any sounds whatsoever apart from a chill late autumn wind whispering in his ear. Strangely, there was a faint smoky smell hanging in the air about him.

"Yer boys." Knotwhistle dragged his leg behind him, bobbing his shoulders as he went and continued toward the back of his charge, the burnished metal rail trams also idle on the tracks. Such teeth were absent from the old man's face as to cave his mouth in and make his chin pop up and down when he chewed, which he forever seemed to be doing.

"What they done to Dustle. He was a good one. The war."

He tilted his leather head to the side a bit as his slowly expanding vantage revealed a touring dirigible cruiser secured with mooring lines to the corrugated roof of one of his railcars. Sylhauna's face appeared over the gunwale, waving. Then the Recorder popped up as well. It would have been most appropriate to ignore the Recorder and address only the girl; but he didn't actually address either.

"Funny business! Old Knotwhistle will get his piece!" He waved a fist as if they'd opposed him in this.

The two of them climbed reluctantly down, dropping to the earth softly since that seemed to be the thing to do. Knotwhistle looked at Sylhauna as if she were a whale falling from the sky.

"His piece."

Sylhauna coughed patiently, awaiting something that made sense to which she might respond.

"Ye ought to know, freaks. Ye cough some up for old Knotwhistle or we'll settle it right now. From yer funny business."

Sylhauna turned her eyes to the Recorder, gaining nothing, "Did we upset him?"

"We'll give ye a manifest change. It ain't right what they did to Dustle, took off his knees. Made him see things. Yer boys. Greasing was on schedule; but they don't believe old Knotwhistle. Say he's just filling out the papers. That ain't what we done back then, old Dustle would chew off yer behind for papers not right. Greasing was on schedule."

She smiled graciously, "Goodman Knotwhistle, maybe now that the greasing is done, you can tell us why everything is so still? We've been waiting to go into the city; and our friend has-."

"Ye agree to cough some up from yer funny business? Tell the company about yer doings, then ye'll be sorry. We can settle this right now. From yer funny business?"

She smacked her lips, "Our friend was working with someone to have us added to your manifest so we could-"

"Funny business! Prolly part of this mess with the rails too. And the tower. Freaks!"

When they had stared uncomfortably at one another long enough to recognize no way forward, Knotwhistle turned and started hobbling in the direction he'd earlier been going which was toward the dispatch station, the same direction to which Ring had made for earlier and hadn't returned.

"What tower?"

"Yer boys. Nothing but freaks for old Knotwhistle. The war!" He continued in that fashion, grumbling vaguely racist things and glancing occasionally and viciously back at the two of them who followed. When he turned, it was as if he'd been discussing them with someone at his side and the two of them were in agreement. There ahead of them were others; but a silence overshadowed the place…an absolute and frightening stillness of the sort when one hears a dear friend has passed away.

"What happened?" Sylhauna's voice cracked and faded as she saw the faces of those sparsely peppered about them: thick and burly cargo handlers, mechanics with faces soiled in lubricants, and wide-eyed passengers with packages and bags piled at their feet. Something was very wrong; and it had the feel of hot steel suddenly chilled in ice water. A handful of idle mechanics and laborers were sitting on the ground or leaning against their machines, staring distantly like they'd each been abandoned and were only now understanding that. Ring was within sight; but he strangely kept to himself some distance off in the moss, sitting cross-legged and alone and avoiding their eyes. He avoided their eyes like he was guilty of something or was wishing things different.

There was a flickering gray light coming from inside a shed's doorway where several dirty and rough workers crowded. Knotwhistle turned to look at the two of them, wearing a cruel jaundiced smile as if he were amused at someone having fallen. As Sylhauna and Misling stepped over the threshold passing the old man, it wasn't clear whether anyone stopped paying attention to the droning newscaster trying to make sense of Balcister's smoking crater on the screen. Inside, a crowd of freight workers smelling of oil and grease sat watching. Their faces bore the pain of what they were seeing; and some were rubbing their eyes.

It was in some fashion and to those there settling or important to keep hearing about the smoke and the fear of further assaults, confusion. No new images were coming from the city, only trickled and possibly false stories. If all the nuanced rumors were true, the entire city was in flames.

"They didn't even threaten us. Why wouldn't they threaten us first?"

"Doesn't matter. Peri will make them pay."

Alson was frozen – locked down tightly, that much was clear. Trains and highways, dirigibles, everything was shut down. There was no movement in or out; and thousands were missing, presumed dead. Balcister was entirely devastated.

"Where is the Judge? Why doesn't he say something? He should say something."

"He can't show his face – they might be watching for him, hoping he'll flush out so they can get him too."

Many of them let it hang there that someone would want to take the lives of their politicians for their beliefs or for their words or for the jobs they'd chosen. Here were neighbors and storekeepers and passersby who would have perhaps laid their lives as sacrifice for their children or for their freedom, and yet were called to do so for nothing.

Quite some time passed as these working men and women, calloused and dirty and angry, sat in shock seeking distance from the newscaster's rambling, watching old images of the shining Plaza and likely understanding their world was to never again be the same as it had been. One of the line mechanics tapped the forearm of the fellow beside him and motioned to his right – this is what started it. Though slight, the motion caught the attention of most of them; and at once a sight more frightening than they'd already seen was there with them an arm's length away. It was enough. They froze motionless and pale.

The Recorder was wiping tears from his cheek.

One of the cooks from the mess wagon, a woman with thinning cottony hair and a twisted nose touched his shoulder in consolation since no one had seen such a thing…a Recorder not solemn and cold, not silent in the corner and transparent, but feeling along with them.

"Sweet boy." She patted him softly as if he were her own son till at last many others joined her; and finally, they each touched him in a comforting web. At last, the Recorder got up and left them, walking into the autumn daylight beyond the machines and concrete to the riverside where he sat before a broad speckled scatter of sea birds.

"Yer boys." Sylhauna had stepped outside and found Knotwhistle there watching.

"Not now, please." Sylhauna shook her head at the old man to sign for him to keep quiet. After a moment, she looked at the old man as if he were her brother.

"It's worse for him, you know. Being a Recorder."

She nodded patiently as Knotwhistle breathed out something imperceptible, "I once tried to run from my shadow because somebody told me it was a hole in the floor chasing me…a little me-shaped hole that moved as fast as I did and knew where I was going so it was always there. Isn't that awful? I wonder is that what it's like for him – never to have a horrible day go away?"

Knotwhistle was yet mumbling insults or threats or something in a very still voice, softer than before. She tried to listen for a while, then at last tilted her head to continue.

"What was the worst day of your life, Goodman Knotwhistle?" His yellowed eyes stayed on her; and his back twisted a little, for it seemed to pain him to stand without moving. "What on earth would you do if it always felt the same as it did the first time?"

As the afternoon chill began to set in, people were scattering like ants after a rain, neither quickly nor with clear purpose, leaving the two of them among the scarce remnant. The old man's chin popped up and down as he chewed on nothing.

"Yer sort of trouble. Last of it. Nothing for old Knotwhistle. Nothing in the sky and nothing going up that hill." It's possible that's what he said given he mumbled such. Nevertheless, he was away again, cursing to the empty air and limping unsteadily away from her.

Sylhauna found Ring rummaging through the dry stores on the dirigible, chewing on something and having tossed unwanted items about on the deck. It seemed inappropriate somehow, doing anything. She stayed quiet and only ran her hand along the bow of the dirigible, the strange carving of the girl and her ridiculous ice sword.

"Eat something, dear heart. It will be a while before we get another chance. In a very short time, our mutual friend is going to get up from his spot there by the water and trudge up that hillside like a pack animal." She could just see Misling hazed against the orange sparkling river, staring at nothing and shaded by cold towering machines; and her expression betrayed a notion that this wasn't at all about to happen. It didn't make any sense that he would do that.

"He isn't a good Recorder, is he?"

"He's magnificent. The way they should be. Eat." He tossed her a ragged goldenrod block of spiced bread.

When he had stuffed a satchel full and filled two steel canteens from the cruiser's brass spigot, Ring sat cross-legged and chatted briefly to review his ventures with Misling to date, "Let me tell you about Farmilion…"

Ring drew sad eyes from her answering to the relationship between the Recorder and his talkative charge, at least the part of which he knew. He told her of their meeting and the little Recorder's nervous manner in the market, his facial expressions when mocked. She chuckled at the part where Ring slid the dirigible down the hill from the tent city and described perfectly Misling's birdlike head turns as the vessel picked up speed. There was a flash of something on her face then, as if maybe it wasn't okay to chuckle yet. He only nodded at her, approving.

"You know what stands out the most for me, though?"

She took a small bite from the spicebread quietly, prompting with her eyes for him to continue.

"You know how they normally are...all stuffed and...like a painting. The little guy always tries to act like he's so burdened and busy...like what a pain in the neck it is to play the adult and remember everything and make sure the old guy...you know...takes his whatever and craps regularly...there's a shine in his eyes when he's with him. When we were leaving the tent city, he hugged him. Looked like a drunk goose, but wow. You don't see that."

Sylhauna saw the Recorder again, still and sad against the water, "How'd he wind up with him?"

Ring shrugged, "Dunno."

"Why does he need a Recorder?"

A pause, "Maybe he's just famous."

"You're gonna help him, right?"

Ring sighed, "Mm hmm."

Nodding, she tossed the remainder of her spicebread to a small grouping of birds pecking on the brown grass and stepped closer to idly slide her fingers across the haunting figurehead on Farmilion's dirigible, "Who's Laoka?"

Eyebrow raised, he watched her a moment curiously, "Head of the Rauchka when they broke away from the imperial courts. What's he got to do with anything?"

She jutted her lower lip out thoughtfully, "Before they were all-" Then she made bang-bang gestures with her fingers.

"Yeah. They were jesters one time. It's what the Salt Mystic made them. Are you sure you want to talk about this now?"

"Anything other than today, yes. I heard you and the Sniper a bit back in the cave. Most of your junk there doesn't make any sense at all. Why aren't they still clowns? What happened? We could use some clowns as long as they're not creepy."

Ring inhaled deeply, considering his words, "The Mystic's idea; and a pretty good one when you think about it. The higher up you go in the world, the less you hear the truth; and it's not exactly humble people attracted to jobs like that anyway. No matter how big a deal you were, their job was to tell you your farts still stank and you're losing your hair…your boobs are sagging. Shaking feathers, cracking jokes, drawing pictures…whatever they wanted to do; but that 'untouchable' law is only as good as the people who'll keep to it."

Ring shook the canteen idly to drop water onto some ants crawling on the dirt below him, watching them suddenly float on tiny pools of surface tension, "When the Old Man got to be somebody after Sarling, when everybody started asking his opinion and trying to find out about him…started rooting for him, Laoka started embarrassing him to knock him down a bit. It didn't go well."

"Why?"

"They didn't like each other. One time he pulled the Old Man's nose in front of his kids and some generals, so the Old Man pulled a knife on him. Drew blood. You weren't supposed to do that, so a little civil war happened: old way versus the new way. Got pretty bad and escalated. Some Rauchka kids slipped something into Nanny Talgos drink that made her simple minded. That's when the Old Man decided he'd delete the entire Rauchka race from the Record. All of them."

"He missed. There's a bunch of them. They're scary though, not funny at all."

Nodding, "He lobotomized their Recorders, dug out parts of their brains. Chained Rauchka to posts in the Salt Flats. He hired wicked midwives to make their babies spastic or retarded. That's the kind of man he was, so they did what they had to do. The Malthus helped; but there was only a handful of them left anyway."

Ring set the canteen aside and stood, shaking out his legs from sitting too long, "So one day under heavy mortar fire at the Leylands and in front of his maps, Laoka turned around at the sound of his name to see two Rauchka grip his wrists and chain them together. He was betrayed. They dragged him to the Old Man, breaking most of the bones in his arms on the way and asked for it all to stop. Talgo leaned in close, whispered something to Laoka that no one else heard, and poured a bottleful of acid into his left ear."

Sylhauna grimaced, "What did he whisper?"

Ring shook his head, "Nobody heard. But remember what I just told you if the idiots in the plazas with the banners and signs start shouting for another Talgo to be in charge. And this thing today…with Balcister…" He stopped short, interrupted.

"Old Dustle." Knotwhistle's voice suddenly drew their attention from below, breaking their fancy. He was standing alone and stupidly, yet mumbling, holding something taupe and draped over both arms. He said nothing further, but rather squinted his eyes and frowned. He looked at Sylhauna and held up for her his gift. It was his coat. He was offering her his coat. When she recognized it as such, she touched her chest with her palm and thanked him. Awkwardly, with nothing further in his plans, Knotwhistle took a step backwards.

"Dustle was a good one. Showed them how to be." As was his way, the very old man trailed his words off as he lumbered away, dragging his leg somewhat like a sack and pointing his face to his side erratically along his path. Ring watched him leave, but didn't comment.

It was a very short time following that Misling stood up and dusted off his pants and walked in a determined fashion directly up the hillside within the rail bed much as Ring had suggested he would.

"You might bring your new coat, Dear Heart. I have no idea what's happening next."

11 SCREAMING

Nested and entwined within the Judge's cliffside palace were cobbled passageways and stairwells opening mostly behind tapestries in great rooms and storage areas. It was winsome public gossip that Stendahl, often left alone growing up, would disappear for days into the old walls such that the kitchen staff would scatter blocks of chocolate and bread and fruit about the counters untidily to find it had disappeared unattended. One favorite recount of many visiting statesmen often smilingly retold in Alson was of diplomats and department heads patiently sitting motionless while the little fellow skulked beneath the heavy oak table thinking himself unnoticed and trying to paint their shoes. Things of this sort are what emboldened many in the markets and parks and public houses to address Stendahl as a young man whom they'd helped raise.

In such a passageway, musty and serpentine leading to the grand hallway, Stendahl dragged almost violently behind him a Recorder. Shoving aside the yellowing tapestry, he made for the parade balcony outside which overlooked the flagged courtyard and beyond that, the city itself. The vicious column of smoke lingered still; and new fires had broken out. Stendahl gripped the Recorder's head by the temples and shoved his face forward at chest level like a lantern, fitfully coercing the struggling fellow to observe the happenings below. In a pained and choked voice out of line from his typical purring velvet, Stendahl shouted.

"Liar!"

When the Recorder struggled free, he took a step backwards and cast the sort of puzzled and yet judging stare Recorders would at times let slip. It said one was caught for all time in the full light of day at being an ass. There were names for such stares. This Recorder scurried from the room, bumping loosely into one of Peri's watchmen at the doorway who'd seen but a moment of events on the cold balcony, having been looking for the young man.

"Get out of the open!" The watchmen gripped Stendahl's sleeve and tried to shove a railgun into the young man's palm. Stendahl was much taller than the soldier-policeman; and although he didn't resist or unduly delay moving back into the grand hallway, he did purposefully let the weapon fall to the mahogany floor.

"What were you doing out there?! Pick it up!"

Grotesquely, Stendahl only looked at the slender bole weapon resting where it had dropped. Having no time to press further, the watchman relented and led Stendahl with his own railgun drawn but exposed on his flank.

"Whatever. Just move!"

At the landing of the ceremonial stairway beside its massive winged silver statue they were joined by a second watchman who slipped into place like a bird in formation.

"Got your back!"

"Roger that, thanks. We'll make for VIP lockdown. Any sign of a breach?"

"Not really. Spurious alarms, maybe."

The two of them continued on either side of Stendahl, professionally and cleanly sweeping the area in protection until at last entering a freight elevator. The first watchman slammed shut the cage door and struck a key from his pocket lanyard against a panel projected from the bulkhead. The elevator hummed mightily and started downward.

"Emeresca...Blade Watch." He was taut and spoke out the side of his mouth in introduction to his fellow, still watching the cage door.

"Trope...Engineering Corps."

"Engineers?" Emeresca chuckled and cast a glance at Stendahl with his tossed white hair and char-black and wrinkled silk shirt. "They're scraping the bottom for you, aren't they, Bubba?"

Stendahl ran his eyes across the soldier, pausing on a coiled sigil on his shoulder patch, "You are Rauchka?"

Emeresca ignored Stendahl's query as if neither the inquiry nor the inquirer mattered, "Trope, what's going on outside? I've been dark." He leaned against the wall and loosened his railgun's shielding straps around his forearm.

"I've been at my battle station since I heard about Balcister. I just went there to the landing…didn't know what else to do. No one's answering. I've been trying to decide if I should go out and find some way to help."

"Last order I got was to go find this guy and get him underground. What did you hear about the assault? Do they know who did it?"

"I heard Venom Watch ran into a Red Witch platoon and got burned down. No survivors. But they also said there were suicide blasts all over town; and not all that's true. I mean, nobody really knows what's going on, do they?"

Emeresca's eyes betrayed a muted awe as his voice trailed, "Venom Watch."

"I know. Should we locate anyone else first?"

"Just stick with me. Peri and the high hats are supposed to meet down there."

Suddenly and entirely out of context, there was a scream from below their feet, a male scream deep and uncontrolled. It was close and utterly horrifying in its intensity. Stendahl stared at the floor and stepped to one side, close up against its burnished interior wall.

"What the crap was that?!" Trope went pallid. Emeresca

slammed his palm against the emergency stop. They stared at one another waiting on something further to happen…something to clarify and make sense of things so as to properly react. Yet the creaking elevator went as still as pastureland.

"Man's voice. The only people here now are watchmen…soldiers. What would make a soldier scream like that?"

"Don't freak out, man. My little brother is a watchman; and he's afraid of everything."

"Was that your little brother?!"

"Calm down. Let me think."

"Perhaps the lockdown is a trap." Stendahl rubbed his forehead. His odd expressions were always difficult to make out; but he at that moment had the look of someone flailing in seafoam, gasping.

"Keep quiet." Emeresca was trying to look in charge. They waited with fading hope that something definitive would happen, even another scream to help along a decision on what to do.

"Are we going to keep going down or what?" Trope scratched his neck nervously, more than would be necessary for an itch.

"I don't know. Just wait."

"They blew up Balcister freaking Tower…I think waiting is a bad call. If I was going to send a message, I'd blow up this place."

"They blew up Balcister to take out communications."

"Whatever. That guy was screaming. I say we go back up and run for it."

"That's a longer trip than we have left! Lockdown has blast bunkers. We could sit out the War of the Rupture down there and sip tea all along."

"You sip tea! He was screaming at something, man. The Red Witch are down there already; and we're stuck in a little box! We should never have got on this thing."

"They're not down there, Trope. They blew up Balcister with stooges…losers they tortured and brainwashed. Nobody's down there."

"Then who was screaming? And who are you trying to convince anyway?"

"We'll surprise them. We know they're waiting on us."

"Get us back up!"

"What about your job, soldier? We're supposed to get this guy to lockdown and protect this facility."

"I build roads!"

Emeresca shifted position to place his back to the control button, ensuring none but himself had sufficient access to make this decision. He tried his throat communications again, receiving no response.

"Emeresca enroute. Anyone copy?" He paused, then spit. "Why aren't the backup comms working?"

Wiping his shining forehead, Emeresca looked at Stendahl, "What's your vote?"

The young Talgo looked on, steady jade eyes not yielding to tears but rather sparkling suddenly with tiny ghosts of the elevator lights, "With swords for eyes and iron for will, he's become a man who was never young…"

"What is he talking about, man? He's saying something weird."

"He's just coping."

"It's a poem." Stendahl's face was pale, his eyes rolled to one side looking back at them.

Disregarding Stendahl and continuing to sieze his honor, Emeresca quickly pawed the controls again to restart their journey downwards. He pointed his face at the floor as if it would soon drop beneath his feet so as to push his fellow watchman from his peripheral vision. Trope surrendered to the decision and gripped his weapon tighter as the heavy freight elevator lumbered down again, doubtless imagining all that was frightful about the Red Witch.

"I've never seen one of them."

The Red Witch nation's fighters were fierce and without conscience, speaking a language wherein objects were named based on how they might kill and actions distinguished by the level of pain or confusion they might cause. Perhaps no thought choked fear from a soldier of those days more than slipping into such hands. The Red Witch nation was born in the dissolution of the Salt Mystic system generations before; and the attendant lapse of the order and ecstatic structure it had long provided gave way to a vacuum which was filled with cutthroats and mercenaries. Whereas the Malthus worked the received will of the state, backed by the insight of the Recorder Pool and the Augur's interpretation, hammering out a reality in human affairs that was deemed appropriate for the forces and players of the times, those who grouped under banners such as the Red Witch were imitations, thieves of style and tricks who only used the manner and not the genius of the noble orders. As such, they were an abomination.

Emeresca sliced the quiet with nervous chatter, nodding toward Stendahl. "My mom thinks you're my little brother or something."

The watchman continued since they were close to the bottom and the silence was worse than rambling, "She likes you more than me sometimes."

"I've heard that before."

Trope knelt facing the cage and aimed his railgun. Emeresca followed suit, preparing for its opening. Stendahl slid himself behind them, pushing against the walls such that his fingers had squeezed into a ghostly white.

"On the balcony…you called that Recorder a liar…what was that?" Emeresca nervously tapped the the grip of his railgun waiting; but Stendahl kept silent, plucking at his lip. The watchman let it go.

There was a massive shake as the elevator grounded against the lowest level. The faint spirits of talking could be heard close by. The ProMat cage peeled open first, then the heavy door, rumbling along its worn track. Stendahl remained behind the two of them, and so was hidden from the view of those beyond the opening.

"Watchmen! Don't move!" The two of them shouted loudly and leveled their weapons at those in the corridor, a volatile and unsteady step away from unleashing a kinetic torrent of electromagnetically hurled slugs.

Six pale young women stood in the corridor watching Emeresca and Trope as if they were street art. The ladies were unremarkable, of the sort one would find at children's sports fields or in shopping areas. Their apparel was loose cotton, turquoise and opal bangles, of the fashion common in those days yet splattered with red gore. They smiled politely, one with curly brown hair and high eyebrows even waved. At everyone's feet being ignored was a dead watchman, torn apart and his head twisted fully backwards. His body was actually in pieces, the skin at the torn parts stretched and hanging loosely.

"Put your weapons on the ground slowly." Trope was assuming weaponry as he spoke; but the strangers had none. The ladies only looked on courteously as if waiting on a bus and willing to share the shade.

"What happened to him! Did you people…?" His voice just stopped. They had torn the man apart with their hands and were smiling at him.

The brunette who'd waved stuck out her lower lip sadly, "He stinks a little."

"What's the matter with you? Are you lunatics? All of you?"

"It was really easy to get down here with him."

"What are you – radicals or something?" Emeresca pointed his weapon at the brunette's forehead. On her flushed cheek was a tiny painted pale orange bird in flight, her eyelashes made up as if she'd planned on a theater evening. It was smeared in something that looked like blueberry preserves and that had chunks in it.

"He brought us down here to protect us. We were crying and stuff. I guess he changed his mind about us. He changed it a lot." She broke into a nervous laugh when she said, 'a lot'.

"Why did you come here?" At that point, Stendahl stepped out where he could be seen and could see. There was a noticeable reaction among the lunatics, an anxious murmuring and lifted eyebrows. Whispers.

She sniffed as one would sampling a candle, "You smell like an old man. But not just any old man, isn't that right?"

"Where are the explosives?" Stendahl's query drove their excited whispers louder. Emeresca and Trope glanced at the Talgo briefly as they gauged his assessment of things and suddenly agreed.

"I like that you're quicker than them. You'd never be goofed on, would you, Talgo?"

"Where are the explosives?" Emeresca poked her under her eye roughly with the twin rails of his weapon, drawing a ribbon of dark blood that made her wince and withdraw sharply. She chuckled and darted her tongue out and in quickly like a lizard.

"We need to do something now. They're wired or something." Trope's voice was cracking and going too high. Emeresca slid the rails to the woman's hip and pulled up on her loose blouse, raising it to the side to reveal horrible enflamed scars across her stomach, still strung visibly with thin black thread.

She pointed her thumb at a black haired lady in a silk yellow top behind her, "My sewing buddy wasn't so good."

"They tricked their way down here to blow up the lockdown, the whole government. I mean, the whole government, man! How do you detonate – is there a signal?"

The black haired sewing buddy defended herself, "You were wiggling. If you'd stopped wiggling so much."

A third, with blonde hair and homely, chubby and with freckles and still holding a dripping piece of the dead watchman like a drumstick, "I didn't wiggle at all; but mine is leaking."

Trope took a step back, almost swallowing at the same time, inquiring of their spokesperson, "Are you drugged…what did they do to you?"

Like a nightmare killer suddenly shaking off a smile and glaring at the dreamer, she who'd spoken for them went cold and solemn quickly and unnaturally. She tapped her temple viciously.

"Oh, they'll do much worse to you, sweetie. It will be just awful." She glanced over to Stendahl, "I wouldn't want to be famous."

Trope frowned and held his firearm forward, "Let's go back up and leave them here, man. We can't know when the detonation signal is coming. Or maybe it's on a timer. We have to go!"

The black haired lady who accused the other of wiggling began shaking violently, in tight fits like a seizure. Without a further word, she began to jam her extended fingertips deep into both eyeballs, up to her opal rings.

"Calm down, sweetie. They warned you about this."

Emeresca grimaced in horror and pointed down the hallway, "They need to be inside the blast bunkers or everything blows."

"So what? Let's go!"

Ignoring them both, Stendahl locked rigidly, leaned into the first brunette's placid face and watching her eyes like there were words written there, "Are you in there too?"

Still tapping her temple, her eyes shaking, "You who have whored your freedom, taste the rape of the chained."

His brow folded, uncertain and cautious.

"Stand fast, Trope. Don't freaking move."

"Get in the bunker!" One could tell Trope didn't anticipate compliance even as he said this. He was flailing, hoping something would change before they all went up sky high. The lunatics simply watched them.

"Get in the bunker!"

"They're too far gone, man."

"We're out of time!"

Critically, slowly and in some curious manner both at one time, the two watchmen turned to Stendahl. Seeking authority and a mandate beyond themselves, perhaps a place to put their guilt, they looked to his ghostly face for direction.

"What do we do, Talgo? Make a call."

Certainly the timing of the explosives was unclear and possibly imminent. It wasn't a time for deliberation; and his was the family that ruled. He was what they had at that moment.

"What do we do?"

The black of his shirt was absolute and looked against his bright hair like a deep shadow over him. For an overly long moment, tensely and without momentum, Stendahl only watched them back. He breathed in deeply.

"Don't hurt them." His voice was soft and frail, a little boy in a crowd calling for his mother but despairing of finding her.

Emeresca's face grimaced in disgust immediately before he opened fire with all his fury, "Whatever."

The hum and rush of railguns sounded, soft transformer buzzing backed with bursts of rushing slugs. The women didn't run or duck, but rather stood in praise with their arms held out as if bathing in sunshine on a cliffside while their faces ripped into fragments. Stendahl turned his eyes away. Perhaps if there had been a struggle, a clawing and screaming or angry brawl peppered with insults and bitterness, what the watchmen did would have seemed heroic. As it was, the action was horrible and one for which Emeresca and Trope neither recounted for their fellows nor came to receive commendations.

When Peri and a small contingent of watchmen arrived a short time later in fact, both the Rauchka soldier and the road builder were sitting in streaks of blood propped against a reinforced bunker door, doodling circles in the fluids and failing to stand to attention at her arrival. The dead watchman's parts were draped in an old squadron flag, purpled and clinging by this time.

"We dragged them in, Marshal. Afterwards."

When Trope saw she was waiting, he added, "There wasn't any…explosion. I mean, I didn't hear an explosion in the bunker."

Emeresca turned to him and repeated something he'd said already more than once, "The bunker is blocking the signal."

She only nodded and turned from them without comment, "The Judge is locked down in the war room. You men get the Procedures-Master and Commerce Secretary put up in the bunkers. Where is Stendahl?"

When neither of the seated watchmen responded, Peri screamed close-in, bending over to shake them out of their reverie, "Grow up, ladies! Get over it. I asked you a question!"

Emeresca's eyes were wide as he looked back at her. She had clearly seen things he had not in his short service. "One of the bunkers, I don't know."

Disgusted, she started down the corridor towards the center of the underground complex, which she knew to be a shining oak and leather library with deep fur carpets and wall shelves full of old books. It was the subterranean keep of old man Talgo, dusty and silent in those days and not a place where even the Judge would tarry. It felt to many like he was still there, angry and pacing.

She slowed at the carved snakes adorning the reinforced doorway, an entrance that hadn't been illuminated in a very long time. Likely, she was imagining the last time she'd been called to speak to the old man in this very room. Though Peri probably anticipated finding Stendahl on his side crying fitfully, he was eerily seated at the old man's thick cherry finish table leaned over a white ceramic bowl, his hand draped over a brass pipework. It was much like she would have found the old man in his day; and that made it solemn.

"What are you doing in here?"

Stendahl's sparkling jade eyes looked up at the old soldier, sad and angry. His hair was sweaty and matted against his neck like wet cotton; and he was tired.

"What's the matter with you?"

When he only looked down into the wide bowl, she saw it as the projection bowl of a camera obscura…part of the network that veined the old imperial palace, the same as that which Wentic had earlier used to see his son in the library. She stepped closer and rested her dry, calloused hands on the moon colored rim to peer inside.

"The Judge's war room. It's hard to make out…what is that?"

Stendahl was making a noise with his lips, like a train's smokestack noise. It was soft, but unsettling and out of place.

"Let's go, little man, I don't have time for this. What's the matter with you? Do you know something?"

Stendahl focused the lens by turning a brass key on the pipework; and it squeaked as it turned. He was softly speaking, "Walking the plain of a world that's dead, a citizen without a nation…"

This was when the world stopped for Peri…the sort of moment when the sound drops out and all that's left is a heartbeat. Cast in miniature, illuminated shapes gelled at once into familiar faces. It was a wide view of the Judge's war room, seen from a mounted wanoa's head on the wall across the palace. The tiny figure of Revin was there, apparently seated on the floor beside what looked to be the dead body of Judge Wentic Talgo. Revin held a railgun in his hand.

Stendahl's face hardened into a frightening mask, anger and pain in creases on his skin as he looked directly into Peri's eyes and spoke commandingly in a cold, spitfire tone she knew well…a tone she hadn't heard in a very long time.

"Marshal, cut off the Counselor's arms and legs and bring him to me alive."

Peri was to say later she'd watched something happen there in the young man's face that frightened her more than anything she'd seen in combat. As she backed out of the old man's keep, Peri was doubtless thinking of a little boy that used to paint shoes under the table.

"Judge, I came as soon as I could. What have you heard?" Revin shouted as two watchmen resealed the wide impact doors to the war room. Wentic had been pacing and scratching wild notes onto the electronically painted walls. A slender blue-steel rail gun hung loosely from his side.

"Revin, excellent. Glad you're here. Let's figure this out." At that, the Judge slid his finger in swirls across the walls, drawing dark black lines behind it. Some of his notes were animated in diagrams intended to perhaps show influences. Intelligence embedded in the paint was trying to optimize and parse his notes, making suggested connections and rearrangements which he was either accepting or rejecting.

"What are you doing? What are you talking about?" The Counselor was unsteady, still huffing from his flight and unsure of what was being asked of him.

"Connections. Looking for connections. Need to figure this out quick. And don't just assume it was Cassian. That's irritating. Have a reason for saying that. These are all the provinces and anyone who might have been responsible. It's Red Witch; but you know what I mean. Who hired them, I mean."

"Grebel is in the city. I saw him myself. When he heard, he acted like he didn't know; but he's here. He was scouting or something, you know. Your brother has Red Witch on his payroll."

The Judge frowned, "So do we. Why were you with him?"

Revin hesitated, "I was in town and saw him."

Wentic kept his suspicion but turned again to his ponderings, "What are you talking about? Get control of yourself. I need a steady hand here."

"Where's Peri?"

"Headed to lockdown with some of the guys. Told her I'd stay here and puzzle out what we're gonna do. After your little jig with Sullion, half the country hicks out there think we're trying to make their economy fall apart. Could be anybody. Could be all of them."

"Are Watchmen patrolling the streets?"

"All over the place, yeah. I've got tanks rolling and battlesuits. It's like the Rupture out there; but Red Witch crazies aren't fighting with tanks, you know what I mean? These guys snuck in and launched their loonies on us and could be gone by now for all we know. You don't fight the Red Witch, Revin. You set martial law and go kill whoever hired them."

"What's that about Sullion, you're blaming me." Revin's eyes were squinted. The Judge glanced at him in quick retort.

"Well you didn't help!"

Revin locked his hands atop his head, thinking deeply and inhaling sharply, "Look, I need to talk to you about what's going on. Don't discount it this time – I have proof."

Wentic raised his eyebrow, "Not your Salt Mystic junk again?"

"Hear me out. Don't ignore it when you know this is how these things culminate. I've studied it, you know I have. We've been under Salt Mystic attack for a long time. Maybe as long as your entire tenure as Judge."

A loud slam sounded from the impact doors, startling Wentic. Revin instinctively placed himself between the Judge and the entranceway in protection. There was another slam and the distinctive zings of slugs off railguns from the other side. Revin was only standing there with his fists clenched tightly and staring, a wildcat defending a cub. After a tense silence, the doors started to slide open again, drawing Revin to leap towards the opening with his fist tightly clenched and raised, high on adrenalin for he had no other weapon.

"All clear." A trusted watchman's voice sounded from the opening just before he poked his head into the clearing.

Revin was relieved, "Whitejohn, what's going on out there?!"

"Sorry, Counselor. Rookie freaking out. All clear." The impact doors slid back shut; and Revin turned to see his Judge aiming a railgun as if he'd never held one before. Wentic wasn't panicking, but rather was perhaps unused to touching violence personally.

Revin slid his hand over the railgun and pulled it gently away, "Let me have that. I can bring one of the watchmen inside if you like."

Wentic turned back to his wild scribbling, "No, 's all right. You guard the door."

The Counselor inhaled deeply to calm himself and shoved one of the weapon's rails into a loop on his belt before pacing, "She fleshed this out. It's about destabilizing a nation by paralyzing its leadership-"

The Judge moaned his irritation; but Revin continued and raised his voice to drown it out, "-attacking its people's work ethic and morality, and…you know…bankrupting them…when the right players inject ideas into the system and the timing is right."

The Judge rolled his eyes, having endured this before, or something like it. In fact, Revin had gone on a number of talk shows detailing his views on the conspiracy, which went further toward making him ridiculous in the people's eyes.

Revin continued, "The last step after…I mean… culmination…is to sell a vision of an easier and prettier alternative to make them just…walk away. You and the others that make fun of all that and call it conspiracy theory and crackpot talk, that's part of the plan. You've made them invisible by making a joke of anyone that…that…points it out."

"Revin, I've got dead people. I don't have time for this. Get out if you can't get off that junk. I'm sick of it! People make fun of you for this sort of thing. I'm tired of defending you."

"Our law was written with debate and compromise." Revin pointed his finger at the Judge for emphasis. "Even in the Old Man's time, that was a virtue. Your people can't pass a resolution or decide on budgets for fear of being seen as weak, straying from their principles. Where did that idea come from?"

The Judge rubbed his temples with his two index fingers, understanding maybe that Revin had to get this out before saying things more useful. Revin pointed again as if he were poking through something immaterial in the air between them.

"I've traced it. Could only have spread from a whisperer in an era transition, crushing expansion…eighteen summers ago…Forum Chief Caslade and all that happened to him. Nobody thinks about that anymore; but it's where this whole idea started that you can't negotiate…that you're a political liar and spineless if you seek compromise. 'Paralyze the leadership.' The people laugh at your Forum, how they're out of touch and helpless. Flip-flopping laws make it so no one can invest and generate wealth – it's stagnating us. Wild speculative bubbles in the economy that pop and destroy the value of our money…those were missiles in Salt Mystic combat."

Wentic growled in irritation and frustration, still squeezing the sides of his head.

Revin sustained his passion, almost as if he'd practiced the very words in mirrors and tested different means and gestures with which to say them, "The magnesium windfall… why are we still paying that out to the people? Those mines are…you know…depleted. Anyone knows you can't take money away from the people once you promise it. What about your civil loan nonsense…you said it was to help the people get out of their debts; but they owe the Forum now. What's the difference? 'Destroy the work ethic'."

"And dirty pictures and naughty theater are making us all sinners, yeah?"

"The madness every year over a new entertainer – each more outlandish than the last. Do you wonder whether they'll ever tire of growing more vapid and uninterested in state affairs? 'Distract the people'. The Mystic said a nation's use of mercenaries signals its decline…what are you doing to our military?"

"Revin, I really don't need to hear the rest of all this. I can't even stage a parade without screwing something up – who could possibly plan at this scale and over this long of a time period? Certainly not my freakshow brother! I know you believe it; and I imagine you can make it sound plausible. Let's drop it because it isn't helping. I have dead people; and we need to do something about it."

"I am doing something about it!"

"Besides pushing crackpot theories about boogie men!" Wentic twisted away from Revin and circled an area of a hand-drawn map he'd scrawled in an area on the wall, drawing a flurry of suggestions from the embedded intelligence.

"Who came up with those ideas? I've traced them and plotted them into the perfect eras, the perfect players to act as hammers. Not just anyone could have gotten the civil loan program off the ground. Lawmaker Po was a reluctant warrior embraced in-"

"Would you please stop talking junk to me! I don't care if you're right or wrong about this, Revin. It doesn't help what we're facing. Maybe you don't know what the Red Witch will do to us here. Maybe you've never seen one up close eating someone's face off them alive. We're in trouble. They will have left behind an army of people who can sit right next to you on a park bench and talk about the rain that's coming until they decide to rip out your eyes. You're never going to know when you've cleaned it all up. How do you fight an army like that without turning into them?"

Revin's voice cracked and squeaked just a moment as he answered, "You attack the vision. That vision is what matters. What the people think will serve their…you know…best interests."

Wentic was at his end with it, "I don't know what it will take to get you off this. You're useless and you've probably caused this. Get out!"

"Tathlum is fake."

The Judge's eyes widened; and he turned back to face his counselor, "What's that?"

"Fake. I made it up, nurtured it. Was a necessary concept."

"I told you to calm down. Stop seeing gremlins and talking nonsense. I've heard that rot from Peri." The Judge eyed him suspiciously.

"It's impossible. Was just an idea injected into the system. A momentum breaker. And it's worked and given us…you know…leverage we didn't really have. Pseudo-science ideas dazzled your military thinkers and kept them from asking difficult questions. All the researchers were trying to get something published or gain status at their universities. It took on a…you know… life, quickly as it was intended. Novelty and uniqueness fired the project; and we all gained from it. Had to happen."

A pause, an unearthly pause, "Traitor." The Judge's voice was cold. His eyes darkened like a rolling thundercloud.

"Traitor?! I can't believe you're calling me that! I've done more to keep us safe than you can imagine."

"I've seen field tests."

Revin nodded, "Theater effects. I can explain why the timing is perfect for something that-"

"Traitor. You've caused all of this!"

The Judge's face showed the magnitude of his disappointment and abandonment, like a cornered man turning to face the wolves. Revin was surprised at the passion he'd engendered with this. Right then, he froze for that moment, clearly in a desire to pursue his argument but just staggered by what he was seeing on the man's face: a Talgo coiling for a strike. It was a sight that had cowered hardened generals.

"You brought them here." He stiffened and straightened his back, quickening, a rising fury like a stalking wildcat.

"You turned the provinces against us. You stole from me. You lied to me. You killed my people. You've ruined us; and you're calling it a kindness."

The Judge's reaction not having gone Revin's way, he had the look of someone who quickly wanted to explain his case with short shakes of his head. Wentic placed his two palms against the Counselor's chest and shoved Revin sharply into the impact doors.

"I'd rather have lunatics in my house than a traitor beside me, smiling and lying. What were you really doing at Sullion?" Wentic placed his palms again on the Counselor's chest and pushed him, almost knocking him over this time.

"What was it? Did you decide the timing? Collect your payment?"

Revin responded, "We're under attack. I only did what would best protect us. It's a new kind of war. This is what we have to do – the fleet can't protect us from-"

The Judge shoved him again, this time slamming Revin's head against a mounted wanoa head, drawing blood, "What?"

Revin's voice was shaking again, in fear and panic and anxiety to make his argument clear, "You're hoping that…ramships or something…are going to make a difference when your whole society is being eaten alive by ideas. It's not a-"

The Judge's fist drove into Revin's throat, cutting short his shouting and causing him to choke and cough viciously. When he saw Wentic was coming at him again, he gripped the railgun hanging from his belt and pointed it at the Judge's chest.

"Don't-."

"There it is, you disgusting thief. Show your colors!" Wentic did not slow his advance or his dampen his anger.

"I'm a patriot."

"I'm a Talgo!" The Judge reached forward again with his palms to shove his Counselor again and with a vicious sneer.

In a panic, Revin fired. A deep bass zip sounded and collapsed a small crater where the slug had bolted clear through Wentic's face beneath his nose and to the left of his nostril, pieces of skin flaking off and smoking as they curled aflame. The crater distorted his face as his eyes widened, drawing an eye and the lips in as if they were falling down a hole. It was a nightmare vision there as everything quieted into a deathly hush but for the Judge's labored breathing.

"I'm a Talgo." That's what it sounded like he said.

For a moment, Wentic tried to speak again as he staggered; but he was struggling to take a breath. It sounded like the air he drew in was leaving the gaping hole in his face. His awareness was drifting; and his twisted eyes were rolling. Revin could only watch it like a fascinating wreck as the Judge's life drained out.

Revin looked at the impact doors, then back to the fallen Talgo. He was in a terror and hadn't at all intended to do this. The only sound was his own breathing. What was left of the Judge's mouth gaped; and blackened and charred blood and gel were bubbling out the wound. Just the history of this man laying here and what he represented were crippling for the Counselor.

"I needed you for this to work. You had a part."

He kept his eyes on the Talgos immobile face, "I didn't do anything wrong. We were under attack already; and I didn't cause any of this."

The Counselor knelt to be closer to the Judge's dead ears, "It's too late. They've worn us down too much to lose our faith now."

He looked back at the impact doors, "I'm going to go out there and tell them something that will organize them, that will make you a martyr. I don't know, I'll figure it out. It's just too late to let anything shake us…we can't fall from within. It can't happen here. Not on my watch."

He stroked a finger across the Judge's forehead, "I'm going to make this right."

After a moment of reflection, the Counselor stood. He glanced at the tilted wanoa head on the wall without realizing its lens and mirrors led to the camera obscura pipeworks. He glanced at his fallen Judge without realizing what was coming for him. Revin may in his mind have seen himself poetically, a giant of history recounted in the Record and at a low point that historians would view as his quality's finest moment.

Then at last, in a voice surging now with determination and swelling confidence of being the right man for the right time, only moments before Peri and her watchmen burst through the impact doors to sieze and dismember him, Revin spoke to no one at all.

"I'm a patriot."

13 STRANGE COMPANIONS IN THE MORNING MIST

The mossy green canals that lazily coarsed the city were washed in the pale lemon light of streetlamps; and Ring and his companions were still following them through the desolate late hours. A soft fog had descended, misting over the promenades and making a watercolor of things. Sylhauna's hands were tucked into the thick wool coat; and Misling had coiled a rough woolen muffler around his neck.

"Vomit. This Recorder is going to vomit." He perched suddenly beneath a nickel lamppost styled in the shape of a silver wanoa clutching a raised torch. Misling was holding his knees and staring at the water, exhausted. Ring and Sylhauna huddled around him.

"It's not safe to hang out under the light. Let's keep moving."

When Misling didn't respond, Ring leaned in, "Is it your lungs or your legs?"

"It is both. Everything hurts."

Ring nodded, "Shake and stretch your leg muscles as you run. And breathe deeply but slowly…don't let your breathing get out of control. You can run forever that way." Sylhauna watched Ring with her head tilted to a side, curiously, perhaps wondering where he would have come up with advice on distance running and self control. The pace of Misling's wheezing calmed eventually; and the Recorder at last looked up into the starless night sky like he was drinking rain. He seemed tired in so many ways.

"There is a café by the fountain where the event readers go. I'd like to hear about your visitation. If we're not there, we'll be in the tower at the bank. Just wait for us." Misling's tone was flat, entirely unlike Hastine's when he'd spoken those words.

"Yeah, I know." Ring notably declined to offer hope or speculation but rather only nodded. The three of them sat huddled together watching the shadows. Further down the wide boulevard was a massive victory arch rimmed high on its top with a handful of sculpted figures composed of programmable matter, silhouetted and silently exchanging heroic postures against the city's light. The evening was chilling; and everyone's breath was just starting to cloud.

"Four lives, right?" Sylhauna sat beside Misling resting her elbows on her knees. He nodded at her.

"Which of them thinks this is a good idea?"

Misling's back tightened, understanding her meaning, "This responsibility is not yours; and your attendance to it, though appreciated, is unlikely to serve you well. The Record would bear you no shame were you to turn away and return to the Cave City to protect your own charge."

He engaged Ring's eyes as well, "Neither is it necessary nor prudent for you to continue. You have in mind great things and should be about them."

Ring rolled his eyes and shook his head no, "Don't pretend to think that's how this works. Although I'm dying to know what you plan to do when we get there."

Sylhauna brightened, "If this were some sort of…like an adventure story…a mystery guy like you would turn out to be…I don't know…special forces or something. And you'd say we were being watched because you could smell them…and pull out…like..a crazy gun out of nowhere that makes people disappear. And set traps."

He frowned at her, "Again with that?"

"Maybe we should keep moving then, or hide or something? This doesn't seem wise."

Ring looked back to them from the corners and alleys he'd been scanning, "Did Misling just say he appreciated us?"

"You know, he did; but he was trying to get rid of you too."

The Recorder shook his head and placed his face in his hands. They sat in silence shivering and watching the alleys and their breath. Across the street was a downward leading stairway framed by two lampposts whose halos reached out like prominences, blurring in the early morning mist. An odd feeling came about them all, like that of stepping into a dark and unfamiliar basement and hearing a breath; and it was Sylhauna who first noticed something new or perhaps previously unaccounted for on those stairs.

"What is that?"

"Steps to the canal."

"I'm talking about right there..at the top of the steps."

Ring and Misling followed her line of sight. It wasn't moving and seemed to be a man, perhaps a statue. Yet it was in the center of the stairway where such a sculpture would have obstructed the entranceway. The vision had the feeling of an unexpected face in a window…out of place and threatening.

"Is that a person?"

Ring stood and squinted his eyes. The three of them watched for movement, though none was obvious. It would have been incredibly unnatural for a man to remain still that long.

"I'm pretty sure nothing was there when we stopped."

"Guys, stand up."

Misling and Sylhauna did so, very much unsure what it was they were seeing. The silhouette was definitely in the shape of a man, though the head was cocked strangely to a side. Strangely, the face lost in shadow looked stretched, elongated as if his mouth was being unnaturally forced open.

"He moved, I think. He's looking at us. What's the matter with him?"

"I don't think it moved. Are you sure?"

"Something's wrong. Let's uhh…let's get moving." Ring touched their shoulders to shepherd them away from the silhouette. He was as still as a cathedral possibly looking in their direction. There in the desolate morning on an abandoned city street and entirely alone, a silent man stood wide mouthed and staring, unmoving.

"Perhaps he is afraid or injured."

"It's the middle of the night. How can anybody stay that still?" Sylhauna stepped behind both of them, watching from over the Recorder's shoulder. Curiously, when Misling stole a glance to his side, Ring seemed as concerned about the area behind them and overhead as with the strange still man with the long face.

"Stay here." Ring stepped to his own side, arcing around so as to be able to see down the limestone stairway but without getting any closer to the figure in the mist. He left the Recorder and Sylhauna clustered together beside the lamppost. The stranger's face did not follow him, but was clearer now as everyone's eyes adjusted to the pattern he made against the reflected streetlights.

"So sweet like jelly." A raggedy and bowed man stood from the stairs, rising from the ledgestone wall behind which he'd been concealed as he'd sat on the steps at the feet of the silent and still man. The new arrival was short and unhealthy looking, wearing a torn hooded baja over a round belly and knit wool cap cocked to one side. Frayed red strings hung from an eyebrow piercing dipping over his left eye; and part of his nose seemed to be missing though that could have been a trick of the light. He had no obvious weapons but had the look of a hard life about him, of the sort that live along the canals or tucked under covered bridges. He was smiling.

"I'm not hiding from you, sweetsies. I heard your little voices, all chitty and chatty. We were just coming through and I heard you, I did. There's nobody else out tonight, isn't that right, you rascals."

"What's going on with your friend?" Ring stayed cautious and gestured toward the immobile man on the stairs, apparently failing to satisfy himself of something as he scanned the new arrival.

"He's just a little darling, he is. That one there. He's Bomar. He isn't right; but he won't hurt you. Not you, my sweetsies. I was listening to you, every dripping word…so sweet like jelly. I just had to see if you little rascals are plain regular folk, you know…that you aren't crazies. Oh, I had to see, my little darlings."

The stranger hesitated, glancing at each of them but mostly Sylhauna and suddenly dropped his smile watching her, "You hurt me, princess. So much. My princess thinks I wants to steal something or ask for money. I don't wants anything from you, sweetsie. Keep your frilly princess junk. So much."

"What's your name?" Sylhauna brushed some hair from her eye; but she remained by the nickel lamppost. It's possible she felt having a name would make him less frightening. Misling separated himself from her and straightened his shirt.

"Oh, I'm Kensi. That's me, isn't it? My mummy called me after her favorite uncle. Was a pet fish too, my darling rascals. An ugly little fish with bumps on its head, yes it did. Filthy little thing that stared."

"What's wrong with him?" She was pointing at Bomar's face.

Kensi stepped around the silent man and hopped up to sit on the wall, crossing his legs casually. Bomar's entire body was motionless; but he seemed to be staring at Ring at this point. No one had seen his head move; and it was unclear whether this was the direction he'd been looking earlier.

"I told you..such rascals..he won't hurt you. Not one little bit. Bomar's just not right-not plain regular folk like my sweetsies. But not anybody's all completely right. Not you either, my princess? He's just got a little more of not being right. I'm not saying I would get that close to him." Kensi warned Ring at the approach, his voice darkening and watched momentarily before turning to Misling and Sylhauna still beside the lamppost.

"What are my sweetsies all doing out here – such a time of night and all full of crazies? Such rascals…you look like kiddies on a field trip."

Misling coughed to gain the floor, "What is your understanding of the events at Balcister? What news have you about what has happened to the city?"

Something about Misling's tone or grammar, or perhaps his demeanor, gave notice of his identity as Recorder. Kensi leaned his head in, perhaps a little excitedly at the notice, evidently straining softly to make out the wheels within wheels on the Recorder's forehead as confirmation.

"It blew up." He chuckled inappropriately. "It did. This morning, darling."

Kensi leaned toward Misling and lowered his voice like he was telling a secret, "Killed thousands..just horrible and going about their rascal days when up it all went."

After watching them a moment, as if trying to gauge what they knew, Kensi quickened and gestured like a storyteller, "Wasn't all either. There were crazies turning 'round in crowds and firing full blast-zip zip zip. Walking to work and not wanting to be rude and crossing the street, then turn around, they did and started killing. Zip zip zip. I saw that at Carnabie, I did. And fires all over the rascal city. Crazies. People like my sweetsies…wandering 'round for hours, nowhere to go. I see a lot, don't I? With sweet Bomar."

"Well what's happening?"

He watched them for a reaction to what he'd said, maybe savoring what news he did have, "I saw one rascal covered in dust…looked like a cloud walking, he did…just kept moving past me wouldn't even talk or look at me…here he'd made it all the way to Carolinestrasse and wasn't slowing down. So far, my sweetsies, isn't it?" Kensi scratched his neck and coughed, then spit onto the street.

He widened his eyes and purred, "To run that far, he must have been real scared, isn't that right?"

"Surely there are rescue efforts, authorities. Have you heard nothing of survivors? What of the Plaza?"

Though the questions were the Recorder's, Kensi glanced suspiciously at Ring who had stepped closer to the silent man, "That's what had him so scared…you treasured little rascal. He was scared because no one was helping, were they? No heroes in bright clean uniforms…no doctors and no neighbors pulling off rocks…no helpers at all and a big pile smoking and people screaming. 'Isn't that what watchmen are for', he said to me. Didn't I ask him why he didn't help, my little sweetsie. Didn't I do that? 'Why are you here with me', didn't I say? And 'What did anyone do for me', he said back. Didn't he? But I heard something. Are you looking for somebody, little precious sweetsie? On your field trip?"

"What are you talking about? There are watchmen, certainly. If no one else, watchmen will surely be coordinating rescue efforts."

Kensi's goblin face crunched into a wicked smile as he chuckled, "We don't feel that way sometimes."

"This Recorder's sponsor was to meet him in the Tower or the Plaza. He would have been there at mid-day for the crowds. You said you heard something – what was it you heard?"

Kensi shook his head, "Recorder…talking to me…going somewhere." Looking at Sylhauna, "Something's punchy about that, isn't that right, little princess?"

He turned back to Misling and ran his hand across his hair stroking a long pony tail, "That's horrible, just rascal. Everybody's got a story. I don't know. I heard from a lady, all made up and old, who waddled and came aroun' midnight and wouldn't give us any money and wanted to see her grandson. She said she hoped the crazies don't go after houses where all the sweetsies are headed. Where her little Eduan is. Can you imagine spooky strangers stepping into little houses while all the precious rascals are sleeping? Right there at the foot of your bed and you have your feet under the blanket because you're afraid a cold hand will touch it in the dark and you open your eyes and there are the crazies staring at you. Oh she did, my darlings. Little Eduan screaming at crazies."

"Someone is responding…there are rescuers! How can no one at all be helping?" Misling's tone was intent. Kensi only shook his head.

"My little kiddie on a field trip…you want to go and see, don't you? There's no one in charge down there, my sweet darling. Nobody in charge like you dream of when you're warm and sleeping and think how good it is to live in a place where there are brave uniforms. And I heard something."

"What is it you heard?" Sylhauna held tightly to the lamppost. Ring still hovered near the grotesque Bomar – haunting and silent.

"That old bird, all made up and old…she told me what she saw down there. She did, my sweetsie; and it tells you who the crazies are, doesn't it?" Kensi grinned; and in the pale light it was at last clear his nose was in fact partly missing. His teeth were twisted and foul.

"There's a bell tower down there, lollipop. A bell tower all filthy and tall; and it wasn't there yesterday was it?"

The Recorder stopped cold, locking into his highest level of attention. He always turned his left ear slightly toward the center of activity when that happened.Ring at last shifted a half-turn away from the gargoyle man, putting Bomar outside his peripheral vision. He again made a cautious scan of the garrets and upper windows lining the dark boulevard, the gables and parapets. Sylhauna was the one to question it though.

"Like a Red Witch bell tower? Like it just showed up today?"

Kensi nodded, "That's what she said, the old bird. My princess. She had to see tiny Eduan to keep him from the crazies, didn't she?"

He looked at her like she was a pastry, awkwardly hesitating, "So much."

After a moment, he continued, "That means my sweetsies go poking 'round in a pile for survivors, somebody's gonna rip you into pieces and wieces. The crazies will, the rascals. But you sound like you know how it goes, my kiddie on a field trip. Ring the bell and you go free, right? Isn't that right?"

He darted his gaze between the girl and the Recorder, "Won't some rascals tell you it isn't true and that awful tower is a trap, right? It's a trap for drawing out resistance rascals, right? And they don't let anyone go. Who knows, princess? Who knows what happens when you ring the bell? Maybe you go free."

She shook her head, "I don't know."

"Well whatever. Good reason to not go down there, isn't it?" He laughed, somewhat of a cackle like a cartoon witch.

Sylhauna caught Ring's attention and, tellingly considering her view of who he was, asked, "Is it true?"

"Where on Carolinestrasse?" Ring ignored her question and asked his own of the street man. He was close enough to Bomar at that point for dark and hard claws to strike out and grab him mercilessly should things go that way. Bomar's dead eyes stared directly into the back of Ring's head, his black mouth gaping like a sinkhole as if he were set to screech like a banshee and draw down leather winged hordes from the sky.

"What are you talking about? Are you being rascal?" Kensi's

tone was less friendly, offended almost. He shifted his seating on the ledgestone to more fully face Ring, eyeing him like a piece of ground beef.

"You said you were on Carolinestrasse when you saw the man covered in dust. You were making a point about how scared he was because he'd run that far. We get that; but where on Carolinestrasse were you?"

A pause, "Near the rendering plant, sweet darling. I think you smell nasty, all getting close when he shouldn't and on his field trip…and looking at sweet Kensi like he's done something rascal. Looking at me. Are you trying to catch me fibbing…like I'm spinning stories for kiddies on a field trip?"

Kensi squinted again, "What are you doing here early, anyway my darling? We weren't supposed to meet till sunrise, were we?"

Misling and Sylhauna tensed quickly, both of them unsure of what it was they'd just heard the strange street man say just then. The Recorder confirmed in her eyes she'd caught something in it as well.

"And don't stand that close to my friend, Bomar doesn't like that…he'll be rascal with you. Sweet Kensi has told you that already and said it again."

"Right. So you've hit all your high points now. You know we're looking for someone and filled us all in on the bell tower. You've kept us and pressed us for information." Ring was as confident here as he'd been at any other point, not reacting to the stranger's implication. He turned back to face Bomar, cold and dead…close by.

"You're being rascal with me…and you'd better stop it. You'd just better stop it or I can be rascal too." Kensi spoke violently, through clenched teeth, aggressively.

"And you made it compelling to go…very spooky. Your midnight woman was full of insight into what's really going on. Of course, you made her up and little Eduan. They told you to make up names to sound authentic, inject details."

Kensi caught the eyes of Sylhauna and the Recorder, lingering his gaze long enough to fully draw their attention to his face and his manner and to ensure they caught the full import of what he was to say, "This fellow here…this rascal…he isn't who you think he is."

"You're inept and really lost." Ring was close enough to Bomar at this point to breathe on him.

"Bomar…"

"Yeah, Bomar." Ring lifted his hand slowly as he continued. Kensi stood erect with fists tight at his side and shaking just a little.

"I wonder whether your minder is close and you were killing time or if you were just trying to get to that bell tower crap you were throwing at us." Ring's voice rose in his passion. Misling and Sylhauna watched the gargoyle man more closely and urgently, as if he were being summoned into a foaming berserker rage to swallow them whole.

"Get away from sweet Bomar, you horrible darling, he doesn't like-"

"Yeah, he doesn't like it. You know what he doesn't like?" Ring reached an index finger up to Bomar's nightmare face and touched it gently to a single tear on his cheek, slowly turning to see it and sense it for what it was and what it meant. He watched the tear as if it held visions of the future.

"Being tortured by a lunatic poser trying to earn his blackening from like minded psychotic filth." Ring looked up at the street man fiercely and with lightning in his eyes, "Wake him up."

"You can't have him, sissy boy. Sissy kiddie on a field trip. Turn your own. Turn your own kiddies and leave my sweet Bomar!" Kensi eased closer, like a boxer appraising a bigger fighter than himself.

"I said wake him up!"

"Worry about yourself. Rascal! You think you're smart and you're winning. You have no idea what you just did. No idea, you terrible fish, just filthy!"

Sharply, like a demon crawling from a pit, a hulking Red Witch fighter appeared in the shadows behind Ring, towering over him…massive and armored, cloaked in a long coat, scowling and smoking from the heat off his body. Ring was a dwarf beneath the monstrous and dark man coming at him with a charged carbine sizzling and popping like a live wire. Once Ring had turned, each of them stood wide-eyed, beholding the monstrous warrior while Kensi laughed like a howling coyote.

"I'm winning now. Isn't that right, princess? Now there are some just horrible things to do to my treasured lollipops. Disgusting little sweetsies, so sorry they ran into Kensi, aren't they? Now we'll cut off strips of you…strips like bacon."

"*Eat his face. Eat it right off.*" Disembodied whispers, several of them, surrounded the Red Witch man like demons inhabiting his flesh - one was never certain what that was. "*We'll crack his back, leave him in the sewage with dung in his mouth.*"

Ring watched the massive new arrival, as if he were waiting to see if there were more. The whispers faded in and out. Possibly, the Red Witch man was awaiting fear and panic and stood before them to instill such, or perhaps gauging which direction they each were to run. Perhaps he was awaiting others.

"*…squishy little pieces of stripped off meat, yummy…*" And another over the first, "*Stupid looking coat…*"

Ring listened and observed only a moment, then gathered himself, "I trust you hear me over your…babbling."

The whispers went into a frenzy, incomprehensible and speaking over one another. Though Ring watched for a reaction, The black face and burning eyes were like stone.

"Minders learn lots of languages. I imagine you understand me." His voice echoed on the quiet nighttime street; and it was not at all clear whether the tremor in his voice was from anger or panic or fatigue. Yet tremor it did, nonetheless.

He swung his thumb towards Kensi, perhaps trying to sound at ease, "It's embarrassing what you've chosen over here. Are you really going to give this idiot a chance to join you?"

Kensi roared viciously, spitting, "You first! I'll cut you and pee in the hole! Get on your knees!"

"Start with his eyes, his eyes!" "Embarrassing." "He said pee, he said pee…"

The Red Witch man only chuckled, booming and thunderous, still having said nothing. He powered down his carbine and slid it to his shoulder strap but pulled something else from a separate holster along his waist and just inside the duster.

"Oooh….now he'll get it…."

Ring held up his hands, his left in a tight fist and his right with fingers outstretched and locked as they train the deadly Frost Troops in the north countries, "Guys, run. Get out of here. No more are coming."

Kensi seized Sylhauna by her throat and knocked her feet out from beneath her with a strong kick. Before she or Misling could react, the Red Witch man swung his armored fist quickly and smashed into Ring's left temple knocking him into a half turn. The blow had hurt Ring severely; and it was all he could do to raise his face again. His eyes held the loose daze of too much wine; but he did raise his face. He looked fiercely up and into the Red Witch man's eyes and lifted his hands again, his legs spread wide.

"Misling, run."

Without mercy or hesitation, the Red Witch fighter slung the new weapon he'd only just drawn like a club and in the opposite direction, metal on bone and vicious. It was hard enough to shatter Ring's jaw and sounded like it had. He was at that point bent over like a man vomiting, thick tinted mucus streaming like a rope from his mouth. When he turned his face up again and tried to lift his fist, the Red Witch man lifted his boot and kicked Ring in his chest hard enough to shove him the length of three people along the street. It was a shocking move and carried extreme force. Ring stopped moving after that. The Red Witch man shoved the heel of his boot into Ring's right cheek.

"Stop it!" Sylhauna shouted. "You're killing him."

The Red Witch fighter as if in response, held forward the new weapon and pointed its long rectangular barrel, flashing streetlights in stretched reflections, directly into the base of Ring's skull at the top of the spine and fired. A mechanical thud sounded with finality; and the force of the shot shook Ring's body.

Kensi laughed in a caterwaul, "Look at that one. Look there."

The Red Witch man locked his red eyes on Misling, glowing like two drops of lava in the soft street lights. He had to lean forward to see the Recorder's face. Glowing red wolf's teeth spread out inside a widening grin. He reached out a massive gloved finger and placed it across Misling's forehead tattoo roughly.

"Hello, little bug."

"Wheels on his head, turn it right round…"

Kensi scooted himself to Sylhauna and sat on her, pinning her arms with his knees, "It's hard for me, lollipop, to steal you away.

Like a sister to me now. Crazy from here. So much. Just crazy and screaming and will do anything to make it stop. But a Recorder…that's just funny, isn't that right? Remember everything, don't they?"

"Remember everything…"

"You killed him." Sylhauna struggled and shouted, almost toppling Kensi. He righted himself by repositioning his left foot wider away from her. Kensi was surprised she'd bucked him so hard and steeled himself tightly.

"So much."

The Red Witch man lifted the weapon again and held it sideways, pressing the barrel into the Recorder's forehead, watching his eyes closely. The stock and body of the weapon were frosted but transparent and held a liquid inside. The barrel wasn't actually open as a gun would be, but terminated in a turquoise spongy Pro-Mat plate.

"Explain this." His voice was deep and cavernous. He was addressing Kensi, perhaps savoring the panic and seeking to flavor it further.

Raggedy Kensi chuckled again, "Liquid computer, my sweet, juicy darlings. To see such bad things and feel them and live a long miserable life in no time at all. Just awful what you'll see and what you'll feel and the crying and it goes on for years, doesn't it?"

"No time at all…stupid coat…"

She and Misling both turned their eyes to Bomar's cold face, stretched and dead like a folded latex mask. Kensi had produced a smaller pistol-style version of the injection weapon the Red Witch man held and suddenly looked at her through its clear stock, grinning as the image of his eye stretched across its curved surface watching her. He gripped her neck to turn her head aside and expose the top of her spine. He wasn't interested in more talk and was eager to get on with it, clutching and clawing at her as she struggled; but he couldn't hold her steady enough to expose the spot he needed.

"Explain, meathead." The Red Witch man said it again, drawing some irritation from Kensi at the interruption and the delay. Unseen by anyone, Misling was clutching his fist.

"Turn it right round…"

"About Bomar?" Kensi was asking the Red Witch man for guidance, his voice screeching in his urgency. When there was no answer apart from maybe amusement on the massive nightmare face, he continued although was getting out of breath with the struggle.

"I call him Bomar because it's a funny name. Snuck into his little Bomar house and watched his little Bomar's. Such a pretty rascal he had, and was helping her with her math, wasn't he?" Kensi leaned forward to put more weight on Sylhauna's bound arms. She was kneeing him in his back savagely and grunting and trying to bite his left knee unsuccessfully. Kensi wasn't really strong enough to keep her down much longer and clearly wanted to get on with things.

"'I'll be right back', she said, didn't she? She had to poop. 'Right back' is funny because I grabbed her, didn't I? Before she could. I grabbed her and I stuck her and it doesn't take long, does it?"

"Out of shape…get on with it…juicy strips…"

Kensi had to right himself as he was almost bucked at Sylhauna's struggling. He was huffing at this point as if he'd been running as he told the story. He looked at the Red Witch man again to see if that was enough as he was losing his balance and getting winded. After a moment, he knew he had to continue for the Red Witch man's pleasure. Unseen by anyone, Misling braced his legs widely, coiling.

"It's like ages go by but it's only a blink, isn't it? Sweet Kensi made it fast so he could see happy Bomar's face when his little girl came back grinning and staring with spit on her chin all bubbling and wanting to slice into his neck. She went to poop and came back like that. 'I'll be right back'; and she was, wasn't she? Your filthy fish is doing that now, isn't he?"

Sylhauna halted only a moment in her struggle to glance over to Ring, still and silent as a fallen marble column. He hadn't made a sound since he'd gone down.

"Talk to the bug." The Red Witch man again directed Kensi.

"Turn it right round…"

"Can I stick her first?" He grunted, almost entirely out of breath at this point. He fumbled and clawed like he was drowning, still trying to expose the back of her neck.

"Can you? Talk to the bug, meathead." The massive Red Witch man chuckled as he picked something from his nose.

Unanticipated by anyone, Misling launched himself into the weapon, smacking it to the side and attempting to claw his nails into the Red Witch man's throat like a wildcat. No one would have known; but it was an assault made hundreds of years before by a young Duke Exeter in his practice before the first battle of his life, shamed by his trainer and eager to earn a command of any sort. Here at this moment, it was a similar act of hopelessness and finality with as much chance of succeeding.

Misling didn't howl or shout a battle cry; but rather only moved fluidly and as brutally as he could. The young Duke had managed to draw blood from a seasoned field lieutenant and earned a place by the cannons in a battle whose name no one remembered apart from the Recorders. Here, young Misling managed to do nothing of any kind and was brutally slapped down with the barrel of the Red Witch man's weapon.

With the barrel pressed coldly against the base of Misling's skull, the Red Witch man chuckled, "Record this, bug."

A theatrical pause followed where they all seemed to freeze, where music would swell and images would slow. It was a moment of surrender and terror. And then Ring said something.

"Faring." His voice was distant, damaged. He was injured severely and could only just lift his head right then. The Red Witch man turned his face to look.

"Don't listen to the fish, my darling!" Kensi was horrified to see Ring alert. "He says bad things, confusing things."

"What's he say? What's a Faring? The juicy strips…"

The Red Witch man's flaring eyes squinted, wondering why this man was conscious at all considering the blast he'd just received to his mind and the beating he'd taken. Ring unsteadily lifted himself to rotate over to his side and face them, now lying on his right hip and resting on his elbow. He was bleeding from his mouth and possibly from his tear ducts as well.

"Under Governor Faring of the Southern Red Witch annex. In his pool. Ask him."

The Red Witch man's face seemed to show delight and surprise as he bent over so as to better gauge the Recorder's reaction, "Faring?"

Misling and Sylhauna were watching Ring with amazement. Kensi's burning stare was fierce, an absolute hatred for Ring. He also looked exhausted after his attempts to hold Sylhauna down. Misling met the Red Witch man's eyes then.

"From his fourth failure at the blackening through his time as Chaselord and ultimately Under Governor, and his capture and interrogation."

It wasn't clear right then whether the Red Witch man had heard of the Under Governor or was imagining him. Neither was it clear he believed Misling at all.

"His last words…?"

Misling paused uncertain, as if that made sense for a Recorder reciting from his Record. He was silent for an awkward moment, either because he was calling up the moment in its Mast entirety, fully preserved like a pinned insect in alcohol with its wings stretched wide, or because he was imagining and lying. Who could tell?

"He dragged himself along the cell floor leaving blood in a trail behind him." Misling coughed and looked at Sylhauna, then back to the Red Witch man.

"Turn it right round…"

"His breathing was labored, like bubbles coming up through mud. It was cold; and mist rose up from where his legs had been severed as a streak of goo poured out."

Misling hesitated, losing himself in the images he was watching, "It was not blood. Something else. Close in, eye-to-eye with the Recorder, his breath smelling of mucus and sewage, the Under Governor said, 'I beat them. Tell them how I beat them.'"

The Red Witch fighter only watched and pondered. It was then, perhaps as Kensi was distracted at the Recorder's recount, Sylhauna finally toppled him by freeing her hand and grasping his pony tail, tugging the street man's head down viciously to the stone pavement. It bounced like a ball and elicited from him a shriek incommensurate with the force of the blow. In a panic, she seized the injection pistol from his loosened grip and slammed it onto the side of his neck where it made a whoosh noise and stuck fast. Then she scooted away, wide-eyed and frightened, watching him.

"Bah bah bah!" Kensi was shouting nonsense in his own panic. He snatched his arm out and grasped her boot at the ankle. She had thought she was far enough away and was shocked at his reach.

"Don't." The Red Witch man didn't shake his stare at Misling for the moment despite what had happened behind him.

"No. Juicy strips…confusing things…turn it right round…"

Kensi looked desperately at his minder, the injection weapon hanging loosely from his neck, "But she's being rascal."

The Red Witch man at last shoved Misling's shoulder and broke his pondering, turning and straightening to walk to Ring who was bleeding much worse from his mouth and the side of his face than before now that he'd tried to sit up. The minder kicked Ring down again, pinning his shoulder to the dusty street with an armored boot and pressed the frosted acrylic barrel against the base of his head, firing twice. Two horrible booms sounded, sending pulses of violence through Ring's body. The minder watched for a reaction.

Ring managed to roll himself and look up, coughing. His voice was horribly distorted through the swelling and bleeding, "It's weird, isn't it?"

Fierce red eyes squinted. The minder looked at his weapon and tossed it to the street, sending it bouncing.

"Follow them." The Red Witch man spoke to Kensi as he picked Bomar's lifeless body up like it was a sack of concrete slung over his massive shoulder. The poor man's face was bunched fabric, stretched and horrible and vacant, rustling loosely against the minder's duster as the fighter walked into the shadows. He was leaving.

"Follow the juicy strips…confusing things…"

"That's my Bomar, darling. My head hurts. It hurts really bad, my sweet Bomar." Kensi was squealing and holding the back of his head and was horrified at the blood he was finding on the hand he was using to comfort himself. His other hand still held Sylhauna by the ankle. When he showed her the blood, she kicked him with the other boot and got up, rushing to join Misling and Ring, though still watching the panicked street man.

"Is that it? Is he not coming back?"

The Recorder locked eyes with Ring, trying to maintain Ring's drifting attention as he held him by the shirt, "How are you unaffected?"

Ring's eyes rolled up; and his mouth widened as Bomar's had. He moaned, then regained control and became alert again, though sorely punished and suffering. His cheeks and jaw were swollen and purpling. There was severe pain in his eyes; and they were tearing up.

"How are you unaffected?"

"Misling? Shelter. Can't stay here."

The Recorder continued, "How are you unaffected?"

Ring weakly lifted his hand to touch Misling's hands, clutched there at his collar, "Can't black out. Don't let me black out."

Sylhauna at that point turned her eyes to Kensi to perhaps gauge his urgency, his intentions, whether he was in fact leagued somehow with the mysterious Ring. She was stepping further from him as she looked.

Kensi still sat like a toddler, holding his head and with the injection pistol still dangling beneath his ear, "He's wicked; and he's one of us. And I'll eat his eyes. I will. The fish!"

Ring was becoming unresponsive and groggy as if under ether. Misling was stuck, uncertain. It may have been he was running back through his Record of the last day, skipping through to bits of dialogue or facial expressions for clues relating to Ring's behavior. It may have been that he was scared out of his mind.

"His eyes!" Kensi hissed and snapped. "My chance!. You soured him on me, you filthy kiddies. On your field trip. Too much talky talky. Next time sweet Kensi cuts your throat and pulls your tongue through the hole. No laughing or explaining or blah blah. Just cutting and pulling and then I'll dance, you filthy fish!"

Panicked, Sylhauna ignored the blathering and poked the Recorder's shoulder to gain his attention, "I know somebody close by."

Kensi stood and started walking toward them, "I'm dizzy, princess. You made me dizzy; and I can't see good. And I'll eat your eyes too."

"Okay, we're leaving. Get out of your head and help me. I know somebody." Sylhauna started to lift Ring's rubber arms, limited by his size relative to her own and awaiting the Recorder to act. He was hesitating, drifting into his memories and reviewing his archives for something.

When she understood what he was about, she tugged on him, "Bigger problems here."

Amazingly and decisively, completely out of character for a Recorder and something that came to great attention and discussion in later times, Misling did in fact come from his reverie, and stepped quickly and aggressively to within paces of the street man, locking eyes.

"A bargain." He gave Kensi a fierce stare, level setting his proposal. "Should you go away right now, should this Recorder never again see your face, your moment in the eternal Record is one of fearful service as a blackened Red Witch fighter defending the Southern Annex against…an incursion of purge troops, in fact falling in battle back to back with the Chaselord himself. Just the two of you against an overwhelming force and glorious. That is what this Recorder will place as your Record."

Misling watched the street man's face, the stirring of fancy and dreams, "Such a destiny, you will agree is unlikely from here for you; and it is free and promised and certain herein. However, should you follow, molest or interfere, should you in any way make yourself known again to this Recorder, your only mark preserved for the remainder of human history will be that you cried like an infant when bested by children and…were defecated upon by the Red Witch when they declared you worthless. Consider your chances."

Though Kensi continued to stare ahead with a foam on the side of his lips, he did register something on this. He kept up the daze as Misling at last spun and assisted Sylhauna. He maybe called after them once to cast threats or venom as they faded hobbling into the shadows; but his voice only sounded like broken wheezing. Just when the three had faded into the mist, Kensi tugged the hypodermic pistol from his neck and began limping in an awkward trot in the direction towards which they'd gone.

"Like jelly."

The sun was still yet to rise; and it was cold…still the early lonely hours between evening and morning. A withered man, not old really but withered nonetheless, was laying in his damp linen, sweating in a fever and shifting position to seek comfort. Beyond his artifact-cluttered room and through a cramped kitchen where the floor was antiqued brick and copper pans hung in haphazard fashion, he could see the night sky and city lights from an open terrace window with a broad limestone sill wide enough to be seated upon.

"Who is that?" It was perhaps the odd rustle or snap; but it shook him.

When there was nothing further, he inhaled deeply as if coiling for a jump and threw his arms out to assist in righting himself, trying to sit up so as to reach a bottle of sana which was sitting on the tableside drawing a moisture ring on a stained piece of laced filigree. He couldn't sustain the position, however and fell back empty handed, squinting his eyes in frustration or discomfort. Whether his left side or his right, there was no comfort to be had; and he at last rested again on his back, laboring.

"It hurts."

The look of his face was of surrender, sadness that it had come to this. Slid to his side and scattered about the floor were models of pillars and pilasters, ornamental gargoyles and intricate architectural pieces in miniature; and he maintained odd bits of latex molds stacked in rows about the floorboard. He placed his hands gently on his stomach to rub the skin thereon; but decided against it and moved them again to the side so their weight should not press upon his abdomen.

"What's that? Are you back?" There was another rustle from beyond his doorway. It was more definite that time; and he knew it.

He stared with eyes round and alert for a time, then tried to sit up again to gain a better vantage. Something fell and shattered somewhere near the terrace, only a few paces and around the corner from where he lay. He inhaled sharply and gripped his linen as if he were falling.

"Is it you? Speak up. Who is there?"

Suddenly, Sylhauna's face popped around the doorframe as she waved, "Hi, Lennox. Sorry about that."

He eyed her suspiciously, with disgust, "Are you stealing? What are you doing?"

She held up a finger to sign that he should await an answer, then continued toward the entrance, "Just need to open your door real quick. Where is she?"

Lennox tried again to right himself, upset and intolerant of this disruption. He protested but was ignored as he strained to listen to noises of the new entrants, not visible from the untidy sick bed in which he lay. He rolled to one side and propped himself on an elbow to gain his view, at last seeing Sylhauna and Misling with difficulty drag Ring down the main corridor past his bedroom entranceway. Ring was speaking a string of words that made little sense, but seemed to be an attempt to wake himself.

The bedridden man's hand suddenly clamped to his mouth as a shield, "What are you doing? Is that man sick? I can't be around sick people. Get him out of here."

There were further noises of settling the wounded man down; and at one point, Misling's face was visible through the doorway a moment as he jaunted by to get water. Misling waved uncomfortably. It drew more reaction from the withered man as he hid his face, having recognized the tattoo of a Recorder.

"Don't tell him my name. Get them both out. Are you listening to me? Don't tell him my name."

Sylhauna came to him in her ridiculous coat and looking tired, sallow and panicked. She sat on the floor by his bedside, opposite from the door and hidden from its view, trying to calm her breathing. As her adrenalin and momentum died down, she rubbed her eyes and took a bite from a fruit she held. They were each silent for a time; and though he likely didn't notice, she was curling further into a ball as she sat trying to entirely shield herself from the sight of any who might come through the doorway.

"You're still smelly."

He drew in a long breath, "Why'd you bring a Recorder here? I don't want anyone to see me like this."

She chewed again, the fruit crunching softly, "'s okay, he's not good at it. Funny thing to worry about."

"What happened to the other one?"

She hesitated, "A better worry. Where is Cristoffel?"

"Why?" Lennox coughed and laid his head against the mashed cushion again.

"Where is she? It's important. Have you seen her since this morning?"

"Is he sick? I can't be around sick people."

"I asked you if you'd seen her." Sylhauna lightly smacked Lennox's hip to gain his attention to her question. When she did so, he turned angry eyes to her in reaction, an expression of ferocity.

"Don't touch me!"

She drew back in fright, wincing like a whipped puppy accustomed to the beating, then took another bite from the fruit, pondering.

His voice was cold and direct, "What do you know about what's happening out there? There were watchmen in tanks outside earlier, bullhorning something about Balcister and staying inside. I think they shot some people. And it smells like smoke. It's smelled like smoke all night. Do you smell that?"

"I must be used to it."

"What do you know about it, I said?" His tone tried to be commanding, perhaps recalling the way he used to sound before he was ill and withered and tied to yellowing linen. Yet his voice broke for lack of sufficient breath.

She turned her head up to face towards his eyes though he couldn't see her, "I could have died tonight. A guy tried to jab me with something. Scary guy."

"Is your friend sick? Some sort of plague breaking out? That's why they're shooting people; and you brought it to my sick bed?"

A pause when he didn't acknowledge what she'd tried to tell him, "He isn't sick."

She examined the jumble of plaster miniatures laid alongside each other and stacked haphazardly on the dusty pine floor: elaborate buttresses and a decorative keystoned arch, an architectural wanoa humped over like a cat set to pounce, and elaborately crossed figures possibly from inset pieces such as might surround an elegant window high on an old building. She traced her finger along one of them to feel its cold texture against her skin.

"Well what happened? Do you not even know what's going on out there? Are you that lost in your freaky little world that you don't know what is going on when there are tanks in the street?"

She took another bite from the fruit and spoke softly, "Don't yell at me."

"What?!" He paused for an answer, which was not offered.

Perhaps it wasn't an answer he awaited, but rather respect or an assertion of strength. It was grotesque and sad, such harshness from his sick bed toward a girl only chewing her fruit and cowering from something that might sneak in from outside to kill them or steal their minds. She sat quietly, still afraid in her way.

"If it's plague, you owe me aid. You'll help me to a ferry and get me to your Cave City. You owe me for all I did for you. I'll stay there till I get better. Fresh air. Get out of the city. That's what you'll do. It's good you came. Get me away from her." Lennox seemed to be transitioning his conversation to a monologue, satisfying himself with his plan for what she was to do for him. His voice even trailed as his thoughts went inward, having settled the matters.

"He wouldn't like you."

Lennox continued as if she hadn't spoken, "Your Recorder person will have to help me to the ferry. I can't walk more than a few steps without losing my wind. We'll just leave at first light. Should be coming up shortly."

"Lennox, have you seen her today?"

"Don't need her. She doesn't help me anyway. Wouldn't help your friend either, if that's what you're doing here. Only wants to sit around staring at candles and statues and sit in the cemeteries. And she stares at me too."

Sylhauna took his chatter as a negative and looked again to the plaster bits and pieces. He'd drawn himself into a darker thread though, one he suddenly in his spooling thoughts desired to pull.

"She stares at me." His voice died off to silence as he appeared to decide at last she wasn't the person with whom he wished to discuss the issue. Sylhauna waited awkwardly.

"Lennox, it isn't safe to travel or even be outside."

His eyes squinted; and his cheeks drew into a skull at his fury,

"You'll do what you're told; and be glad of the chance. You're not getting shed of me or your responsibilities. You'll do what you're told. You owe me. For all I did for you."

Lennox appeared to start a lean forward again, to try and look more fierce and authoritarian than he might should he remain prone. The pain locked him into only a sort of seated position propped up by one elbow. His face paled even further in the exertion; and he locked eyes with her to complete the show.

"Everything you did." She watched him, maybe waiting to see what emotion would swell up on his face, whether he believed what he was saying. After a moment of that, she stood up and scratched her cheek. Sylhauna tore off the last flesh of the fruit, watching him still. Then, she turned and left the room. He turned his head to direct an ear toward the doorway. When someone returned, it was Misling looking tired and disheveled.

"Lennox Weshire, is there something of importance you wish to preserve in the Record?"

He groaned a bit and turned his face away. When he'd thought better of his new circumstance, he peeked from behind his outstretched hand which shielded his face, then stuffed a folded pillow behind his back to support a seated position, motioning for the Recorder to come over and sit beside him.

When Misling was at his side, Lennox waved his pallid hands in front of the Recorder's eyes as if shooing away scattering flies, "Can you stop that? I just want to talk to you. Just don't remember all this. Can you stop it?"

Misling creased his forehead, "That is not how it works. This must be swift. Do you have something you wish to preserve?"

Dismissing that with a wave, "Forget that. She's being funny. I need you to take me to the Cave City to get away from this plague. Thinking better of it now, we should start right away rather than wait till first light. That way there won't be a lot of people on the ferry.

Could be infected."

Misling only watched, no reaction whatsoever. Seeing that was so, Lennox at last raised his voice a bit and pointed to a side closet, "I have some changes of clothing and towels in there you should pack. Might draw some water into a bottle as well, to chill my forehead on the trip up."

When he found he'd still drawn no activity, he shouted, "Don't just stare at me! I asked you to get started. Do what I'm telling you, I'll explain it. Gather up the clothing and towels!"

There was a ceramic clap from the inner room possibly from near the terrace. It wasn't clear what had sounded; but the fellow's reaction showed his nerves that it might be the person for whom Sylhauna waited.

"Start moving now, Recorder. There's a satchel in the closet corner, maybe right inside on your left. Just start packing whatever's in there. We can sort it out later. Stop staring at me; and get moving."

The clapping sounded again, much like what a mog might sound like arriving onto the terrace. The withered man knew that and clearly thought it was so. Misling only watched him curiously, unaffected by the possible arrival. Suddenly, Lennox sealed his eyelids and threw his head back to weather a wave of pain and nausea. It drove his crown into the cherry headboard, pushing it back in a squeak as inexpertly crafted fixturing gave way to his force. There were muffled voices, conversing too low for them to understand yet clearly betraying a new voice.

"Don't let her come near me." Lennox at last opened round and spider-webbed eyes. He was stiffened and cold. The Recorder only watched and listened, yet with a slowly dawning solemnity. The wave of pain had not let up; and lines stood out on the fellow's cheek as he clenched his teeth to bear it. A soft blue vein bulged from his right temple like the breathing of a lizard, inflating and dropping a number of times as he braced himself.

Whispering to secure his words from being overheard, "Take me to the Cave City. I can get better there. Sylhauna owes me that. They shot someone outside. Told somebody to get off the streets and go home; and I couldn't understand what the others said back. I'm talking about watchmen; and they shot somebody for not going inside. It's plague. And I'm attended by one who will murder me. You can't let that be!"

"What have you done, Lennox Weshire?"

As voices ghosted from the inner room, Lennox shuddered, "Pack my towels."

Misling stared; and the voices were louder. Lennox was cracking. After a moment, Misling turned to leave the room. The man in his sickbed started again to halt the Recorder's departure.

"If you'd seen her cry in the corner, curled up and staring, you'd know what I know."

Misling stopped.

"I never told her to squat in the corner."

Misling squinted his eyes, though disgust would have been inappropriate and beyond his calling. He watched and listened. The withered man cast a worried glance towards his kitchen and rubbed his palm against a radiating forehead. He swallowed hard and tried to avoid the Recorder's eyes, but decided at last to look directly into them because perhaps he wouldn't get his help otherwise.

"I starved her and locked her up. And other things." Lennox watched coffee brown eyes and hesitated. Misling gave nothing further.

"I've done worse. I've done much worse that I'm not going to talk about. And I can't sit up without wetting myself and there are watchmen shooting people outside and it smells like smoke and awful things are happening and it's coming back around to me. She's going to murder me or stir something vile into my food. If you're still a man, don't let her near me. I'm so sorry for anything I did. Tell the Record I'm sorry for anything I did; but don't let her near me. Pack my towels!"

Misling pulled away at last and turned from Lennox towards the voices behind him. He glanced only once back towards the withered man who kept up his urgency as the Recorder left the room, beckoning for aid.

"He's cold." A teenage girl with night black hair tied into a pony tail was knelt beside Sylhauna in the other room watching Ring. His face was not that of poor Bomar, not stretched in nightmare fashion or betraying a tortured trance. He was however bleeding and swelling and was rattling off a continuous stream of words in another language without addressing anyone, like something rehearsed or memorized beforehand.

The vortex engine of her mog was still coasting down, sounding much like a far off lonesome train speeding into the distant country. Cristoffel was shorter than Sylhauna and was caked on her arms and fingers with dried latex. Hanging loosely from a canvas toolbelt on her waist were a score of fresh rubber molds. Misling absorbed her appearance and demeanor, trying to align what he'd heard from Lennox with what he was now seeing. She only glanced up at him, then away again when she saw his tattoo. It was an instinct. Sylhauna leaned closely in to Ring's face to the point where her eyes were only a finger's width from his own.

"The other fellow was in some sort of trance. They said it was liquid computers. Do you know how to break liquid computers?"

Cristoffel only looked at Sylhauna without saying anything, then stood and withdrew a syringe from a well stocked nursing kit atop a rolling shelf. She jammed the needle into one of a series of neatly organized packets in the kit and drew into the syringe a viscous gray fluid which she in turn injected into the side of Ring's neck. A tiny drop of bright red blood swelled up, then trickled down his neck.

Sylhauna tried again, "Liquid computers?"

Cristoffel shook her head, "Bone maintenance and for the swelling."

"Is he going crazy right now?"

The quiet brunette shrugged, "'Hauna, I have no idea. What are you doing here?"

"I was doing what I'm supposed to do, fruit and biscuits. Just fruit and biscuits and no dairy. Then he said I had to go with them because they're going to turn the world upside down. But then Balcister blew up and he-" She pointed at Misling as if he were a piece of furniture. "-he had to go find somebody with a cool blimp because he could be dying. And then the crazy street guy said he was going to make us nuts and Bomar's face was all stretched out. Then the Red Witch guy beat the crap out of him. And they tried to stick me with the stuff; but I bounced his head off the road."

Cristoffel's expression was that of irritation, "Gibberish. And who is he?"

"Like we know!"

At that, the new arrival shook her head, "You shouldn't have come here. You'll just upset Lennox."

"Yeah. We did that. We need a place to crash, though. Weren't you listening?"

Misling stepped to the terrace to view the foggy streets, still misted and fuzzy in the smokey yellow lamp light. His motion caught Cristoffel's eye; but she caught something else just out of sight and looked away as if she'd seen something.

"Weren't there four of you?"

Sylhauna shook her head no; and Cristoffel just let it go, "Who did that to him?"

Sylhauna only watched, "If he goes to sleep, he goes crazy. Most people can't do that; but he's special or something. Can't go to sleep. Ever. Till you fix it."

Cristoffel clearly thought nothing of Sylhauna's response, perhaps accustomed to nonsense from her, "Shouldn't you have taken him to a hospital?"

Sylhauna showed disgust and impatience, "What if we were waiting in the crowded hospital surrounded by…hurt people and everybody was moaning and crying and looking for their brothers and wives and everything…and maybe somebody there in a big droopy hat or a mask chains all the doors and starts shooting…or even he gets a doctor and he's laying down on the table to be worked on and then…the doctor looks down at him right before he puts him to sleep and starts…laughing with an evil laugh. That's no good. You fix him."

It was then the bullhorns sounded again, an amplified watchman's voice backed by the machine hum and clanking of urban riot tanks rolling through the street below. There were too many echoes and too much muffling to comprehend what was said; but it had the sound and feel of a siege.

Each of them but for Ring quieted and only breathed silently. They waited and watched one another with fright in their eyes, each unwilling to make the sound that might draw attention to them there, huddled in the second floor room with the lights on and the terrace wide open. Cristoffel placed a hand on Ring's chest to try and quiet him. The metallic screech of the tanks was getting louder; and the patrol was apparently headed in their direction, perhaps even below them. Misling was still at the window but had stepped back a pace, shrouding himself from view such that only a soft wrap of pastel light bathed half his face stopping at his long nose.

Cristoffel leaned into Ring's face to whisper, "What happened to you?"

He licked his lips and locked eyes with her, motioning to the syringe she'd just used on him, "This stuff…how long does it take?"

"I have no idea. I've never used it. You need real help. What happened?"

He smacked himself in the forehead a few times and rubbed his eyes harshly, "I can…I can only make out every few words you're saying here; but I can tell you're nice. Don't take me to a hospital. Not now. Just don't let me black out."

He was trying to keep a lock on her eyes; but something kept drawing his own eyes away, like he was being summoned harshly by a cruel taskmaster just beyond her. Something cold and dark was drawing him inward; and he was fighting it and losing.

"The Recorder…"

Overhearing, Misling stepped from the terrace and knelt beside Ring.

Ring licked his lips again and nodded, "I need you to listen. You have to get me to the Augur. When we're there, everything will make sense. It's important, just believe me on that."

Misling watched him carefully, with a look of anxiety and perhaps suspicion. His was a function of obeying and assuming second place, of complying quietly and sitting when told to sit and standing when told to stand. Something of substance was crusting over in his experiences and taking form. The purpose for his life was to record it.

"No."

Sylhauna's eyes clicked onto the Recorder again, for it wasn't a decision she'd anticipated; and Ring hadn't expected to be refused.

"No more. One question, one straight and direct answer."

The bullhorns and tanks were directly below them, screeching and clanking. The amplified voice warned of going outside and of subversion; and it warned of even looking out to the street, to lock windows and doors. It warned of retaliation.

Ring stared at the Recorder, who was unmoved by the actions of the watchmen below. He squinted his eyes shut in an attempt to clear his vision and shook his head, then blinked several times before looking again at Misling. This was discordant to those accustomed to what Recorders should be, to those who'd seen them standing alone in the corners of funerals or behind a desk as legal documents were signed, trotting alongside wealthy children in their bright jumpers…to those who'd been taught to ignore Recorders as a transparent functionary of society with no opinions and certainly no will all their own. Here was one who demanded. It was maddening.

"Shut off those lights!" Lennox's voice sounded from the other room, shouting yet still in a whisper. Sylhauna glanced in his direction, but ignored it overall.

"I'm losing." Ring's voice was weakening, softer like he was starting to dream, like he watched dark fairies pleading for him to follow.

"No more." The Recorder's eyes were tearing up again. He sniffed.

Cristoffel patted Ring's forehead and stroked some hair from his eye, "Needs to sleep."

"He can't. He'll wake up and try to kill us all. That's what happens."

She glanced at Sylhauna, "Stop saying that. He's badly hurt and needs to rest. He probably needs blood too."

"Will you hold to your promise?"

"Shut off those lights!" Lennox raised his urgency, as it had become clear the tanks were no longer moving. They were right outside the terrace opening, down two floors on the street. The bullhorn voice kept on, warning of sudden moves and of not dealing with strangers.

Ring licked his lips again, reluctantly eyeing Misling with irritation, "I don't have a lot of time."

Misling leaned in urgently, his eyes still wet and sparkling in the terrace light, "At the airpark, when this Recorder was awaiting his package, you were watching from the steps. Already watching, there is no doubt of that. You may have noticed him by chance because he was looking back perhaps or from the novelty of a Recorder's sigil, and thought of fame…or maybe you did not disembark from the ship at all but rather had been hiding from sight, waiting."

Misling awaited a reaction or perhaps gathered his Record, more closely examining what Ring's expression had been there on the airpark tower. Ring only looked back, blankly.

"When you followed to the market, your incitement of the crowd was an act of whim, perhaps with a hope to impress your amusement into the Record…or you were surveiling the market for its security."

Bullhorns outside were becoming louder, more focused. Ring's eyes followed the jagged track of a dripping tear on the Recorder's cheek, sliding down to his lips.

"When this Recorder left you at Balcister…"

Sylhauna inhaled sharply at the mention of the tower. Cristoffel followed little of this. Ring's own face was sallow and swollen, but clear of acknowledgement one way or the other.

"…you could have had interest in experiencing Balcister for the first time as many do when they come to the city…or you desired to meet with confederates and inspect the building prior to an attack.

There were people in the alley."

Lennox escalated his voice, clearly becoming more frightened, "Shut up in there! They're going to come up because of the noise and the lights! Shut up!"

Misling watched Ring's eyes, his expressions, discerning clues to decide the matter in some favor. As only a Recorder can, he evaluated Ring's tone and body language not only now, but in those other times as well with equal clarity. "What you knew of Farmilion was personal and betrayed details you could not have known. The street man, Kensi…his arrival was a matter of chance along his…patrol…and you were attacked viciously, or you were truly expected to meet up with Red Witch agents at sunrise as he suggested, suffering a betrayal instead from one who would have your position at the Blackening."

Cristoffel stood and stepped closer to the terrace, though still out of the shadows. She wanted to see why the noises outside had just then and quite suddenly gone silent.

"Ask him, then!"

Cristoffel leaned closer into the soft ambient streetlight, her young face gently painted by pink and yellow from the lamps and signs outside. No tank noises. No bullhorn. Yet they had not left.

"Did you have anything to do with the destruction of Balcister Tower? Answer it clearly and without dodging the query's intent."

Ring hesitated. He looked at the tray ceiling and inhaled slowly and weakly with the trembling wheeze of painful breaths.

"Guys, shut off the lights." Cristoffel waved her hand to gain attention for her directive. "They're watching us."

None spoke at that point. Neither did they step or move their hands for a moment. Cristoffel at last leaned gently into the terrace again and peered over the limestone balusters. A long deadly time settled upon them while they waited for something to change. Cristoffel was first to whisper because she'd seen something.

"The soldiers. They're looking up here through scopes."

The only noises to be heard in the apartment were the rush of fans and an animal somewhere howling in the distance for scraps. Here was a frightening uncertainty and a sad realization that the awful weapons of war were aimed at the great city like a butcher's knife turned inward. Tanks and riflemen and unattended flames on Alson's streets weren't visuals anyone imagined there, not to those who'd strolled along the covered walks or snuck unseen to private outlooks on the gabled rooftops or laid idly about the fountains in Balcister Plaza. It was sober and had the feeling of a nameless doctor saying there was no hope, that time was short and nothing but pain remained.

After some time, the bullhorn sounded again and warned of staying inside, of retaliation. The tanks clanked and screeched at last; and the noises muffled slowly and drained away as the procession continued down streets further away.

They each looked at one another, fear and panic in their eyes, till the Recorder leaned back into Ring's face, unrelenting, "One question. One straight and direct answer."

Ring looked at the Recorder with some regret and pain, took a deep breath again, "She didn't threaten you, Misling. The little girl in the field. She didn't say anything like what you thought she said."

The Recorder's face rumpled in surprise, his eyes blank, "What?"

"Just a little girl. Probably said something about your forehead. You heard something else because…" He grunted as he combated searing pain. "…because you've got memories sealed you can't unlock. Nothing to do with Farmilion…something really sealed you don't even realize. It's a security thing…an alarm."

"How do you know this?"

"Get me to the Augur…" Ring's voice was trailing, signaling defeat.

"Answer directly. Did you have anything to do with Balcister?"

Ring locked eyes with the Recorder, "I don't know. Maybe. I really don't know."

The Recorder was dazed, off his hard line because of the distraction of this new information. Perhaps it was nothing and a diversion. Perhaps it was a key to everything. He couldn't have said. In fact, he decided something different all together.

"Then enjoy your rest!"

Like lightning, the Recorder raised himself and spun towards the mog vehicle Cristoffel had parked on the terrace and clambered inside. He was instantly fumbling with controls inside, swiping his fingers across simulated buttons and slider bars with a death-grip on the joystick beside his knee. He could have been funny in his helpless urgency were it not for the understanding that his sponsor was possibly buried under Balcister's ruins.

"Hey!" Cristoffel bared her teeth and made to stop him; but Sylhauna beat her to the mog's door to block the way.

"Easy. I've got him."

She pushed against Sylhauna, confused, "No. No, you almost fell off the wall last time! Look, you can come back for a little while; but this is all too much to ask. Get these guys out of here; and get out of my way. He's not taking that mog anywhere."

Misling managed to flash a blinding white headlight and turn on the air conditioning looking for the vortex engine's engagement sequence. Lennox was shout-whispering again from the other room.

"Stop it in there! Shut up; and get out!"

Sylhauna's voice was urgent, "He's lost someone at Balcister. I can take him there. Nothing bad will happen; and we'll stick to the rooftops. No one will see us." She leaned back, still fending off Cristoffel to guide Misling's fingers to the proper screen on the projected controls, pointing at a large black throttle symbol.

"Stop helping him rob me. Get out of the way!" The heavy machine hum of the vortex engine spinning up sounded, eliciting greater intensity from Cristoffel.

"Cris, I need you to back off. We have to help him."

Cristoffel examined Sylhauna's eyes with a familiarity, with perhaps a sense of having heard something much like this before, at least in the urging and drama of it all, and having given in then as well. There was something to her voice, to the way she was standing up like this, to the idea of helping this stranger, that fleshed the idea with significance much like an event might feel should it have been dreamed or spoken of beforehand. She weakened her grip and took a step back.

"'Hauna, this isn't a puppet show full of daffodil fairies. Those guys in the tanks – they'll shoot you. They will, I promise. Because they're scared."

"Well so am I, Cris; but we have to help him."

Cristoffel's voice sharpened, "Why? How long have you known him? He's like a freaking robot – who is he to you?"

Sylhauna's face went cold at that, "You remember our first week here…with him?" She motioned toward Lennox's room. Cristoffel's squinted her dark eyes, indicating perhaps she did indeed and held no love for the memory. Sylhauna's curly hair formed a serpentine coil laying across her right eye; and her tone was more solemn than perhaps Cristoffel had known before this.

"That feels like a really long time ago; and he's not even that scary anymore. I don't even dream about him now. But this one here with his silly tattoo and his stupid way of talking about himself…with him, things like that never go dim. If he lives it, he always lives it..even other people's versions. And he's living it right now. So we're gonna show him some kindness; and we're gonna help him find his friend. And whatever junk that guy in there's been putting in your head, you need to forget! In fact, you're going because I don't know how to drive this thing; and I don't know how to get to the Plaza anyway!"

Cristoffel was surprised at what she was hearing; and she honestly didn't look to know what to do at that point. She looked at Misling, who was still as a rock by then, maybe as interested in Sylhauna's passion as the rest of them. It just wasn't what any of them were expecting from her. His expression was that of a boy who'd broken something.

"Well I'm not taking him."

Sylhauna bared her teeth and held out her hands as if squeezing a coconut between them, "Yes you are. Get in. Help him get to the Plaza and stay hidden. Do it!"

Cristoffel watched Sylhauna, then took another look at the Recorder and Ring, trying to understand what it was here among them that was bringing out this woman before her. It took a minute or two of locked eyes and just trying to frame out in her mind what was happening before she at last, with a resigned shake of her head, motioned for Misling to slide over in the swivelseat of the mog.

"Move over. And don't touch anything."

Ring was seated at this point, trying to stand but only observing. He'd been saying something about the Augur, about not going to Balcister; but no one had heard him. Lennox was desperately whispering from his bedroom, equally ignored. Sylhauna only stepped back another pace, her eyes shining.

The mog's articulated legs raised to position its flighted wheels on an illuminated limestone cornice; leading it ultimately to the outside stone-clad walls of the building as the vortex clung tightly. Misling and Cristoffel swung sharply in the seat as it unlocked and the vessel's orientation shifted. Misling raised a solitary hand, looking back to Sylhauna as if to say thank you. She watched them as long as they could be seen, darting quickly across and up the outside walls to disappear over a green copper dome, the sound of the vortex engine fading. When she turned to see the man with whom she'd sailed the cornfields, he was cold and asleep.

15 INTERLUDE: THE PAIN SELLER

"You have no idea what you're doing. Is this even how it works?" An arm-length soapstone carab figurine cocked at an angle within the supplicant's lap chided the man as he sat cross-legged on an overstuffed cushion desperately staring at a haunting fresco as if it were a hearth. The supplicant only glanced at the figurine coldly, perhaps unused to speaking with statues and perhaps agreeing with it.

Honeycombed within the subterranean reaches beneath the Augur's unearthly temple was a series of stark apartments such as this, intended for those seeking audience. The only ornament apart from a glass bowl brimmed with illuminated glass spheres was an incredibly intricate full length fresco on the far wall upon entering, painted in swaths of bright lemon and orange and peach. He would have remained in such an apartment staring at the image, the slender tall boy with the eyes of a very old man, for probably weeks awaiting the call to the Augur's terrible presence.

"I will not be ignored." The carab man laughed, sputtering like an old man who'd choked on his spit.

The supplicant inhaled slowly, then upturned a warm bottle of sana, the color of juniper and frothy at the surface. He swallowed with a scowl for he didn't like the taste, then shoved it back into a hollow between cushions. He stretched open his eyelids and blinked hard a couple of times because he'd lacked sound sleep for some time, then he stood and examined the image from very close up, leaving the carab setting sideways on the cushion.

"Please be quiet."

The false man rolled its milky stone eyes, "Make up your mind."

He traced the youth's frescoed chin to its neck with his fingertip, and leaned in closely. It was an unearthly boy and a very old image. Its eyes were sparkling and dark, tender but wise and the face in some eerie way, wicked. It was a young face, a god of wine and madness full of mischief, painted sharply with such realism as to set one's back tingling and give a feeling of being watched in turn. As was common to all references for emanations, the image's long fingers had no fingernails – a nuance kept as tradition from the days when emanations walked the streets in wide liberty and such visual cues were important to sort one's standing with whom one was speaking. A sliver of the illustrated stone wall came off in his hand, betraying the wall's age. He crumbled it to a crunchy powder within his fingers and let it fall like a mist to the floor.

There was a squeak from the corridor, which he ignored or perhaps didn't hear at all in his depth of concentration.

He touched the image's crisp white eyes, "You don't scare me."

More sputtering from the stone man, "That's just a picture, big boy. When you're standing at the Circle it's a whole different meatball. You're not gonna make it!"

The supplicant turned to gauge the carab's expression, pointlessly. Hadn't he himself said that, since the figure's life was only imagined? "You're confusing me. What could you know that I don't?"

The carab man hummed disgust, though the statue looked suddenly empty and as it had been when the attendants handed it to him on his arrival, "Loser."

It was at that point the squeak sounded again, a high pitched honking that sounded somewhat like a rusting cart in the corridor. It may have been happening all along, it would have been hard to say. Either way, it was inappropriate. The supplicant could see nothing beyond his doorway to explain it.

Availing nothing, he sought clarity from the figurine, "Am I imagining you or is this some kind of test? I don't understand. Are you the Augur, peeking in on me? Preparing me?"

Cold soapstone rested lifelessly, a ridiculous puffy beard jutting upwards and thick eyebrows clouded carved, blank eyes. The supplicant waited, then turned back to the hearth, to the fresco that stared harshly back at him..or maybe it was laughing silently. He honestly couldn't have said.

"How long are you going to keep me in here?" He stared until his eyes crossed, waiting and tracing his fingers against the wall. After a moment, the squeaking sounded again from the corridor. It was more consistent this time, and louder.

The carab figurine spoke again, "A private chamber, they said. Virgin solitude and monastery silence while you contemplate the great mystery; and you get the one with the squeaky air conditioning. Your thundercloud just follows you everywhere!" The carab man chuckled again, but was shushed by the man in the room.

At once, a damp headed and shiny faced fellow poked in through the doorway as the squeaking stopped, "Know you're busy and whatnot, all that, just need to sit for a blink."

The supplicant froze in disbelief at the fellow's trashy behavior. "Just a blink, mind you. You won't go SHOO me, there's a good man!"

The new arrival shuffled in, tugging on a rickety cart decorated in thin copper filigree and wobbling on one wheel. Inside was an oversized portmanteau, its leather faded and cracking in spots. The cart jostled slowly up and down as he rolled it near the cushion where the carab was. The man wasn't terribly old; but he was out of breath for the effort all the same. He wore a changepurse around his waist which rattled and clinked when he moved.

"What are you doing? You can't be in here."

The new arrival only waved his hand in dismissal, "Not more SHOOing, please. Never seen such in ten years. Nobody wants to chat, to make gentle conversation…nothing but 'storms in the symbols' and whatnot. Pure junk and rude, after all my time served!

Let a man earn his keep, right?"

"They said no visitors. You can't sell me anything if that's what you're doing here. I paid a lot of money to be here, you'll get me pulled out!"

The fellow nodded as if in agreement, "How could anything be in the reading if you didn't put it there? Answer me that! Let a man earn his keep. Bad for business, I say. Let it go." He rested his feet on the cart and his head on the cushion, breathing out dramatically to signal his pleasure at finally finding a place to roost. Quiet improperly, he broke wind and only after a moment apologized.

"Sorry about that."

Stitched into the leather on the old portmanteau were the words, 'Pain Seller' in an ornamental script. Surely inside were his wares, whatever they were. The supplicant noticed the stranger didn't close his eyes long, but rather lifted his head and scanned the room with the eyes of a salesman.

"Ask him what he's selling." The carab figurine chimed.

The merchant sat up, acknowledging the supplicant's modest clothing, threadbare and patched, and his duffle bag in disrepair and clumped in a corner beside some dirty shirts. He paused on a nickel and malachite bracelet hanging from a loop on the duffle. Here, as he gauged the supplicant's means and despaired somewhat from what he discovered, here he had not found a man of substance.

"You're rambling. You really need to leave before someone-"

The pain seller only looked tired, locking eyes with the supplicant, "Knock it off, you're glad I'm here."

He pointed at the fresco, watching the both of them from its cold stone wall, "'Cause that thing is driving you crazy. Am I right? Watches me pee, even. I'm fed up with it. Come on, you're glad I'm here. Let's just sit for a blink. Just a blink, mind you."

Having conceded, the supplicant went quiet. It was a fair point. It was in fact the pain seller who next spoke.

"So, do you know what you're going to ask it?"

"It's personal."

The pain seller chuckled, "Umm hmmm. You're going to ask it what might have been. What might have happened to you should certain things have gone another way. Yeah?"

Surprised, "How did you-?"

Nodding toward the duffle, "Second-hand military kit bag…bracelet's a woman's…" He squinted and turned his head to one side as he evaluated the supplicant's face, his own nose and cheeks red and roadmapped with tiny red veins. "You have the look of a failed businessman about you."

"Well, I said it's personal."

"Yeah." The pain seller nodded and leaned forward towards his cart. "Been hitting these halls for ten summers, gooseberry; and there's a bit of a pattern to it. D'ya mind?"

He gestured to his portmanteau and cart, his eyebrow lifted and a sly grin on his pink face. He sought permission to open his little portable shop. The supplicant was a bit dazed suddenly, having thought of something. He poked a single finger forward and jabbed it into the merchant's shoulder to test its solidity.

"Real enough, ay? D'ya mind, I said?"

"Did they send you in here?"

"Nobody sent me, gooseberry. They'd flip if they saw me at this. Ten summers running; and not a sniff of my underarms! I'm some kind of record, no doubt. Can we get on with it then? I'm real; and nobody sent me. We're good on that, right? No SHOOing? No storms."

"I'm not answering any of your questions. If the Augur's what it claims, then it doesn't need to send parlor trick faith healer spies to pry information out of me before the Audience."

The merchant looked insulted, "You've been in here a little too long, don't you think? A little too long, I think. Watches you pee, gets in your head. Doesn't it? I'm just trying to get a little something for myself and sell a bit. Captive audience and all that. Sell a bit. Just a blink; and I'll have this open. You'll see. D'ya mind?"

The supplicant smiled thinly, perhaps deciding to play along, and signaled for the merchant to go ahead with his thing, whatever it was. Of course it was incredibly discordant to hawk trinkets or souvenirs within the hallowed Augur's temple; and though no one had shown him the written rule prohibiting such, there was certainly one. The merchant clicked an old mechanism unlocking the case and set the suitcase to open vertically like a reliquary, still resting on the old cart. He hesitated.

"Any thoughts before I open this? What might I have inside?"

The supplicant only passed his hand as if swiping away a web, "Pills, I suppose. Some sort of illicit medication."

The merchant hummed, grinning, "Huh uh, no pills or draughts, gooseberry. Not me. Pain Seller, it says. What sorts of pain, you might wonder?"

"I don't know. Get on with it, whatever it is."

"Come on, then. Have a go at it! You're a brainy one – thoughtful type and wandering in search of yourself. 'S my take, at least. What sorts of pain might you think? What in the world might I be on about? Think like a philosopher. Think where you are!"

"Alcohol or pornography, something a wife might addict herself to while her husband travels on business?"

"A try, no doubt. A try. No draughts. No booze. Nothing my mother, bless her, wouldn't approve. So much closer to the mark. Think where you are!"

The supplicant waved his hand and shook his head in surrender, "Cheating love letters…"

With a showman's grin, the merchant creaked apart his case and laid it wide open, pulling from their recessed positions a number of tiny shelves and racks and at last setting up his cheap store before the two of them upon the cart. Hanging from hooks and jammed within drawers were postcards, old silvers, tiny picture frames no bigger than a man's thumb, doll's clothing, statuettes, a velvet bag of toy coins, a shining white pair of infant shoes, a mummified shenna - stiff and missing a leg, opals and papers, and assorted bits and pieces one might find in a poor neighborhood's pawnshop. There were curled photographs on old canvas, the way they would print them before electronics. It was an argosy of useless flotsam and mementos.

The supplicant was unimpressed, "What a bunch of junk. You're talking about other people's pain. You've got…what, sob stories for all this stuff? Why would anyone pay for that? I've got my own problems."

The merchant's head was turned to one side slightly, the sly grin still wide, "Try something, gooseberry. Why don't you?"

"No one could make a living like this. Who would buy stories of other people's grief?"

With a determined and maybe frustrated frown, the merchant reached into his case and pulled from a stack an old photograph on yellowing canvas inside a tin frame with strings of maple leaves engraved along its length and width. The colors were faded; but it portrayed a woman, not young and not yet old, dancing with a much younger man. The merchant held it forward and awaited acknowledgement.

The supplicant said, "A wedding maybe. Some sort of social. His mom, I'm guessing?"

"Do you want to hear or not?"

"I don't know. Yes."

The merchant lifted an eyebrow, "You've got to settle down, then. Listen more closely and think like somebody waiting in a place like this. You've got to see what I tell you. Can you do that?"

"Okay. I get it."

"See Audra's face, her expression. Look at that. It's a strange turn to have a snapshot of the very happiest moment of a person's life. Strange turn! Sixty three autumns, all that happens to a person through their whole life; and this short dance was the treasure. Isn't that something?"

"Who's the boy, then?"

"Don't presume. Not his time yet." The merchant rested his hand, lowering the photograph till his wrist settled on the case. The supplicant's eyes followed, scanning Audra's eyes closely, her face and her poorly fitting dress.

"Audra was gentle. She didn't say anything if she hadn't something kind to say. Not like her parents who only screamed at each other, screamed at nothing at all. It was her way to gently pick up the pieces of whatever they'd shattered, one by one. They were always breaking things. She'd stack them into piles humming to herself, then sweep them neatly into the trash before the mess itself became the fight. That's who she was, gooseberry. Who she was. Anyway, they both went away when it was clear Audra's white-haired grandmother could be taken advantage of. Grew up lonely, didn't she?"

The supplicant took the photograph and frame from the Pain

Seller's hand. Audra's eyes were bright, her smile full and wild.

"She took a wrong-headed husband, though. When he talked about dreams and the country, about getting out of her town and seeing brilliant lights in her eyes. He never hit her really, but came to say things about her habits and her body, about what she was doing wrong and how short she fell. Scattered his time with friends and rebuilding machines, and forgot things he'd promise to do for her and her birthdays. That dress there in the picture…something he bought her once twenty six days after her thirtieth birthday. This was the first time she'd actually been somewhere to wear it."

The merchant leaned in and looked as well, as if to remind himself of the dress.

"Their boy was full of life and preferred to be where his dad was, always moving and busting things apart to see how they worked. That was his way, wasn't it? Audra took him to fields and recital halls, to libraries and dances. Even so, the boy preferred his father's company at exhibits and theaters, for looking at big machines. 'My son is clean and healthy, that's what matters', she'd tell the neighbor beside them, who never found himself short of things to say about Audra's lonely days. Always something to say.

"Fairly sudden when Audra's husband took a job in the provinces and never spoke to her again. This snapshot here was taken at the social hall the day Audra's boy passed his trade exam and one year to the day since she'd last heard from his father. Just before the flash went off, one heartbeat before as the cameraman was stepping into place, the boy told Audra she was the most beautiful woman in the world."

The Pain Seller leaned back and rested his head against the soft cushion, "It was only twelve summers later when Audra found herself in a hospital bed being told she wouldn't be leaving. Her boy was there – she asked if he remembered the photograph being taken. He didn't and couldn't remember the day at all. She smiled, shut her eyes, and gripped this tin frame. And that was all."

The supplicant was quiet, sad. He looked slowly around the apartment, to the motionless carab man and the crumpled duffle, the illuminated beads and painted hearth. He glanced for a moment to the ceiling, silently pondering before he spoke again.

"Is that real? Did you make that up?"

The Pain Seller only looked back at him silently, no sign of an answer either way.

At last, "I'll take the picture."

"You see my meaning, then. You asked why someone would buy pain. I've answered your question, gooseberry? Is that not right?"

When the money had exchanged hands, the two of them sat quietly for a time. The supplicant examined the photograph, scratching his chin and studying Audra's face, maybe rehearsing the story for himself or perhaps just experiencing her as fully as he could. The merchant stood and stretched his back at last, cracking and popping at his joints uncomfortably.

"He's a liar." The carab man spoke up finally, having absented himself from the discussion for some time. Strangely, the merchant cocked his head and took notice of the figurine at almost exactly the same moment, as if he'd heard something though that was clearly impossible. He gripped the statue by its waist and lifted it at arm's length, twisting it this way and that to observe its artistry and frowning all the while.

"Cheap imitation. House specials are getting cut-rate, know what I mean?" With that, he shoved the carab face-down into the cushions and stepped idly to the fresco on the far wall, his hands linked behind his back in ponderance. The supplicant eyed him suspiciously, for such a thing shouldn't have happened the way it seemed to just then.

"So, do you really know what to expect in there? In the Circle?"

With an expression of sudden insight, of having decided

something in his favor, the supplicant stood quickly and joined the merchant beside the image still carrying the frame, facing him, "Yeah. I think so. Is there something you want to tell me?"

He whistled softly, then pushed out his lower lip a bit, "Omens all over the place. They're all on about it here. It's all they'll talk about. Black eyed emanations standing in rows seen by hundreds at Spenecia. How could that be? Weird patterns in the readings nobody meant to include but that show up over and over. Cracks in the Record – Recorders that suddenly can't remember specific things. Some say the Salt Mystic is even coming back, how about that? What's really going on – can you tell me that? I live in these halls, my very new friend. These halls are still at the center of everything, aren't they? And something awful is happening."

"Talgos killing each other. Whatever. Happened before. Will happen again. What does that have to do with Audra?"

The Pain Seller turned his bloodshot eyes to the supplicant, watching him and evaluating him, maybe turning over what the young man had said looking for truth in it, "Nothing's going to step out of this wall. And that dime store thing over there, it can chatter all day; but it's all coming from your head. But when you get in there…if you get in there…it's not. Fourteen Recorders, gooseberry; and they've got the thing in their heads. All of it, back to the beginning. It talks, sounds like one of them speaking; but it isn't. It isn't at all. Did you know that some people, after their visit to the Circle, they never laugh again? Never laugh. That's the sort of place you're going."

"What are you getting at?"

"All they bring it is pain, gooseberry. It's all it knows. Every generation gets worse and more lost the further they go without beliefs. Sad, isn't it? Ever wonder how those today, ones that can't hold their families together or hold on to their money, raised by absent parents chasing their own appetites, how they'd handle the sorts of terrors our grandfathers saw? And the war hounds, what sorts of atrocities might they come up with given such little conscience?"

He widened his pale eyes, "I believe in the omens, those signs. They're real; and it's the Augur screaming. It's screaming at us all; and whatever the Talgos unloose on us will swallow us whole. Something awful is happening; and it's our fault…'cause we let it."

Silenced and thoughtful, the supplicant only watched the Pain Seller with a creased brow. The fellow took on the expression of wrapping up, of being done with things, and suddenly started collecting his shop and pulling in the little shelves, swiveling in tiny racks into the tightly compacted case. He snapped the shiny latch, greasy with fingerprints; and it took him twice to get it to hold. He started for the darkened hallway from which he'd come.

"More'n a blink, I imagine. No doubt. Sorry 'bout that. I do chatter. Still, was a lot of fun; and you needed the break anyway, isn't that right?"

The supplicant still was standing listlessly, the fingers of his right hand clutching the frame. He tilted it so as to gain vantage again of the scene, the inexpensive dress and the sparkling of the woman's eyes.

"Why did you sell me this?"

Chuckling, and a little mischievous, "It's what I do, gooseberry. What I do. All they bring here is pain. Nobody brings good news to the Augur. I just like the idea of thinking about somebody else's rather than your own. Draws you out of your world, know what I mean? Too late for Audra…maybe not for you?"

With that, the Pain Seller shuffled off into the flickering darkness, his ridiculous cart squeaking and honking as he went. The supplicant scratched the back of his neck and sat cross-legged at the peach and white feet of the image, looking deeply into the photograph as if it were a river at summer.

16 WHILE YOU SIT MUNCHING GRASS

The arsenal ship rolled along the wide Salt Flats, with irregular chunks of white and gray speckled in bits of fire by the low orange moon. It was early dawn and still chilled; and the enormous vessel with some thousand souls was moving quickly on its tracks, incredibly quickly given its size. Cassian Talgo was watching from an acrylic bubble window a squadron of dusty ramships launching from lowered ramps along the stern swirling in a current like splattered mud. They darted with the speed of mayflies, now stopping, now reversing, and at times slamming viciously into one another from great distances, shielded and unharmed. In a broad arc along the east and running north was a strand of foreign flatrunners, patched and older in the turquoise and black of Rangleward Province.

"Best place to be is behind those Ranglers when they're rolling. Clumsy people."

Cassian turned at the voice to see a haggard female commander he knew well and was relieved at the sight, "Fantine, I'm glad to see you." He gripped her hard shoulder in a gesture of familiarity.

"You really gonna let them roll with us?" As she spoke, she crunched something she was pulling from a bag.

"Not you too."

Fantine shrugged carelessly, "Heard you had runners from the Fountain City and Danclia on maneuvers with us too."

He nodded, unsure of her implication or whether there was even an implication. She was kept for her viciousness in conflict, not deep insight. For his part, he was known for massive overpower as a means of establishing certainty in conflict.

She crunched again, "Maybe they'll just run into each other instead of us."

He changed the subject, "Have you heard anything from Grebel?"

When Fantine shook her head no, Cassian nodded gently and looked back at the swirling ramships – particularly to see two vessels emblazoned in red which were playing at a very long range game of chicken. He lingered his eyes on the two of them, quick vessels riding on pocked ferro-ceramic spheres that zipped in any direction including laterally and operated as battering rams. These two accelerated to capacity before plowing harshly into one another, stopping dead in their place without rebound.

Cassian's voice was distant, "I heard he's in Alson. Hope he's okay."

Fantine only chuckled, signaling her reflection that Grebel would be okay seated in flames facing undead beasts, for she'd known him a very long time and had seen terrible sights in his company. Cassian watched her leather face, the tendons of her jaw popping in and out and the thick vein on her temple throbbing; and he drew some comfort from her amusement.

"Where's your boy?" Fantine fished around in her little bag for crumbs of her snack.

Cassian turned to watch the ramship pilots behind them, milling around and joking with one another in the hangar. A group of them were slamming their fists together knuckle on knuckle as a game of endurance and laughing as a man would drop to the floor howling in pain. These sorts of pilots were typed as adrenalin-addicted brutes in those days, enthralled with the speed and closeness of battle in which they were engaged. It was said Ramshipmen felt the heat of enemy vessels burn.

"He'll be in the war council shortly. I sent my Red Witch to bring him."

Still swirling her finger in the bag, "Maybe instead of sending that black-headed donk out to babysit we could drown him till he admits what his freak brothers are up to. A suggestion."

Although it was a disrespectful comment, Cassian only barely reacted. That was just Fantine; and he knew it. "Commander, I need your help."

She crumpled her bag and dropped it to the deck, wiping the side of her dry lips, and pausing afterwards with an expression of casual interest.

"It seems my entire government, and now even the press, are ready to go pillage Alson. It's all over the news. An old woman, old enough to be my grandmother, grabbed my arm in the street and told me she's glad she lived to see the day when we paid them back."

"Ooh rah."

He hesitated, understanding the depth of contemplation he stood to gain from her, "I don't want to lose sight of my son in all this."

Fantine raised a gray eyebrow at him but didn't say anything. She may have understood where he was going with it.

"He stirred something up at Denai and may have gotten into some sort of gunfight, it's hard to tell. I don't even know what he was doing there. I just know that with everything going on, he's going to get lost. I don't carry any notion around that I'm a prize father; but it's getting to a point where…where I need to do something different."

"Grebel's your man. You don't want me in this."

"Grebel isn't here; and you are. I need you. I'm drafting him with a field commission; and I'm assigning him to your fleet, a Black Fire gunner."

She showed her yellowed teeth, "You couldn't have had a worse idea. Do you know how much trouble he could cause in a job like that, especially when we're in the soup?"

He eyed her with impatience, the look of an administrator shooing away details, "Grebel has talked about it before – it's perfect for him. Some action, no doubt. But keep him under your eye and stay away from the hottest parts if it comes to that. I need you in this."

It was then a thin man in a red jacket, shoulders encircled in gold aigulettes, stepped up to Cassian. A name badge on his chest read, 'Rhodomontane'.

"The commanders are waiting in the conference room, sir."

Cassian pulled a watch from his pocket and shammed examining its face, "Oh, I've lost track of time. Thank you." Fantine seemed to notice he wasn't surprised at the time at all but rather was avoiding something.

He dodged her stare as the aide stepped away; and she followed as he began walking past the ramship pilots. Someone called, 'attention on deck', locking them all into neat rows at attention, only relaxing upon the War Marshal's departure through the hangar bay door. In the mess hall as they passed, Cassian watched young soldiers at the tables, laughing or scarfing down a quick meal before going on watch, or scanning the corridor for a friend. The silence wore on him, and also perhaps the kid faces in the mess hall with pimples and sweaty socks unaware of the rotting amputations and trapped screams of battle that waited for them; and he at last stopped in the passageway beyond the reactor room offices to face Fantine.

"They're about to tell me to slaughter my brother and his people. I don't have the bandwidth to argue with you about this."

She nodded, sucking her teeth a bit, "Yeah, I'd say so."

"Like kids yelling for the show to start. Inexcusable. It's somewhere we haven't gone before – hitting first. What will the

Record say about people who cross lines like that?"

Fantine grimaced like she'd been asked to hand him a rubber chicken. He looked at her with disapproval before surrendering that line of thought, "Cyprian wasn't born for peace; and he'll get in this somehow. I know that. He'll steal a ramship or fall in with some special forces during the assault. I don't know. He knows all the field commanders – they'll go along with him no matter what I say. But he will get in it. That's why I need him under your eyes."

She watched his eyes a moment, squinting, "What do I do with the diapers?"

"What I need is for someone I trust to watch out for him."

"What you need is sloppy seconds because your handmaiden has disappeared. I don't know why Grebel puts up with you. What happens to me if the boy dies?"

"Don't let that happen."

Fantine wasn't unfamiliar with distasteful orders; and here as she watched the face of the ruling Talgo, there was a tone and a bearing she knew well and which she'd followed. She'd served with the Old Man at the battle of Sarling and with Cassian in the battlesuits during the Rupture and well knew what it was to be called upon by a Talgo, even a weak one whose voice shook and who couldn't control his own son. She considered her history and his; and with a look of more ease than one would expect from such a circumstance, she nodded.

"Yeah, all right."

Uncertain towards her, he lingered his eyes and awaited more. She grinned wickedly, though all her grins looked wicked, "I said yeah. He's gonna be in there, right?"

Cassian watched the door latch to his council room as if it were the face of a dead child, "He's supposed to be."

"I'll make it happen. 'Black Fire'…unbelievable!" She eyed him, a vein bulging on her neck. "You know what you're gonna do in there?"

Cassian hovered his hand over the latch, inhaling sharply with an indication he had no clarity at all what was about to happen inside. She was annoyed with him and squished her nose somewhat to show it.

"Just turn us loose, Talgo. Stop bucking it. We'll clean it all up nice and neat for you."

Like a tiny boy on a high dive staring at the glittering water, Cassian watched his hand on the latch cautiously and pondered before at last snatching it down and stepping into the crowded council room, alive with murmuring and chatter.

Inside and seated around a wide oval computronium table were a number of uniformed soldiers as well as Rosgrove, one of the men with whom Cassian had conferred at the commissioning service in the craneyard. To the left, an incredibly dark skinned statistics officer named, Oblave was distracted in his analyses, energetically swiping his fingers across the tabletop shaping performance and strategic data into pivot tables and agent-based models like a pianist lost in his sonata. A war recorder was sitting quietly on a stool in the far corner, her forehead sigil framed in splattered red signifying her Record as consisting of the condensed battle experiences and personal accounts of every major conflict known to history. Cyprian was not in the room, which Cassian immediately noticed.

Fantine grimaced at a tall, awkward looking fellow dressed as a provincial farmer. She intentionally bumped into him as she passed to seat herself, "Boadshise."

A civilian representative of the Salt Flats tribesmen, Boadshise's presence at any discussion involving the militia was required by law; but he wasn't well liked. In fact, Fantine had almost knocked him from his chair just then.

Boadshise recovered quickly, only frowning slightly at Fantine, "Marshal, what have you found out about the attack on Alson?" His dialect was country and considered low class.

Cassian scratched his chin, "Nothing. Radio silence. Razor and Claw are seeing quiet on the borderlands. We know it happened. As for why or who hired it out, it's guesswork. And it's pathetic guesswork."

"Who's watching the Brigadier?" Mandibo, an officer in blue to whom all engineers reported spoke up.

Rosgrove responded, "We lost him after the Resthouse incident. You know he disappears when he feels like it."

"The Brigadier may have hired the Red Witch."

Fantine's mouth twisted, "Riiight."

"Did we?" Boadshise uncrossed his long legs to turn in his chair and view not only Cassian but some others in the assembly. Curiously, Cassian surveyed his officers to gauge their reactions as they did his.

"We did not." The Marshal was not as certain as his words implied. "Look, back up. The purpose of this council is to decide on a course of action. Oblave is here; and our War Recorder. What I want to do is go over the shelf plans for defense of the city first in case there is a similar attack here. Then we can get to the offensive plans. It all needs to be updated and optimized through the Record."

Cassian could not have drawn more disgust from the room if he'd tossed putty onto the table and suggested they mold clown faces. There was a buzz around the table indicating extraordinary disinterest in endless logistical and scenario gaming and an unearthly bloodthirst to just get on with it. It was the sort of tension familiar to those who worked closely with Cassian.

"It's not gonna happen, Talgo." A round faced man on the far side named Thessany who was one of the founders of the Twister Corps and had ridden tornados, was leaned back in his chair, resting a boot on the tabletop. "Doniphan's already mobilized. They'll have mogs in Alson in a few hours."

Cassian was furious, his voice higher pitched, "What?!"

Thessany just raised his eyebrows and grinned, "Those people are jumpy, what are ya' gonna do?"

To Fantine, "Did you know about this?"

She nodded, "Oh yeah." Then she turned to Thessany, "Pretty good mog pilots too. I've seen 'em fight upside down."

Cassian glared at her as if she'd jabbed a fork under his ribs, then glanced to the empty seat where Grebel regularly sat.

"What are they doing in this?"

"Wentic's been sitting on those guys for years. You know that. Thinks because he sends them money they're his pets. But pets bite, don't they?"

Oblave looked up from his data tables, "It's a good thing for us. Will soften the battlespace before our ships arrive."

"Peri won't sit in the showers, boys. She'll have tanks and battlesuits on the streets by now; and the jig'll be up for your mog-slappers." Fantine mouthed, 'mog-slappers' with pursed lips and a ridiculous drawl.

Boadshise shifted in his chair uncomfortably, "Aside from pleasuring the high hats in this room, what are the people actually going to get from all this?"

"Shut up, saltlicker. Who's talking to you?" Thessany leaned forward to slam the legs of his chair to the floor. "Do you think they even care what we do?"

"Times are tough, Boadshise. They're out of work and chasing healthcare."

"Yes, you've all made a wreck of things. You've been reading my newsletter." Boadshise's tone was long and sarcastic and irritating.

"Well who cares anyway?" Mandibo interjected. "I've got kids, man. I can hardly pay my bills. Every time we tick off one of the hick nations around us I can't go on vacation and have to pay three times as much for groceries. I'm sorry hilljacks died and all that; but they deserve it for what they've done to us. Doniphan's right to get there first."

He gestured to Fantine, "You know what I'm talking about. We need the land. Let's take it."

Rosgrove raised a finger to gain attention, "What about the rumors of the Salt Mystic coming back? Where is that coming from?"

Thessany rolled his eyes and groaned, "Sorry to interrupt your nursery school lesson, Rosgrove. But who cares."

"It matters. It's all in the White Fleet right now; and my office is getting hammered asking what we know about it."

"Oblave", a lady admiral named, Phryne who led the submersible and vortex navy interrupted, "is there anything in your datastream telling you a mysterious two thousand year old woman is possessing someone with the intent of obliterating our way of life by standing around talking like she did the first time around?"

She hesitated while the dark man only watched, unsure what to say to that, then, "There you go, Rosgrove. There's nothing in the datastream, so you can stop worrying about it."

"It isn't that simple, lady!" Rosgrove grunted. "If this thing takes off and turns religious, the Provinces could split or flip sides. You'll not know who you can trust."

"As opposed to the family cookout we're having now, I suppose?" Boadshise picked something from one of his front teeth.

"Look, Talgo." Thessany raised his voice to cut through the chatter, "Grow a pair. Launch and take Alson while they're down. If it's the right thing to do, it's the right thing to do now. You're gonna put our people at risk if you wait and do it anyway in a few days. It's irresponsible to dally like this and let their forces gather. Let's get moving!"

Those who'd known Cassian would see he was drowning, having relinquished the flow of events and uncertain what other information he might be missing. They all quieted at that point and watched him; and it wasn't lost on them that his eyes were starting to sparkle in the light, watering only slightly. They just watched him, fascinated like awaiting a fizzing bottle to explode…much like the two watchmen had observed Stendahl in the corridor beneath the palace. That was always the way with Talgos, one felt it best to prod them and step back, to be a spectator to their fires and their bluster.

"Well I'm sorry to interrupt your plans for Armageddon; but we're going to slow this down just a little bit."

"I'll bet you are." Thessany rolled his eyes, perhaps used to Cassian slowing things down.

It was at that moment, when Cassian locked eyes with Thessany deciding whether to call out his disrespect, that Cyprian strolled into the room. He no longer wore his coat, but still had on a close-fitting polymer weave shirt with molded graphite armor plates sewn in. As it ever was, his carbine hung backwards over his shoulder. Those at the table watched him with interest, never sure whether he'd sit quietly or set something on fire. He glanced at a handful of them, though not all in the room, and shut the door behind himself. Then he pulled up a chair and sat blocking the door. He was carrying a canvas bag in one hand.

"You're late", Cassian said.

Without a reaction, "That's right." He tossed the bag onto the tabletop; and it slid a few inches before coming to a rest slightly off-center and closer to Thessany than anyone else. There were dark stains visible on one side. Cyprian folded his arms comfortably.

"You can't expect these people to respect you if you can't…can't show up on time." Cassian was shaken, not just by the current of the discussion thus far and his son's arrival, but by the bag. What was in the bag?

"You were discussing slowing things down, I believe."

Some of them grinned at that, the implication that maybe here was a Talgo that didn't approve of slowing down.

Cassian took a breath, "The fact lost on this room is that the world has moved on. Having bigger bombs doesn't mean what it used to. If we're the aggressor; and we alienate the friendly states, we'll have bigger issues than..expensive groceries."

Thessany leaned in without reaching forward, trying to eye the loose opening of the sack in front of him.

"Boadshise, speak up. Where do your folks stand on this?"

The provincial was observing Thessany's face, glancing up to Cassian at the mention of his name, "Strangely, they're ready to kill something. I've never seen it like this before..." He got the attention of the War Recorder, "…but for the Record, I disapprove."

Many of them had sidearms; but it was nonetheless unsettling to have Cyprian blocking the doorway. What was he doing there? Mandibo was particularly nervous at that and kept eyes on the young man, entirely dropping from the discussion.

Rosgrove's voice was raspy, unsettled, "Can you uhh…can you move so you're not blocking that door." He was of course ignored.

On the other side of the table, Fantine was rested back in her chair with her fingers locked behind her head, "I'm getting really lost in this discussion. What are we supposed to be talking about right now? Are we trying to decide if we're going to launch when it's happening already? I just need to know who's reporting to who. I'd just as soon not get divebombed by a bunch of Doniphan mogjacks when I roll into town, under friendly fire from Rangleward probably lost but along for the ride wondering whether some freaking Red Witch donk is going to show up. Can't keep all of it straight. Pick a Warmaster and let's get on with it."

Thessany turned his eyes from the sack to Cyprian, grimly seated in the doorway and armed, like an assassin coiling to scatter lightning into the assembly and turn them all into charcoal. He slid his hand to the railgun on his thigh and glanced back to the sack. Mandibo followed Thessany's eyes and slumped in his seat as if clearing a way to slide beneath the table. Tellingly, Cyprian noticed all of this.

Boadshise slid out from the table and uncrossed his legs, "I didn't buy a ticket for this wreck."

"What's in the bag?" Rosgrove at last said it.

Cyprian watched him silently, waiting for someone else to ask, then when Cassian raised his eyebrows as if to do so, "Those are the testicles of the Red Witch man you sent to bring me here. Just letting you know I got your message."

A rumble of disgust and shock murmured in the room, though there was nothing else to say about that. Cyprian had said much by bringing that sack. Cassian relinquished his passion, his fire for combating the momentum of events; and they could actually see the decisions on his face to turn them loose. Thessany had been the harshest of them and was quiet now, only waiting on someone else to speak first. Cassian breathed out slowly, unwilling to give more attention to that which was beyond his control.

Boadshise shifted uncomfortably, perhaps looking to cut the threatening mood, "Maybe we ought to ask our gift giver over here what he thinks about kicking off the end of the world. He seems to want to be in the mix. How do you feel about your dad alienating the Provinces and getting us surrounded by those who will feel we're propping up the scenery for their genocide?"

At that, Mandibo leaned forward, trying to gain Cyprian's eyes past Admiral Phryne who was much closer to the doorway but with her head bowed to the table, "What do you think about a quick strike into the Spenecia Region now while Doniphan softens the City? That's their weakest in-road; and it will give us a straight line into Alson."

Oblave took note of Mandibo's stated strategy and started sliding his fingers across his simulations rapidly, pivoting tables of numbers about like a harpist on strings and launching optimization viruses into the trickling current of data. Admiral Phryne lifted her head and sighed, somewhat relieved at the more tactile turn of the discussion.

"A marshaling point at Spenecia would be huge for our supply lines. I can defend that."

Rosgrove bristled, "None of that is new. Spenecia's been off-limits to us for years. Why are we willing to break their sovereignty now?"

Cyprian's demeanor was that of a lioness in the weeds, drawing as many of them out to engage him as possible, and making sustained eye contact. He settled on Fantine, whose eyes were shining in amusement. He'd spent long hours watching she and Grebel drink and punch each other, wargame and curse till early morning hours. Something passed between them at that point that none but the two of them would know, yet they understood one another. That much one could tell.

Thessany sat upright, more settled, though with a finger still resting on his weapon beneath the shimmering tabletop, "Let's hear it, Cyprian. You brought balls to the table. What do you say?"

Oblave coughed as he often did – he was forever with a sniff or chest cold, "You're showing up a lot in the datastream. Turning out to be a key variable. I actually need to know where you're planning to be."

"He'll be at a Black Fire cannon in my flag squadron." Fantine was grinning loosely at Cyprian to see his reaction to this news. "He'll love it. Lots of chaos and…big explosions."

Nothing rattled Cyprian; and he only acknowledged he'd been referenced with a tiny nod towards her. He was letting something build, maybe just an anxiety to hear from him…a significance to his opinion when he'd been so long viewed either as Cassian's son forever shouting or disappearing or as an unwelcome celebrity, odd and bringing unwelcome attention. Whether he was pleased to hear of this gunner assignment would be difficult to tell.

Admiral Phryne took note, "Is there some sort of kettle drum you're waiting for, or can we hear your position on this? Black Fire is a technical job…requires coding and accuracy, obedience to commands, and is easily liable to turn on the fleet…we've got a right to know whether your heart is in this. Or if you're being coddled."

He turned his cold eyes on her, calling to mind the same look he'd given her as a small boy when she smacked him hard enough to turn his head away after his injudicious comments about her hips. She remembered that incident, no doubt.

"I couldn't care less what you do, any of you."

An offended murmur swept the room like a rolling thundercloud. Cassian watched his son with disgust, giving him room to make of himself an irritant.

Mandibo's face squished menacingly, his cheeks coloring like water with a freshly dropped teabag, "Come on!"

Cyprian surveyed them, "You people are herd animals; and you're not paying attention." He turned to sections of them as he said three words slowly and emphatically, "Flaccid…stumbling…poufs."

Some of them looked to Cassian to see whether he'd put a stop to the tirade; but he was drained of vigor and possibly as curious as they to see how far this young man would go.

"You're babbling on about what to do now when you know that answer. Like you have a choice at this point. What should be stuck in your throat is why did you sleep and suck milk while it came to this? Your government can't agree to the time of day. Your children are stupid. Your payroll is overdrawn. And your sailors are burning down in resthouses…without a squeak from you. Did you even notice that?"

The faces around the table were irritated, shocked…silenced by his audacity. He looked like his eyes were flashing with sparks, burning with intensity. He sat forward, drawing a nervous twitch from Thessany.

"Big boots track mud, don't they?. Why let the same idiots that brought you to the end of the world lead you into it? Don't ask me what I think if you don't want to hear. You don't come out well – any of you."

Fantine's eyes were wide; and she was smiling like someone waiting for a playground scuffle. When she looked at Casssian though, there was nothing to him then but a young boy shifting a knife with quivering hands over a pregnant shenna. He wouldn't respond; and Cyprian knew it. Cyprian stood and slid his chair from behind him to clear the doorway, then turned his eyes on several of them. Thessany sat tensioned like a spring. With a dark and challenging tone, the young man spoke the following words; and yet something bizarre occurred at the same time.

"But sure, I'd love to be your new gunner. I'll help clean up your turds and your vomit while your credit collapses and your banks fail and your people riot … while you fat ridiculous wads, you sit munching grass."

The War Recorder, silent till this point, spoke softly the last part of what he'd said at precisely the same time as he'd said them as if she'd already heard – the very same time, their voices exactly in unison in the manner which would be difficult even if practiced beforehand. Cyprian noticed; but in his temper and impatience only waved her off.

With that, he slammed the door open and left in a storm as perhaps he always left a room. For those with the Recorder, the lingering question was what she thought she was doing. Only a handful of times in history, and then only in silly myths tied to blusterous overblown characters and melodrama, had the Record been said to catch up to events or even supersede them as prophecy. Although nonsensical and out of step with reason, it was in popular literature and theater often a banshee foretelling horrors.

Cassian was pale, drained, "Recorder, why did you say that…just now? What were you doing?"

The War Recorder only watched him in response, dully and as would someone staring beyond and lost in thought.

Phryne watched the War Recorder with suspicion, as she would a dog on the side of road and needed a stick with which to poke it. She whistled and lightly shoved the Recorder's shoulder, "Hey. He asked you a question."

"This Recorder is not aware she had spoken."

But for Fantine, who was gently lifting the sack's opening to peer inside with the expression of smelling something foul, those around the table eyed the Recorder quietly. It was exhausting when Recorders got this way, useless. Fantine was in fact the next to speak.

"Sounds like something the Old Man would say…"

17 AS ALWAYS WITH TREASON

The breaking dawn light colored the chilled mountain city in pastel oranges and pinks as the wide formation of watchmen stood in loose congregation in Wentic Talgos Alson courtyard, whispering and straining to see what was happening on the palace steps. Stendahl stood beside Peri on a dais backed and bookended by a handful of officers, an image carefully structured to display continuity and order no matter one's loyalties. In a stark and brutal display of cruelty, Revin sat limbless and in anguish like a nightmare gargoyle clinging to a rooftile, propped and lashed against a marble column with his wife sobbing uncontrollably beside him. The short stubs where his arms and legs had been were roughly tied with knots at their ends; and black rivulets stained the remaining skin. He was flapping them madly and kept his face raised to the sky with clenched eyes. She was convulsing like a cat dying under a tire and held within her chubby arms something metallic and ill-shaped. She wouldn't look at him. Behind them all and past the landing atop the grand staircase still shone after so many centuries the ancient translucent illusion-man strapped to the stone like a torch.

Deep in the line of soldiers, out of earshot from the droning Procedures Master on the platform speaking of the Judge and what he'd done for the nation, chatter was inevitable and rampant. Here was a nation under mysterious siege, with its government hidden throughout the night and thousands dead. Many of them didn't care at all that the Judge himself was gone, but only that now there was uncertainty in authority. They were told fighters were coming and to stand courageously and do calmly what they'd been trained to do – that their nation may perhaps ask of them to die for its defense. It is fact and was captured in the Record that many shuffling their feet in the courtyard that day broke out spontaneously in stirring patriotic songs.

"Man, that's really messed up." A female watchman on the left of a small group was looking out at the platform whispering so as not to be widely heard. Her companion, a fellow with red hair whose uniform was heavily wrinkled in his haste to join the gathering, glanced to her quickly.

"You always say that. You always say, 'that's really messed up'. What are you talking about now?"

A third, beyond them and with earring holes and ornamental scarring on his neck interjected, "What's messed up?"

Her stare was unbroken from Revin's wife, "What's she holding there? Can you tell? Looks like some kind of messed up idol. Is that what they cut his stuff off with?"

The third whispered back, "No, man. You don't know what that is?"

"Yeah, I know what that is. It's why I'm standing here like a chump asking. You don't know either."

"It's gold."

The one in wrinkles chuckled, "You don't know anything."

"It's gold, I'm serious. The Old Man used to kill traitors by pouring molten gold down their throats like lemonade. Except when it cools, it turns solid again and takes the shape of all the guts inside; and they dig it out of the corpses to show it off. My pops told me Little Man Boneghost drank when the Old Man caught him stirring up mischief in Locust Watch…said you could see it pop out of his eyes like tears and his neck spilled open. They're making her hold it. Later, he'll be drinking that. Maybe her too."

The three of them quietly hesitated, then the girl watchman observed, "That's disgusting."

"Yeah." A fourth, a fellow named Eber who all of them knew as a clown, whispered back. "Yeah, it is. Also works."

The four of them stood in silence, eyeing Revin's suffering with blended sympathy and gratification, perhaps a flavor of justice. The Counselor was broadly disliked among the Watchmen, yes; but here was a vicious strikeback not seen in Alson for a generation or more. They weren't close enough to really see his face; but he was swaying and shaking with the fading life of a man in shock. He would drink when the time came, that much was certain.

"Who made that call – Stendahl or Peri? Have they said who's in charge?"

The girl grimaced, "What could possibly qualify that grinning idiot to be in charge? His last name? He's a freak, everybody knows that. Peri's got the ball – that's obvious."

Wrinkles chuckled, "You're stupid. As long as there's a Talgo around, they're in charge. Everybody knows that."

"Shut up. We're about to get hit hard; and there are nutjobs all over the city and all you morons can do is jabber on about which talking head sleeps in the big room. There could be wackos in the formation right now, did you think of that?"

Eber leaned forward, "I heard from my buddy the two of them were arguing this morning."

The scarred fellow grinned, "What was the freak's opinion – curl up on a library shelf and rattle off poems?"

"Hey guys," an extremely tall, gangly fellow named, Cope whose mouth was always idly wide open broke in with a whisper. "Who is that bald guy up there? I've never seen him before."

Several of them turned their eyes to the landing above and beyond them to a frowning man in a long dark gray peacoat with the old style leather uniform in illuminated malachite bracers and greaves, staring grimly at the assembly a handful of paces away from the blabbering Procedures Master, who was dull and old and uninspiring by comparison.

Wrinkles whispered back, "That's the new Chaselord."

"Chaselord?! That's a Red Witch thing. What are we doing with one of those?"

The mysterious fellow looked like a devil from the shadows, alien and brooding, trolling the anonymous faces which paved the courtyard looking for one whose soul he might swallow.

"They're worried we're infiltrated or compromised."

"What if we are? What's he gonna do about it?" Cope's whispered tone was urgent, confused. The girl watchman turned subtly back to see his expression, perhaps curious that he knew so little of the consequences of a Chaselord's appointment. She glanced at Wrinkles and the scarred fellow with raised eyebrows. Their own expressions spoke darkly of what such a man might do.

"Nothing, Cope. Just don't attract his attention. Stay away from him; and if he asks you anything, don't even make jokes. Just be as normal and as professional as you can; and answer only what he asked you. Blend in."

"Why? What's he supposed to do?"

"Shut up, Cope."

Eber's attention was elsewhere, his eyes still locked on the dais in the area where Stendahl and Peri stood before a backdrop of officers, "Look. I told you. They're arguing right now. Look."

Strangely, and outside expectations for Stendahl, he and Peri were indeed having a discussion of some kind on the landing, only the two of them and in disregard for the challenging and cautious words of the Procedures Master about best practices in urban warfare and the passion of defending one's very home. He talked of passion like he was talking about which blend of fescue seed was best for the season…like he was reading it or didn't understand the root of his message. From their distance in the courtyard, the watchmen could neither see facial expressions nor gauge any context for the words exchanged between the Judge's fatherless son and the leader of all Alson's watchmen.

"How can you tell they're arguing? Looks like blobs from here."

"That's because you're freaking blind. They're ticked off at each other. Look at his fist."

"Do we get to watch Revin drink?"

"Uggh! You want to see that? What's the matter with you?"

"Standahl doesn't argue. That doesn't even make sense. You're seeing it wrong."

Wrinkles shoved his hands under his armpits in an attempt to warm them in the morning chill, "They look like they're arguing to me. Eber, sneak up there and see what you can find out. Pallius is in front – that suckup will know something.

Cope interrupted, "Are you serious? What if the Chaselord sees that? Eber, you can't sneak around right now. Stay here."

The girl watchman frowned, "Don't do it, Eber. Cope's right. This isn't the time. There hasn't been a Chaselord in thirty years."

"Come on, Eber. Pansy. Go talk to Pallius. He's not even close to the stairs. Find out what's going on."

Each of them glanced quickly to see what puckishness might be in Eber's face, whether the familiar wrinkles framed his eyes as when he'd send new recruits off to the parts depot looking for imaginary repair materials or when he'd call the depot asking to speak to watchmen with profane names in hopes of their repeating him aloud…'Baws, first name Icy', and that sort of thing. They knew well his breathless tinkly giggles when he was up to his business. At this moment, that was in fact what they found beside them. He grinned like an elf, plotting.

The girl darkened her tone, "Eber, stop it. Not now. They're watching us for anything not normal. You don't know what they'll do to you if they think you're turned. Stay here."

He smiled wider, "No problem, guys. I've got this." Then he was gone, vanished within the ranks of uniforms.

"Oh crap oh crap oh crap." Cope was droning in fright, their implications toward the Chaselord having made an impact on him. He was leaning forward in a useless effort to track Eber along his route between and into the line as needed, trying to avoid being noticed.

"Cope, straighten up. You're going to attract attention."

"Why'd you do that, man?! You know Eber can't help himself. He's going to get us all busted. I don't know what they'll do – this is bad."

The girl watchman craned her own head to try and pick Eber from the crowd; but he was only apparent occasionally, darting in and out as watchmen either allowed him through or tried to obstruct. Some along his path didn't desire to accommodate this sneaking about and aberrant plotting and tried to trip him up or shove him out into the open. Yet he was skilled and deft, here hopping over a boot, there dodging behind the line as he went. She quickly looked back to the grim Chaselord staring and cold. Someone had taken the sparkling mass from Revin's wife; and she was curled beside her husband on the landing, trying to console him, stroking his back and whispering into his ear. She looked absurd, round and sloppily dressed hunched beside a flapping and slaughtered man.

"Oh, man are we going to be in the gravy if he gets caught."

The group of them went quiet for a time, waiting for some sort of shock which didn't seem to come. The Procedures Master had stepped back and left a General to explain the logistics associated with the squadron briefings which were to follow and where those briefings would occur. He said things which were intended to be inspirational and something of note for historians perhaps, recorded along with the defense of Alson from siege and invasion and maybe her finest hour. Not many in the courtyard that day came to recall anything the fellow had said, unfortunately, for one reason or another.

At last, Wrinkles broke the silence, "I'm wide awake."

The girl watchman creased her forehead, "What are you talking about?"

"Shut up."

Wrinkles hesitated a moment in reaction to the voice from behind him, "Something my little girl scribbled on the driveway last night."

"I didn't know she could write yet. What's your point?"

"Would you two shut it!" The voice from behind was more urgent, irritated. The girl and Wrinkles ignored him.

"I don't know what she was doing outside. It was after we put her to bed…doors were locked. Thought she was asleep all night. We were all pretty nervous after Balcister…stayed up watching the news. Somehow she got out and wrote, 'I'm wide awake' on the driveway in chalk. Saw it this morning when I left, bright yellow, scrawled in long fat letters. I don't know how she got outside."

A pause, gathering thoughts, "Was she in bed this morning?"

He nodded, "Yeah, she was. She has a fever or something. It was her handwriting…all caps. That's something she does."

"You must have missed it yesterday going home. You were distracted and didn't notice it.

Wrinkles pondered, for the idea wasn't new to him but rather was unacceptable, "Yeah. I must have."

"You think something happened to her?"

He spun his head as if she'd thrown a rock at his temple, for it was his fear, "Do you think? What could she mean, 'I'm wide awake'?"

The girl watchman nudged his arm, recognizing too late when she shouldn't have spoken, "You missed it yesterday going home. She's with Elia all the time. No way was she alone. And Elia was fine, right?"

There was no answer following that, as he perhaps was considering whether in fact Elia had been all right. It would have been difficult for him to say. Anyway, a massive black iron pot was being carried in by massive torturers upon the dais leading towards Revin; and it was attracting attention. The general had ceased speaking; and others were sliding dark stocks around Revin's neck.

Cope leaned forward again, "Where's Eber? Can anybody see him?"

"I think I see him over there. It looks like he's next to Pallius now. That's him, right?"

The girl was watching Wrinkles, trying still to gauge how certain he was of Elia's wellbeing. It frightened her. The scarred fellow kept his eyes on the Chaselord, who stood with his hands locked behind his back and still scanning. Something he saw in a turn of the Chaselord's head drew his eyes to a cornice framing the courtyard, then another on the far side. There was something moving up there.

"He's got snipers." Scars pointed softly, his voice cracking a little too loudly for the circumstances. "Guys, the Chaselord has snipers watching us. I swear – look up there."

Each of them followed his pointing finger to the tiny silhouettes. There were men atop the buildings, no doubt. Here was something none had foreseen; and its implications were paralyzing if that is what in fact those men were doing up there.

"On us?" The question left off there in all its depth and urgency.

Revin's wife was being held by a giant Interrogator by then, as she'd tried already to run away now that the stocks were in place. Revin was a man thirsty for conclusion, flailing his stubs and shouting for an end to it, shouting something of the Talgos and what they bring with them. Peri and Stendahl were silent at this point, standing in respect for the moment and to see justice play out. It was strange to notice; but Stendahl with his white hair and the pale skin of his face stood out in view like a crisp-white dead tree on a green-treed mountainside; and many of those there that day watched him closely and were fascinated.

The Interrogators with Revin were rosy and fleshy and unnaturally broad, their wide white grins surgically affixed and visible even from such a distance. Those men were withdrawn from society for hearing voices or expressing secret and unearthly desires, made cannibals and deviants and provided terrible addictions in the service of torture and extraction of intelligence. Typically, they were chained as they worked. Here, they moved quietly, securing Revin's neck in place and positioning him while another held his wife by her hair. The General was saying something about faithfulness to one's homeland and what happens to traitors. It was of course silent as snowfall at this point, all eyes locked upon the landing where the massive black pot slowly was brought to him on poles. Occasional flashes of lemon light squeezed from the pot's opening as it swayed when the Interrogators stepped. Revin had by then ceased shouting and crying for his life, ceased threatening doom from his plots and intrigues, and was cooperating. To anyone with any sort of empathy, it would have been incredibly saddening to watch the man turn his head up and open his mouth wide to assist those charged with his murder in their work.

There was a collective shock in the courtyard as Revin drank and as his throat opened up, a spirit passing through the formed masses speaking with the voice of the ocean and saying, "Enough". Perhaps their grandparents had seen similar things in their times; but no recollection at any dinner table could call to mind what it was like for those there to see such retribution towards a man so closely in the employ of a Talgo – their Talgo.

After Revin's pierced corpse went limp, punctured in places with seeping golden drops and charred, the interrogaters threw his wife off the dais and into the courtyard as they might a chewed apple core. She wouldn't drink today; and they were done with her. She was also with this act being told she may not have Revin's body, which was perhaps just as cruel. Once the horrible sculpture cooling within him was removed, he was to disappear with no tomb as did all traitors in the days of the Old Man, to take away a rallying marker for other intrigues or martyr-worshippers. Revin would never be seen again; and everyone understood that. Stendahl was crying; and many noticed and wondered.

"That is so messed up."

Cope leaned in again, his unpleasant breath on the girl watchman's neck, "What happened to Eber? I don't see him anymore. Is he coming back?"

In fact, there was a gap in the line where both Eber and Pallius had stood moments before.

"Pallius is gone too – maybe they went out of the open to talk."

Up above, on the rooftops, the snipers seemed to be at attention and sighting something in the courtyard.

"That would have been stupid."

There was some murmuring and confusion sounding from the direction to which Eber had gone, where he and the other had stood speaking.

"Where did they go? What's going on?"

The general spoke again and was dismissing the watchmen to their logistics briefings, wishing them good fortune and courage in the defense of their city and in the oncoming battle. The crowd was breaking up and dissolving into disparate threads, lingering chatter of what they'd seen and heard, with occasional blasting screams for speed and discipline from the field officers to get moving. Suspicious and afraid, the girl watchman, her eyes squinted, glanced to the landing where the officers and the Chaselord and Stendahl and Peri still stood. Now, they needed snipers on their own defenders; and Interrogators were on full display in the light of morning for all to see, executing state officials. Now, the government was muddled and split with nameless attackers coming to lay waste to the city's bright streets with everyday lunatics smiling in shopping malls. Now she stood in a crowd of soldiers who might soon be dead being asked to risk her soul to fight for those people there.

She glanced back to where Eber had gone missing, then back to the landing. A soft yelp of surprise rose from her throat when she saw that the Chaselord was staring directly at her.

18 SIEGE

"All right, riddle boy. Out with it!" Cristoffel examined Misling's blushed face as if he'd eaten the last cookie. "What have you been saying to that girl to get her so worked up?!"

The mog vehicle was rumbling along the concrete panels and limestone curbing of a vertical street on the outside wall of a tall building climbing upwards toward an illuminated sign which read, "Unleashed", bathed in the flickering light of tall blue and white gas jets: some sort of business offices in the smaller financial district the poorer kids called, "The Spooks". Newer buildings in Alson were required to maintain such streets. Misling and Cristoffel weren't yet to the part of town wherein Balcister had once stood, not yet even past the step streets and cluttered and rambling art houses of Bethani. In fact, she had for the most part kept to the upper parts of buildings and in the shadows of arches, soaring towers and gabled friezes high above the city. Though there was extraordinarily little traffic, they weren't alone as they'd perhaps anticipated they would be. Only an occasional scattering of folks like small crickets were appearing on the streets down below as the sun was rising.

The Recorder looked back at her innocently and with caution, still unsure of this girl, "Lennox Weshire believes you are poisoning him."

She turned her head to face front, "Good."

The world went on its side quickly as Cristoffel twisted the worn control stick to its left, steering the mog vehicle across the clay rooftiles of an elevated walkway joining buildings. There was a sharp set of pops as the swivelseat spun loosely again in its bearings to the new orientation. The Recorder watched her until it was clear this wasn't something she'd discuss.

"Well?" Cristoffel's tone was curt.

Misling coughed as he considered perhaps the level of detail or
how to frame out what he needed to say, "She is kind to help. There
is someone who is very special, a man of importance, who was to be
in Balcister yesterday. That is where this Recorder must go…quickly.
It has been too long already."

She glanced at his face like she wasn't accepting something he'd
said, "Your dad?"

He chuckled…almost, "This Recorder's father is laying drunk in
a plains town beanfield hallucinating and soiling himself."

Momentarily on their side again, they twisted horizontally to
range across an expanse of concrete wall on another tall office
building, where just beyond was a cluster of crowded rooftops
leading out of the Spooks.

"You know what I mean."

Like a thundercrack, a shot fired so close to them she heard the
wind from its passing. A clay drainspout shattered into pink and
white fragments, spraying dust. With instinct, Cristoffel jammed the
controls forward and moved the vehicle high and around to the far
side of the building, high into its tower where they'd be shielded from
view. They both sat motionless, only after a moment at last looking
cautiously down to scan the wide streets and broad panorama of
cityscape before them. No sign of a shooter or patrol.

"Too sloppy for military."

Misling shoved his face into his hands again at the delay, "What
was it then?"

"Gun freak maybe…gang. It's Alson, who knows? We'll sit here
a few minutes. Take it easy."

The Recorder shifted uncomfortably in the seat, restless like a
caged grizzly growing angry at its walls. Cristoffel however, she took
quick notice of something beside them and reached into a

compartment deep into a canvas bag therein. It was as if she'd heard something.

"What do you know of rescue efforts in the Plaza? Of survivors?"

She was still reaching around for something and was distracted because of it, but still grunted, "I'm sorry; but it's pretty unlikely. You can't be surprised to hear that."

"But of rescuers?"

Cristoffel glanced at him, "It's a nice thought." She fished an old leather-bound field notebook from a cluttered glovebox and rested it on her lap. Then Cristoffel turned her eyes up to the brightening blue autumn sky as if to find shapes in the clouds.

"There may be people somewhere who would…would run up the stairs into a burning building… maybe someone who'd help carry people out instead of shoving them out of the way…but not here. Whatever is left at Balcister is on its own. If you have to see that, then I'll show it to you."

The Recorder was cold and shivered at her words, at her full-on admission of the world in which the two of them live where strangers didn't take such risks. It wasn't so much something with which to dispute, but rather to lament that it was so. She soon flipped open the book and slid out a pencil to scrawl hastily written notes, at one time glancing around as if identifying a location. With that done, Cristoffel snapped a rubber band around the book to secure it and slid it back from where it had come.

"I've been shot at before. It could be part of whatever's going on…or it could just be some buck-tooth taking advantage of the confusion. I get that you're in a hurry; but we're not going anywhere just yet."

The look on Misling's face was that of exhaustion, with his eyes reddening and tired. For a moment, he rested his head against the back of his seat and inhaled deeply, then thought better of it and leaned a bit sideways to scan the streets below looking for a shooter or strange reflection as if he were suited for such a search and would recognize those things should they present themselves.

Cristoffel however, she didn't spare any time for a look to the streets or the surroundings. In fact, once she'd stowed the notebook away, she pulled from her bag a dusty and streaked can of something and pried its aluminum lid up with a slip of steel hanging from a frayed leather lanyard on her mog vehicle's door. Misling took a distracted interest in her busy-ness and observed whatever she was about despite the presumed danger of mysterious railgun fire from below. The can was perhaps three quarters full of a beige milky liquid; and drippings from it had dried in pretty jags along the length of the can. With the lid pried up, she spun herself in the swivelseat and unloosed her safety belt to stand and prop her boots against a decorative cornice, ornamented along its perimeter with unusual concrete human heads and faces. The heights were dizzying to the Recorder; but here among the bright building novelties and elements, Cristoffel seemed to be well accustomed and comforted.

She upturned the can and let the beige milk flow over an evil looking sculpted head jutting from the cornice. The head was maybe the size of a man's torso, perhaps larger; and it wasn't at all obvious why an architect would place such a work at heights like this. Who would see it? Neither was it clear, Cristoffel's purpose; and Misling was at once annoyed with her.

"Why are you defacing that figure? What on earth would incite you to pointless vandalism when you are hiding from gunfire? There is no time for this!"

Her forehead rumpled, "Huh?"

Misling leaned in her direction and made a respectable effort to grip the can and take it from her, though his concern for the heights and upsetting the mog stole much of his intensity.

"Back off! Look, sit in that seat and shut up or this trip's over.

You can get out and climb down."

He watched her with that look, the one saying she was an ass; and tried once more to reach for the can before she could again pour. She smacked his hand and, with blurring speed, pulled from her waist a longknife and touched it between his eyes.

"Touch that can again! Touch me again! I swear I will send you down the side of this high rise! Why are you messing with me right now?"

He pointed at her work, the tan and frothy milk she'd spilled over the haunting sculpted head before them. She rolled her eyes and dismissed him, slipping the knife back into hiding and replacing it in her caked fingers with a brush, its bristles splayed in a hundred directions but still serviceable. Still propped against the architectural pieces on the building's outside walls, Cristoffel quickly brushed the material into a film fully coating the sculpted head's outside surface. When satisfied, she poured the remainder of the can from the crown of the figure's head and allowed it to flow a moment before repeating the brushing.

"Latex, moron. Making a mold."

Misling stared back at her as if she'd admitted to conspiracy.

"The idiots are going to blow up the city. You know it; and I know it. All this is gonna be gone. It's heartbreaking. If I capture them, then all this talent, these weird little…beautiful things…they won't be lost."

She dabbed the grinning face's nose again with the brush and waited as if this was something she'd outlined before and had thrown back at her as foolishness. He was only watching, listening.

Cristoffel shrugged, embarrassed, "The hard luck guys that built this city back in the day…they deserve that."

Only later would it become clear what happened at just this

point, as the two of them perched high above the streets in hiding and the creamy latex settled gently on the statue…the fear of harm and the desolate and lonely sense that old and important things could indeed one day vanish. Only later would it make sense what was going on in the Recorder's racing mind as he understood Cristoffel and saw around him a city of illimitable purpose and depth, gorgeous and strange, familiar and ridiculous…and it cast into a fire like dried leaves. "Fear above all - capricious kings", the Salt Mystic had once exclaimed; and with the chilling autumn winds and haunting doom of hidden men firing slugs at them, the Recorder perhaps saw then more clearly than ever that lunatics were in charge.

"We are leaving." His tone was cold and severe, quite unlike him.

On her face, for just a blink, was a flash of disappointment that he didn't share with her just then, that it didn't make as much sense to him as to her, before she noticed he'd changed something very slightly about how he spoke just then.

"Did you just-?"

Zing. Another shot pulverized a corner two arm-lengths from them, indicating the shooter had moved or perhaps had a partner. Cristoffel quickly leapt into the vehicle and, without securing a belt, kicked up the anchor and shoved the stick forward and to the right. They turned the far corner of the building so quickly, the mog's wheels popped off the wall slightly before snapping back into place on the far side, frightening Misling out of his mind.

She strapped herself in and scanned beneath them and the surrounding buildings, "He's moving or something. Need to go now, I agree. Not sure how though – we'll have to drop a bit to get anywhere."

Misling's eyes were wide, for he saw the problem with lowering closer into range. Cristoffel was quickly eyeing any and all escape routes, understanding they would have to in fact jump from the walls of this building to another in order to get away without going very low. There was a wide, gradually sloping steel roof arcing downward on an adjacent building perhaps within reach. When her eyes settled there, the Recorder only grimaced fiercely and settled deeper into the swivelseat, gripping sharply.

"Hold on!" With that, she backed the mog lower and to the very edge of the face to which they clung, till the flights rested hard against the concrete corniceworks, inhaling deeply and squinting her eyes with adrenalin and focus. Another zing poked a hole through the vehicle's front hood; and the Recorder reacted by shutting his eyes – maybe soliciting some reserves of courage from someone in his Pool, which is said to be possible. Either way, his eyes stayed shut from the moment the vehicle sped from that corner till it launched in freefall and ultimately locked onto the steel roof close by and slipped around another corner.

"Oh, no." It was then, the smoke caught Cristoffel's eyes; and she braked to more fully understand what was happening. Her voice was suddenly lifeless, at once losing the lilt and ease with which she'd only just then spoken of beautiful things. Misling straightened his back, even loosening the security belt in order to get his head higher to more fully see what was before them.

"Wasn't a shooter at all." She rubbed a finger roughly against her right temple.

In the distance, in the direction from which those railgun slugs had come, there was flame and fury, shrouding gray and white buildings in bright sparks and pulsing shockwaves. Dark clouds of Black Fire swelled and blossomed like poison tea flowers as speeding mogs darted and clashed and quicktanks thundered in the street. Pulverized fragments of city peppered the brightening blue skyline.

"It was stray fire. We're not just at war. We're in it."

Misling broke from the surprise before Cristoffel and rested his hand gently on her shoulder. She faced him with panic and anger, perhaps not expecting from a Recorder the sort of determination and reserve he was giving back. When he spoke, it wasn't with a nervous squeak or soft fear, but rather commanding.

"Balcister. Now."

She pointed her wet right hand, palm up, gesturing toward the swelling Black Fire clouds and smoke, the swirl of Doniphan's assault, signaling that was their direction should they continue. Though her eyes were clear she wanted off the hook for this, something was holding her to his decision one way or the other. It's not even clear now what that was; but it is what happened.

He settled back into the swivelseat and secured his belt, "Stop for nothing. Please."

Cristoffel at last secured herself as well and shoved the controls forward as if she were slaughtering an animal. It wasn't important to say anything – they both knew she was going to stick to this or she'd have turned back already. The two of them bounced and jostled as their vessel rushed along the outsides of the financial buildings leading out of the Spooks, dropping lower and remaining shielded on far walls as much as possible. She was angling to the east of what looked to be the hottest part of the battle but still not too far out of their way.

She shouted without turning her head, "Reach into the compartment where I got the brush."

Misling held a climber's grip on the door's handle and cautiously slipped open the glovebox, "For what purpose?"

"You'll figure it out."

At a sudden shift, he jammed a shoulder against the back of his seat, losing his fumbling hand's way in the jumbled mess of the deep storage hold. He slid aside thick cloths, a gamebox and a handful of packaged bars of granola and at once froze his searching fingers – surprised at the unexpected shape.

"You feel it?"

A carbine - small and compact, the sort used by light infantry or gateway guardians. The Recorder's physical hands had never once touched such a weapon, though many in his mind had and with them, done terrible things. He did not withdraw, but rather gently pulled it from beneath the settling clutter. The cloths fell back like the curtains of a play. He watched the side of her face only a moment; and she didn't turn to see. There was nothing to say – they were headed where such a weapon was needed; and she had one. He examined its russet brown shielding and the palm-length trigger within the armlets. It wasn't new and had been through such times as this.

The Recorder inhaled deeply and surveyed the way before them. Massive plumes of Black Fire still swelled ahead, framed in smoke. They were just then speeding along the top of a covered walk and were much lower than they'd been till that point. He gripped the carbine's trigger softly, slipping the leather armlets around his wrist and forearm, and shifting himself in order to sit up straighter and to see in front and behind them. They were close enough now to make out the individual mogs racing along the outer walls of the buildings, engaged in vicious dogfights with Alson's forces. One building in the distance suddenly fell into a white rising cloud, collapsing and carrying mog vehicles and screaming men down to the streets below. Balcister was beyond this.

"We're going off-road."

Before he could question her, Misling saw she'd positioned them overlooking a shorter building, possibly a shopping arcade, with a large skylight above an atrium. Misling then noticed what she'd apparently seen - a Doniphan vessel had caught sight of them and altered course to intercept. Misling roughly unsnapped his seatbelt in order to face backwards, extending a quivering arm in the direction of their attacker. He jammed shut his jaw in determination, for this was a touching of violence he'd not till then known.

"Doing it", she said, as if asking him to disagree. The Recorder, quite inappropriately and like perhaps no other Recorder before him in all the years since the Mystic dreamed up the idea, screamed a warcry and squeezed the palmgrip successively, sending ball lightning bursts out in a flurry towards the Doniphan attacker. It was the same moment that Cristoffel shoved the controlstick forward to launch their vessel into the air and shatter through the arcade's broad skylight, falling through and forward with incredible momentum, landing safely on a high whitewashed wall painted with smiling advertising faces. The Doniphan followed, for a moment lost in the debris and shock.

"The elevator door. Shoot it!!" Cristoffel shouted.

Misling spun to see what she was talking about and gripped the carbine's trigger again, actuating the carbon breaker at least ten times in a row and perforating the thin elevator door with balls of elemental fire. She drove at speed along the inner wall, beyond brightly ornamented shelves and bursting shop displays, toward the elevator door he'd decimated and plowed through it. Misling was unable to see what had become of the Doniphan.

Cristoffel drove them along the masonry shaft wall, downward at high speed, into darkness only eased by pale headlights. She was weaving this way and that to dodge cables or electrical boxes, and was staring ahead fiercely. The attacker was either coming behind them or would be waiting when they emerged.

She slowed the vehicle and at last stopped, "I need to think. Do we go back up or keep going? I need to get to the canals. Where did he go?"

Misling rubbed his forehead, trying to catch his breath, "Both are choices a soldier would make."

"And your point is?"

The Recorder settled the carbine in his lap, "Sneak out a side window before he can call for assistance."

Cristoffel nodded and positioned them in front of a lower floor's door mechanisms, visible to them as a thin vertical sliver of light and shapeless motorworks. Misling fluidly punctured the door as before and created an escape on perhaps the second or third floor. Within a few moments of cautious navigation, she'd found a wide display window easily maneuvered open and slipped the vehicle through and outside to the exterior walls again. All around them on the street and below were the black and gray masses of Black Fire: tiny replicating automata making copies of themselves from whatever they landed upon in a nearly uncontrolled chain reaction. It was a terrifying rust which ate flesh and steel alike; and Doniphan had for some reason brought it to Alson's beating heart.

They made it through a shaded alleyway on the horizontal street to a narrow stairway leading down to the green canal. Cristoffel didn't hesitate to take them down the steps and along the walls rising on either side of the canal. This wasn't any safer than where they'd been; but it was at least for the moment, quiet. She looked at the Recorder with eyes wide, disbelieving what had just happened to them.

He watched her as well, not saying anything but sharing the relief.

Then Cristoffel broke out laughing, throwing her head back. She laughed till it was awkward with the Recorder watching her. She looked at Misling again, inhaling deeply as if having finished a rich dessert, then leaned in to kiss him fully on his lips. Not knowing what to do with such a thing, Misling sort of narrowed his eyes and tried to pucker a bit to help it along. When she was through, he rubbed his chin nervously and shifted the carbine in his lap.

Cristoffel smiled, "You scream when you're blowing things up. That's hilarious."

He chuckled then…actually chuckled, perhaps for the first time, "You are a terrible driver."

His smile surprised Cristoffel; and she laughed again. Smiles were fading when he softly raised a finger, signaling that they should go. She nodded and started up again, continuing along the canal walls for some time, unmolested. The engines and blasts of battle were still within earshot all along.

"We're close. It's around this next bend."

He nodded, though she couldn't see that.

"Are you planning on having me just drop you off or what?" Strangely, when she didn't get an answer, Cristoffel glanced at his face to see that he hadn't thought that far into it.

"That's what I figured. 'Hauna is awesome at finding people like you."

Misling's face was exhausted and drained, "I cannot leave him."

She examined his face, pondering, and nodded. After a few minutes, once she'd parked her vessel on a mooring platform and shut down the vortex engine, Cristoffel slipped out of the vehicle and motioned for him to go ahead of her up the stairway to the main thoroughfare which led to the Plaza. It was silent. When the two of them reached the top of the stairs, the view opened up of a rubble field smoking in a gentle smolder in what was once a proud and beautiful courtyard crowned with the jewel of the city. There was a faint scent of smoke and old damp masonry.

"No…"

Tall and haunting, rising in silhouette against the rubble and with the feel of stark nightmare when something wicked intrudes on nostalgic dreams of home, there stood a misshapen bell tower. It was roughly in the courtyard's center and stood as tall as four men, a black iron bell housed in its upper reaches. It was of no ordinary materials or design; and as they watched it became more obvious what a horror they'd intruded into.

"It's made of people…" Her voice broke in sickness, for the tower was composed of contorted living people standing upon and clinging to one another. Heads, arms, and shoulders jutted from its mass — some frozen, some moving slowly as if awakening, and some with heads darting quickly about. The bell tower stood overlooking what was once mighty Balcister; and it was constructed of madmen.

Sylhauna was talking with some soapstone figurines on a shelf as she stirred eggs in a copper skillet, digging the cottony puffs off the sides with a spoon. She sprinked some herbs from a dark walnut shaker and admired the swirl they made with one of her huge buckled boots crossed behind the other and her head tilted to one side. The kitchen was tidy and smelled of cinnamon. The miniatures represented some of the Salt Mystic's fundamental archetypes, commonly called the 'players'. She turned down the blue flame of the stove and lingered her eyes on one, then picked it up, bringing it to her face for a closer look.

"Hello, Libertine! It's quite pleasing to see you again." Her accent was intentionally ritzy and glamorous. Suddenly, she whispered with a suspicious glance away and a jerk of her thumb, "Famous guest. When he wakes up, I'll ask him why he gave you such a dumb name, okay?"

A muted banging explosion sounded from outside, possibly a surrounding neighborhood; and her shoulders winced at it. She quickly recovered her cheerful tone, "They'll be fine. She knows all the hiding places." Sylhauna replaced Libertine in its position on the old shelf and spun Peacemaker one way, then the other idly.

"Don't you?"

Tiny bubbles needled the eggs in her skillet, calling for her attention; and she stirred them again. Dreamer was beside Peacemaker, in the form of a little girl with flowers in her hair trying to hand a mushroom to someone. Sylhauna didn't address Dreamer or touch it, but rather turned the fourth and last piece all the way around to put its defiant frown and crossed arms to face the dimpled shale backsplash. It was the image of the Rebel; and she didn't care to see it again.

"I miss you, little buddy." Not lingering on a thought unpleasant to her, Sylhauna lifted the skillet from the flame though the eggs were still runny and sloshing around in the gray skillet. She raised the volume of her voice to reach Ring in the other room.

"I like them a little squishy and shiny; but not everybody does. I know liquid computers and all that; but when you wake up, do you think you'll want them squishy or kind of dry? Dry is safe, I think. As long as they're not plastic." She waited, thinking, then decided for herself and placed the copper back on the flame.

"I don't really understand something about you, though. If you're the Salt Mystic and you're back, there had to be a 'you' already, right? Did she suck out your soul or are you in there somewhere – do you know what I'm saying? Or are you faking everything, because that would be kind of mean?" Not really awaiting an answer, she glanced back to the figure of Dreamer holding forth her tiny mushroom.

"No, thank you; but how kind of you to offer!" She lightly bowed to the figurine, then shifted subjects again at an idle thought. "But since you're her and more…you know…mystic than Bomar, you can just wake up normal and not foaming at the mouth and stuff. You can just wake up and not be crazy, right?"

Suddenly, she jerked her eyes back towards the wall separating her from Ring at a snap or click coming from there. Hearing nothing further, she gripped the skillet's handle and lifted it from the eye. It is telling of her that the instinct was to bring along a skillet and not a knife; but there she was.

"Lennox?" Cautiously, Sylhauna peered around the corner into the living room wondering at what she might find there; and there stood Kensi in his rags and dust.

"Like jelly." He was leaning over Ring, jamming one of the needlepacks from Cristoffel's kit into Ring's arm with his finger mashing just then on the plunger and despairing at the lack of visible reaction. "I'll have to tell. I'll have to tell."

Sylhauna stood in desolate fright, the runny eggs dripping onto the floor. It was all over her face that she was considering bashing him on the side of his head with it; but she only stood there, uncertain.

Kensi chuckled without looking at her, "You come at me with that and I'll jam it down your throat, my little sour tart. You believe me, don't you? Settle it, princess." He was laughing wickedly, entirely amused with how well things were turning out for him. Sylhauna bit her lower lip, then softly placed the skillet onto a countertop behind her. She looked back at the goblin face.

"Your Record's going to have you getting crapped on."

His eyes showed little recognition, though he was for a moment stalled out by it. He patted the bloody place on the back of his head gently while she stood motionless, perhaps trying not to remind him she'd done that.

Kensi squinted impatiently, "We'll cut your fish's throat and pull his tongue through the hole, like I said. Just like I said. No talky talky. Your kitchen will have my knife for me, won't it lollipop? You rascal. Maybe you should have grabbed that instead. Really glad I followed you now. Had to hide, didn't I?"

She shook her head no, "Not such a big deal. We did too."

He watched her, then took two steps in her direction, "You're weird."

Backing, her hands up, "Just get out of here." Sylhauna's voice quivered as she tried to sound less frightened.

Closing in, his eyes smiling, "After we've eaten."

He was wearing on her; and she was almost in full panic by now, stepping back into the wall and watching him. She cast a glance to Ring still laying lifeless, then to the apartment door, then the terrace opening and balcony beyond. Then something else happened.

Quite suddenly, Lennox lumbered out of his bedroom, unsteady and leaning very heavily on the doorframe, "Get out!"

Sylhauna was horrified, "Are you serious? Why would you come out here like that?"

He grunted, clearly suffering, "My house."

Kensi clicked his teeth and took a step towards Lennox, not realizing or foreseeing what the ill man was prepared to do. He was moving with the surety of someone feeling powerful and controlling with the mischief of a mad god. Lennox however, held in a hidden hand a solid piece of plaster gripped solidly. The dull sound was awful when he slammed it with all his strength into the right crown of the street man's head. Were Lennox a healthier man, Kensi wouldn't have survived that blow. As it was, Kensi buckled in severe pain and was dazed enough for what followed. In his panicked rush, Lennox gripped Kensi by a greasy and bloody clump of the street man's hair and dragged him clumsily to the bathroom, shoving him inside. He slammed it shut and locked the door. Exhausted by the effort, the ill man leaned weakly, doubled over and resting his palm against the writing desk while trying to calm his breathing. She unfortunately stepped closer to him.

Lennox looked up at her, disgusted, "All you bring me is problems."

Sylhauna's eyes softened, hurt. Yet he saw her with disdain. Lennox clutched Sylhauna's hair and gripped the bathroom's doorknob to open the door again.

"Stop it!! Let me go!!" Too quickly for her to fight or understand what he was doing, Lennox had shoved Sylhauna into the bathroom as well and locked the door behind her. Then she was alone in a cluttered toilet space with a small sink, weathered cabinet with a mirror whose silvering was wearing off, and the street man who sought to torture her. She banged her fists against the door, a door with scratches and streaks on it; but it was solid. Kensi was recovering and watching her, clasping the pooling bloody places on the side of his head. He stared at her as she banged madly, wolf-like and wild in her fright. After a moment, he ran a pointed finger down one of the old scratches in the door. Fingernail scratches. His smile grew shining yellow teeth.

"Door locks from the outside, sweetsie. You don't see a lot of that."

Sylhauna went berserk, smashing her fists against the door hard enough to bloody herself. Her eyes were wild; and she'd lost control. Kensi's eyes were on her as he steadied himself, not so much enjoying her reaction as just bearing it. When he shifted his position as if to move toward her, she stopped banging and pushed her back against the door as if that distanced her from the street man.

"I hid a key in here once, under a tile behind you. May still be there."

He nodded dismissively, "Sweet Kensi's had a rough night, sour tart. He's thinking maybe the princess knows where these old fingernail scratches came from, isn't he?"

Sylhauna was silent, trying to calm herself. He nodded, "Bet that's really scary then. Cause here you are again. With a rascal." As he said that last word, his eyes twinkled in joy.

"Were you lying about expecting him?"

Kensi stood up slowly. He wasn't well after all the beatings he'd had. She inhaled sharply, trying to keep him talking. Yet Kensi's filthy face collapsed into a skull, vicious and mean, as he sharply sprang at her and clutched her neck with both hands. He squeezed and shoved her into the wall, lifting her off the floortiles with the force of his attack. Her face purpled almost immediately as she choked for air.

"Would you like Kensi to keep talking? To be stupid and gloat and tell you what I'm doing and how many there are and where I was born? Fish!!"

Sylhauna's eyes were rolling backwards in her struggle. She wasn't getting any breath past his clutch at all. He stuck his tongue out like a hungry snake, scraping it against her left eye.

"If he hadn't made me talk before, I'd have you dreaming cold dreams right now, fish! Instead of choking and dying in the toilet!"

Veins stood out in his neck and on his forehead like roadmaps. She opened her eyes quickly and rolled them left and right, searching desperately for a way forward. No one was coming to help; and she was entirely on her own. Her breath was depleted, her arms weakening at her sides. No sounds came from the other side of the door at all. Sylhauna was devastatingly on her own in this; and it was ending here. Her eyes stopped on the fingernail scratches, long and curving and worn.

She reached her right hand up, incredibly past his locked arms, and in one motion shoved her pinkie finger into the ring he wore in the pierced eyebrow, the one with frayed threads hanging from it, and jerked downward as hard as she could. She'd torn flesh; and he withered immediately in howls of pain as bright red blood sprayed about them. Kensi was flapping his body as she doubled over and wheezed in.

He howled like a dying animal, "Aiiieeee!!"

She madly lifted her right boot and jammed it into Kensi's face, striking the back of his head against the back wall twice. He reached out and tried to grip her boot; but she already had struck him again with her fingernails, digging into the wounds on his head as if digging for potatoes. She was screaming with ferocity and abandon; and that too was confusing him. He only shook his head and flailed his arms, too dizzy from the head batterings to find his way up and at her. Sylhauna struck him again in his face with the boot; and he slammed viciously into the wall and went still. Knowing it wouldn't last, she quickly leaned forward and over him, his disgusting breath still puffing into her face, and reached back to the floor and jostled an old cracked piece of tile around till it slid apart from the place where it fit. Kensi was starting already to mumble something, slurring his words. The key was still there where she'd placed it perhaps years ago.

Yet she dropped it; and it made a tinking sound as it fell. Kensi's eyes rolled open again. Sylhauna wasted no time at all and clamped her teeth down onto his wounded eyebrow, biting down and trying her level best to rip his flesh. The pain drove him to fury; and he rammed into her, knocking Sylhauna to the floor. It only put her closer to the key though; and she slipped her grasping fingers around it right away. She sat up on her knees and fumbled with the key in the keyhole, having only a blink to work the mechanism, and managed it open. Then, in another fit of fury perhaps recalling that of other days she'd spent in this place, Sylhauna drove her boot again into the street man's face.

Outside the room, as the doorway squeaked open, Lennox watched in shock from the floor where he'd been resting after prying open his cellar door. He'd dragged Ring down to this point and was planning to dump him into the dark cellar and now had the look of someone caught sneaking liquor from the cabinet. Seeing Sylhauna emerge from that toilet wasn't a development he'd foreseen, for didn't he know her?

He at last grinned politely, "'Hauna. You need to understand how scared I've been. How sick I've been."

Sylhauna's eyes were cold; and she didn't watch him long. Across the room, stepping back into the kitchen, she gripped the skillet she'd held earlier and held it up above Lennox's face as if preparing to strike him. His eyes were wide, disbelieving. She pointed to the cellar, motioning for him to get himself down there at once.

"I'm not going. You'll have to-"

Perhaps most who knew her would have expected a hesitation; but Sylhauna really didn't think about it so much. Instead, she swung the skillet and smacked his cheek with a gong-like bell sound. He didn't pass out; but he did roll himself down the creaking wooden steps into the dark cellar below the floor. He was moaning for mercy, dazed and miserable. Kensi offered little resistance as she pulled him by his feet, grunting from the exertion, to the same cellar steps and dumped him in as well.

Kensi was mumbling again, like a drunkard, "Fish. I'll eat your eyes."

Sylhauna kicked the thick door closed, swiveling the latch around to seal it off. Then as if to get distance from what she was doing, she slid a thick bristled rug from near the terrace over the cellar door, concealing it from view as two muffled voices barked from below. It was then as the immediate threat had eased that the terrible dread settled on her; and she sat cross-legged on the floor, hunched over till her forehead rested against her feet and just breathed, her hands clutched tightly to her ears to shut out the thump thump from the cellar and the hum and crashes from the window. She didn't cry.

It took her a long while, long enough for the thumping to die down and her breath to settle, before Sylhauna looked back up at Ring to see him still cold and still. Reluctantly, she gathered her strength and stood. She no doubt wondered at what it could mean that the cellar door was silent now, and perhaps also at what Ring might be like should he awaken after all. Entirely out line, she just straightened a pillow on the chair and some bits of junk strewn on the writing desk like she was cleaning for a visitor. Then she took a look at the medicine packets on Lennox's tray.

The packets each had their own sheathed needle or Pro-Mat dermal transfer patch; and they were arranged in overlapping rows like packaged tea bags. Fumbling as if she knew what she was doing, Sylhauna accidentally flipped two packets off the tray and to the floor, which is when she noticed her fingers twitching. She at last closed her eyes and rose her head as if smelling something.

"Bare feet crossed on a pier, in front of a sparkling river at sunset. Birds are honking." Calmer, Sylhauna gripped something from the tray, perhaps what she'd been looking for, and turned to

Ring. As an afterthought, she slipped into the kitchen and seized the copper skillet just to hold it.

Leaning in close, Sylhauna whispered, "I believe." When nothing happened, she yelled as loud as she could directly into his ear. There was the slightest puff of breath from his nostrils but no sign of awareness. Knowing a man rolls his eyes beneath the lids when dreaming, she peered over his nose and saw nothing. What did that mean? Her scream resurrected the muffled booms and murmurs from the cellar door; but it was too blurred to tell whether it was two voices or one.

Back close, lips to his ear, "I believe." That's when she shoved the adrenalin packet into the side of Ring's neck and squeezed like she was killing a rat, disgusted and not wanting to touch anything but shoving through anyway because she needed the rat dead. When she pulled back, she held the skillet up between them. Then his eyes banged open. They weren't sparkling as they had before; and he held the look of someone uncertain where he was as he noticed the room and the thumping cellar door, then the taint of blood still strawberry red and wet on the side of her mouth from Kensi's brow.

"Sorry." She wiped her mouth with her sleeve and watched him like he was going to eat her.

What was probably the sound of a mog falling whistled and crashed from the terrace; but it was far away and could have been something else. He noticed that, then looked back tellingly to the cellar door, thumping and thumping. When he checked her face again as if to ask what that was, she lightly shrugged, frowning. Unsatisfied, but moving on anyway, Ring struggled to a seated position, shifting his legs over to start to stand. He moved with the aches and favoring reflective of his wounds, grimacing harshly when he fell into a cough. Staring at his feet, he waited out the echoes of the cough, then stood ever so slowly, really not even straightening above a slight bow at that.

She held out the skillet, "How long were you gone?"

He poofed out his lower lip when he saw her weapon, then shuffled into Lennox's bedroom rooting for something. She followed him at a distance, at last seeing it was a cane he sought. He brightened when he found it; and with it, he made for the door gingerly.

Facing the now open door and with her behind him, Ring made a 'come-here' gesture with his other hand and said, "Let's go."

"Where are you going?"

In the hallway now, quickening his step, "The Recorder. Can't do this without him. He'll figure it out pretty soon, once he's not worried about whatever happened at Balcister anymore. We need to go."

Protesting, pointing first at the terrace noises, then the cellar, "But-?"

Ring stopped, "Your old guy is in there too?"

Sylhauna's panic returned, a guilt that seized her. She didn't say anything. Having neither a need nor a patience for her answer, Ring only knocked soundly on the neighboring door, frowning. He banged and banged impatiently, till at last the door cracked inches open and a gray-browed eyeball slipped inside the crack to peer suspiciously at him. It spied Ring, then rolled to Sylhauna, showing the slightest hint of recognition because he or she did a doubletake at Sylhauna's hint of a wave. Then Ring became an entirely different person, illuminating and inflating right before her with unbelievable vigor.

"Call the Watchmen. We're all in big trouble! I mean it. Crazy lunatics crawled up from our cellar, right next to you here! I mean it. We heard weird noises; and some kind of chanting; and suddenly heads popped up. They're crazy!"

The eye was huge now. It was a man's eye, a little more obvious now that the other eye was shifting into view and a big rumpled round nose. He was getting it; but Ring spelled it out anyway. "We managed to lock them back up down there; but there's scraping noises. I'm sure they're digging to your cellar now – call the Watchmen!"

The fellow made a sort of surprised yelp, then slammed the door. That's when Ring turned and shuffled down the hallway, his work done, scraping the cane in staccato bursts as he tried to hurry. Maybe fascinated, perhaps relieved, Sylhauna surrendered and started following him. That was how it was with Ring, one just followed him. He was quiet down the stairs and still grunting

"They tried to kill me. Both of them!"

He only nodded, "You get used to it."

She scooted alongside him, still holding the skillet, "Cris is going to be furious at me. I was here a day; and look what happened to Lennox!"

"You did nothing except be incredibly brave. I need you. It may be a while before I can form long term memories again – and I'm a mess. We'll probably have to steal something to move faster – can you steal things?"

Hurrying, surprised at his speed and leaving his question hanging, "The Recorder, what's he going to figure out?"

Not looking back, "Five visitations, dear heart. And he's the fifth."

20 THE BATTLE OF ALSON

"Since when does Doniphan have enough guts to come in here after us?" Peri stood an arm's reach from the screen alongside her statistics officer, the graphics alive and popping with the datastream — feeds from street cameras and sensors, text from battlefield correspondence parsed into trends, nanoparticle sensors belched into the skies…the whole of it analyzed real-time with living algorithms making optimized strategy of what in other times would be havoc. They were inside a command tank, rolling deep within Alson's streets and surrounded on all sides by a mog and quicktank urban battlegroup. Full panoramic views were displayed about them, giving the feel of windows. Oddly, Stendahl sat cross-legged at their feet, a massive leather-bound book propped open in his lap over which he was leaned in closely as if expecting to see mysteries in its words.

Peri rubbed her chin, frowning up at the thundering mog battle high above them on the gray office buildings, "Amelin, my friend, we need to wrap this up fast. Spenecia - that's where they'll hit. This is all smokescreen. All of it."

Amelin was following a textual analysis that draped suddenly across the streetmap before them, but stumbled against Stendahl's left knee. He was utterly irritated and grimaced, "What is he doing in here?"

She barely glanced over, "Because half of you think he's in charge. That's how civil wars start."

Patting her hand in the air as if smoothing a sand castle, "Don't worry about him. You just figure out what happens if I encircle the Spooks to the northeast with…" She snapped her fingers and glanced over some reporting above and to the left of the street map, "…Blade Watch. All the way to the bridges. Run the scenario."

As Amelin commenced swiping his hands across the tables of data, Peri folded her arms and frowned back up at the battle above them. Suddenly, she turned and touched her index and middle fingers to a moving icon which indicated one of her quicktanks on a street corner nearby – a viewbox appeared across the map swirling with the jumble and smoke of what the tank's pilot saw.

She gritted her teeth, "Clain, you get in the soup now or I'll have you drinking gold too! Get moving – they're headed east and south now, possibly in the direction of Bethani. I need you."

Peri touched another icon, then a third, watching the harried first hand views of those in mortal danger in turn as she proceeded. Amelin stepped back from his results, unimpressed with whatever he saw. When she glanced at the table of data, she agreed and frowned at him as if the probabilities were his fault.

"Am, what do I pay you for? Make something happen – you understand me?!"

Holding her hands out in desperation, "Why do I not have Black Fire support here? Morro, do you see what's happening above me?"

"Yes, ma'am." The tinny voice sounded from nowhere.

"Then bring it in tighter."

Her frown was deeper as Peri watched the fierce combat above them, dark plumes swelling and lilting in a carnival of devastation. She was trying to position quicktanks as an ambush from street level and drive the Doniphan attackers into the trap with mogs. Unfortunately, the battle was spreading too rapidly; and Black Fire was swelling out of control in pockets making routes unavailable.

Watching a massive ebony plume, "Why would they bring such an abomination into my city?"

Amelin nodded, "Because it works. Their distortion is set to…almost nothing. I mean…this is why it's illegal."

The two of them winced as the view above them blotted in multiple places, as if a pot of clotted ink had been kicked. A mog went off the building from inside one of the swells and into the open air, soaring down to the street.

"Ave, I want a crossfire on this guy and I want it now." Peri pointed like Ave from his thundering tank could see her. "Bogey seventeen…the squirrely one that keeps popping around that walk! Break away now!"

Amelin looked at her, "He's our protection."

Ignoring that, Peri returned to her street map, "I want a hard line of battlesuits…" She drew a line with her finger across a major thoroughfare, where carnivals and masked fairs occurred in early summer. "…here. At Carnabie. I'm talking Choke Watch, First and Fifth Squadrons, and…something with big guns…"

Amelin's forehead crumpled, concerned with her orders. She hesitated, thinking; and her eyes widened when she thought of the guns she wanted, "…The Hag." Peri pointed at Amelin as if it needed emphasis, "I want The Hag there."

"That's pretty concentrated. You sure that's wise?"

She shouted, "A hard line at Bethani! Nothing gets through. Acknowledge!"

"Choke Watch, aye."

"Fifth, aye."

"First, aye. Ma'am."

Peri's eyes were angry, irritated at the loss of containment when Doniphan should never have gotten this far. They shouldn't even have been able to get into the city. She was further annoyed when the final acknowledgement didn't happen.

"Mallow, I told you to get to Bethani." A pause, after which she touched her two fingers to the fat icon moving along to the south of her, opening up a view of smoke and explosions. The vessel was in a harsh engagement. "Mallow, break away now. You hear me?! Mallow!"

There was a long pause, an uncomfortable one, then, "Hag, aye."

Peri's eyes held fire in them, "You don't let them past you, understand? Nothing gets past you!"

Another pause, "Ooh rah, ma'am."

She hardly had time to fold her arms again before a massive black plume flared overhead; and two mog vehicles locked in combat fell off the wall and started falling directly above them. There was a vicious crash upon collision; and Peri and Amelin jumped back in reflex as if they'd been standing on the street itself. The two of them hesitated nervously, eyeing one another, gauging whether the Black Fire that came with the vessels would eat into their war engine. It was a horrible silence; and much of their view was choked out by the wreckage.

Peri glanced down to Stendahl, still reading his old book with his finger tracking down each line. He felt her watching, because he looked up at her, his deep green eyes flaring in the tanklight.

"The man with the horrible name stands alone, victim of his own reputation."

Her eyes squinted, ever curious at this strange remnant of the Old Man and his family. Then quite suddenly, the dark wreckage was swept to the side, brightening the compartment somewhat.

"You're all good, commander." A voice sounded at the same time as the coarse and hardened face of a battlesuited soldier appeared in the ceiling above them, giving a quick salute with the suit's wide arm. The image flickered spottily. She cast her eyes once again to Stendahl, who'd returned to his book as if he'd said nothing to her. Amelin had no patience for it and quickly called for her attention. His voice was almost squeaking in his urgency.

"You're taking too much firepower out of the loop. They're spiraling out in multiple directions – what good is this hard line of yours even if it holds?"

She gestured to the street map, "Look. They came with no supply line. No reinforcements. That line holds; and it gives me a plow. Then I start sweeping them like mice into the guns. We have to stop them somewhere. It happens at Bethani."

Peri tapped her fingers harshly to another fat icon on the swirling map opening another window into fire and corpses and wreckage, "Tanker 77, where are you going?"

The bright green icon was drifting to the west in a jagged pattern, unresponsive. "Tanker 77! Respond or you will be disclaimed. Where are you going?"

When she saw there would be no response and the vehicle was to continue along its way out of battle and beyond those who needed it, Peri shouted, "Chaselord, Tanker 77 is disclaimed. Burn them down."

The voice over the radio was business-like and calm, "Chaselord aye."

Amelin raised his voice, "What are you doing? What if his comms are down?"

She only pointed at him, "Not now. You just plot the optimal space for my ambush."

"How about a better scenario – like what's happening south of us now that you've pulled out Blade Watch?"

Harshly, with no patience for him, "Stick to the numbers, geek. I've got this."

Stendahl gently closed his book and stood, idly stuffing his hand into his pockets but saying nothing. She glanced at him, then back to the map dismissively. Amelin watched his face a moment, as if looking for him to join a side in the discussion, but received nothing. Peri was starting to pace, once again stopping to tap various icons to view the battle from the soldiers' perspectives, calling now and again out to some with minor direction or encouragement.

It was said of Peri during the War of the Rupture as massive imperial cities collapsed in flames that she had sisters in her pocket. Flitting about the front lines of chaotic battles like a dragonfly, she would appear in places as if there were several of her; and it engendered a fierce loyalty and devotion few even senior commanders could match. Many one-eyed and limping soldiers for the times afterwards told stories around their own dinner tables of being left for dead and abandoned, 'but not by the Lady Commander…no, aye, one of her was always in for a scrap'. It's possible she'd have been more at ease driving one of the tanks or climbing a high rise; but here in the command tank at her map and analyses, the Marshal, now again the Lady Commander, was very much alive. She stepped to her left to more closely see Bethani, pulling her fingers apart on the screen to zoom in the streetmap. Most of the forces she'd marshaled for the area were arriving and forming up.

"All watches and squadrons, possible crypto breach. Radio silence till further notice. Radio silence till further notice."

Amelin grimaced, "Why did you do that?"

She only grumbled and zoomed in closer. The Hag was arriving as well; and the forces had formed an arc in the crossroads there, a wide crossroad with brick streets and often decorated with sparkling banners and floating lantern decorations. It was a place of artists and observatories, with a wide canal lined with old trees beneath which teenagers would shade themselves on hot summer days.

Peri inhaled nervously, blowing her cheeks out as she exhaled. Standahl was entirely silent, only watching her and the map. "Did you get my ambush site yet?"

He nodded, "Yeah. Two stages. Vangeline, then Auberdon to the southeast."

"Quantum crypto – text it to them."

As Amelin leaned in and tapped his message, Stendahl casually watched as if trying to read a newspaper over the fellow's shoulder. It was more of a pastime to him than fierce combat, it seemed. Peri was tense and lost in a hundred skirmishes at that moment, entirely ignoring the Talgo beside her.

"Mallow, don't screw this up." She wasn't speaking to anyone, only herself and perhaps to the ghost of the Old Man who occasionally taught such strategies with salt and spice shakers on his feast table. An uncomfortable silence blanketed them after this, as her pieces were slipping into place and they awaited an outcome. If the line held, then it would be a turn of the battle and something for history.

"What if the line doesn't hold? Are you willing to pull more guns out of the mix to try again?"

She ignored him and instead touched a finger to the Hag's icon, seeing for herself what Mallow and his light crew saw on that carnival street with Doniphan mogs swarming ahead and gathering. Peri's neck was tight; and her finger was just barely shaking.

Quite uncommonly known of Peri, while still very young in her career and a junior officer with but a handful of men in her division, the troop landing ship upon which she served, her first ship actually, was attacked. Every officer but herself was killed whether through smoke or fire; and the wide-eyed boys left behind held trust to her cold commands and quick battle decisions. They went through much together, losing no more men and returning safely; but it was the homecoming so many of them would keep secret afterwards. It was the homecoming as the pier came into view with its crowds of family and friends waving when the boys went to find their missing commander shaking and crying in the bathroom stall, staring at the deck. Many of the same boys served the rest of their careers under the Lady Commander and never told that story.

"We can't afford to move more, Peri. Mallow has to hold the line or else abandon this strategy."

She glanced at Amelin, then back to the map and viewbox. It was silent again as the mogs approached, then Mallow's voice returned.

"Commander! We have a-!"

With ferocity, Peri engaged the comms, "Mallow, repeat your last! Hag!"

The icon representing the gunship began to drift, not even in a stable direction. At the moment of collision as Doniphan attackers were arriving, the Hag was drifting out of position.

Amelin's voice betrayed his concern, "He broke radio silence…"

There was a flame in Peri's eyes, "Hag! Get back in position! Get in position or so help me, I'll kill every last one of you and your families. Respond!"

Amelin looked at her face then, perhaps trying to gauge her threat's truth and deciding she meant it after all. The view window was showing the Hag to be headed for a sidewalk, perhaps a shop window – there were papier mache mannekins staged in a macabre dance scene from preparations for the holiday, colorful and bright but haunting now with leering smiles and crisp wrinkled eyes staring.

"Mallow…mark status!"

She widened the view to see the street map again, timing the approach of the enemy vessels. They were upon them and under fire already. The viewbox maybe showed the shop window in pieces and the gunship wedged inside. It was difficult to tell. Peri closed her eyes and bowed her head in disappointment, resting a moment to try and stoke her fires again to recover. A shirtless soldier had crawled from the vessel with blood across his mouth and chest and on his hands, and was pressing his grinning and smeared face into the camera – a huge bloodshot eye swelled to fill the window.

Amelin spoke first, "Mallow's dead. The Red Witch got to his gunner." Hesitating, feeling it important to state what she was thinking already, "Your entire fleet is compromised."

Peri dropped her head further, steadying herself. She didn't need to hear this from him.

"Any one of your ships could go rogue at any moment."

She rubbed her palm harshly against her forehead, thinking. After blinking a couple of times, she looked back up to the streetmap, seeing the swarm piling up. Peri was perhaps going through options and strategies, recalling experiences like this which could offer insight into a way forward yet discounting them all one by one. Her face showed abandonment. Stendahl stepped closer to the map silently. It was bad; and it felt that way.

Peri at last lifted her face, tired and looking older somehow, "All right. Here's what we're going to do…"

Quite suddenly and unexpectedly, a shout came from the comms, "Surface, boys! Get up in the light o' day and start poppin' some heads! You heard me, you soft fatties. Surface and open fire!"

It was a familiar voice; and Peri's eyes widened at its sound yet not in joy, more of anger and a striking of horror. She charged the map again and touched a finger to one of the Choke Watch quicktanks only just in time to watch a camouflaged submersible arise from the canal in a boiling torrent of whitewater, firing glowing slugs of lightning into the sky like a runaway firework.

Amelin surged, "Datastream shows mini-subs rising from the canals in several places throughout the city, with a mass at Bethani."

Peri pointing at the swirling neon screen before her with the face of someone terrified and falling through clouds, "That's Velo Boneghost!"

There was laughter from the comms, maniacal and eerie laughter. Peri nodded, certain now who it was, "What's he doing out of prison?! In my subs?!"

She looked at Stendahl furiously, "We executed his son! He's a traitor and a killer! What have you done!?"

Stendahl waited to answer, as if giving her a chance to understand had she not yet what would become of Peri's line at Bethani and the entire tide of battle now with these additional and well placed forces, "I did what you did not."

Amelin uncomfortably interjected, not liking the expression upon the Lady Commander's face, "They were in prison cells, Peri. It's unlikely the Red Witch could get to them."

The war engine went softly quiet for a time as the three of them watched the battle play out further, as the swarm began to cluster tighter and start moving in the direction of Vangeline Park where an ambuscade awaited. The line was holding; and the plow was working. Peri at last put her eyes on the young Talgo there beside her, looking at him with wonder and fascination, perhaps with anger. Loyalty to that family was deep and strange and not the sort of thing people of those times would be able to explain if asked. Stendahl picked his lip idly, only watching her from the side of his eyes without looking directly at her. He hummed as the mogs crashed and danced as if he were listening to the conflict as a majestic song soaring with violins and crashing with cymbals. At last he grinned strangely and turned to face her.

"Peri, I am the new Judge of Alson; and you are Commander of my fleet." It was a bold claim to the title, not at all legal or understandable apart from the family into which he was born.

Amelin's surprise caught his throat; and he made an involuntary grunt of surprise, quickly looking to his Commander to find her reaction. She would have been upholding her duties and pledge to the city were she to have dragged him into a prison or put him on a martial law trial for seizing the Judgeship without the mandate. Instead, she watched him as one would a dangerous storm best not viewed at all yet enthralling for its darkness and might. He was calm and held the tone of someone acknowledging a light rain.

Amelin was lost in this, "You can't just-"

"You will maintain Alson under lockdown with everyone in their homes and proceed to Spenecia with every Watch you have, leaving behind two quicktank squadrons under the command of the Chaselord."

Stendahl's expression was fierce, electric. His eyes were piercing as he assumed control of the room, as if he were swelling in size and importance right there before them. Incredibly, very much a point of discussion for historians to come in character studies and debates, Peri only nodded. She nodded and gave him control of the entire city and the Judgeship. Like that.

"Instruct him to reactivate the suicide chambers throughout Alson — all of them; and make it known through the patrol loudspeakers and the news."

At that, both Amelin and Peri grimaced with disgust, having no doubt hoped those nightmares were never to return to service. Perhaps stranger than this, it was then Stendahl's face turned vicious like a snarling hound, "And inform him that before nightfall every Rauchka among our fleet is to be hanged. No delays or trials. Hang them all."

Peri's eyes squinted, even more confused at this new turn, "Rauchka? I have good men who are Rauchka!"

Stendahl only looked at her imperiously a moment, with older and more soulless eyes than to which she was accustomed, "Hang them, Commander. And don't let anyone past Spenecia."

When he placed his head in his hands like a man enduring pain, she glanced again to the streetmap and flashing battle histograms and data, then back to the young Talgo, "I'll stop them at Spenecia or die there."

He nodded though failing to withdraw his head from his hands, "And Boneghost I will go to the Augur."

Peri's eyebrow rose curiously, "It was Cassian who hired the Red Witch. He'll be the one at Spenecia."

Stendahl spoke again from within his now whitening hands, "He didn't hire them. There is a third hand playing the strings; and as always, the Rauchka are betraying us."

"How do you know that? Sure enough to hang them all?!"

He turned his eyes up to her as if to burn her down with them, exploding, "Because that's all they're capable of!" The suddenness of his retort shocked her.

"And what's the Augur going to tell you?" Peri's voice was weary, drained and compliant. She'd heard this Talgo hatred of the Rauchka before and knew of the Old Man's long and ugly history with them.

Stendahl gritted his teeth angrily, his stare wicked, "Nothing at all. I won't even ask a question."

Peri pulled her head back from him as if stepping away from a fire, seeing something more now coming over the young Talgo – something not to be near.

He faced her, "Every time there's a revolution, the Augur is at its heart; and I tire of that. And so I will end it."

"What's happened to you?"

"You will kill our attackers; and the Chaselord will kill our betrayers. The lunatics will kill themselves. And when the one behind all of it is laughing in his circle, thinking himself phantom enough to escape more killing, I will put an end to all of it."

Stendahl stood taller, towering over Peri and looking for all the world like an avenging spirit, "We were violated; and I will have vengeance. And I will have a lasting settlement to cower those who pick bones from the ashes of our violaters: a terrible settlement to stand for generations against anyone who'd plot again to assault these mountains. I am the Judge; and I will slaughter and destroy and never leave from bleeding them till all who'd cry mercy know there is to be none."

He looked at her with a terrifying familiarity, "I'm going to the Augur; and I'm going to kill it."

21 A NEW WARMASTER

The maintenance shop smelled of old grease and acetone, draped about its battleship gray walls with dusty sheaves and belting, random electronics, and odd bits of ProMat frozen in jumbled geometries. Thessany was shoving his head into the machine belly of a tornado engine when Cassian walked in. He only glanced up to see who'd entered, then without acknowledging his Marshal, stuck his greasy head back into the steel cavity and among the flights and cabling therein.

Cassian watched a moment, "Don't you have people for that?"

The Twister Corps Commander was quiet a moment, then, "We can't all wander aimlessly. Shouldn't you be running the government or something – or does Grebel do all your thinking for you?"

"I need to talk to you."

"Talk."

"Get your head out of there. I have to face you for this."

"Bot in-feed chutes don't straighten themselves, Talgo. This is where I entrain them. If that doesn't work, I can't control the twisters and they fizzle out. You ought to know something about fizzling out." He chuckled to himself.

Cassian held his temper, "I'm going to name a Warmaster."

Silence. Thessany stayed inside the cavity, though likely he stopped working to listen. There hadn't been a Warmaster since the final days of the War of the Rupture. It was a position of incredible authority and importance, seizing control of a nation's entirety of resources for war; and whoever inherited this title now was following the Old Man himself in succession.

"It will be effective immediately; and the new Warmaster will be commanding all the forces at Spenecia as well as forces arriving next week from the Steel Horde and Vendle."

Thessany whistled, "Talgo, how big a freaking war are you trying to start?"

"It's coming unplugged now, Commander. The Frost Troops and fleets from two other provinces are joining Wentic's forces. All the jealousies and grudges are coming back out. This is the sort of thing I was worried about; but it's getting way too late to stop it now."

"Right." He grunted as he pried a steel bar against something.

"Thessany, get out of that machine and face me."

Taking his time, Thessany did at last withdraw from the cavity and slowly slide off his thick work gloves. He rubbed his palm against the side of his head, either straightening a shock of hair or wiping grease, then leaned back casually against the engine, grinning.

"I'll be your hacksaw. You don't have to beg – it would be unseemly for you."

Cassian watched him unpleasantly, as if tasting something sour and not to be swallowed, "You're not my first choice."

"And you're not mine, rich boy. But your babysitter isn't here, so…"

After a moment, Cassian took a few steps toward the vortex engine, its gargantuan mouth worn in streaks. He couldn't bring himself to say something, so he was working up to it and occupying himself in idleness while he did so. There were still some splattered wads of bots stuck fast inside the cavity, clots of computronium goo running software to sense wind speed and direction, to emit millions of tiny puffs for course and temperature correction, and all of it in a fiercely complex network designed on a large scale to sustain and guide tornadoes in combat. Cassian wiped a smear of it across his pants leg; and it sparkled as it tried to boot up.

"I want to know what you think about the Salt Mystic. Is she coming back? Is she somehow behind all this?" He turned to look again at Thessany, maybe to gauge his first blush reaction. Thessany grimaced in frustration.

"You're a clown."

Cassian gritted his teeth and spun to stare the Commander down, "I'm your Marshal; and you will show me respect!!"

Thessany frowned, "You've always been a clown. The Old Man should've just picked one of you and handed the whole thing over rather than leaving us this mess. I mean…we're rolling to battle…right now. And you're clucking about fairy tales and nonsense."

He held out his hands as if pleading, "Honestly, who cares – one way or the other? If you mope around like you always do and give the bumpkins time to think about it, they might all switch sides! I would. A better idea, you embarrassing gilt-headed flimsy – how about you strike everywhere fast enough to make them dizzy and leave them wondering who's sticking with you? They'll be too scared to even talk to each other. That's the sort of strategy the Old Man would have put to it."

Cassian's eyes were growing cold and vicious, "And you two were pretty close, yeah?"

"I never met him, Talgo. All I've ever heard is he was a scheming, backstabbing liar who'd slice your ear off if he could sell it. But I'd give a year's salary if he was here instead of you."

With a terrible elephantine shout, Cassian rushed into Thessany, knocking him into a bulkhead. His first punch entirely missed Thessany's chin; but the second, weaker punch contacted him in the neck at the adam's apple. Although choking for breath, Thessany drew up his wrist to block another strike, then drove a knee furiously into the Talgos stomach. It was clear the Twister Corps Commander hadn't expected such a reaction from his Marshall and had been surprised by the sucker punches; but he was more seasoned in such situations.

Cassian tried to sieze Thessany by his hair and drive his head into the wall; but Thessany slapped both hands, palm open, onto the Talgos ears as if clapping. The sudden pressure change and pain froze and disoriented Cassian long enough for Thessany to drive his knuckles into Cassian's left eye socket. It sent him falling backwards and to the deck where Thessany drove a boot into his stomach further depleting his breath. Thessany swung his next kick a wide arc into Cassian's side, then fell on him like a predator bird.

Following two more punches to his mouth, Cassian suddenly shielded himself by placing his hands over his face. When Thessany tried to peel them apart, Cassian managed to strike like a snake and twisted his hands around, jamming his thumbs into Thessany's eyes deeply. The Commander tried to break free, to slam his fists into Cassian's forearms to break the pressure; but he couldn't push away. At last, Thessany rolled off to relieve the pain; and when he did so, Cassian contacted a bloodying punch to Thessany's lip. Following on from this, the two went at each other shouting and hurling insults another moment, with Thessany slowly gaining insurmountable advantage. Then when Thessany was kneeling over an exhausted Cassian, poising to drive his knee into the Talgos injured side again, bashing the Talgos face viciously again and again and drawing thin splatters of bright red blood, there was a tap on Thessany's shoulder.

Grinning a wide nightmare grin, an Interrogator stood watching the Twister Corps Commander, his ghostly head cocked to one side curiously. This was of the sort who'd executed Revin, of the sort in common use in the Old Man's time. He was not chained. Thessany's reaction was immediate and one of a man avoiding plague-soaked rags, jerking back to seek distance.

"What is that doing here?! He's not chained. Talgo! What's wrong with you?!" Thessany was scooting backwards in a panic.

Cassian sluggishly arose from the deck and wiped his bleeding lower lip, at once watching Thessany's fright with very little relish. The Interrogator was ignoring Cassian and stepping closer to Thessany, ever grinning and with eyes as blank as fresh paper. Thessany was backed against the bulkhead at that point, desperate to be away from this maniac and his wicked clown smile. His eyes darted across and about the Interrogator, looking for weapons and watching his flicking hands.

"They don't stop, Talgo! Once you give them a name. Get some men in here, now!!" His voice squeaked in its intensity for at that moment, Thessany truly feared for his soul.

Quite suddenly, like sparks popping from a fire, an inexpressible joy shone in the Interrogator's eyes. He inhaled sharply and clenched his fists. Thessany slid along the bulkhead rapidly, still seeking distance.

"How could you take him off the chains?! Don't you know what happened to your mother?! Call him off!"

Cassian smiled thinly, "You're my new Warmaster. I'll see more respect from you moving forward. Yes?"

Thessany gestured to the advancing Interrogator, "You gave him my name. You gave him my face, Talgo. They don't stop. What are you gonna do about him?"

Cassian wiped the pooling blood from his lip again, "Warmaster, that's just something for you to worry about. Honestly, I'm not sure I care what you do anymore. I'm exhausted with all of you. You want to take Spenecia? You want to set Alson on fire? Have fun. It's yours."

Thessany glanced to Cassian, "You're leaving?"

Grimacing suddenly from pain in his side, "I'm leaving. You and the rest of them can sleep at night thinking you have it all settled as long as we have bigger tanks. Then when some country girl in rag clothes starts ranting visions claiming to be the Salt Mystic coming back and you're surrounded by fanatics looking to erase you from the Record, remember how you busted my lip and called me a clown and wished the Old Man was here."

"You're going to the Augur."

"That's right. We don't just need more firepower. We need answers. Blowhards like you always forget little details that come back and bite you in the end. That's why I'm the Marshal and you're the guy sniveling in a corner like a little girl."

Thessany frowned, wiped sweat from his forehead, "How many more of these things did you let out?"

Cassian shook his head, "Wentic will be there too. I know him. It's the first place he'll go. Maybe he and I will just kill each other there and save all of you the trouble."

"I'm my own man, Talgo. If we do this, I make it happen on my own, no puppet strings or dancing for you or your weirdo family. What about your boy? I'm not responsible for your boy."

Talgo hesitated, pondering. The Interrogator glanced up at him seeking direction. When Talgo failed to acknowledge him, the lunatic looked back at Thessany as if he were a piece of steaming steak, then stepped into a corner quietly though never again breaking his stare or his horrible smile.

"Yeah." Cassian stared intently at the deck as if he'd been asked a question of much importance, "Yeah. Someone has to be responsible."

Thessany pointed at Cassian accusingly, "Fantine'll watch him; but you put him on the battlefield. Not me."

"Someone has to be responsible…"

Thessany straightened himself and centerlined his shirt, dusted off his pants leg, "That's right. I'll do my duty; and I'll win Spenecia. But if something happens to him, it's on you. Just want that clear. It's on you."

It was awkward and calm for a moment while Cassian nodded thoughtfully and stared downward. After some time, he turned his eyes back to Thessany showing them to be bloodshot and perhaps watering. "You know…he was born for it; and he'll flourish. You probably agree; but I guess…" Cassian spoke slowly, evaluating every word as if it were to be engraved and therefore needed to be of substance. "…I guess, if I were to be the new Warmaster, the question that would be whispering in my ear…is whose side will he really be on?"

It was then, the War Recorder stepped into the room followed quickly by Admiral Phryne and Oblave. Another small fellow was with them, one dressed like Rhodomontane and who wore about his left eye a device with which to record something. The lunatic Interrogator watched them silently, calmer now and breathing less intently. Thessany at once brushed off his pants leg again and tried to slick back his hair, for he recognized what was about to happen.

"It's about time, right?" His voice wasn't convincingly assured as he'd maybe hoped; and Thessany was still catching his breath from the adrenalin of his tussle with Cassian and from seeing the horrid Interrogator. Phyrne's expression was of urgency as if there wasn't time for this, as if she needed to be elsewhere. Oblave coughed and wiped his forearm against his mouth, perhaps a little excited to be present for such a thing.

"Let's get moving, Cassian. I have a fleet underway." Phryne placed herself in position opposite the grinning Interrogator and framing the Recorder, Thessany and Cassian. She frowned with distaste at the Interrogator in the corner, watching them. The little fellow with the eye-camera started circling slowly, though cautiously avoiding the Interrogator. They were each settling into a ceremony, hallowed and honored for centuries and of great importance, though Thessany was probably not anyone's ideal for the person at its center.

Cassian nodded reluctantly and motioned to the Interrogator but addressed the cameraman, "Keep him out of your shot."

Then he looked at Thessany as if he were a firing squad, "Twister Corps Commander Meridian Thessany, defender of Tanith, do you seek to be Warmaster?" The tone and wording were of ritual, familiar to those present.

With a calming smirk, settling himself for the moment, "No, I do not."

Cassian nodded again, "Good. It is to be required of you then. May your Record be selfless. Meridian Thessany, defender of Tanith, do you fear dying in the causes you will uphold as Warmaster?"

"Yes, I do."

"Good. Then you will be prudent. May your Record embody wisdom. Meridian Thessany, defender of Tanith, will you show mercy and brotherhood to your enemies should they run from you or lie in defeat?"

"No. I will not."

"Good. Then our children will not fear the shadows. May your Record bring terror. Meridian Thessany, stand solemn." Cassian took a step towards him, fishing from a thigh pocket a small vial of a clear liquid that shimmered inside its glass. Phryne and Oblave softly gripped Thessany's wrists, which he offered willingly, understanding this part of the script for assignment of Warmaster. Each of them had studied this in school and knew it well, though it had changed somewhat from its early origins.

As Cassian lifted the vial above his head, Thessany glanced again to the Interrogator, "What about him? Somebody's got to watch him while this happens."

Ignoring him, Cassian continued raising the vial and with its soft aperture revealed it to be a small eye dropper. He touched his left hand to Thessany's chin, guiding his head upwards and tilted back. Each of them stood silently while three drops apiece of the liquid went into each of Thessany's eyes. It may have burned, or perhaps he was reacting to the Interrogator's presence while he could no longer watch; but Thessany blinked harshly several times and shook his head like a dog trying to dry himself.

"I mean it, Phryne. Watch him." As they each observed him, Thessany continued shaking his head and looking around, blinking. They knew his vision was enshrouding already and perhaps wonderered what the scene looked like.

Cassian replaced the vial in his pocket and stepped backwards, "Defender of Tanith, do you know what you are to see now?"

"Yeah, yeah. Just do what you have to, okay?"

Cassian smacked his face, drawing a sudden and vicious defensive posture from the Commander, "Follow it or we're done here! If you can't respect the history, you can't respect the land. Follow it."

"Don't touch me again." He was blinking again, occasionally widening his eyes as if to clear them.

Talgo acknowledged the cameraman, "Edit that out."

Then back to Thessany, "Do you know what you are to see?"

It was clear at that point that Thessany was suddenly looking at something else, a scene and a world far removed from the arsenal Ship maintenance garage in which they stood. He surveyed the room as if it weren't there and was scanning to an invisible horizon all about him something that was awful and of significance. He was quiet and no longer smug or confident. What he saw left him struck and humbled, perhaps like someone first sitting quietly in a very old and echoing cathedral. Thessany had looked slowly all about himself, wide-eyed and fearful of what it was he saw.

Softly, "I didn't know it was this bad."

More urgently and louder, "Do you know what you are to see?"

A long, awkward pause, "I see the dead. I see the rubble. I see what the last Warmaster did that I might be free."

"Look then. And do likewise. Will you recite the General's Blade?"

Thessany licked his lips, still awed by what he saw – and disgusted, "May need a little help with that."

Cassian clenched his teeth, "The loyalty of the people…"

Thessany turned again, perhaps disbelieving the horror of what he saw, or maybe anxious to absorb its worth before it faded, "The loyalty of the people is the sharpness of the general's blade."

He hesitated, thinking and still seeing things far away and long-since gone, "I will not dull this blade in open wars without end nor by incautious pouring of my nation's blood. I will not seize it to turn against my overseers and take the homeland for myself, as if a man were not surrendering his soul for such desires. I uhhh…"

"I will fear the people…"

He nodded vacantly, "I will fear the people that I might not bring them pain worse than that from which I defend them and that I may know when to lay down what I have been given. And I will be vigilant towards those who rise against us to know why there must be a blade at all."

Thessany barely waited long enough for Cassian to take his cue, "Say it, Talgo."

A long pause, "You stand as Warmaster. Do your duty."

When he'd finished, they each stood quietly while Thessany surveyed the phantom and vanished landscape before him. It was unlike Meridian Thessany to be without words; but he saw a world that stretched to the horizon with rotting dead and twisted machinery…and of still-living soldiers mangled and straining against the silence. The panoramic was known to have been taken following one of the last battles in the War of the Rupture when the great cemetery which had once belonged to this portion of the ritual was scorched and cratered. None born later could imagine such devastation and loss on this kind of scale without seeing it firsthand like this. That was of course the point.

At last, the new Warmaster began rubbing his eyes sharply and shaking his head again. The imagery was wearing off; and he was anxious that it do so.

"All right, gawkers. I said your poem; and I watched your eyeball thing. Get back to work; and let's make something happen. I need to see division reports on these folks from Vendle and the Steel Horde, Oblave. Get me whatever you can find."

He contorted his neck far to the left, then to the right in an attempt to crack it and relieve its soreness, and again rubbed his chin and lip where Cassian had drawn blood, "Phryne, you still here?"

"Yes, Warmaster."

He smiled at the address, still not quiet seeing her but looking in her direction nonetheless, "You and I need to draw up how we'll enter Spenecia. My twisters are gonna get close. You need to be ready for that. How about meeting me in the dome when I'm done here?"

She nodded as she turned to leave, always in a hurry, "Yes, Warmaster."

With his eyesight still occluded, Thessany listened to the shuffling and footsteps as at least some of them left him. He turned again to face the corner where the terrible Interrogator had earlier huddled. He called to Cassian, suddenly uncertain if he was gone as well.

"Talgo, when are you leaving?"

There was no answer. Listening closely, Thessany leaned forward to reach for his right ankle. "How about you, freak? You still here, grinning like an idiot? I still can't see…why don't you do something? Take a little bite?"

The tiny puff of a breath was what he'd needed; and when the Interrogator took it, Thessany followed the sound, withdrawing a knife from inside his boot and piercing it clean through the Interrogator's windpipe to the wall behind him. No struggle. No hesitation. The horrible man just slid down like melting ice on a window, spewing blood and gurgling.

Thessany pulled the knife and ran its sides along his thigh to clean them, then leaned against his extended left hand onto the wall where the Interrogator had stood. It was beyond the wall of course, that which he saw as he steadied himself: the fields of the vision.

"I didn't know it was this bad."

22 THE BELL TOWER

Cristoffel and Misling were running, seeking shelter within a
colonnade which was part of a narrow aisled marketplace and was
now caked in white and blue dust that swirled and prominenced in
the wake of their flight like vampire smoke. When they were hidden
from view and breathless, Misling turned to see the haunting Red
Witch bell tower, its twisted denizens still moving awkwardly and
without purpose. From the distance, it was difficult to make out
individuals within the tower, for there must have been more than
thirty, nestled together and doubled around one another, stacked and
laying and clutching, ramped in filth and urine. Four motionless men
stood at its pinnacle, arched toward one another and holding the
heavy black bell between them.

"'They'll hear you breathing'" Misling whispered. Cristoffel
turned to see his expression, trying to understand what he knew. His
tone was different; and she could tell it was a quote.

His eyes left the mysterious tower and drifted across the
rubblefield, with its rippling crater and flotsam of steel; and he knew
what this meant. There were no rescuers, no machinery hauling
wreckage away…no one at all apart from the tortured souls stacked
upon one another. She patiently let him look for a short while, then
tapped his arm and whispered.

"Are we done here?"

"What if he is one of them?" The Recorder pointed to the tower.

Cristoffel closed her eyes, perhaps having hoped he wouldn't ask
that question, "That's even worse. What are you gonna do – shoot
him? We need to go back. Or maybe I'll put it this way: I'm going
back. I did my part. You can't say I didn't."

He looked at her, "Lennox Weshire is a weight upon you. Leave
him."

She rubbed her eyes, "Don't go over there. Don't."

With that, Misling took steps toward the desolated plaza and toward the tower, his breath shallow and quick and the carbine shaking in his hands.

Hesitating, then following, "Keep your distance, okay?"

He locked eyes with her; and in a look showed his gratitude for coming with him. Then, gripping the carbine with whitening fingers, the Recorder advanced to the tower and ever slowly came to within a few paces of it. The two of them were at last close enough to see individual faces, some pale and stuck like plaster masks and others twisting and darting their eyes back and forth. Misling frowned with determination, looking for the old man's familiar pink nose and laughing eyes.

Beside him at once was the little girl from the barley fields, pointing. She vanished away when he turned to look.

"What? What are you looking at?"

Misling only eyed the plaza immediately behind him to gauge her reality, whether someone had slipped around him. Seeing nothing, he turned again to the tower to see eyes upon him. Here and there, along its disgusting levels eyes were turned his way; and babbling whispers sounded. Standing this close, he could see how those on the tower were intertwined, contorted and interlocked in impossible complexity and forming a solid structure with no visible gaps. Its base was wide, sharing the weight of those on the upper levels across perhaps a third of them. Anyone would have been drained of strength with quaking and pained muscles following only a short time in such a formation, yet here they had been for possibly hours. It was a terror to see.

Misling was intent and focused, hunched over like a back-country tracker as he made his way around them, awkwardly gripping the carbine as if he feared dropping it. Cristoffel also surveyed the surrounding buildings and alleyways, sidewalks and corners, looking for those who might seek to watch or sneak. After uncomfortably noticing Misling was within arm's reach of the tower, she grabbed a pinch of his shirt and tugged him back a step. He allowed it; but he failed to turn and look at her as the strangers' faces upon the tower fully absorbed his mind. Then he stopped suddenly and went entirely pale, quaking.

"No. No. No. No." The Recorder's voice was broken, lifeless. He stopped, disheartened to an extent difficult to imagine or describe. Then he closed his eyes to steady himself.

Cristoffel touched his arm, the one opposite her carbine, and stepped closer to see what it was he saw. With a cluster of dirty faces in a mass, it was difficult to see the one upsetting him. She sought an older man, with a kind face. Contorted and tortured as many there were, it may have been any number of them. She took another step towards Misling, perhaps setting herself to take from him the carbine and end this unnatural and vile thing that was happening to the Recorder's sponsor…to spare him what was to come. Misling opened his eyes again; and she followed his stare.

"Selisa." He spoke her name. With the suddenness and shock of a loud pop in a fire, the bright white eyes of a woman with filth and ash on her rough cheeks twisted to look at them. Her head was pressed into the chest and thighs of others upon the tower; and her expression was wild and disconnected, hallucinating.

Selisa spoke, her voice that of a horrible nightmare monster, "Have you come to ring the bell?"

Misling hesitated, unwilling to respond and lost in his despair, so Cristoffel answered – perhaps unwisely.

"No."

Whispering and a cackle shot through the tower, contagious. All eyes were on them.

Cristoffel leaned a little closer to the strange woman, "Do you want me to help you down?"

Selisa grinned, sprouting pink teeth, "Climb and join us."

Cristoffel frowned, growing colder. There was a feel of attraction to the tower somehow, as if it really did make sense to settle into a place there somewhere…to stay warm and protected like a sheltered hearth at winter.

"Climb and join us."

Two others whispered, "Climb and join us." Then whispers spread across one side, up to one of the bell holders. Selisa's filthy hand struck out like a lizard's tongue, clutching with her nails digging long white furrows in Misling's wrist.

He held forward the carbine, his voice squeaking, "Let go!"

Selisa tugged with incredible strength, grinning and snapping her teeth with wide rolling eyes. Misling shook his arm and pulled, going nowhere. A balding man in a torn business suit who was perhaps a salesman before he became this, slithered out, making a noise from his mouth like lobster pincers clicking, with thick saliva trickling down from his fat lips in strings. All clicking teeth and smiles, he brought his face up to Misling's cheek – saying nothing.

Cristoffel tugged on the Recorder's sleeve, trying to help but really just panicking. He was still slinging his arm trying to free it; but Selisa held tight and only cocked her head to one side curiously.

"Kill yourself."

Misling sidestepped to try and separate from the drooling Cheshire cat the salesman had become, with the clicking having stopped and only smiles remaining. He aimed the carbine at Selisa and shouted.

"Let go!"

All the eyes of the tower were watching; and some of those close by were starting to unravel and separate from the rest as if preparing to come down, with the look of unbridled enthusiasm.

"Shoot her!" Cristoffel yelled, backing away a step. The salesman was horrifying her like she'd seen his snake smile in dreams before.

Selisa's voice cracked, "He suffocated. Cursed you at the end when he drowned in concrete dust. Climb and join us!"

"Let go now!" He shook and shook availing nothing; and his hand was cloud white.

At last it was another darting hand that prompted the Recorder to fire. Another snake darting from the nest and snapping; and it sent him into full self defense with a merciless grip on the carbine trigger. A sizzling ball no bigger than a child's fist, yellow as sunrise and smelling of ozone cannonball-roared into Selisa's head and blew it apart in brightly flaming pieces like a scattering of dry leaves in a campfire.

The hand still clung to him; but he was able to shake it this time.

"Run!"

The salesman and others had withdrawn and were climbing down. It was fast, much faster now that Misling had fired than before…with purpose. There was a little girl in pajamas, covered in muck and eyes blank who was leading the way; and they were apparently intending to spread out to surround and encircle. Misling and Cristoffel had started for an alleyway behind them but stopped sharply at what was emerging from it now…people running at full speed like roaches on all fours. They were screaming gibberish as if it was real words, carrying the force of a blind and furious mob, as fierce and stupid as the worst of them all and entirely out of their minds. Trying to fire behind him, Misling was blasting wildly and contacting very little. Without strategy, they were just running. No duke or Chaselord was with him then; and nothing in his memories rose to his aid. There were just too many; and it was happening too fast.

"Fire that thing! Shoot them!" Cristoffel shouted, though he was trying already. She'd pulled her knife but was doing nothing with it. They had to shift directions again when more came from a second alleyway, led by a dark woman with bloodied fingertips, with some of her fingernails torn and hanging in shreds.

"Baby Jorey! My baby!" The dark woman's voice was hoarse and fading, like she'd been yelling for days. Yet her eyes were wild; and she wanted blood.

Misling and Cristoffel were at last encircled; and he managed to burn down the screaming woman. He'd hoped maybe they would fear him because of this; but that wasn't so. Then the carbine only snapped. It was overheating and shutting down. He looked at Cristoffel sadly, for it was only going to be another moment before they were buried beneath this horde like animals on the plain being feasted upon. And it was his fault.

"I have killed you. I am sorry."

She looked back at him and grabbed his hand, ultimately facing the clicking bald man who patted the pajamas girl and the nightmare mob behind them.

Then, a smoking carbine barrel jutted from the alley, "That's enough." One ball of fire screamed, then another – each precisely tearing into the chest of one of the attackers. They began dropping, one after the other.

Grebel's face was behind the barrel, frowning, "Chumps."

When he'd dropped several more, in textbook and mathematical precision, the crowd ceased its advance and took on a panicked immediacy like horses in thunder, mad eyes and poised to run. He calmly rested the barrel against another's forehead and exploded the fellow's face in a crimson starburst. Then they began to entirely disperse. As he saw their numbers dwindle, Grebel stepped into the clearing and held his arms out in a taunt, beckoning. The girl in pajamas was last to turn and walk away, her face coy and wicked. He watched and held the position long enough to ensure no takers, then turned to face the little Recorder and Cristoffel disapprovingly.

Grebel saw the carbine in the Recorder's hands and frowned deeper, then looked at her with contempt that she'd allow such a thing, "Maybe you'd like to go back and ask your buddies on the Tower where they have their hair done! Build a fire. Sing some songs."

He smacked Misling's arm, "The most dangerous handheld weapon known to man; and you hung it on a panicked nerd."

She chuckled nervously, still looking up at Grebel. He creased his forehead, "What's funny?"

"I'm standing here getting yelled at by Grebel Lant. I don't know what to tell you. Bad day."

He looked at her a moment with his cold, military scowl, then softened and chuckled. In fact, he was fairly tickled by what she'd said and broke into a laughter uncommon for him.

"Come on. I need help."

Inside the winding corridors between buildings, where a chilling breeze funneled through and whistled, they followed Grebel and at last came to another street, one with a barricade pile of furniture and debris. Inside the wide marble and palm-shrouded atrium of a botanical museum sat perhaps twenty people talking. They were at café tables and benches, having conversation; and several glanced at the Recorder and Cristoffel as they arrived only to return to their chats. Grebel ignored them with disdain and was bound for a hallway farther in; but Misling stopped right there, dumbfounded. He had resigned to being torn to pieces only moments before, surely within earshot of these sitting here; and they could sit with no conscience at a sandwich shop. Few seemed injured.

"What are you doing?" Misling lost his temper; and this was

entirely a new thing in the world. A tattered and grime-smeared Recorder with a carbine slung across his shoulder yelling – those at the tables were frightened at the day, surely; but here was something none of them had seen before. He had their attention in a vise.

"There is rubble in the plaza." He pointed toward from where he'd come, "There is a Red Witch tower right there. What are you doing here?"

Grebel and Cristoffel had stopped at Misling's voice, curiously. By this time, Grebel was smiling widely at what he was seeing, with his arms folded. She looked up at Grebel and saw that was so, but didn't know how to react herself.

The Recorder kicked a table over angrily, spilling its contents, "Could you not be bothered? Is this not your city?!"

Sana and water splattered across the tiles making green and dark crowns and starbursts, soaking the bread and glass shards that had fallen. He looked across their stunned faces, their blank expressions and self-absorption, burning their appearances into the Record; and they would have known he was doing that. Farmilion wasn't there – only downtown office and merchant people failing to do anything beyond celebrate their own salvation. No one spoke up, though some turned their heads down.

Misling turned another table over with his boot and frowned at a tall and incredibly athletic fellow who he judged should be perhaps lifting rubble. "Is this not your city?!"

He left them with the horrible silence and let the question wash over those at their cups, stomping away to continue down the hallway and saying nothing to Grebel or Cristoffel as he passed. Grebel glanced at her after Misling was beyond, only raising an eyebrow at such a sight as he'd just seen. The bland crowd murmur rose instantly, echoing down the atrium.

"On a different day, that would have been hilarious."

Cristoffel didn't smile, but shifted subjects, "I'm really glad you showed up when you did. What are you doing here?"

Gesturing to move her along, "Come on."

Past the fountain blossoms and a stagnant landscaped stream, the corridor opened up to a columned room with a skylight meant for sculptures that had been laid to their sides and stacked against walls, now housing perhaps fifteen injured men and ladies, resting on folded blankets or coats and shaded gray and pale blue with Balcister-dust. Cristoffel scanned for a short fat man with a pink face and unfortunately saw nothing.

"You've set up a life station."

Nodding, "Your camerahead was right – almost nobody showed up.

"I'm here."

Grebel's soldier face betrayed maybe surprise at that, "I need you to help out in the kitchen. These guys need some hot food, know what I mean?"

 Irritated, "Because I'm a girl I'm going to the kitchen!?"

He frowned impatiently, "Because you can walk and everyone else is worthless! And if you start drooling or acting weird, I'll light you up like a fireworks show."

"Do you know what's happening?"

Grebel re-evaluated her, hesitating, "I think so. Where did you come from?"

Cristoffel pointed with her thumb in the direction of the Spooks, "We came through a mess – mogs all over the place. They're tearing the city apart."

He raised an eyebrow, "The financial district? Green and yellow…sort of a…" He shaped something in the air with his finger, "sort of spikes on the cannons?"

Shaking her head apologetically, "I don't know."

He only nodded, "Yeah, it's Doniphan. Have any family in Spenecia?"

"No."

"That's good." He appraised Cristoffel again, having to look down at her young face because of how tall he was. She'd been different than those he'd encountered that day, as had been her odd companion.

"Go talk to your Recorder first. I'm guessing he just lost somebody. Never seen one act like that. You can tell him from me though, ain't no survivors from Balcister that weren't turned."

Cristoffel surveyed those lying in pain and those unconscious, with only a skinny, oily-faced boy in office clothing tending them with cheap cups of water. Grebel walked away as she did so; and though she called out to ask where he was going, he didn't answer. Cristoffel was a bit awed by someone so familiar and of such celebrity being in this square with them. Although Grebel hadn't been in Alson for years, his was a face everyone knew – the tribesman from the Salt Flats who commanded the heaviest assembly of war vessels ever put together and never lost a battle or skirmish. His stride was confident as if he'd purchased the city and was inspecting its cleanliness.

Then she discovered Misling under a table, holding his head in his hands.

She coughed gently as she joined him, "That woman…where did you know her from?"

"Her name was Selisa."

Misling paused and at last locked eyes with Cristoffel. He was trying to establish a memory for the woman he'd slain. "Selisa. From the tent cities, loved by Hastine. A rough woman, sarcastic and good at riddles."

Cristoffel saw that she had to nod her acknowledgement, that she was now to remember what she could of the woman who'd died on the tower by his hand.

"She was to have been in Balcister with Farmilion."

"Were you able to…?" She gestured towards the plaza and the evil piling of souls shrouded within it.

Shaking his head, "He was not there. After all this…" His face bore an unbelieveable sadness, "I miss him."

Cristoffel only nodded; and then they were silent for a time. There was a smell of smoke; and grit was in their teeth. Cold breezes were starting to chill the evening as shadows lengthened. Frosted and curved through the skylight, and high along the limestone and concrete buildings, windows were empty and rooms vacant, mog-roads desolate and quiet.

Misling at last said, "That was Grebel Lant from Tanith."

Her eyebrows rose at his change of subject, "Yes, it was." She was careful to take her cue from him on the depth to which they would discuss this matter.

Pausing, "A thing of interest to the Record."

"I would think so, yes."

Still holding his head, slumped like a dying cowboy in a saddle, "Will you just say things? Just talk."

Understanding him, that a Recorder could be distracted by

recording, Cristoffel coughed as she discerned a good place to start. "I don't really know what I can-"

"Please."

Trying again, slowly at first before building to some speed, "I thought of something earlier. Not sure why. When I was very little, there was this prize hunt at school; and I couldn't find anything. Everybody else had sacks overflowing – I was just last to all the good hiding places. I remember thinking if I cried again, they'd laugh at me. I was always being laughed at for something; and I didn't want to give another reason. There was this really old principal, with the kindest eyes I'd ever seen. We all knew he'd lost a son and a wife – his son's name was tattooed on his forearm. People kind of avoided him because it was hard to know what to say to him. Anyway, they weren't supposed to help us; but he got my attention and sort of…pointed…barely lifting his finger. He'd showed me a huge pile of prizes behind a tree. Even now, I can't think of anything I've been more grateful for. Some people live up in the parapets and on the rooftops. They don't have any money; but there are some I know who remind me of him. Just kind and…deep…people who've lost someone or who've been through something but have the distance now to…accept it. It's comforting. I've always thought Recorders must be like that, at least the old ones."

Cristoffel waited then, uncertain whether she was rambling or being unhelpful. She was tired and hungry; and it still wasn't clear this place was any safer than where they'd been.

He lifted his head to see her, "It is not difficult to hide after lights-out at the Academy, to sit and listen to the Lord Recorders speak to one another. They are such people." Cristoffel only nodded.

.

Misling brushed hair back from his forehead, clearing the symbol there. She examined it curiously as he did so, "When Farmilion came to select his Recorder, there was an assembly announcement, posters all over the walls. They had placed the very best of us in a lineup; but I was told to sweep the great hall to be kept from his view. When his face stuck from the doorway, he was grinning as he always was. Such a tiny little fat man, smiling and pink in the face. 'How about an adventure…or lunch?'"

Misling's impersonation was incredible and startled Cristoffel. "He was not in the wrong place as I had thought and tried to explain to him, but rather had ignored those in the procession and on purpose wandered the hall looking for whoever had been passed over."

Cristoffel's eyes softened, smiling, "He sounds amazing."

The Recorder nodded distantly, seeing a day long gone. She pulled the black hair from her pony tail and let it fall to her shoulders. Looking up, she shook her head gently and puffed from her lower lip to clear hair from her eyes.

"You were pretty hard on those people sipping their tea in there; and maybe we ought to do something different. Grebel asked me to help out in the kitchen, so let's go see what we can do for the people who've made it. Okay?"

Misling was still distant, drained of vigor and likely swimming in his Record, both times past and here with her. It took a moment for him to catch something in what she'd said.

Raising both eyebrows, "Is that what Grebel Lant said, 'help out in the kitchen'?"

Cristoffel cocked her head, then tried to ease him, perhaps fearful of his disappointment, "It's just a way of saying it."

"Implying there are others here not yet seen."

"Don't get carried away!"

The Recorder scurried from beneath the table. She tried to keep up with him; but he moved quickly and with a purpose. The burnished nickel restaurant sign betrayed the kitchen's dimly lit entrance; and steel chairs honked against the floor as he shoved them roughly from his way. He kept on till he was standing before the kitchen doors themselves and was within earshot. There were the clinking and rushing water sounds of men inside preparing some sort of food. He stood and listened, inhaling nervously and shutting his eyes and hoping.

After a moment of silence and unclear murmuring from the room, the bang of closing oven doors, a voice sang out.

"You wiry, thin little man – what would you know of sausages? You might as well strangle the poor fellows out there as feed them those wretched, mangled blasphemies you've manufactured! Haven't they suffered enough?"

Misling's eyes opened and shone like a tiny child at Christmas, blinking in the brightly colored lights. He grinned ridiculously and stood perfectly still, savoring the fat old man's voice.

"Your casings have split, as perhaps should your head for wasting such beautiful treasures. And the heat of the oven…what in the world are you used to cooking, you backwoods uncultured wreck of a cook? The shepherding of good sausages is in low heat and patience, much like the great lovers will say of women. It is fortunate for those poor wounded fellows I am here to set in order your efforts!"

Cristoffel saw what was happening and grinned. It was beautiful. The Recorder stayed motionless a moment longer to bathe in the relief and the resolution, letting it warm him like sweet oil soaking into bread, then pushed open the doors to step inside.

Farmilion was stirring his steaming water and frowning at the split casings, while the thin fellow beside him covered in smoke and dust peered hopelessly into the pot. The Recorder heard none of what the other fellow said and instead, watched the tiny man happily. When Farmilion looked up and saw Misling, his cheeks and rumpled forehead softened and colored like rose petals.

"My dear little professor! You have come back to me!"

The words brought incredible relief to Misling as they hugged, the Recorder quickly realizing that Farmilion had an awful limp now and was bandaged about his right hip with dark red stains showing through the cloth. Farmilion didn't want it mentioned, and with his eyes drew attention away from his injuries. The Recorder sniffed, savoring Farmilion's smell and the feel of his belly as he patted it with his open palm.

Farmilion puffed his big lips out at Cristoffel, "And you've a girl!"

Misling pointed at her, "She kissed me."

"Did she, now?" Farmilion raised a white bushy eyebrow, his thunderous laughter warming like steaming cider. Smacking the assistant on his shoulder, "Why are you just standing there?! Can't you see they're thirsty?"

23 YOU CAN'T CHOOSE YOUR FAMILY

The evening light was dwindling as Grebel sat on the rooftop, his legs dangling over the guttering and overlooking the plaza. He was watching the filthy Red Witch tower in the dimming light and was alone till Misling wandered from the fire escape to join him. Grebel grinned.

"Well, there's the table-kicking firecracker! How was the celebration?"

Squatting beside, his legs crossed, Misling joined him. "Happy. Farmilion is explaining again what happened to him at Balcister."

"He turned left; and the other guy turned right. I heard it. Twice. And the other one stayed back to eat berries."

Misling only nodded, not wanting to elaborate on how many times he'd heard it so far. Grebel was sucking sausage grease from his fingers and Misling watched him do so. It drew Grebel's attention; and he sort of shrugged to the side to eat the last of it in peace. The Red Witch tower was still and quiet; and from this distance it looked like poorly crafted stoneworks.

"I don't normally speak with creeps like yourself, little guy; but I'm giving you my firecracker special dispensation. We're in a big toilet bowl right now; and everybody else is just gonna pile on now. Gonna get bad – you and yours ought to get out of here and keep on going."

"Are you staying?"

He gave a disgusted look, indignant that he'd be asked, "There's somebody I've gotta pull out of this mess before he makes an ass of himself."

Misling nodded, "Young Talgo." Grebel didn't answer, but

rather just sucked his teeth and watched the misty plaza. When he felt the Recorder staring, he looked up, irritated.

"Ask it."

Relieved at the permission but still waiting on something, Misling looked only like someone waiting on the floor to give way. The two of them were eye to eye for a moment, Grebel growing more annoyed.

"Get on with it, you painted shlong. If you've got something to say, say it." Misling knew exactly what he was on about, but only looked on patiently as there was no need to ask. The flatsman was asking it himself. "Why the Talgos. Right?"

He picked something off his boot, "I don't know, man. I'm stupid. Somehow, getting in the middle of wherever they are always seems to be the right thing to do."

"A poor and unpardonable excuse."

Eyes widening at the affront, "What did you say to me?"

Misling looked to the rubble to avoid the eyes of one of the most powerful men in the world, one who'd commanded the forces of an apocalypse and killed millions in war. "Because you have chosen a place for your guilt does not absolve you of it."

"You mouthy little rodent…"

"Please." Misling turned to him. "I have lived five times over."

Grebel stared, as most did with this Recorder when he said things like this. He wasn't a man accustomed to such directness and was perhaps just as likely to shove Misling from the roof as answer. "Yeah."

Grebel well knew he was speaking now not to a brown-eyed young man with a nervous stutter and an awkward manner, but the eternal Record and uncountable generations to come. It was breaking him.

"Yeah." He nodded slowly, and bit his lip a couple of times before at last jutting his lower lip idly, like he'd answered himself on whether it all mattered at this point. "So, I was going in to see the Old Man once at the worst of the Rupture, when everything was burning…standing by the snakes and straightening my uniform. I'd just left the previous Warmaster's command room and had found the guy play acting in some kind of costume. I'm not making this up – he was shadow boxing and reciting lines or something with his staff handing him props. Un-freaking-believable. The Old Man was next in line, so I was hoping…I don't know.

"There was this thread poking out of a buttonhole on my shirt; and I was trying to spin it around the button rather than try and snap it. He noticed stuff like that. Funny I still remember. I was worried the button would come off all the way. Anyway, that's what I was doing when the big doors opened." Grebel's voice was ponderous and sad. This wasn't something of which he'd spoken; and it was coming unstuck roughly. "The women who came out, not all were old and toothless. Some were even pretty. There were maybe twenty of them; and I remember it was like a funeral – the way they looked. Midwives, I found out later. He'd just told them to poison and choke the Rauchka newborns but not enough to kill. That's how far the crap with the clowns had gone. This one white-hair comes right to my face and says, 'there is no forgiveness for this'".

Grebel shook his head, "You'd have thought he'd be in there mad, throwing things after telling people to do something like that. You know he was chuckling. I asked permission to enter; and he was bouncing a ball on his foot and kicked it to me."

"Yet you go to shelter his grandson."

"You can't choose your family, chief."

Misling raised an eyebrow thoughtfully, "You did."

The old soldier glared, a vein pulsing on his temple, "So he's still spinning that ball in his hands like a little boy when we're at the big map; and he goes through the most incredible tactical plan I've ever heard. It was pure genius; and I knew it was unbeatable as soon as I looked at it. He'd just ordered the maiming of infants and was saving the world now. It was Sarling. It's how we kept Sarling and turned the war."

Grebel shrugged, asking not of this Recorder but of those to come who would hear his words nonetheless, "What was I supposed to do?"

Misling let it get quiet again. Voices distant enough to be only murmuring were coming from the plaza where a pack of teenagers stood around the Red Witch tower, as many had throughout the day intrigued by the challenge and question of the black bell at its top.

"You are not alone in following, Grebel Lant. There is powerful momentum to Talgo."

"Maybe." The old soldier had drifted back into his thoughts.

Misling's painted forehead crumpled curiously, "Was he working with the Augur?"

"Nahh. He told me to bomb it."

"'Is the Talgo mystique a tool of or product of the Augur, or perhaps its master'…have you heard that question, Grebel Lant?"

"I've heard it; and it's crap. Look, don't get deep on me, chief. You lucked out today and got somebody back. That's not gonna happen again. Tomorrow, you'll wake up and think none of it was that bad and isn't this an adventure. You'll think maybe just go pick a little at any leftovers from your trip here; and it all feels important…that you're the only one that can make a difference. I know it well; and it's a good way to wind up with a mouth full of mud and a hole in your back. The very thought is occurring to about two million people right now while we're talking. Get your people and scoot."

"Yet you chose to try. And still do." Misling gestured in the direction of the atrium below where the lifestation was.

Frowning, "Everybody wants to leave a mark, right? I just don't want mine to be a scar."

A little girl's voice, "Ask him about the clown prince." Misling jerked his head in shock to see the little girl from the barley fields sitting cross-legged next to him, hugging herself. Grebel hadn't heard and did not see her. She wiggled her eyebrows at him and smiled.

Hesitating, steadying himself, "Did you…" She was still there, not a memory – not in Mast. There. "Did you know the Rauchka clown prince, Laoka?"

He chuckled, "Yah. I knew him. Idiot; but he was a good guy. Could burp his way through 'The General's Blade'. That always cracked me up." Grebel was smiling, looking off into his own dim record. Misling saw the barley-field girl as real as the ledge and the night sky and was puzzling at her implication.

"What was he like?"

"Had a way of getting people to do things for him. He hung out with an old Malthus twig and picked up some of their tricks, especially when the Old Man really started going after him. You know what he told me one time? I'll tell you this, you let me know if it's possible."

Grebel chuckled idly, still not seeing the girl and not realizing Misling's growing realization, "We were lit one night. Absolutely lit, swimming under this hideous Salt Mystic statue in the Fountain City when he tells me the old buzzard hid things in the Record…like traps. He said they get triggered sometimes to right the ship when we make a turd of things. And get this…he said he was one. Is that possible? Could she do that?"

The Recorder stared back, uncertain, "It may be."

"Hmm." The barley-field girl was grinning, like she'd thought of an inside joke. Her nose was pink. Misling noticed her nose was pink.

"Would he have attacked Alson like this? Would he hire the Red Witch?"

Shaking his head, "Not ever, chief. Not in a million years. He was a softie. That Malthus twig I told you about – a fossil losing his memory. Couldn't' remember to wipe his own butt at the end; but Laoka did everything for him, like a son. Weird and sweet, right?" Grebel noticed Misling suddenly examining something, something below him perhaps on the ledge. "What are you looking at?"

"The iron ring. The…Ring."

"You're losing me."

"That is what he wanted us to see in the reading: the Rauchka all over the pattern leading to the Rupture but nowhere at all now…hiding in plain sight and fighting to hold back the tide." He glanced to the girl for her to confirm; but she was still only grinning. "He was letting them know he is back."

The old soldier shook his head, "Okay, I don't know what just happened to this conversation. Look, you want to know who hired the Red Witch? Nobody. Nobody hired them. It's momentum, chief. You said it. No conspiracy, no evil master mind. Bad momentum."

Grebel stood, rubbing his hands together to warm them, bowing his head in ponderance. Nothing in his face or manner showed he felt clean of fault in any of this. At last, he shook his old head with some finality, "And both sides just let it ride till here we are scraping it off our shoes. Shame."

"Yes, as before. And the clowns are all that have been standing against it, maybe for a generation or more." Misling squinted, looking at nothing and trying with his very soul to understand how his strange friend could embody not the long-dead Salt Mystic, which maybe he'd never believed anyway, but rather the clown prince, Laoka with all the ridiculous history against the Old Man that entailed. He was to admit years later in explaining these events, that it wasn't so much what Grebel had said or Ring's knowledge of the Recorder creed that persuaded him what he now knew…but unbelievably, that farting noise and wiggled fingers at the statue of the Iron Eye outside the cave city. Somehow that made it make sense.

Grinning slightly, but entirely disagreeing and all but turning to leave the Recorder there on the dim rooftop, "Revin's talkshow all over again. Great. If that pinches it off for you, chief, then good for you. A pipe dream; but good for you. Maybe we all should have stood against it. How about you leave it to them, then, and get your fat little friend out of Alson and up in the woods somewhere?"

"But what does the Augur have to do with any of this?"

"The Augur didn't start any of it." The barley-field girl answered when Grebel didn't and before she vanished again into the twilight- before the old soldier stood to part ways from the Recorder for the last time. "It's just where it's all going to end."

The apocalyptic battlefield of Spenecia spread like a prophet's vision, with screaming battlesuits and ramships already smashing into each other. Searing orange explosions the color of tigers flashed and dimmed in thick clouds of white and gray smoke; and midnight blooms of Black Fire swelled to the sky, then fell back to the scorched earth. To many in later generations, even those not yet born at the time, images from this conflict came to be familiar and primal. Students of war marveled at the speed with which Peri marshaled her defense forces and the collision of traditional strategies with innovative new means of fighting. Weapons and methods that had long been agreed as illegal went into full play; and larger than life characters stomped through the battle stories with vigor. It was a day of shame and of majesty; and to those later generations, certainly the root and beginning of their suffering.

The Flatsmen fleet led by Thessany had trundled to the farmhouses and cropfields of Spenecia in an open-mouthed arc of war engines and quicktanks with battlesuits on the outer wings and ramships swirling like hornets in the center, his arsenal ship following behind and sheltered. They found Peri's defensive fleet there already, laid out in a wedge aimed like a bullet at them with skirmishing ramships leading. First hand accounts from the day describe those hesitant few moments when the two forces faced one another as haunting and wicked, like the world was about to do something it shouldn't and each side wondered at the sheer force of arms their enemy had brought to bear. In fact, what actually kicked off the first volley was white-haired Mervyn Loelto, one of the Old Man's guardians and confidantes who should have been rocking before a fire somewhere humming to his new great-granddaughter with the tiny purple birth mark on her arm, but instead rode an armored wanoa right into the no-man's land between them all and pointed his freshly polished carbine into the sky. Strangely, the Alson and the Flatsmen commanders waited till the ancient fellow with the uniform a bit tight and his arm shaking had signaled before they launched.

If Alson fell here, they would vanish from the Record; and they well knew it.

Thessany

"Once I find Peri, this little puppet show is over. Know what I mean, boys!"

Thessany laughed and raised his volume as he stepped to the full size viewscreen like a museum mural full of tanks and cannons and dying soldiers, yet still only the opening movements of a larger arrangement, "You hear me, you flower chewing, perfume wearing cross-eyed's?! Where is the crafty little shrew!?"

The seven of Thessany's command crew ignored him, busily staring into sensor monitors or speaking into screens displaying in trickling text and popping windows the full datastream of the Spenecia battlespace.

"I'm the Warmaster; and I'm coming for you." The command center hummed and droned with low voices; and faces flared in the electric blue and green of their displays.

Thessany leaned in to one of crew, a chubby young man whose uniform stretched tightly upon him, "Tubs, build me two twisters."

Far below, from the belly of a massive tank, an earthshaking hum sounded. The tornado would begin no bigger than a child and white with dust like a swirling mist. Yet as the intelligence swarm entrained within, Thessany's engine built a threatening black tornado that swelled and separated from the hangar like thick soup dripping from a spoon. A second black whirlwind emerged soon after; and the two of them remained alongside one another whipping and flicking and roaring, till they flushed like a cuttlefish, ripples of silver and flash rolling from the ground up. Incredible amounts of steel shrapnel dumped from chutes along the hangar entrained into the funnels, raising a sparking and deadly sheen.

Thessany watched the coloring and smiled, "Clear out these

ramships; and slam them into that wedge. I want to get to the war engines in the rear. That's where she'll be."

Tubs did as he was instructed, lifting speeding ramships like specks of dust and casting them aside, by really just swiping his finger across a console screen. Anything lifted into the whirlwinds started shredding and catching fire almost immediately because of the shrapnel, so it was lifeless refuse that was thrown back to the battlefield in most cases. Peri's ships were scattering to make way for the tornados; but they were fast and wide and held out little hope of escaping them. Thessany pointed his fat finger and magnified the view of a red-haired Alson lieutenant on the mural screen who was crouched in some weeds outside the battle, a field commander shouting orders to several huddled in a half circle about him and pointing with his hat in explanation. He was a young officer, looking like he was trying to settle the nerves of his men.

"Toss him."

Tubs shifted with discomfort, not seeing this as funny. He was starting to sweat and smell. He and the old sensors officer looked at each other before Tubs would continue; but he ultimately did as he was instructed with a flick of his hand. Quite suddenly, one of the tornados compressed like a spring into the sky and fired a tendril of intelligent wind. Then from close enough to feel his breath, the men in the weeds watched as their young lieutenant shot backwards and into the sky, and ripped into pieces as the tornado that had plucked him settled back to the earth.

Gaining the attention of the sensors officer beside Tubs, Thessany pointed, "Find her."

Peri

"Amelin, you irritating pile! I always knew I would wind up dying next to you." Peri eyed him with a sparkle. They stood again on the deck of her command vessel, with the Alson fleet's datastream spread before them on the screen where she'd seen her failure at

Carnabie. Amelin looked tired and had beard stubble worth several days. He tried to smile back at her.

She grinned, "Cheer up. At least Grebel is still missing. If he was over there, we'd both be crying in our beers."

"How do you know?"

Pointing, "That's Thessany's formation. He thinks I'm as hotheaded as he is, that we'll try and rush his circle and break up the lines before they can enclose. It means he'll bring up that arsenal ship from behind it as soon as we do that."

She took a pace step, then halted in thought, "Unfortunate though. Cassian would have been easier. He's so…black and white. Optimizes everything. You can read him. Thessany is just..fond of toys. But he isn't a thinker…all his moves will be textbook War College stuff. Run that as a filter when you're answering me on what his wings will do." Amelin nodded and swiped across the flickering datastream, sparkling like sunshine on water.

Quite suddenly, "Twisters inbound! Two of them. Imminent to the front lines!"

His alarm did little to help. The marbled sky filled with the killer tornados that assaulted her ramships in the fore and tossed them like toys. Peri and Amelin braced their hips against and gripped a brass bar that ran the length of the bridge at its rear, in order to steady themselves against the boneshaking that hit almost immediately. Bodies and vehicles were raining on them.

"What are your orders?!"

Peri inhaled slowly, "Patience." Their war engine took another brutal assault, shaking and almost capsizing. Thuds and bangs from what pelted them were deafening; and everywhere even at this distance was the terrible roaring. They had to yell now just to hear.

He looked up sharply, "Scatter pattern or pull back – which will it be?!"

"Sshh." She held a finger to her lips. Amelin creased his forehead, angry at her reaction and lost in what to do. He saw in the readings and status updates what damage was being done already.

Because she wasn't talking to him, Amelin could only just barely hear her say, "All right, you little whiz kids. Make something happen."

"Are you praying? What's the matter with you?" He yelled; but she ignored him for the moment. The voices of her commanders were talking over one another on the comms, requesting support and orders. Some screamed in agony. The war engine shook, knocking them again almost to their side. It just wasn't the kind of punishment they could long sustain.

"Got one." She punched a fist into her palm, watching the datastream keenly. Curious and angry, Amelin tried to confirm whatever she'd noticed. When he looked back at the visuals, it came together for him.

"You have somebody hacking tornados."

"Yeah. And they were in freaking prison. We might not get another one if Thessany figures out how we did it, so get moving. I want a steel whirlwind smashing into his face as soon as you can make that happen...him personally, not the fleet. Go after him; and he'll get stupid."

"How do I-?"

Frowning, she braced again for the slam of debris and vehicles outside, "Quantum crypto on the command net. Renegade Squad."

Not having heard the name and thinking little of it, Amelin creased his forehead and looked at her, questioning. She shrugged, "Who cares what the little guys call themselves? I have a tornado!"

Some striking images were captured and came to be representative of this battle in later times - sparking mountains of swirling whirlwinds colliding into one another like gods wrestling, slamming steel and debris and tanks as they bounced off one another. And much like it would be with gods, they stalemated.

"No good. They're locked together. Canceling each other out. Every time we try to pull away, they step in. He'll just launch another, Commander. Does your 'squad' have more than one trick?"

"I don't know anything about geeks. But he won't know either, so we'll not see another launch till he figures us out. Too risky for him. No, they'll hold for now. At least he's locked up or this would have been over already. Are we still seeing what we did with the Hag?"

"Only two battlesuits so far; but we know there can be more. Our ships are down by twenty percent; and we just got started. Peri, we don't have the meat to hold them off. If we just sit here, he'll grind us down with sheer numbers. If we rush him, he encircles or brings out the arsenal ship. And he'll do that anyway, by the way, when he gets tired of waiting. We have to pull back now so we can stand again later. Give up Spenecia."

The Lady Commander smacked her thigh three times, pondering options. She was looking into a wall where there was nothing as if the Old Man was there, telling her to push harder…to be audacious and crueler than those opposing her.

She exploded, "Is any of that freaking tathlum crap real?" He returned a grim frown as she asked for a miracle he could not offer. She cursed Revin and his golden corpse.

The colossus tornados flashed with lightning and sparks; and the ships laid out on the Spenecia fields spread to accommodate a wide berth about them. Opposing ramships were careening again into one another, shielding the larger vessels from their assaults. Here and there, Black Fire blossoms unfolded; and puffs of white hot explosions rose. The war was still on; and it was being lost. The winds had died down enough for them to be able to speak at a normal volume again.

Amelin's voice was tired, "It's a bigger battle than I'd thought it would be."

"Yeah. Me too." Holding her hand to her cheek in thought, "What are we doing here? I mean, who really hates enough to want this?"

Listening to her and watching the datastream, he had to report and so interrupted, "Another gunship has gone rogue. Just drove into the tornados."

Nodding, she was unmoved by what he'd said, "There's something I…but we're not going to get the chance."

"What is it?" Amelin saw in her gray eyes a sadness and something fading again within her, like it had when Stendahl had seized his father's position. Like none had seen with her before in Peri's long service, she was flickering – growing pale and drained and then catching fire again in bursts. He was frightened because she was one of the last of the old guard and a rock. If she fell, what were they left with? She didn't answer him.

"Commander, we need to pull back into the city. Guerilla warfare. Use the buildings as shields and buffers, strike from hiding. It's the only thing to do now."

"I'm sorry you think that's an option. This is the easy terrain access to Alson. If we fall back, there is no end to the firepower he can stage here and pummel us into dust. Spenecia won't stop him - they're trying to keep their heads low and wait us out. We're not going anywhere; and he knows it."

Peri at her screen, her favored position where she could see the grit on their faces and upturned tank tracks, the confused teenage riflemen ducking in panic at their first time under fire and the entirety of what she commanded, she looked noble like a warrior queen and sad.

"If you're asked to die, you'd like it to be for a worthy general." She tracked a finger across, in the shape of a curve arcing around nothing in particular. "I don't think there's a single Talgo out here."

"We're not fighting for them." Amelin said this; but his tone didn't bear out that he was certain of it. She didn't acknowledge either way.

Thessany

"Tubs, you get me a better firewall on these twisters or so help me, I'll steal your sandwich!" Thessany smacked his shoulder. "And come on! Why haven't one of you ginks found Peri yet!?"

"The transponder code you gave us for her is transmitting from more than twenty five locations. They know you have it." The older sensors officer beside Tubs responded, with thinning white hair and a scarred neck, likely called back into service for this. A fading and blurred squadron tattoo draped around his forearm.

Thessany smacked his palms together, "That squirmy sweating little prat lied to me. That's impressive. Glad I didn't pay for it." Kicking the white haired fellow's seat, "Well, recover. How are you gonna find her now?"

The old-time squadron man glared back, "Don't kick my seat."

"Simmer down." Thessany squatted beside him, his knees stiff and sore. "Look, you're all kinds of old and should know these hilljacks pretty well. Why is no one rushing my wings? Isn't that the obvious move? I've taken out forty of her ramships already. How long could she wait?"

"She knows you'll grow impatient and do something different to give her an opening. That's what she's waiting on. You should study their commanders if you're going to be anybody at this job. She outsmarted you already; and tornados are supposed to be your thing."

"I like you, Cobweb. Straight shooter. Don't mouth off to me; but…keep being honest. How about this…push the rammers out deeper and stretch out the wings. Thin…three or four tanks deep. Make me a big wide mouth; and then go ahead and bring Big Daddy out."

"Are you not listening to me? That's exactly what she wants you to do. If you stretch out like that, they can get easily spooked and scatter if anything happens."

"Spooked by what? I'd find it snuggly comforting if I was out there with a city on tracks armed with every weapon that's been invented watching my back! What if she gets through to my second twister? I've changed my mind about you, Cobweb. You don't know what you're talking about. You're missing the bigger picture."

Gesturing to his fleet coordinator, "Did you hear me, Bubbles? Tell Aussilo and Mithens to push out deep and fast and stretch the wings. I need a wide net. And bring out the arsenal ship…right down the center to the point of that wedge and just barrel through them. They'll scatter right into us."

Cobweb shook his head, "Classic mistake. You're like a book to her!"

Smiling, Thessany stood, his knee making an awful dry twig-crack as he did so, "It pains me to leave you in darkness, geezer. Peri's all they've got. All those other yahoos out here are a bunch of political posers and yes-men because that's what Wentic built. When they rush my arsenal ship; and they'll do that – of course they will, what else are they gonna do – you know who's gonna be leading the charge. I find her, this whole thing is over now."

"You're flushing her out." Cobweb watched Thessany with a very slight admiration. Maybe there was more there than bluster.

Thessany grabbed a ceramic coffee mug, a blue and yellow glazed one with an offensive cartoon graphic of a man violating a skull on its side. He took a sip and leaned in closely to Tubs. He leaned in quite closely and held the mug under the young man's nose, such that the steam and scent of it were unmistakeable, not quite close enough for his nose's tip to get wet. Tubs nervously stared directly into his console, swiping and tapping in a rushed and determined tack to regain full control of the tornado guidance intelligence. He was trying to ignore his Warmaster, though that was getting impossible.

"Tubs, I've never had to deal with losing my twisters before; and I'm just wondering why this problem is new with you." Tubs held his eyes firmly to his console, unsure whether to say anything or defend himself would help. A clear streak of sweat dropped in a jagged trail across his cheek and down the bridge of his nose to drip off in a plink into the black coffee inside.

"Look up at that." Thessany meant the battle scene on the gargantuan screen before them all. Tubs reluctantly glanced, then returned to his prayerful bow. "If we're not steering all my twisters before I finish this drink, I'm going to put you in the rustiest unarmed wagon I have and send you out into that…after I cut off your romantic hand. I want my tornados back."

Peri

"Commander, he's doing it. The arsenal ship is emerging from the battlegroup's rear formation." Amelin was pointing at jumbling numbers and text in the datastream as if it was an image. His young voice betrayed his fear. "Their wings are coming forward."

Peri nodded, "He'll come down the center with it. What about our twister – can you break it away?"

"They keep heading us off. Your hackers are saying we'll lose control of it any time now."

She cursed and punched the screen, "How about the droptroopers. Has anybody gotten past their rear guard?"

"Negative. They're shooting them out of the sky."

"Push, man! Tell them to push!"

"It isn't a matter of pushing. We've lost another fifteen ramships; and there are deserters now. Pull back!"

When she didn't answer, he raised his voice, no doubt thinking of how she'd withered just hours before at Carnabie, "Commander, we're outgunned and outnumbered! We need to do something different or we're done now!"

She stood directly in front of the main screen, sliding her hands across the jostling text and symbols looking for something. "Start looking, you slug! Look in here and find me something I can use!"

Leaving his console, Amelin joined her where she stood, hopelessly peering alongside. She looked older just then than ever, clumsily tossing bits of data and code like rummaging through an old chest. He'd told her before her use of the datastream was more blunt sledge than detailed clockwork; and it was her way now at Spenecia, with a grotesque desperation and cursing at nothing. She cursed Revin; and she cursed him. She smacked the screen when she didn't know how to inject an ant-colony model into some logistics data. Peri was looking for something; but it was easy to imagine there was nothing there to find.

The war engine shook again at a collision. Ramships had made it to them.

"Commander." Amelin put his hand on her wrist. It was actually the first time he'd ever touched her. She looked at him, a bit wild-eyed. "I can find it. I can. You have to tell me what you're looking for."

Peri glanced at her wrist where he held her. There weren't many she'd allow to do what he was doing just then. "I can take out the arsenal ship. Sheet diamond all around except for the top where the vents are. Typical Tanith engineering, not thinking about mogs. I'm gonna take eighteen of them right on top of her and punch through the roof. Then we'll board, blast as deep in as we can, and freaking blow ourselves up."

He frowned at what she'd said, letting her go. "A suicide run?"

"But I need distractions. I need chaos. There has to be an absolute mess out there for us to get anywhere close to driving on top of that thing. Find me something I can use!"

Like nothing he'd tried to avoid before, Amelin sadly took on what she'd asked. He dragged a search algorithm from the toolbar ring that had appeared when he stepped closer and dropped it onto the popping and bubbling datastream. No doubt, he was trying to think of ways to talk her out of leading the charge and knowing how that would turn. Anyone there would have seen him testing in his mind what he might say as he helped his Commander find something to help her die.

Thessany

"Who's spooked now?" Thessany patted the old fellow's shoulder with pride. He took a long sip from a coffee mug, nodding slowly as he watched the Alson vessels jostling to draw back from his arsenal ship but smashing into his waiting ramships and cannons. Then he punched the air in frustration at what he saw on the screen when a small group of his quicktanks was swallowed up in an Alson Black Fire barrage. Three speeding ramships crashed directly into the swelling mass with all hands apparently lost before the blooms shrank back. Thessany was winning overall, but didn't act like it.

He spread the image to see closer up as two light battlesuit squads climbed up a ramp of fallen Alson tanks to finish them, their mechanical heads popping up and down as they rambled up,

"Cobweb, I know you think I'm a loose wheel that never cracked a book or chatted up a Recorder; but I've been around tanks and guns a bit. I'll tell you one thing I know about them." He paused to watch their acoustic cannons pulverize the drivers and internals with enough energy to set them afire. "They're awesome."

"What are you going to look for to know it's her?"

Thessany thought about it, then, "Progress."

"Slade Watch has pierced through to the war engines!" A second sensors officer shouted, a little louder than was needed. "They're pounding them now."

Thessany threw his coffee mug into the wall, shattering it into three jagged chunks and splattering what remained of its contents, "There you go, rammers! Somebody showed up for work today!"

A chaotic swirl of silver and red ramships massed like bees against the war engine cluster, speeding and crashing into hulls against a hail of fireballs, mortar and streams of Black Fire and leaving behind smoking craters and tears as they sped back to withdraw. Their Alson counterparts were veering back to aid; but the battlefield was a mess and cluttered with wreckage, impeding them. One of the war engines tottered on its tracks, puffs of charcoal-black smoke drifting from its undercarriage; and men were jumping from it to abandon their machines.

"You have a bit of a strategy here." Cobweb acknowledged.

Thessany's brow rose as if this was inappropriate to say, "That's a bit uppity, Cobweb. Know your place." He addressed his coordinator again, the one he called, 'Bubbles', "Tell the long range mortarboys, target those holes where my rammers have ripped them. Get some Black Fire inside. If they cluster to shield each other, they'll catch and start a reaction. That will be hilarious. Man, I'd hate to be her!"

Cobweb leaned to get the attention of Tubs, "How much

longer?"

Nervously, stuttering, "They're good. Really better than I've seen. I should know who they have over there working against me if they're this good; but I don't. Hard to see what they're approach is; and it keeps changing."

Thessany avoided the conversation, having made his point already to the poor fellow and being assured of his enthusiasm for the job. Instead, he watched the ramships pounding and pounding, ripping graphite hulls like wounded animals. Another war engine took a battering that knocked it on its side off the tracks. There was little Alson's forces could do to react to this; and many of the quicktanks and battlesuits were indeed drifting inside Thessany's wide and long net as he'd predicted.

"Keep Big Daddy out where you can see him, Bubbles. She'll be out after him any time now."

Peri

"Found it!!" Peri's voice was incredibly excited, like a little girl who'd found in her yard a treasure. Anyone beside her just then would have only seen an aged lady commander pointing at a cacophony of swirling data. Amelin squinted as he interpreted that to which she was directing him.

"What are they doing? They're wearing Tanith colors."

"Who cares. Publish this now, in clear data. No encryption. Blast it as loud as you can with coordinates so they can confirm."

Amelin rushed to his console and ran his fingers across to do as he'd been instructed, "How did you know that was happening?"

"Didn't. But I'm thrilled. Blast it wide, Amelin. I mean it. Send this everywhere. I want it on the news back home. I want it fed to spies. I want it everywhere, now. A freaking miracle; and we're not letting it go!"

Shaking his head, "How is this a miracle?"

Ignoring his question, she grabbed a cracked and faded leather satchel and slung it across her shoulder preparing to leave, "Tell the geeks to pull the twister up when the mogs come out."

"What?!"

Peri hesitated in front of him, eye to eye perhaps for the last time and looking to instill some calm into the one who would be her stand-in, "Amelin. Listen to me. Stay calm. You know what I'd do up here. Send the orders just like I was still here. Tell the geeks to pull the twister up as soon as you see the mogs. Pull it up into the sky and leave it there. I respect you; and I need you here. I really don't have time to baby this or coddle you. Just make it happen, okay? Stop asking me questions and do what I tell you."

"Commander, you can't lead this mission personally. Send them in without you. It's irresponsible."

She frowned at him, cocking her head to one side to evaluate what he'd said, "It's just the opposite."

25 MYSTIQUE

Deep inside the buzzing and smoking cauldron of the two fleets at Spenecia, Cyprian Talgo let loose a horrible fury from an open-cabin quicktank. Maneuvering with unorthodox speeds and angles and cackling ferociously like a psychopathic emperor, firing balls of lightning from the carbine in his right arm and Black Fire mortar rounds with the triggers in his left, he was havoc. The swirl and fire of combat was all around him, burning men and squadrons being driven apart in blank confusion. He'd seen a day of horrors with perfected weapons and tactics, the War Recorders and battlefield algorithms making certain the experiences of centuries of conflict folded into what happened here. He'd heard battle cries that swelled in men's throats as they charged into hopeless collisions that were expertly crafted and psychologically tuned to best inspire them to ultimate war. Here in Cyprian Talgo was another perfection, and one most unwelcome.

"Talgo!!" An unearthly nightmare shout came from behind him, just before his quicktank started sparking and popping. Turning fiercely, quicker than even well seasoned and leather men who'd helmed such tanks their entire fighting lives could do, Cyprian at once faced his attacker with mortar and carbine aimed at a dead-stop. It was a troop tank with an acoustic cannon, a rolling tower of the kind lying in ruin beyond the tent city; and four Red Witch men climbed from it, carbines drawn. Cyprian's vessel was sputtering and dying in billowing clouds; and, choking, he jumped over its gunwale to the charred Spenecia ground onto crushed crops. They were just now on the perimeter of the conflict; and perhaps the Red Witch had waited until that had been so.

Cyprian clenched his teeth as his eyes slitted, observing the Tanith markings on their ship yet their attack upon him. The four of them were towering black demons, grinning phosphorescent red teeth flaring in the morning light. Wildcat stalking, they stepped apart from one another to spread against him.

Nodding, "Revenge. Cassian's bodyguard. " Cyprian smiled

maliciously and held his arms out like a man crucified. "Is that right?"

Watching their day-glow eyes and carbine arms carefully, with serenity and utter command, "He screamed, boys. Oh yeah. Offered me all kinds of things…unnatural things… if I'd just… stop…hurting him."

The disembodied staccato whispers from the Red Witch men broke through the chaotic battlefield din in pieces; and they were each repeating, *"Kill us an eensie Talgo" "Kill us an eensie Talgo"* This sight, advancing Red Witch fighters massive and stalking, eerie demonic whispers and carbines drawn, this was the image of nightmares. He was outnumbered and outgunned by men who'd surrendered their humanity to be death and madness. He had backed up such that they couldn't form a circle; but their arc was wide. Only incredible confidence and recklessness would drive him to have his arms out and away from his carbine's armature shield with four guns drawn on him and coming from multiple directions. It was a Talgo move and suspicious, and probably did much to delay their firing upon him.

One of the central Red Witch took a step, with a long ugly face and ears that stuck out far from it, with lips that jutted out over buck teeth. The blackening could hide much; but an awkward boy who'd been pushed down and laughed at, who'd been left cold and alone with his books and had snowballs shoved deep into his shirt amid giggles and horsecalls could sometimes be seen peering back now and snapping his monster jaws.

"Kill us an eensie Talgo."

Cyprian flinched as the leftmost man glanced at the smoldering quicktank, discerning whether the young Talgo had left something aimed at them as a trap yet seeing only the Black Fire cannon sideways on its swivel, the mortar tube directed to the tank's broadsides and upwards. The first of them to think of it, he was the shortest; and his long coat was threadbare and patched. Seeing him flare his arms from his sides as if used to trying to look tougher than he was, it was easy to see in this one an angry boy, a survivor, cross-legged on wet concrete streets crouched over hiding whatever potatoes and fish he'd pulled from the dumpsters behind late evening restaurants.

Louder, "*Kill us an eensie Talgo!*"

One of the remaining two tensed his shoulder, readying his strike. He and the Red Witch beside him resembled each other — the shape of their heads and eyes, the way they stood…brothers, likely. Their coats and body armor were new and unsoiled, perfectly aligned with Red Witch standards. Fists clenched hard enough to shake, the two stared at him with blind religion, bringing to this showdown the hate and tyranny that perhaps had been explained to them years before as they sat wide-eyed hearing what vengeance was needed in the world. Here they stood facing one who'd been cradled by the most vicious Warmaster of history; and they well knew their part.

"You might as well have labeled yourselves." Cyprian's demeanor was amusement, squinting in the orange morning light, as if he'd just heard a good pun that was sneaking back up on him as funnier now than when he'd first heard it. He licked his lips and turned his carbine into the shield position, bracing his right leg back. He slid his longknife from its sheath and gripped it, blade upside down parallel to his left wrist and forearm. Incredibly, he sniffed the battlefield smoke and char, stealing glances at the collisions and smashes, the flames and madness of Spenecia in total war like he was sampling a holiday candle, savoring and pleased.

"*Kill us an eensie Talgo!*" They began shooting, in the manner of an execution.

Cyprian fired distraction shots into their faces and rushed one of the brothers first, the one who'd tensed his gun arm, and with such speed that he was up streetfight-close to the Red Witch man before he could react to it. A bright splatter of blood spewed; and bursts of light hissed and popped inside their tight conflict. The brother couldn't get his arm extended and tried to kick out with his knee to push Cyprian back; but he still couldn't break away and wound up being turned with Cyprian so his back was to the others. Then

Cyprian's two quick blasts burned off both the Red Witch man's arms at the shoulders. It was sudden enough to cause the others to hold their fire, shocking in its violence and finality. Cyprian hugged his victim, resting his cheek on his armor as if cuddling a stuffed bear. The screaming was chilling as the maimed man twisted and contorted in agony. Cyprian opened his eyes and looked directly at the remaining brother who shook with fury.

"Sounds like it hurts."

The Red Witch men knelt as they recommenced firing, trying to lower their target profiles. They were trained to block return fire with shots rather than shifting to defensive positions for shielding, which was economical in motion but took much of the attacking fire out of play. Cyprian used this to advantage, staying behind and firing around the injured brother as he shoved him forward to rush his counterpart. The kneeling brother was not holding back his fire now and held his teeth clenched, gripping the carbine with both hands and firing as quickly as he could. Yet he bowled backwards as Cyprian came upon him, dumping the armless and burning man onto the barrel. Too quickly to see, Cyprian drove his blade upwards into the second brother's groin inside the thigh and was away before the fountain of blood hit the ground. The brothers burned together and went still.

"That was really fast!" Cyprian danced a bit, shifting from left foot to right and back in excitement and smiling, his eyes shining. "You guys can tell I'm messing with you, right?"

He pointed his carbine forward, gesturing, "You. You're the streetsmart guy. The survivor. I'll make you a deal – you stand still while I kill him; and I'll let you go." The black face was hard to read; but he was still and only watching. It was unprecedented, a lone man defeating Red Witch every time he faced them.

Cyprian pointed at the other, the donkey-eared one, with his knife, "You look stupid and probably have always looked stupid. An absolute moron who thinks he found a place for himself. I'm going to do something entirely awful to you; and honestly, he's just going to watch." The Red Witch man understood; and he registered this. Here he was after his blackening, the most horrible of men and with the face of a night goblin; and there was still laughing. It was wearing on him.

Cyprian rushed the donkey-eared Red Witch, firing as he charged. The two of them dueled fiercely, sizzling lightning exploding like fireworks, though Cyprian was not slowed in his advance. Blocking and parrying, ultimately devolving into close-in combat, the Red Witch was hopelessly outclassed and came to panic. His red eyes swelled when he saw Cyprian's blade shoved deep into his now useless carbine forearm as he found he couldn't clench his fingers. Then Cyprian drove the white-hot barrel of his carbine like a spear into the Red Witch's stomach and ripped out a gooey mass. It was his intestines…Cyprian was gripping the man's intestines and disemboweling him where he stood, ripping them out like a ribbon as he stepped back. The Red Witch glanced pleadingly to his motionless comrade, then dropped weakly to his knees and fell. His eyes were lingering on the parts of him when he went still.

Cyprian looked then at the remaining man who'd sought to execute him, the one who now held out his armored hands in surrender and who wore a cancerous fear in his red eyes. Cyprian was walking forward, like he wasn't planning to honor the deal he'd suggested. The look of him was bloody mess and black char with fierce exhiliration, in every way the avenging fury the Red Witch people tried to be. He stood threateningly staring up into the Red Witch's dark face, then at last smiled.

"Go tell your friends."

Thessany

"Talk to me, Cobweb! What are you seeing out there?" Thessany leaned over Cobweb, uncomfortably close and impatient.

The sensors officer pushed him back gently, "Nothing advancing to the arsenal ship that looks coordinated. I don't see any patterns at all yet. Slade Watch is being engaged by Alson rammers now; but we outnumber them three to one there."

"Okay." He looked around himself idly, thinking. "Okay."

An acoustic cannonade was firing blurry hypersonic pulses into the smoking sky to burn droptroopers alive inside their ballistic spheres, like it was a turkey shoot and almost mechanical. The underbellies of the high altitude dirigibles were barely visible, but dotted the clouds in a manner not seen since the Rupture. Thessany only nodded, waiting on Peri's move. He glanced at Tubs briefly to see him still hard at work combating Peri's hackers with no victory as yet, then back to Cobweb.

"What about Spenecia's fleet - have we heard from those guys? Which freaking side are they on?"

When Cobweb shrugged, the second sensors officer spoke up, "They're condemning both sides, staying neutral. Warning us off their sovereign territory."

"Remind me of that later." Then as if strolling, Thessany stepped up to stand beside Tubs, again uncomfortably close. "I'm gonna need you to add a second command screen to that console…need to be able to work it from two sides."

Tubs looked up, still sweating and scared, "Why?"

"Because my butt cheeks could do a better job than you!! He

shouted loud enough for Tubs to shrink down in his seat, involuntarily pulling from the noise.

"I'm close. I'm really close. Okay? I've got a hundred and fifty viruses working on this; and they're all morphic and sentient. One of them is going to jam the command injection, then-"

"Stop talking geek to me!" Jamming his finger into Tubs's forehead, it drew a white halo and red ring around the fingertip like a small pimple.

"Hey, you've got to see this!" Cobweb tapped something on his console and then pointed up to the big screen. "What do you think of that?"

Cyprian Talgo was standing on the battlefield, roaring twisters in the background and his own vehicle smoking and in ruins, staring down four Red Witch in Tanith colors, their troop tower bearing Tanith markings. Turncoats were attacking the Marshal's son; and Fantine was nowhere to be seen. Thessany was irritated.

"What the-?" He watched momentarily as Cyprian blew off the arms of the first of his attackers and held him close in a mock embrace. "Whoa! Where's this coming from? Cobweb, validate this. Get coordinates. I don't believe it."

"Confirmed. Happened just now, actually. He's still out at the same spot."

He pointed feebly, confused and interrupted by what he was seeing, "Well who are those guys? Why are they wearing our colors?"

"They're ours. Part of..." Tapping, scanning down a list of codes, "...Ghost Dogs. We backfilled The Ghost Dogs with Red Witch. And that's them."

Cyprian was mesmerizing; and everyone in Thessany's flag staff just then was transfixed at his unnatural speed and ferocity, what he did to the two Red Witch to make them burn together.

"Did he switch sides?" Bubbles asked from his console, staring intently. It drew Thessany's attention to the fact that all of them were distracted, staring as Bubbles was.

"Hey! Will you get back to fighting my war please?!" He smacked one of those closest to him on the back of the head. His face suddenly bore concern as he watched the young faces around him that perhaps that was happening outside as well. Thessany glanced back to the image of Cyprian, pointing with his knife and speaking with the Red Witch.

He leaned again toward Cobweb's ear, "Find out what's going on there. What do you know about these Ghost Dog witchers…and get me Fantine. She's dropping the ball pretty bad here."

Thessany pointed at one of his sensors officers, "Block that crap! I don't want it transmitted anymore. You hear me?! Jam the air with noise; and make it go away!"

"Fantine isn't anwering. Her code is off the grid. No sign of her."

The Warmaster frowned and mumbled to himself, "Fantine's made of rock. He couldn't kill her." His tone dropped again, with uncertainty and rising confusion, "Why would he?"

"Whoa!!" Bubbles interjected again; and several joined him in surprise as they saw Cyprian tear into the Red Witch man's guts and unspool them before him. This was another image that survived the battle for years thereafter; and many there watching it live could have said that would be so.

Thessany grimaced, also transfixed. "Bubbles, I need a cofferdam around that boy now. Drop in uhh…drop in a troop tower or something and cordon him off. Take him out of play. He's a wild card; and I can't tell what's going on."

"Neither can anyone else." Cobweb noted. It caused Thessany to understand the whispers around him on the bridge, his battle coordinators suspecting a Talgo has turned on them…the most frightening and unpredictable Talgo. "Didn't they put him on a Black Fire cannon? You might want to take that thing out."

"Yeah." Thessany nodded, deciding something of consequence. "Do that. Him too, now that you mention it. Take him out too."

Bubbles was horrified and showed so on his freckled face, "Cyprian? You want me to fire on Cyprian Talgo?!"

Thessany shouted, "You freaking shoot him! I want him dead; and I want that cannon of his out of commission. I want that video jammed! And I want my worthless paperweight freaking tornado back too! I swear to you, if I don't start getting some professionalism here, I'm gonna start cutting hands off! Get me some satisfaction!"

Cobweb tapped Thessany's arm to gain his attention, "You're about to split your fleet right down the middle. This is what she wanted. Pull the wings back."

Jamming his finger harshly on Cobweb's console, "The only thing I want you to do right now is tell me which of theirs are headed toward my arsenal ship. Find me the one in front that knows what it's doing; and blow it up with the nastiest gun you can aim at it. That's what you should be worried about right now."

"Warmaster, the compromised twister is rising. It's going out of play."

His eyes suddenly bright and cheered, Thessany snapped his fingers. "That's a safety. They may have triggered the safety. Have we got it back, Tubs?"

"Negative, sir. It's just rising. Looks like no one has control of it."

Thessany laughed nervously, "Steer ours out of there. Get it to the war engines with Slade Watch! Now!"

Cobweb hummed something, then waved his hand rapidly to gain Thessany's attention. His voice sounded young, "Got her."

"What?! What do you see?" Thessany almost jumped at what he'd heard just then.

"There's a mog stuck to the belly of a datastream support ship. One of ours. I think I'm seeing a second on another ship. It's mogs, Warmaster. They're riding in on mogs!"

Peri

"Bogle, you're veering too far out. Change out to another ship." Peri twisted herself backward in the swivelseat to gain what vantage she could of those joining her assault. She'd only just transferred to the ship she rode now and was considering a quicktank veering in already. It was only clear much later in other times to analysts and historians endlessly reviewing the datastream and interrogating the War Recorders what disarray the battlefield was dissolving into already;but she was herself only surprised at how far she'd gotten unnoticed. The arsenal tank loomed massive and overshadowing just ahead of her; and it was bathed in close-in fire and attacking ramships. Waterjets were blasting off any Black Fire streams that could make it to the hull; and the sheet diamond was undamaged and clean.

"Push! Just push. Almost there." She couldn't tell by this point how many of the eighteen with which she'd launched were going to arrive with her.

"Commander, we've been spotted! Apel and Moo are gone. We need to pull back!"

Disgusted, "Negative! I'll shoot you myself. There's nothing they can do but peel out when they see one of us. We're too small for what's out here. All mog hands, listen to me!"

Leaning just a little out to gauge the arsenal ship's monster height and incline, "I don't know what you think you'd go home to! Anybody you're thinking about back there, they have you to protect them; and that's all. You're it. So act like it. On my mark, we're gonna scramble. Drop from your ships and climb that tank to its top. And if we manage to board her, bring your payload. Kill everyone you can."

"Commander, they've seen us. This is a dead mission."

Peri frowned, perhaps agreeing but shouting nevertheless, "Scramble!!"

From vessels all around the gargantuan arsenal ship, mogs dropped and drove up the steep sides in a wide mass. Cannons swiveled toward them; and close-in railguns were whirling; but nothing was able to fire at an angle to strike them. White waterjets pummeled them, driving two of Peri's mogs from the walls and screaming to the ground where they were quickly set on fire. She quickly counted thirteen mogs arriving with her at the vents and smiled thinly, surveying the battlescene all around them. From here, it was even larger and more vicious than she'd considered before in the command engine; and Thessany had directed seven gunships to encircle her. She was looking into their barrels when one of her pilots blew the vents open. Then they all dropped inside. The ducting she and the others had entered was big enough for them to drive through, so they remained in their vessels and pushed in deeper.

"Commander, what's the matter with them? How come we've gotten this far?"

The large ducting they'd entered ran ahead into a manifold that split into smaller ducts, too small to continue. The mog in front of her burned through the ducting wall and led the way through, after which she and the others followed. It was unclear now how deep inside they were; but they had dropped into a pedestrian corridor with graphite hatches on either side and which led further down to more hatches. Then quite suddenly, they were fired upon.

"Repel all boarders!" The shouts were from all sides, men armed with railguns, ricocheting shots plinking and popping all around.

Her pilots served with credit and returned fire bravely; but in the hailstorm and insanity she watched six of her men fall before she gave the order, "We're too restricted. Abandon your vehicles and bring your payloads." Then she selected someone to die. "Alekos, hold them off!"

Alekos looked at her grimly, understanding what was happening, and nodded before kneeling in place to fire until he was dead. Peri and the remnant of her assault team ran ahead, concentrating their fire to break out of the entanglement. The hatches wouldn't burn with ball lightning, so they would turn to fire behind themselves while one of their number would work the hatch each time. It was slow and dangerous; and she lost two more men in doing so, one of which gripped her ankle and tried to say something which only came out as babbling. The corridor opened up ahead of them to a series of office compartments and auxiliary machinery rooms which looked deserted at first, before a grenade blew apart one of the men beside her and gunfire returned. And this was as far as she got. Though the archives from the day may say otherwise, Peri and her team never got farther than this. In the end it was her alone.

She slid the payload to her front and hugged it like a babydoll. Her attackers came from their shielding places with guns aimed, shouting for her to kneel and set it aside. She saw young faces with panicked eyes and unsteady hands, as she'd seen before many times. When one of them, a leader of some kind, stepped closer to her with his unarmed hand outstretched, she admired the deep blue of his eyes with a growing serenity.

"Peri, just put that down and step away. We'll take you into custody. Nobody else has to die."

The Lady Commander scanned the corridor and her fallen men, perhaps seeing that was always the way it was with Talgos. It always ended something like this. Then he said something to her that frightened her more than anything she'd seen that last day. The blue-eyed man with his gun outstretched got close enough to Peri to whisper, still holding palm upward as if beckoning for her surrender. He came to her, glancing quickly behind himself as if he didn't want the others to hear.

"I'll fight for Cyprian. If he's joined you, tell me. We can get out of here together."

Her eyes widened at the loyalty even here, the sick fascination no matter its lunacy. There in his smooth face she could see this man would turn on his fellows because a celebrity was interesting to him, held intrigue and mystery that made him feel more. It was an absurdity she could no longer stomach; and she knew it. When she twisted the actuator, the canister in her arms blew apart into a swelling clot of Black Fire that stuck fast to the both of them and swarmed over the corridors and hatches with blinding speed. Muffled screams died down almost immediately as they were swallowed whole.

Thessany

Thessany's neck tightened with clenched teeth when he saw night-black tendrils flicking out widening rust-holes in his arsenal ship and puffs of gray and black smoke clinging to men streaming from it like ants from a kicked hill. He looked at Tubs fiercely, as if the entire day thus far could be laid in the fellow's hands.

Cobweb's voice was still calm and professional, well practiced at dealing with commanders and bad news, "Warmaster, Cyprian is gone. He's disappeared; and the fleet is in disarray. Just pull back and regroup in the flats. We've got to find all these mogs or we'll just be moving around her mines for her. Pull back."

Thessany's jaw was tight, his face cherry with anger. He at last turned from the icy stare at Tubs and looked at his command team as a sentencing judge.

"Jamnia, Evergreen, Systelion…who knows how many hilljack lovers…all on their way to kill you and yours. This was our chance to keep the world from getting chewed. When your grandkids are holstering their standard issue to try and finish what you started, let 'em know where you sat…gossiping and…" He scowled at Tubs, "Typing."

Cobweb was more urgent now, "Warmaster, give the order. We don't have control of the fleet right now. Let's go."

Disappointed and furious, Thessany stepped closer to the screen like it was his gallows, "We're smarter than this, Cobweb. I don't like it…there's something more than generals out here with us. I said no puppet strings; but I feel 'em. What's gotten in everybody's heads?"

Formations were in disarray; and the wings were smearing out like melting ice cream. The hijacked twister was lengthening to the ground again, its distracting ruse complete. He looked again at his panicked command crew, mostly shiny faced and probably frightened more of him now like chided kids, than what was to come over maybe years of bloody and swelling war. Maybe for a wink just then, Meridian Thessany at the battle of Spenecia considered shoving everything he had at the battlefield, letting whatever was out there clouding and whispering deal with his full fury. In the end, he did what he had to do though; and none came to question it.

"Pull back, Cobweb." He frowned and turned to walk away from the screen. "Just pull everything back; and let's clean house. I need to know what we're really dealing with."

The Brigadier

The Brigadier in his dusty white uniform squatted atop a grain silo surveying the Spenecia battlefield. The arsenal ship was by now a misshapen black and silver goo; and the fleets were spreading out, thinning.

"Hope you got what you wanted." Fantine's voice came from

the rusty ladder, as she lifted herself over and joined him there, remaining standing. He glanced at her, then back to the east where supply vessels were retreating.

"Who wants any of this."

Fantine nodded, "You got real lucky today."

"Maybe"

She smacked his shoulder and spat in a mocking voice, "Maybe! I put half a lifetime into making that hammer down there. You're hitting too early!"

Without looking at her, his sun-leathered skin dark and chapped, "You'll have to manage Grebel when he comes back. Does he suspect anything?"

She shook her head no without answering; and he understood her answer without looking, "You've done well with him for a very long time, don't let up here at the end. The boy will be a myth throughout the provinces by this time next month."

"If we all live a month."

The Brigadier rubbed the back of his stubbled head, past an old white scar, "Have you noticed how much easier this is getting?"

"What do you mean?"

"To lead them. It used to be complicated: impossible assassinations, faking ancient books, I bankrupted a town in the western desert once – took two years and lost a man doing it, almost lost my hands too. I think I could change the world with just a pretty face now. They're more easily led; and that means we're running out of time."

"Maybe; but you're a little too plucky for somebody with this many variables."

The Brigadier stood and dusted off his backside. He towered over her and was intimidating in his demeanor and bearing. Even now, he likely had snipers watching him for signs to bring down calamity upon those to whom he directed.

"That won't be a problem soon. Stendahl and Cassian are headed to the Augur."

Surprised, "You think slaughtering the Talgos at the start of a war likely going global is how we'll level everything out? You've forgotten how bad things were."

"No. I'm remembering."

Fantine hacked up phlegm and spit on the earth, swirling it into a spiral with the toe of her boot. "Laoka wouldn't approve of any of this."

His eyes were bloodshot, tired, "I didn't ask him."

"He'll be headed to the Augur soon, with that Recorder. What are you going to do if he's there when you want to take the shot?"

A flash of fury that set her back, "Stop calling that punk, 'Laoka'. I don't know what he is."

"There's a lot of people who think he's the Salt Mystic coming back…why's he doing that? Maybe he's somebody else's hammer…"

"Doesn't matter either way. Time's up."

Hands in his pockets, he turned back to the Spenecia fields. The ramships still battered each other as buffers; and both tornados were sheathed, clearing the overcast skies. The big tanks and gunships were largely retreated by this point. Just looking at it, there was a feel of gloom and importance, that the one chance the world had to finish something with precision and be done with it one way or the other had slipped, leaving grudges and vengeance smoking. It felt like a morning rain over a failed wedding.

He looked at Fantine one last time before leaving, his voice cracking again in its weariness, "You can't always fix things and work from what you have. Sometimes, you just have to break it."

Early morning, Misling was swirling the last of cold coffee and sitting alone slumped low in the chair. His hair was cowlicked grossly, with a fat lump on one side; and he looked lost. The celebrants from the day before were gone.

"Sleep okay?" Cristoffel faded into existence from the dimmer hallway, barefoot and with her dark hair tied back again.

"No. Bad dreams."

She yawned at him, "I know what you mean." Now that she was closer, there was a scent of vanilla. He sniffed softly, trying not to let her notice though she did. "Did Grebel leave yet?"

Misling nodded, "Not long ago."

When Cristoffel sat across from him, she was a comfortable and simple sort of pretty he might have said reminded him of home. Her arms were folded. There was still a smear of blue-gray Balcister dust in a cirrus cloud shape over her right eye; and when he was noticing that, he saw she was staring at him, like she was awaiting an answer. His hesitation may have been a quick check to see whether she'd asked something; but no, she was just watching him with a little dimple of flesh between her eyes.

He understood her and nodded, "I have to."

She nodded too, not disagreeing with him. "I'll go with you."

He rose an eyebrow to ask why, considering the perils he'd brought her in a very short time and only the promise of worse to offer. She glanced at him, "Because 'Hauna will go with you; and she's an idiot. And those two things are related. Should be safe at the Augur, right? Sacred ground?"

The Recorder only looked at his dusty boots in answer. After a pause, he looked back at her sadly, "In the Plaza, when the carbine overheated…I let you down. I let you down and had no way out, no brave stand to make. I offered you an apology, a poor exchange for your trust. I led you to slaughter for nothing."

"Nothing?" Cristoffel pursed her lips, "If you were me, would you walk away from this…to caretake for Lennox? I don't think it's for nothing."

She inhaled deeply, closing her eyes softly, then opening again to look directly at him, "From what I've heard, it's for everything."

"A surprise! Marvelous, isn't it?" Farmilion's voice boomed like a thunderclap and joyous. He rushed in, his belly wobbling. His face was pink as ever; and he was grinning. "Such wonders! Like an architect crafted every turn of the events!"

Misling stood from the chair, wondering at the old man's thrill. Farmilion's smile was full, almost driving his tiny eyes shut with the wrinkles it made on his big face. It caught Cristoffel as funny; and she chuckled at the sight.

"Only the beginning, my marvelous sprout! My sturdy sapling, digging roots deep and spreading your long branches…" He grabbed Misling's arm and lifted it up, forming it into something like a treebranch. "…defying the thundering storm that would strip him bare, saying, 'I have a name; and you will say it!'"

Cristoffel laughed fully, though Misling was lost in this. "Are you drunk?"

The old man chuckled, "A little, if I'm honest. Yet totally beside the point. Come and see!" He gripped their shoulders and drove them like cattle to the corridor opening into the atrium. With no explanation and no pause for it, Farmilion pushed them gently along to the museum entrance in the light of the morning and gestured forward like a showman. It was his dirigible, brass-colored balloons shining, with Sylhauna waving from in front of it. Ring was seated inside the railings, leaned forward.

Sylhauna hugged Cristoffel, "You did great!"

"Where's Lennox?"

"He's okay." Sylhauna left it at that, with a glance that maybe Cristoffel would need to question later.

The Recorder smiled at Sylhauna in thanks, though she hugged him rather than letting that be all. She gripped his shoulder and whispered, "We're all going."

When Misling started for the dirigible, the others saw a bit of drama in it and went quiet, stepping back to see what the two would make of their reunion. Inside the rover, drained of energy and wheezing with every breath, Ring was slumped and pale. Most of the swelling of his jaw had eased, though purple streaks still colored his chin back to his left ear. The back of his neck was cherry red and puffed; and his smile was thin and fake. He propped himself up with the black wood cane he'd taken from Lennox. Misling grimaced at what he saw in Ring just then.

"Feels like a long time." Ring's voice was weak.

"How long for you?"

He shrugged rather than answer it.

"You did say parts of this would be bloody."

Ring thought about this, then tried to chuckle though it hurt him. "Yeah. I did. That came a little quick though."

They looked at one another then, perhaps trying to see past the bluster and pretentions and how men were supposed to see each other. Perhaps what was most clear on their faces just then in the ruined plaza and with the old man and the ladies watching them cautiously was pride of each other that they'd come this far and done what they'd done.

Ring stiffened, "One question, Recorder. One straight and direct answer. I never really gave you that. No more cheats this time. I'll tell you anything." He beckoned towards himself with curled fingers, "Hit me with it. You deserve it."

Misling raised his eyebrows, glanced to those watching, then up to the morning sky to consider what he'd been offered again. When he put his eyes on Ring again, frail and small and clutching the cane and looking so much older than when they met in the airpark, he knew what he would do.

"Do you need help?"

Ring recovered himself, like he'd dodged a heavyweight punch. His eyes widened; and he grinned. It was the grin from the first day, the one in the market alive and sparkling, with magic and cheer full of promise and secrets.

"That's your question?"

The Recorder smiled, then turned, amused with himself. Farmilion thought this was hilarious and laughed as he passed. Sylhauna chuckled as well, but stopped him to ask quickly.

"You're going to ask him more than that, right?"

"It will be a long trip; and he is uncomfortable with silence."

"You seem really happy with yourself right now. I didn't know what to expect when we came to get you. Have you figured him out, then?"

Misling glanced back to the rover, "He gave me a name. That is the only thing I know that is certain of him. And it is enough."

EPILOGUE

Stendahl looked out over the stairway railings as he descended from the zeppelin to the Augur courtyard. There were Salt Mystic runes and etchings on the cobblestone, puddled here and there with cold autumn rainwater. The little city that had centuries before spilled over and swelled from the temple was still and quiet around him, though he could just see the occasional market vendor sweeping his stalls or the odd innkeeper shaking out rugs from open windows. The paraball fields were soggy, though a lone man was out there among its hills inspecting the ground and plucking weeds.

Tallest among all was the eerie temple itself, shining even in the daylight and fronted by the gargantuan white fountains enshrouding the Salt Mystic statue nestled inside and submerged to her knees. Children quickly found on pilgrimages here that if they stood in just the right place before her, the Salt Mystic's gaze directly into their eyes was chilling and frightening and not easily forgotten.

A short squat fellow was awaiting him at the landing, holding a massively tall hat in his hands respectfully, "Stendahl Talgo, welcome to you!"

Stendahl frowned, not knowing he'd been expected. "Who are you?"

"Name's, Onyx. Sexton here. Somebody's got to be, don't they? 'Why not me', I said, years ago when I still had red hair and a lift to my step. Hungry?"

Velo Boneghost was in armor, illuminated in places and jeweled much as the Chaselord's himself. He was just stepping from the dirigible and had to lean way over to avoid hitting his head. He was probably the ugliest man Onyx had ever seen; and Onyx didn't quite hide he felt so.

"Plenty of lunch to go around. As long as you don't mind

pickled meats. Everything's pickled here, who knows why! Lick your lips all you like, never rid yourself of the tingle. Any bags?"

Stendahl stepped directly up to the strange greeter as if he was going to eat the man's nose from his face, "Why am I expected?"

Eyes widened, "Loads of you are! Goodness, yes! Think of where you're standing. What's inside that over there. Of course, you're expected. What comes here that isn't?"

"Who else?" His voice was just different from before, darker and less fragile.

Onyx coughed nervously, still holding his ridiculous hat and glancing to Boneghost, "Well, your uncle, Cassian only arrived hours ago. Long enough to dry his boots maybe, not much more. That horrible woman from Denai came yesterday, the one without a name but they call something anyway. The Lord Recorder, though he's a bit standoffish if you know what I mean. The duke of the Fountain City is here since last week, eating everything in sight. Fog Men showed up this morning – not sure what to do about that."

Boneghost flinched at that, frowning harshly. Stendahl understood none of this.

"Loads of people! I told you. More coming soon. In just a blink. More here before you know it. Then we'll get started."

Boneghost gripped Onyx by his shirt, practically lifting the poor fellow from the ground, "Get started with what?"

Onyx answered, his voice rising an octave and speaking quicker, "The audience, Velo! The audience! We're all going to see the Augur. What else would you come here for?"

Stendahl tapped Boneghost's arm to signal him to release Onyx, then started for the entrance to the temple. Flickering lights cast upon him as he began down the rock stairway, descending into the earth and entering the temple of the Augur, as old as known civilization and with the feel of all that is evil and all that is good mortared into its walls.

"That's right, Onyx. What else?"

"Poverty and ignorance bred a tramp called, Blame; and she keeps her young close. Fear her. Because the life's blood of a nation is the character of its people, and because the neglect of souls is the needle that poisons it, I have left you wonders in the Record. The fault and the regret are yours if they must arise."

-The Salt Mystic

ABOUT THE AUTHOR

Brian Bennudriti has degrees in Physics and Business, and has worked in nuclear operations, mergers & acquisitions, and management consulting. He's a Plankowner on the aircraft carrier, USS Harry S Truman; and his initials are probably still scratched in a few places there. He lives in Kansas City with his wife, two kids and two dogs because you can never have enough chaos in your life. Brian wishes he could write Gormenghast's characters with M. John Harrison's words and Harlan Ellison's adrenalin, stealing everything else from Hemingway and Stephen King just because they're awesome.